Do You Want Chips with That?

Malcolm G. Scott

AuthorHouse™ UK Ltd.
500 Avebury Boulevard
Central Milton Keynes, MK9 2BE
www.authorhouse.co.uk
Phone: 08001974150

© 2009 Malcolm G. Scott. All rights reserved.

No part of this book may be reproduced, stored in a retrieval system, or transmitted by any means without the written permission of the author.

First published by AuthorHouse 1/27/2009

ISBN: 978-1-4389-3960-5 (sc)

Printed in the United States of America
Bloomington, Indiana

This book is printed on acid-free paper.

Foreword

This book is dedicated to my Mother, Doris, who gave birth to me in nineteen hundred and frozen to death and was the inspiration behind the main character's Mother, although I may have exaggerated just a tad on some of her endearing foibles, and added some, for which I have already been berated!

Sincerely, she is the best Mother in the world – I know because she told me so herself.

A big thank you also to my editor, Dr Joan Burton, of University of Tennessee, Knoxville, USA who kept me honest throughout the book's development. It is one thing to recognise deficiency in other's work, but when it comes to your own, it needs an independent eye to keep it real! However, I did put up a good fight when we disagreed on some issues, prior to accepting her commands.

This is a work of fiction. Where real people have inspired characters or character traits, the names have been changed to protect the guilty.

M*AY* 2000

Wednesday 3rd May 2000

9-00p.m.

It's my birthday again! Happy Birthday to me! I am now 34 years old...
Gulp!
... living and working in a shag-free zone in rural Cambridgeshire.
Today is the first day of the rest of my life, and I am stuck here, sitting in an aluminium box, 12' x 7'6", staring out into the twilight at a hedgerow through a hole in the side. (The side of the trailer, that is, not the hedgerow!). The fast food trailer, within which I am ensconced, is the source of my livelihood, and the hole is the hatch, through which my customers dispense the fine coin of the realm, which funds this livelihood. **Arnold's Kebab Shack** serves me quite well in that department and has for some four years, although, truth to tell, if there are many more nights like tonight, the rest of my life will seem like an eternity!
It hasn't always been a shag-free zone, of course, but my record with women does read more like a chronicle of disasters, and I am currently between relationships. That's a four-year "between," and I'm beginning to think that there may never be another!
Is it possible to lose the use of your manhood if you stop having sex? Does it lose its power by means of disuse atrophy? If, by magic, some voluptuous goddess demanded to burgle my Calvins, would I even remember what to do?

If you'd have told me ten years ago that I'd be living out in the sticks, I'd have recommended you took psychiatric advice, yet here I am. I moved out here from Luton about five years ago, to be with Lorraine, a very attractive and, in the interest of political correctness shall we say, 'full-chested', woman, whom I met at a Luton Town home match, in the bar, after the game. She had started supporting my beloved Luton, when a friend of hers was dating one of the players, and Lorraine had gone out with his friend. Travelling sixty-odd miles, every time we saw each other, was getting us both down, not to mention costing a fortune. She said she 'wanted us to be on a more solid foundation,' so I moved in with her. Big mistake! I adored her and loved being with her, while we were sixty miles apart, but it began to fall apart almost immediately we were together 24/7. Whenever we were together, we would be arguing about one thing or another, until I was driven to distraction. I would rather have my tongue ripped out by the roots than admit this to my mates, but it quickly became apparent that sex and Luton Town Football Club were not enough to build a relationship upon.

The stress soon outweighed the sex, and we only stayed together about eight months, until I left and got a flat, before one of us did time for murder! I could have, would have, maybe should have moved back to Luton but, by that time, I had bought the trailer and started the business and was in a sort of comfort zone. I got lazy and couldn't hack starting all over again. There were other benefits, of course. Sixty-odd miles are just far enough away from Mother to be able to get there, if I am desperately needed, but just far enough away not to be on tap as it were. At least, from here, I can run, (or should that be ruin?) my own life.

Where are all the customers tonight? It's like a ghost town! But soft… what light from yonder lay-by breaks? It is two headlamps and that means either a customer for me, or someone parking in **MY** lay-by, to use **MY** telephone box, or **MY** Tardis Toilet. Not that it **IS** my lay-by, (or indeed my telephone box or toilet), but as I spend a fair bit of the day **in** it, I do claim some affinity **with** it.

"Hi, what can I get you?"

"Halfpounder cheeseburger please."

Strange accent!
"Three fifteen, please. Do you want chips with that?"
"OK."
"Four fifteen then, thanks."

McDonald's have a lot to answer for, but since I have been "doing a McDonald's" myself, and asking that question, I have to admit that my chip sales have more than doubled. That said, it still pisses me off greatly when I venture forth into said establishment, and they do it to me. I mean… do I **look** as though I don't know if I want chips or not? Ha! Ha! I **do** love irony and paradox!

Whilst on the subject of our erstwhile, alleged rainforest usurpers and destroyers, (if we are to believe the vegetarian lobby), am I the only one who goes into McDonald's and gets aurally assaulted by the combined choirs of Disney World and Lilliput, in a chorus of, "Can I take your order please?" when I need time to peruse the menu? Yet, when I know exactly what I want, am in a great hurry and approach the counter full of hope, anticipation and assertiveness, all personnel are suddenly busy on matters of such national importance that they refuse to let you catch their eye? Is it innate, this ability, or do McDonald's offer degree courses in patronization and provocation? Perhaps those qualities are what the first two stars on their name badges account for! I wonder what stars 3, 4, and 5 are for? Off the top of my head, my suggestions would be boredom, insincerity and how to be a credible automaton.

"You sound a long way from home?" I ventured expectantly.
"Not really… I live just down the road."
Ouch! I asked for that!
<u>Mental note</u>: Assess intelligence BEFORE attempting intellectual discourse.
" I meant your accent- a bit West Country… Dorset … Avon?"
I pride myself on my ability to place accents, from my numerous years on the road as a company rep with a large wholesale greetings card manufacturer.
"Dorset… I was born near Bournemouth."

Yeeeeessss! Mentally performing a moonwalking end zone dance, in the mode of an American Footballer who has scored a touchdown; this followed by piston-like air punching, born of self-satisfaction and smugness with oneself! Oh yes, my mind is a very surreal place to live!

"Nice part of the world!"

"S'pose."

Just then a tangle of humanity walked by, adults and children alike, obviously from the shallow end of the gene pool. The parents were doing a reasonable impression of Wayne and Waynetta Slob, wearing flip-flops upon filthy black feet and adorned with designer (NOT!) tee shirts, which had not had a rendezvous with detergent for many a day. They were followed by four snotty-nosed kids, the first three, all boys and with their arses hanging out of their trousers, scrapping with each other and using disgracefully foul language for ones so young. The fourth, of doubtful gender, was running along like Dopey, the least intellectually endowed of the seven dwarves, trying desperately to keep up with the rest and bawling tiredly as it went. The "Wayne-like" character looked over at me and shouted, "All right Arnie?" but didn't wait for a response before moving on.

I get so annoyed when people assume that Arnold is my Christian name. Why did my father have to have a Christian name for a surname? Mother, of course, would go ballistic if she heard anyone failing to call me Ben. Having said that, when she wants to make a point, I suddenly become Benjamin, or if I am in trouble, I get the full "Benjamin Francis Arnold" treatment from her! That's another bone of contention, having a middle name that sounds more like a girl's. That came from my mother's obsession with Francis Albert Sinatra. Mind you, it could have been worse. She might have called me Albert!

"There ought to be a name for people like that," I ventured. "I'll bet they've got two fridges and a washing machine in their back garden and a microwave oven and four old dismantled cars on their front… one of which is ALWAYS a Cortina!"

"There is."

"Is what?"

"A word for them."

"Really?"

"Where I come from, they calls 'em 'Cackers'."

Brilliant! What a truly amazing and descriptive word. It should be universal. I must make it my duty to disseminate this exquisite noun to a more widely appreciative audience. In fact, as today is the first day of the rest of my life, I will make some birthday resolutions and that can be the first.

"Very descriptive."

"S'pose… bit o' sauce and some salad on there please… no onion, ta."

I complied.

"There you go… enjoy your food."

God, some people are hard work. Now… where was I? Oh yes… birthday resolutions…. (in no particular order…)

1) Bring the word "cacker" into general use.
2) Be more polite to customers, even cackers! (Ha! Ha! I **do** love that word).
3) Stop procrastinating.
4) Do the rest tomorrow! (What rapier-like wit!)

I was watching Oprah Winfrey on Sky TV today. She had a very interesting guest on; an author called Sarah Ban Breakneck, (or some such ☺), who has written a book called "Simple Abundance." She suggests that, if you are as dissatisfied with your lot as I am, you should write a gratitude journal. I'm gullible enough always to be willing to give a fad a go, so I will start listing things for which I am grateful. We'll see if it helps… tomorrow!

Oh number 3; you are going to be hard work!

(Mobile rings…)

I refuse to accede to my American colleagues' request to call it a cellphone!

"Hello? Yes it is Arnold's… Two chicken kebabs? £7-90…would you like chips with that? No?"

OK! You can't win them all!
"Thanks, that will be about 15 minutes. 'Bye."

Thursday 4th May 2000

Birthday resolutions (continued). – *Again in no particular order, but number 2 is quite important!*

1) Attract more customers.
2) Attract more females (one would be a giant step for mankind!)
3) Extract more money from the people in number 1.
4) Do not attract debt or debtors.
5) Get a life (see number 2).
6) Improve vocabulary and diminish swearing at moronic customers.
7) Write the gratitude journal…(Oprah will be proud of me).
8) Take an unusual word each day and use it at least once in context.

Word of the day: Kakistocracy…. Government by the least qualified members of society! (That'd be the cackers then!)

9-38 p.m.

Dave Kingsley has just been to the trailer. He is a local football referee, whose inept abilities I have suffered on many an occasion. I am most certainly no stranger to his yellow card. It has to be said, however, that his links with the human race, at best, could be described as tenuous. In fact, it may be my inability to prevent my sharing this opinion with him, which has allowed me to "make his day" on more than one occasion. In one match, last year, he awarded me first use of the showering facilities, after what I thought was merely a witty exchange. He failed to notice a defender, (who was built like a brick shithouse and had muscles in his spit), scythe me down violently in the penalty area, (allegedly!). I ran after him and was about to deliver a barrage of abuse, when reason took over, and so I made a polite enquiry.

"If I called you a useless prick, would you send me off?"

" You know I would!" he replied confidently.

"What if I **think** you're a useless prick?"

" You can think what you like!" he said, laughing.

"Good! Because I **do** think you're a useless prick!"

Perhaps the raucous laughter of several players, nearby, caused a sense of humour bypass in him, because the red card appeared like magic from his top pocket! Local football is an example of a Kakistocracy! (Hurrah!)

It is amazing the number of people who think that, because they are the remotest of acquaintances, they qualify for free food, or at the very least, a serious discount.

Does it say "Arnold's Soup Kitchen" above the hatch?

They rarely actually ask, but the inference is always there.

"Hiya Benny boy…!"

How much do I hate that? Even my closest friends wouldn't dare!

"…How's it hanging?"

"Downwards, fortunately! If it aligned in any other direction at the sight of you, I would be extremely worried!"

"Chicken kebab, mate. All the trimmings!" he laughed smugly.

"Three ninety five thanks."

(Puzzled look), "Eh?" (Realisation), "Oh, yes… right", (parts with cash, very reluctantly!), "I came by Friday, but you were well busy. You must be fucking raking it in!"

"Yeah right! My other car's a Ferrari." I instilled as much sarcasm into the comment as I could summon.

"You've got it made 'ere, there's always a queue."

"Did you come to that startling conclusion all by yourself, from one drive-past, or did you need help?"

"No, I come past a lot, you're **always** busy! Your own boss as well! I could do with a bit of that, you lucky bugger!"

It never ceases to amaze me how many people think that this is an easy life.

"How many do you see here now, then?"

"Yes, but I bet you'll make a killing when that pub turns out?"

"Not always. Funny that, though."

"What is?"

"The harder I graft, the luckier I seem to get. Do you think that I just open the hatch, and people rush towards the van, throwing money at me like rice at a wedding?"

"Looks like it from where I'm standing!" Self-induced paroxysms of laughter take him over. "Come off it, Benny boy! You must pull a few quid in on Friday and Saturday…and you aren't stuck at a bloody desk from nine 'til five every friggin' day, with only an hour for lunch."

I found myself struggling not to smack him in the mouth!

"You don't know you're born! Do you think this trailer cleans itself, restocks itself, then tows itself here by magic?"

"That's no great hardship."

I was now really fighting the temptation to render him senseless, with the aid of a turning utensil, then realised that this erroneously assumed that sense was currently present.

"I **could** go on but I won't, and I sure hope the washing-up fairy comes in the night again and leaves these dirty utensils sparkling brightly for tomorrow's trading."

Such erudite sarcasm flew harmlessly over his head.

"Can you hear the violins playing?" He mimicked a violin being played. I think this was a feeble attempt at wit.

Although having decided that it was pointless to continue this discussion, I found myself drawn back in by this comment.

"How many hours did you work this week?" I asked.

"40."

"So you did 5 hours overtime then?"

"No."

"9 to 5 is 40 hours a week, but you get an hour a day for lunch, don't you? So you only **worked** 35."

"That's splitting hairs a bit."

"Well I was open for 42 hours, **plus** getting it here and putting it away; cleaning it; going to Cash and Carry; putting the stock on; taking delivery of gas and frozen foods. Then there is the business side; accounts, books, appointments with the useless dickhead who masquerades as my bank manager. OK, I do all right, but I work bloody hard for 60 or 70 hours a week for it! So now play your fucking violin!"

Oops! Direct contravention of birthday resolution six!

"No need to get arsey, Benny boy!"

"I'm not getting arsey…"

Yes I am!

"…just making the point. 9 to 5 seems like a piece of piss to me. Trust me!"

So shut the fuck up!

Tension diffusing mutual laughter ensued, but the point was made, and we both knew the score, before he tentatively said goodbye and exited, stage left, with his, (probably prehensile), tail between his legs.

Do not engage me in a war of semantics! You will lose!

10-00 p.m.

Damn, I knew it was hot in here. It would really help if I opened the vent in the roof! My head has been in a sauna for 5 hours. I wonder if it has shrunk…?

A rather attractive female customer arrived and did not recoil in horror and disgust at the sight of me, so I assume that the head is relatively unscathed by its ordeal and that my craggy good looks have remained intact.

"Hello. How may I help you?"

God, I sound like I've been taking sincere pills!

"Two chicken kebabs please." "£7-90 please…do you want chips with that?"

"Erm… OK."

"Nine ninety then, thanks."
Bingo!

Things to be grateful for

1) My ability to remain calm under duress and resist maiming ignorant acquaintances.
2) McDonalds' idea of selling extra chips by the inertia method.
3) Tea (and more tea).
4) Shrink resistant heads.
5) Wonderbras, and girls who openly display the results of the efforts of their Wonderbras. (Courtesy of the young woman who arrived just before closing time, apparently hiding two ostrich eggs within hers).

Sunday 7th May 2000

Word of the day: Bummalo… A small fish of Asia often used in dried form to make "Bombay Duck", a dish served with curries.

11 p.m.

Brian, Gordon, Jamie and I, collectively the Far Canal quiz team, have just won the pub quiz at the Queens Arms (again! Yawn!). We usually fare quite well every Sunday, but it sometimes seems a bit of a foregone conclusion, and it is difficult to get them to concentrate their minds on the quiz, instead of inspecting the quality of female participants elsewhere in the room.

The word of the day came from one of the questions in the quiz. It was in the fun round, and I almost fainted when Gordon, the accountant, knew the answer and I didn't! I'll never be able to use it in context, other than as a definition, so I'll admit defeat right now!

The evening was made more memorable for me, however, because a woman, whom I had never seen in the pub before, distracted me, totally, all through the quiz, due to the enormous wart on the end of her nose.

Perhaps Oliver Cromwell is an ancestor of hers? This is the area from which he hailed, after all.

Even more distracting was the fact that it had two long hairs sprouting from it. I didn't mention it to anyone else, until after she had left. Jamie said he knew her and her husband. I blame the guest beer of the evening, a strong brew from Shepherd Neame Brewery, for my being so gullible, but I took the bait instantly and virtually invited him to tell us more. Jamie, not normally noted for his wit, or his ability to tell a joke, whispered, (while looking furtively around the room to ensure no unauthorised ears were party to this information), "Her husband says that when she sneezes the hairs on it crack like a whip!"

The whole party collapsed with laughter.

"No! Wait!" He said, indicating in the words of Jimmy Cricket, "There's more!.... Last year, she got the flu and sneezed so much she knitted a balaclava helmet!"

He should have quit while he was ahead. There followed one of those awkward moments of silence, (in the manner of Reeves and Mortimer on "Shooting Stars"), when you could imagine a lonely bell tolling very slowly in the distance. This plaintive sound is almost overpowered by the whistling of the wind, blowing tumbleweed across the main street of the desert ghost town. The longer the silence continued, the more we all wanted it to continue, as it became funnier and funnier, and no one wanted to be the first to break it. He endured it, for what seemed like a minute, but was probably only about 20 seconds, then broke it himself with, "Oh fuck you then… bunch of tossers!" and repaired to the Gents, leaving us laughing like drains.

Do drains laugh?

I voiced the tumbleweed imagery to the others to much amusement. This, henceforth, will be known as Jamie's tumbleweed moment! Trust me to end up as a straight man for a bloody Burnley supporter! (Even if he wasn't clever enough to benefit from my inadvertent lead!)

Things to be grateful for

1) I am not a Burnley supporter
2) I do not have a wart on my nose with multifarious musical and craft talents.
3) The Far Canal team wins the quiz again to the humiliation of The Bar Room Brawlers and Hugh Janus and Co, who finished 2nd and 3rd respectively!
4) Jamie will probably never tell another joke.

Friday 12th May 2000

Word of the day: Indigenous… of people born in a region.

9 a.m.

I hate Fridays! They are so busy and, therefore, so stressful in the anticipation and in the organisation required for getting open, with the correct stock on board. The only part of Fridays that I like is counting the money at the close of business! Oh…. and talking about money, I must ring the air base concession company again, re getting permission to trade on the air base.

3-40 p.m.

The ratio of American to indigenous (hurrah!) customers is increasing by the day. It has come as a bit of a shock to me that the average American is, on the whole, a pretty nice person, (political correctness prevents me from saying "guy"). Most Brits only ever come across camera-adorned, tourist-type Americans who, it has to be said, do very little for Anglo-American relations. I mean the tourists who flock to the "right" attractions, wearing shirts which require a volume control, and who insist on being the centre of attention at all costs.

Apparently, the loud shirts also make them hearing-impaired, because they communicate at an average decibel equivalent to that of a town crier's, often propelling too much information about the shortcomings of their bowel movements, and sundry other digestive problems to, not only the target of their ramblings, but also any unsuspecting life form within a ¼ mile radius. The British tourist merely shouts at non English-speaking foreigners, because, (as we all know), it obviously helps them to understand what we are saying!

I was staying in the Hilton hotel at Stratford-upon-Avon once, which, as the birthplace of William Shakespeare, (Stratford – not the Hilton Hotel!) is a Mecca for tourists of all nationalities, but seemingly, especially Americans and Japanese. That was in my rep days, and my personal preference was to wake up gently in the morning and have a nice breakfast, quietly, with my newspaper, easing myself into the rigours of the day. On this morning, two elderly American ladies appeared at opposite ends of the dining room, like the main protagonists at a world title boxing match. They commenced to take part in a loud exchange. They could have met in the centre of the room, but for some reason that was not obvious, they chose not to.

"We're doing Scotland tomorrow!" began the purple-rinsed variety.

"We did Scotland Thursday… we're doing Wales today," replied the silver-haired one.

"Been to Windsor Castle yet?"

"Yeah, we went last Sunday."

"Strange though, about the Royals?"

"What is, hun?"

"Why they have so much money, and land all over the United Kingdom, yet they built that Castle right next to Heathrow Airport."

"Yeah!" was the thoughtful response, "Didn't occur to me!"

Doh!

I have to say that I now have a large contingent of customers from both local US Airbases, and they are a really friendly and supportive bunch. My viewpoint has been totally reversed. Another thing, which is very helpful to business, is that when Americans find good quality and receive good service, they tell all their friends about it, so word of mouth advertising works very swiftly with them. I guess that the reverse is also true, if they get bad service, but that does not affect me, as they seem to love my fare. Also, as fuel is so inexpensive in the States, and it is such a vast country, they are used to travelling quite long distances to use a facility they particularly like, so it is not unusual to find a customer who has come 12, 15, or even 20 miles, on a friend's recommendation, to buy food from me. God bless 'em, I say, and long may it continue.

These Americans have been cajoling me to apply for a concession to trade on Newton Molecliffe air base, so they can have kebabs for lunch. They inform me that the food on base is so poor, that they are convinced that I will make a fortune. Apparently, it is not difficult to improve upon the quality of food served in their cafeteria, as it is largely cooked ahead of time and kept hot under lamps but, as I cook to order, everything I supply is always fresh, wonderful and wholesome.

Well, as wholesome as fast food can possibly be! (And come to think of it, I'm not particularly fast either!)

I applied last December and am meeting with, what appears to be, intransigence and apathy from the company with whom I have to deal, if I wish to take a concession. I will try to ring them again on Monday as, again today; I am getting just an Ansafone. I used to be apathetic once, but I got cured of that and now I don't give a shit about anything!

Is their no end to my wit…? Or perhaps, no beginning?

Things to be grateful for.

1) Tea! (Twinings Lady Grey variety … Mmmmmm! I admit to being a closet tea snob!)
2) American customers.
3) My inexhaustible patience with the Airbase powers-that-be.
4) McVities' Golden Syrup Mini-cakes. (Delicious – especially with a number 1!)

5) Luton Town Football Club.
I still think there is more to be pissed off about!

Saturday 13th May 2000

Word of the day: Paranoia... abnormal tendency to suspect and mistrust others.

2-00 p.m. resting before tonight's trade

Friday night went quite well. Takings were above average and were improved by a larger than usual number of customers at pub closing time. Also, they behaved very well, which was a bonus. The evening had two highlights, one of which was putting a Watford supporter in his place. He came at the end of the evening and immediately noticed that I was wearing a replica Luton Town shirt. Now, Luton and Watford supporters like each other about as much as Monica Lewinsky likes dry cleaners. This particular one immediately began giving me a hard time about Watford's and Luton's relative positions within the football leagues, even though Watford were about to be relegated from the Premier League to the Nationwide League. This was not a clever move, as the twenty or thirty customers milling around the trailer, at the time, began to tease him more than he wanted! I began telling a joke, as is my wont when I get an audience!

Jesus came to Earth and met a blind man, who was crying. He asked him why he was crying, and the man said he had never seen his wife's face. So Jesus touched his eyes, and he was able to see her for the first time. He then met another man, who was crying and, when asked, the man said he was crying because he had lost his arms in an accident and could never again hug his daughter. Jesus touched him and his arms were restored. Jesus met another weeping man and asked him why he was crying. The man said, " I am a Watford supporter". Jesus sat down and cried with him!

This brought an abundance of laughter among the assembled clientele, and the Watford supporter was suitably humbled.

The second, and most significant, highlight was my being asked out by a young woman called Louise. Her last steady relationship was about a year ago, by all accounts, and she has not been out much since. She is very pretty and seems like a really nice young woman, although, to be fair, she had been to a friend's hen night and had imbibed one or two libations, which had rendered her a little unsteady on her feet. I am meeting her tomorrow, to go to see a film or something. I hope she remembers when she sobers up. What would be even worse would be if she remembered, but was horrified. I admit to being a little insecure where matters of the heart are concerned. Still, nothing ventured…!

Damn! Word of the day 1: Ben 0. – Although I could have just put it in the last sentence and picked up my point!

Things to be grateful for

1) Alcohol's ability to make me seem attractive to Louise.
2) The peaceful passing of Friday night's late trade.
3) Being asked out by a foxy babe.
4) A nice hot shower, when I smelled like a burger and chips.
5) A nice warm bed to fall into, after the shower.
6) Falling asleep while thinking of number 3 in a rather rude manner.

Sunday 14th May 2000

Word of the day: Anticipation … the act of looking forward to

7-45 a.m. in the land of dreams
(Telephone rings at the bedside)

"Hello Benjamin, it's Mum!"

"Really? I thought I recognised that voice! Hello, Mother!"
"I hope I didn't wake you?"
"You know you did. You always do on a Sunday."
"Shall I ring back later?"
"Not now I'm awake! It's OK. The phone was ringing anyway! How are you?"
"Fine, but you know Mrs Middlewich? At number 32….what did you say about the phone?"
"Nothing!...and no, I don't remember anyone of that name."
"Yes you do… her son plays rugby."
"And that is supposed to make me remember someone I have never heard of? I don't know her, or her son."
"I'm sure you do... her husband died of a brain tumour?"

This, or a very similar version of it, happens every week at about this time of day. I would never be awake at this time, unless the phone rang, or had already rung even earlier!

After a long Friday and Saturday nights' trading, I would love to have a lie-in… just once!

The amusing thing is that I am sure she thinks that I deny all knowledge of these people merely for comic effect.

"Mother, I have not lived in Luton for over 10 years. Things do change, you know. I really don't have a clue who you mean. Anyway, what about her?"

"Oh, it doesn't matter, if you don't know her."

Are there serious penalties for matricide?

I need this conversation, on a Sunday morning before 8 o'clock, like a goldfish needs a motorbike. My being unable to persuade her to reveal this precious gem of information, over which she saw fit to wake me up, she finds that she has nothing to say…

No change there, then.

…and decides to say "goodbye," and all is again calm.

I like my own company occasionally, but I have to admit that it does get lonely living by oneself, with only a mad Birman cat for company. He answers, or truth to tell fails to answer, to the name of Jason.

He is in your face when you ignore him and want to watch TV, but when you think you will stroke him, he runs away like lightning.

I have known a few women like that!

Talking of women, I cannot remember where I left Louise's phone number………. Argghh! God! I hope I didn't write it on my hand, or I would have showered it off last night!

Why does that make me think of a song? Oh yes. "I got her number, written on the back of my hand." Who was that by? It's going to do my head in if I can't remember.

10-30 a.m.

Thank the Lord! I have found her number, written on a Tesco receipt for three iceberg lettuces, two cucumbers and a Cadbury's Crème Egg. Now, do I ring her **now**, or leave it till later?

10-31

I'll ring her now… get it over with…or should I? It is Sunday; maybe she likes a lie in, like I would! No. I'd better leave it a while.

Hmmmm… contemplating her night attire. I wonder if she wears any?

Stop that, you pervert, and concentrate on the job in hand.

Argghh! More innuendo, I can't stand it at this time of morning!

10-32

But what if she is already up and going out for the day? To her mum's perhaps, if she has a mum. I'd better ring, or I could miss out.

10-35

No, I'll ring at 12. That's a civilised time to be up and receiving calls. Yes, noon. I rather like that.

10-37

But the pubs open at 12. Maybe she will go for a pub lunch somewhere. Argghh! Better ring now and bite the bullet.

10-55 a.m.

Phew! Just rung. She has been up for ages and was reading her Sunday newspaper. She does still want to come out with me and said she has wanted me to ask her out for some time now, but thought it would never happen if she waited for me. She is right, of course. I flirt with all my female customers, but I am a little scared of being thought a bit naff, if I hit on my customers, although, it has to be said that I don't meet many women nowadays who aren't customers! I am already feeling high with anticipation, (hurrah!), of tonight's main event. I will do my grateful list now, in case I don't get the opportunity later even though, with a bit of luck, I may have a lot more to be grateful for by then!

Today I am mainly grateful for

1) Paul Whitehouse and The Fast Show being repeated on satellite TV.
2) Sunday and Monday off work.
3) The opportunity of a hot date.
4) Cerruti 1881 eau de toilette (and its magical power to turn me into a babe magnet)
5) Mother. If I didn't have her who would worry about me?
6) Father. If she didn't have him, she would be running my life for me, full time!

Monday 15<u>th</u> May 2000

Word of the day: Excruciating.... Pertaining to mental torture often related to the infliction of pain.

9-00a.m.

What an absolute disaster yesterday proved to be. I have not looked forward to an evening as much as that in a very long time. I rang Louise at about 10-40 yesterday morning and we agreed to meet at her house at 7 p.m. to leave immediately, (I didn't want to put undue pressure on her, by going in before we had been out), and then to go to The Brasserie, a new place in town, for a nice meal and then, if the mood took us, we would consider either going to the movies, or to the pub for a drink. Very civilized plans for a first date, and I have to admit to having had butterflies at the prospect.

At midday, I thought I would pop down to The Red Lion for a quick pub lunch and a diet coke...

Didn't want to arrive smelling of alcohol...

... paid for, as it turned out, by taking £10 out of the Trivia Machine.

Genius will out!

This remarkable performance of general knowledge recall reminded me that I had promised to take part in the pub quiz on Sunday evening, for my usual team, The Far Canal. However, realizing that, in a head to head contest of the most enjoyable things to do on a Sunday night, participating in a pub quiz, with one Burnley supporter and two accountants, came a poor second to a planned assault on the charms of the beautiful Louise, I thought I had better give Jamie, our team captain, a ring, to let him know. Finding my mobile phone to be as dead as my previous 3 months' sex life, I successfully negotiated the thirty yards walk to the telephone box and broke the news to him. This was the moment that the wheels fell off my day, my week, my world, my car, my trailer, my Land Rover, my mountain bike and my (rather trendy) inline roller blades. I have it on good authority that even Saint Catherine lost hers; such was the import of this fateful moment! On the way **back** to the pub, my footpath negotiating skills inexplicably left me, and I tripped on a crumbling piece of the path and, as I tried in vain to regain my balance, my foot came down heavily on the edge of the footpath. There was a three-inch drop from the edge of the footpath to the grass next to it and, as my foot turned sideways, my entire weight bore down upon it. There was a noise akin to that which emanates from a chicken joint, when you rip it apart, and a loud crack, followed by my feeble cries of, "Goodness me… well I never…" and "oops, I wish I hadn't done that!" (Or words to that effect). There was a flood of excruciating (hurrah!) pain, during which I was writhing in agony on the grass, not knowing what to do to alleviate it. After about 10 minutes, during which time not a soul appeared to assist me, I attempted to put weight upon it, but it quickly became obvious that this was not a good plan. Eventually, a lady walking a small dog, which looked more like a rat on a string, passed by and took pity on me and rang for an ambulance. Lady and Chihuahua then departed, and I was alone once more. After an interlude of thirty minutes, during which time my ankle assumed the proportions of a large grapefruit, the ambulance arrived and, suddenly, there were fifteen or twenty onlookers, who found the arrival of the ambulance demonstrably more interesting than my predicament. After some inspection by an ambulance man, I found myself nestling inside the vehicle, which left the scene with, in my opinion, a distinct lack of urgency!

Where were the blue lights and sirens?

I arrived at the hospital at 3-50 p.m. and spent ten minutes, hopping around on one leg, whilst being registered, then sat in the waiting room for a further half an hour, before being called to see the triage nurse. During this time, I tried to ring Louise from the pay phone in the waiting room, but it would not take coins. The nurse asked me how it had happened, drew black lines on my foot and said that there was about a one and three quarters to two hours wait to see a doctor, but it looked like an x-ray would be needed. You did not need to be a rocket scientist to work that one out. I waited a further hour and twenty minutes, before being called and placed in a cubicle, to await the doctor. Initially, very pleased that this appeared to be a shorter wait than the nurse had predicted, I became extremely displeased, as the awareness grew that it was just a clever ploy, to give you the impression that you were actually getting somewhere, as I waited in that cubicle for another one hour and twenty minutes, before seeing a doctor. After an hour, I caught the eye of a nurse… a***nd quickly threw it back to her, (the old ones are the best),*** …and she checked to see if I was actually in the system. She assured me I was "on the board." By this time, I was beginning to sweat from the stress and impatience, which was welling up within me, and I was ready to explode.

The Doctor arrived and took all of fifteen seconds to conclude that this was not the original design of a human ankle and that X-rays were in order. I asked why, when the triage nurse and I had agreed, some two hours and forty minutes earlier, that this course of action was required, a doctor could not have given me the requisite fifteen seconds of attention and sent me to x-ray immediately? He looked at me vaguely and said, "I will put you over here and send for a porter to take you to x-ray," transferred me to a wheelchair and left, seemingly baffled by the question. I sat for five more long minutes and looked at my watch. It showed 7-15 p.m. and I was feeling even more stressed, as my phone was out of charge, (and it is forbidden to use mobile phones within the hospital anyway), and I was now within the care area and unable to access a public phone. I wondered what Louise would be thinking about being stood up, and I felt lower than a snake's arse. Finally, arriving at x-ray some three hours forty-five minutes after my arrival at the hospital, I rang the bell and waited twenty-five more minutes to be called in. Back in the cubicle, where I had previously waited for the doctor, a nurse immediately came to attend me. She said that unfortunately, the doctor, whom I had seen earlier, was performing a procedure…***probably on a nice sirloin steak and a glass of red wine!***

… and would be twenty minutes, so I was returned to the waiting room once again. One hour and twenty minutes later, after pleading with the receptionist to find out what was happening, I saw the Doctor, and he showed me the x-rays. There were flake fractures on both sides of the ankle, and he predicted that the ligament damage would take longer to heal than the bones. At last, I was given a "back-slab" plaster to stabilise the injury overnight and told to return at 11 a.m. tomorrow. I finally got out of the hospital in a taxi at 10-10 p.m. after ringing Louise's number and getting her Ansafone, (Answering machine? Answer phone? Voicemail? Recorded message?). Well, whatever the fuck it **was**, it sure as hell wasn't **her** in person. She was out. She obviously went without me. I have rung again this morning, but again the recorded message is still all I can get.

Did she stay out all night? Or has she just got up and gone to work? Am I paranoid?

Anyway, I left a message, and I have told her what happened. I hope she understands. It's up to her now. In all, it took six hours and twenty minutes to be seen and plastered! As a student of the subject, the irony is not lost on me that a hospital's clients are known as **PATIENTS!!**

Things to be grateful for today:

1) Fuck all!
2) Nada!
3) Nix!
4) Nowt!
5) NOTHING!

Tuesday 16th May 2000

Word of the Day: Frustration... dissatisfaction caused by inability to complete desired task.

10-30 a.m.

The word of the day sums up my feelings! I am sitting in the hospital cafeteria suffering the frustration, (hurrah!), of having been informed that they stop cooking breakfasts at

9-50 a.m. I even know one of the staff and still can't get a full English breakfast.

What happened to all-day breakfasts and the customer always being right?

No cooked food is available now until 12 noon, other than sausage rolls. I have had to settle for a cup of tea and have sat down to read a newspaper.

11-10 a.m.

I meet the orthopaedic surgeon who informs me that I will need a cast for at least 6 weeks.

"You will need to go home and rest for 6 weeks keeping your leg elevated." Then seeing my look of horror, "it is not going to happen is it?"

"No, I am self employed, no work - no money!"

"I hope you are going to sue the council."

"Hadn't thought about it, but now you come to mention it, I may make enquiries."

A seed is planted.

I move to the plaster room, where I am surprised to find that the cast is made of a resin-like material and is not plaster at all. I am issued, army-style, with a pair of crutches…

I did stand and wait for a while for my boots and webbing, but none were forthcoming!

…and released, untrained in the art of crutch hobbling, into an unsuspecting community!

9-00p.m. At home…

I have been laying here like a spare part since returning home. However, my brain has been working overtime, calculating the large five-figure sum that I deserve for this horrendous injury! I have also sent various items of stationery down the side of the cast to alleviate the intense irritation. I am now missing several objects, which may still be enclosed within the cast. I have still been unable to contact Louise… ***Does she not want to be contacted…?***

Things to be grateful for

1) Sky TV.
2) Downstairs toilets, or in my case, having only one floor with a toilet on it!
3) Knitting needles, (borrowed from the lady in the next-door flat,) and wire coat hangers to send down the cast for a scratch!
4) After hours of mind-bending torture, I finally remembered the "I got her number" song is by Elvis Costello, but I'll be buggered if I can remember its proper title.

Wednesday 17th May 2000

Word of the day: Procrastinate… defer action, delay decision

I am not doing this today I am really depressed and can't be arsed! Won't be using the word either as it sounds like a sexual deviation!

Friday 19th May 2000

Word of the day: Contemplate… give thought to, consider an action as possible

9 a.m. Lying with my leg up!

I am still in great pain and unable to contemplate, (hurrah!), work, but I am already beginning to panic that I will not have the money to pay my bills, unless I return to work soon. I really cannot afford **not** to work on Fridays.

Louise finally rang, expecting me to be at work, so was suitably embarrassed to have been talking to me in person instead of to my voicemail, when I picked up the phone. She informed me that, when I did not turn up, she went to the pub on her own, thinking I might have got it wrong…

A little bit of typecasting there?

…and when I didn't show, she was engaged in conversation by someone who later asked her out. As, by then, she thought I had deliberately decided not to turn up, she accepted. She was sorry about the leg and that "we" never got off the ground, so to speak, but she felt that she couldn't just dump this other guy just like that. She was very apologetic, but I can't say that my pride and self-esteem were not dented. This means that I am out of the picture before I got into it! Oh well! With this leg, I was not going to be performing in any sexual Olympics for a while, anyway. I decided to listen to the radio, and even that was out to piss me off when the 'I've got her number' song came on and it turned out to be by the Jags. Good job that wasn't a quiz question as I was convinced it was Elvis Costello, and Jamie in particular is a right pain in the arse when a team member is 100% certain of an answer and it turns out to be wrong!

Things to be grateful for

1) I may still have a chance with her. (If I can think of a way to get her 'bloke' off the scene)

2) She seemed to believe me (So she should! Even I can't make up stories like this one)

3) I have a few weeks to plan another attempt at winning her.

Sunday 21st May 2000

Word of the day: Inconsiderate…. thoughtless, lacking in consideration for others (especially, it seems, mothers!)

9-00a.m.

Mother has been ringing every five minutes since I broke this bloody ankle. My answering machine shows 8 messages since I cleared it at 11 p.m. last night and switched **off** both its listen facility and the telephone's ringing tone, so I could get some sleep! I have also begun to practise the ancient art of call screening, by means of the answering machine. In the interests of honesty, I should change the outgoing message to state, **"I am almost certainly in and listening to your message being left. If I do not pick up the phone before you have finished leaving your message, then either I am too busy to take the call, or I don't want to speak to you, in which case, please take the hint and fuck off!"**

9-10 a.m.

Messages 1 to 6 were from Mother, asking if I had died, or was I merely trying to put her in an early grave from my lack of consideration etc. Number 7 was from someone wondering whether I would be interested in taking the trailer to a sporting event, on Sunday, as they had been let down at the last minute…

I don't think so!

… but the message which wrenched me from my complacency was no 8.

" Hello Benjamin. You have not answered the phone for several days. You are just so inconsiderate! (Hurrah! Word of the day 0: Mother 1). What is the matter with you? Are you in hospital, dead, or lying on the floor of your flat unable to reach the phone? That's it! I am coming down there! Your father will have to drive me. You obviously cannot take care of yourself! I'll be there at about 11."

Panic began to fill my body, and I was temporarily frozen to the spot, as the implications of that statement gained clarity in my mind. Was it too late to call her, to put her mind at rest and, thereby, prevent her coming to run my life for me? **YES IT WAS!** I rang and got **her** answering machine… argghh! She is on her way! I am seriously contemplating taking up smoking again!

I looked around the flat. It looked like a scene from "Men Behaving Badly." On the sofa were the remains of 1 pizza…

Double Mozzarella and extra Pepperoni on a Margharita, if my memory serves me correctly.

… nestling in the comfort of its original carton, where it has been since Tuesday. A tower of assorted aluminium trays, previously containing an assortment …

Over four separate days it has to be said.

… of Pilau and Egg Fried Rice, Chicken Madras and Chicken in Oyster Sauce, Mushroom Bhaji and Chow Mein, were standing, precariously balanced, on the coffee table. The, now combined, residue of each of those meals, which lingered, fermenting in the trays, ensured that the aroma of each exquisite dish was still vaguely discernable in the overall ambience of the sitting room. It made me feel quite hungry. A selection of cans decorated various areas of carpet, adjacent to various seating positions; these cans sporting a variety of names of purveyors of analgesic, not to say anaesthetic, preparations, ideally suited to someone with a seriously throbbing ankle. Such names as Boddington's, Caffrey's, Murphy's, and Guinness were particularly conspicuous. Again, in my defence, it should be noted that my usual level of house pride has dissipated, somewhat, through the ravages of this injury, and I **had** lost my duster.

The bedroom was not too bad though. Nothing amiss there that couldn't be disguised by a quick fluffing of pillows and duvet, but this sitting room is a disaster area. Drastic action was needed. I opened a can of Caffrey's…

Which usually helps me view the world in a better frame of mind.

… and sat down to formulate a plan of action.

9-40 a.m.

Who can I get to clean it up for me?

9-43 a.m. er…?

9-48 a.m. ummm…?

9-50 a.m.

I could leave it and let Mother do it?

9-50 a.m. *and ten seconds.*

No better not, the flak would be more painful than the effort of cleaning it myself. OK, it looks like it is down to me to do it.

10-45 a.m.!!

(Eyes open slowly and inquiringly)…. OH FUCK! What happened? She's going to be here in a minute, and the place is a shit heap! I am dead!

I hopped around largely on one leg…
Long Ben Silver?
… thrusting cans and food packaging into a dustbin liner, at a speed that I usually reserve for playing football. There is just time to merely threaten the carpet with the vacuum cleaner and drop the bulging refuse bag o ver the balcony into the service area, where it lands with a resounding "crash" and, carry out the aforementioned fluffing activity in the bedroom, before, finally, repositioning the three piece suite into some semblance of a normal arrangement. I had just collapsed on the sofa exhausted, but smug with myself that I can now gloat at my independence and lack of need for a nursemaid, even with my leg in plaster, when the door received a tentative knock, which I answered.

" So you haven't died then?"
Wonderfully warm and loving greeting, as always, Mother!
"No, Mother! Reports of my demise are premature!"

"DON'T be facetious with me, Benjamin, you are NOT funny! We have been worried sick, haven't we, George?" Dad manhandlesd a suitcase into the flat, which screamds, "I am staying for weeks." I gulp at the prospect.

"Yes dear, I'll get back then," my father ventured escapologically.

I know that word does not exist, but it should!

I am not, though, about to allow my only ally to escape that easily.

"You don't have to go yet, Dad, stay and have a cup of t...."

OH FUCK! Bollocks, fuck and double fuck! ...THE KITCHEN!!!

"I'll make it, Benjamin. Sit down, George.... and stop making an exhibition of yourself!"

Dad wasn't listening but, instead, picked up on the torturous grimace on my face, as Mother strode menacingly towards the kitchen. **That** kitchen. **My** kitchen. Dad silently mouthed the words, "What's wrong?"

I shook my head at him in resignation to my fate.

Things to be grateful for

Can't for the life of me think of any at this moment, unless it is that the National Health Service is free, because I could be needing it again soon!

Monday 22nd May 2000

Word of the day: Pungent... having sharp, strong taste or smell

5-45 a.m.

I am rudely awoken, at some ungodly hour, by the strange sounds of activity in my kitchen. I am about to investigate, with the assistance of a brass carriage clock which, if a burglar had been foolish enough to wander in here, he might have been about to find embedded in his head. As I realize that the disturbance is Mother assaulting my ovenware in the kitchen, like a demented drummer in a steel band, the alarm on the clock is somehow set off. This causes me to jump out of my wits, drop the clock, (which shatters into an infinite number of pieces), and almost pass a large brick of personal effluent into my underwear, though not necessarily in that order. Mother is drawn to the noise, like a moth to a flame, and castigates me, in a loud stage whisper, that it is early, and I should have more respect for the neighbours. I would like to boast that I told her that **she** was the one making all the noise, and who caused the whole scenario anyway, but I can't, because I didn't. I tamely got back into my sleeping bag and went back to sleep, as I was told, ("like a good boy").

7-30 a.m.

I am unaccountably propped up on my sofa-cum-bed with a tray…
Where the hell did that come from? I don't OWN a tray.
… precariously balanced on my lap. A mug of tea and a round of buttered toast, laden with enough marmalade to feed Paddington Bear for a fortnight, are even more precariously balanced upon it. There was a pungent, (hurrah!), odour of bleach permeating the flat, and my eyes began to water profusely.
"Come on! Get it down you! Time you were up and about! That's all the food there is in this flat! What do you live on for God's sake?"
Why is it time I was up and about, you silly woman? And stop shouting, I am not deaf!
I know! I only said it inside my head! I wouldn't dare say it out loud. I admit it!
"OK Mother, gimme a minute," is the censored version of those thoughts that is voiced!
Now, I am not opposed to having breakfast brought to me in bed; in fact, I could very quickly get used to that, but 7-30 is a bit much!

And how am I supposed to tell her that I don't need to be looked after? She is in her element, beavering away in a good cause, as long as she can have a good moan along the way! Anyway, I am still reeling from the verbal lambasting I received at the hands of her very sharp tongue yesterday afternoon…

If tongues can have metaphoric hands!

…even my dad flinched.

Talking about tongues, I read somewhere once that a Chameleon's body is only half as long as its tongue. Oh my God! My mother is a Chameleon. No! She can't be, otherwise she would blend into the background, and I wouldn't be able to see her! Ha! Ha! I wish!

Talking of yesterday's events, I was accused of placing the entire neighbourhood at risk from Salmonella poisoning, merely by leaving the window open, so that the spores of the mould, evident upon the unwashed plates and cups in the sink, could "migrate all over the area." I hadn't the heart to tell her that Salmonella is a bacterium and totally unrelated to moulds of any description! Also, I value my life more than that!

She harped on that she had never even SEEN so much mould, in such a variety of colours. My mitigation, of being unable to walk, simply played into her hands, and I could have bitten my tongue off, chewed it up and spat it out!

"Well **I'm** here now!" she beamed, "I'll look after you until that leg is sorted out!"

No one was allowed to eat or drink anything, until she had cleaned the kitchen thoroughly, from top to bottom and, in her words, fumigated my entire crockery and cutlery collection.

Such as it is, for it is indeed a collection, and not a matching one at that!

As boredom set in, waiting for her to be satisfied with the condition of my kitchen and its contents, I suggested to Dad that we might "pop over the road," to the Red Lion for a swift half. However, she was having none of that, and we were imprisoned in the sitting room, awaiting her reappearance, which occurred some forty minutes later. She emerged, brandishing a large pot of tea and three mugs, which shone immaculately. Dad drank his tea quickly, once it was poured out, despite the fact that it must have scalded his throat, and then made his move to get away. He bolted out of the door, like a rat up a drainpipe! As he went, he cursorily shot me a conspiratorial and sympathetic glance, then made his dash for freedom, leaving me to my fate. After further, and frequent, castigations about there being no "proper food" in the house, I finally took the bait. It was always going to happen, but I surprised myself at how the stress of her being here had got to me so quickly.

"How on earth can you clean this place, when there are no cleaning products in the flat, other than bleach?" she began, as though I were about five years old. That was it!

"Mother! I have to use very professional and powerful cleaning products on the trailer, **which** I store in my garage, and they are better than anything you have ever **seen**, let alone **used**! I am a professional caterer, for Christ's sake! I have to abide by rules and regulations. The Environmental Health Officer has to visit my trailer, and inspect it, and he **always** says how remarkably hygienic and spotlessly clean it is."

I see the look on her face slowly changing from irritation, through a sulking phase, to a hurt look, until it seems as though she is about to cry, and I lose momentum and begin to feel a knot in my stomach.

Damn, I didn't want to hurt her feelings, but she can be so… so…. so provocative!

She is, however, made of sterner stuff than I had given her credit for. She was merely crafting a ploy to make me drop my guard then, with a smug smile, she completely devastated me with her "final" sarcastic riposte.

" Well, it's a good job he didn't come and inspect **this** kitchen then, isn't it?"

I had forgotten which gene pool had supplied my own sarcastic wit and wisdom, but in those few words, she reminded me! I was, of course, never going to win this argument, as she was holding all the trump cards, so I suggested we eat at the Red Lion.

It was about 12-15 p.m. when I made the suggestion, and the Red Lion is approximately 30 yards from my front window. So close indeed, that I could throw a pebble against the pub from here. However, from the moment I made the suggestion, until arriving across the road in the pub, the clock had ticked around to 1-55, and the pub stops serving food at 2. It took her longer to get herself ready to go over the road than it took her to clean up the entire kitchen. What strange and mystical creatures women are. When I made this observation to her, she looked me up and down critically.

"A shave wouldn't have gone amiss, you know!"

I couldn't resist it.

"You had time. You should've had one then, Mother!" I fought with, and then swallowed, the maniacal laugh, which half emerged from my throat.

A withering look was all she said!

The kitchen staff, at the pub, smiled sweetly, as we began to place our order, but as a member of their particular "trade union," I know that they would have been inwardly seething at our last minute arrival. I gave the waitress a knowing look and shrugged resignedly. The roast beef was passable, while not excellent, but I felt fortunate that they had served us at all, at that time of day. I was only allowed to drink coke, (which pissed me off intensely); because of the "drugs" I have been prescribed for the pain in my leg, (although the Caffrey's did a hell of a sight better job yesterday than the mild analgesic I was given by the hospital).

All afternoon, as we watched a succession of old rehashed programmes on UK Gold, (because "I haven't got Sky TV, have I, Benjamin?"), she tutted and muttered to herself about, "what a state to get into" and "not fit to be left on his own," mostly stated in the third person, as if I were not there. I wanted to respond, oh, how I wanted to respond, but I took the line of least resistance and made no comment. After all, she was perversely enjoying her martyrdom so much. At 8 o'clock, I tried to slip away, as would be my usual wont, to the Queen's Head for the Sunday evening pub quiz, which starts at 8-30. The Far Canal would have been there, expectantly awaiting the arrival of their star team member, especially where sporting questions are concerned. I could have murdered a pint, and the Jackpot was standing at £53 this week. My heart sank, as Mother made it quite clear that such action was totally inappropriate, on both the grounds that I should not be thinking of drinking when I had a broken ankle and that she was not here to sit alone all night, while I was out enjoying myself. My protestations, that I would be letting my team down, were met with a deep sigh, and the words, "They will get on **perfectly** well without **you!**"

That put me in my place, then!

Finally, at about 9-30, and out of complete and utter abject boredom, I pleaded pain and tiredness, and I retired to my sleeping bag on the sofa. With the smug parting words, "**That** proves my point. You would have been **far** too tired to go pub quizzing!" she wandered off, to sleep in my bedroom, and no doubt unpack that huge suitcase she had brought.

7-30 p.m.

I **must** get back to work tomorrow. She is driving me totally round the bend! She went out shopping this afternoon and came back armed with an arsenal of J-cloths, yellow dusters and assorted polishes and cleaning agents, proving that she did not listen to a word I had said! Now the entire place has a strange perfume of a combination of bleach, lavender Pledge and summer bouquet fragrance Pot Pourri air freshener, and all the sharp corners on the furniture, hi-fi and television equipment, have little bits of yellow cotton fluff hanging off them! Please let me die in the night! I cannot stand much more of this, and I haven't the intestinal fortitude to top myself!

Things to be grateful for

1) Dad has escaped Castle Colditz and is probably having the time of his life.
2) Perhaps I can use my "sentence" to reorganize my menu, ready to have those leaflets printed that I have been threatening my customers with for 18 months.
3) Mother will be feeling totally fulfilled.

4) I could start back to work tomorrow… I **must** start back to work tomorrow!

5) Mother will then see I am coping very well on my own and go home and torment Dad again, instead of me. (It's his own fault… he chose to marry her. You can't choose your parents.)

6) Things will be back to normal by Wednesday.

Things to be ashamed of

1) Writing "Things to be grateful for number 5".

Tuesday 23rd May 2000

Word of the day: litigation …the act of going to law, or being a party to a lawsuit

9-30 a.m.

I have just rung the air base people again, and again got the answer machine. It gets so frustrating! My American customers keep asking when I will be on base, and I have to reply simply that I am not holding my breath. I am due at the solicitors in Peterborough at 11, to discuss the possibility of a little litigation (hurrah!), against the Council, regarding the violent attempt by their footpath to render me one short in the leg department. The firm of solicitors advertised their service on the appointment card for the fracture clinic, at the hospital. Good bit of marketing there! They advertise no win – no fee, and this is the only way I could afford to proceed at this moment, so I hope it is all above board. Funny how I'm not confident that it is as simple as it seems. We shall see.

11-45 a.m.

Just as I had thought! It is not as simple as it seems! It seems every other ad on television is a company specializing in helping victims of accidents to gain compensation, but their advertising makes it appear that it doesn't cost anything to try. The upshot of my meeting, with a middle-aged woman, with a double-barrelled name, at Findham, Cheetham and Howe (or whatever their name was!), was as follows: -

The charging rate for a solicitor to work on my behalf, as set by the Law Society is £120 per hour…
HOW MUCH?
… and the guesstimate is for a total of about £1200, but this cannot be guaranteed. It could be twice or three times that!
I have three ways to proceed:a) Take the risk of failure myself, and pay the bill monthly, as we go, at £120 per hour. b) As a) but be billed in full at the conclusion of the case, if unsuccessful. c) No win - no fee, where the solicitor assumes the risk and, if we are unsuccessful, then the solicitor waives his fee of £120 per hour.

This assessment appointment was free, (hurrah!) and, if I agree to proceed in suing the Council and win the case, then the Council will have to pay my solicitor's costs in full; however, if I lose, then not only am I saddled with MY solicitor's bill, but the Council's as well.
"Luckily", began Miss Bleedham-Dry, (or at least it should have been her name), who was the "accident specialist" at this firm, "The Law Society have introduced an Insurance Policy which, upon acceptance, once we have assessed the strength of your case, could pay your costs for you, in the unlikely event of our failure to win the case."
"My goodness," I found my facetious side replying, "How lucky I am… and how much exactly is this stroke of good fortune going to cost me?"
"A one-off fee of £370, which, of course, you get back from the Council if you win."
"And which, of course, I whistle for if I lose?"
"Well… yes."
"Are there any other costs I will have to fork out?"

"Just the medical report. We use Mr Choudhery, who is a private orthopaedic surgeon at the hospital, a top man in this field. He knows what we are looking for, and how to word the report, so that the court, if it ever gets that far, can assess the compensation thoroughly. Mostly, these cases never come to court, because the Council's insurers settle out of court to save expenses. We will have to wait about 4 or 5 months for an appointment, though, he is in great demand."

"How much?"

"About £350."

"And who pays that? …Don't tell me," I continued preventing her attempted reply. "It's me again, isn't it?"

"But you'll get…"

"…it back if I win!" I finished her sentence for her. "…but swallow it again if I lose!"

I showed her my photos of the place where I fell and described the event, in full, while she took notes. Finally, she told me that, in her opinion, I had a very strong case and should proceed, as she felt that I would be looking at a possible £4000 to £5000 in compensation. Having gone through all the financing methods, the only one I could realistically go for was the no win no fee option, even though I would have to find £370 for an insurance policy and £350 for a medical report.

"So my total maximum outlay, win or lose, will be £720?"

"If you lose, yes. You lose the £370 and the insurers pay all your opponents' costs, and you would not be reimbursed for the medical report. However, on a no win - no fee basis, we, your solicitors, are assuming the greater part of the risk and could end up with nothing for our labours if we lose. Therefore, we double our fee to £240 per hour and, if you **win**, the opponents pay the standard Law Society rate of £120 per hour, and we recoup the other £120 per hour out of your compensation payment." She sensed the incredulity I was feeling, as my chin was, at this point, in my lap, and my mouth was open so wide that her words were echoing in it!

"But only to a maximum of 25% of your award," she continued, as though that made it all right! "So let's say our costs related to 10 hours. At £240 per hour that is £2400. We get £1200 from the Council, and you would owe us a maximum of £1200 as well. If you were awarded £4800, or more, we would deduct the full £1200 from that, leaving you with £3600, plus all the portion of the award over £4800. However, if you only got, say, £2000, we would only take 25% of that, which is £500.

Oh! That's OK then!

Blah, blah, blah, complicated or what? So, they are trying to motivate your greed and then rip you off for a good piece of it, because they won't take the case on a no win - no fee basis, unless they assess it as a very good risk, and then get double fees when they win. If it looks like a loser, they don't take it on in the first place! I am in the wrong job! Either way, I can't afford to do it. She told me not to worry about it and patronized me by saying that she realized it was very complicated for me to take it all in. She would send me a letter summarizing the meeting and take it from there. As long as I don't get a bill that will be fine. Shame, though, I could have done with a few grand!!

6-00 p.m.

I am Back!!!! Working flat out on the trailer, and my regulars are all telling me how they've missed me. Words of encouragement and support have flooded in from them.

"Where the fucking hell have you been?"

" We have been starving to death, you lazy bastard!"

"What are we supposed to do for food, if you take time off like that?"

How sweet…how touching… God it's good to be back!!

Things to be grateful for

1) My customers missed me
2) As soon as I opened there was a queue.
3) I am able with a little pain to work again.
4) I am a legend in my own mind!

Wednesday 24th May 2000

DON'T EVEN GO THERE!

Thursday 25th May 2000

Word of the day: can't think of one

9a.m.

I have just rung a company who advertised, on TV, that they specialize in accident claims. The wording of the ad was a bit cagey, but it seems that they are a bit less greedy than the solicitor I went to see. I have given details and they are sending me the name of a solicitor in my area. Wouldn't it be ironic if it turned out to be the one I visited?

Wednesday 31st May 2000

Word of the day: Autonomy... the right of self-government, freedom of will

10-55a.m.

Mother has just left. Freedom! Autonomy rules. (Hurrah!). I love my mother to death, but I am so pleased to be back on my own, without a minder! To be fair, she has been a diamond in cleaning and cooking, but I daren't go out, or do anything other than work, and she even managed to make me feel guilty doing that!

10 p.m. On trailer.

Some builders from Doncaster are working on a big house in the next village and one arrived, at about 8 o' clock, to order food, and it was strange to see him drunk only to the level of staggering, as opposed to his usual level of inebriation, on Friday nights, when he can hardly stand at all. He was still loud and opinionated, however, and there were about 4 other customers ahead of him. He began to play with the rotating server containing the kebab sauces.

"What's this one then, cocker?"

I am not a fucking spaniel!

"Chilli sauce, it's a **very** hot one. It'll take your head off!"

" I doubt it, cock, we have some really hot chilli in Donny! …And I eat loads of spicy food…I love Vindaloos and all that. Give us a jumbo sausage in a cob."

Now he's calling me a dick and wants his jumbo sausage in a male swan? Are these people from another planet?

"£1-60 please,"

"I bet it's not even hot to me."

Much to my annoyance and to the other customers' disgust, he dipped his forefinger into the chilli sauce, licked the tiniest drop off it, and ventured his opinion.

"That's angel's piss compared to the chilli up North! I thought you said it were 'ot?" I noticed that he had not tasted very much of it and could not possibly have realised its full strength from such a small sample!

"I doubt if you've got any much hotter than that one!"

"Angel's piss, I'm telling yer!" he laughed.

He continued to assault the ears of all and sundry, while all the food orders were cooking. I demonstratively emptied the, now contaminated, chilli sauce from the container and refilled it with a fresh supply. My displeasure was quite obvious to all except its intended recipient. The others gave me sympathetic glances, and furtive shakes of their heads, in disbelief at his delicate social skills and, after what seemed an eternity, his sausage was cooked and I served it to him, as quickly as I could. I did not wrap it, so he could eat it right away and, preferably, disappear in a cloud of smoke up his own arse! He ladled a huge quantity of the (very hot) chilli sauce over the long ¼ lb sausage and began to eat it, making puffing noises, as the residual heat of the food scalded his mouth.

"Yeah…. angel's piss!", he continued, as he tasted the sauce. "Fookinell, oop 'ome they'd laff at yer, callin' this 'ot!"

Beads of perspiration were forming on his forehead and balding pate, belying his comments, but he continued in the same vein for a few moments, digging himself deeper into a hole, as everyone was aware that the sauce was too hot for him. I have had not too dissimilar conversations, (or listened to similar dissertations), before, so it was with some amusement that I sensed the power of the sauce welling up in him. He bade us all farewell and disappeared behind the trailer, and I thought he had crossed the road to the green and had gone.

However, another customer whispered, "He is at your dustbin trying to get that sauce off his food!" Everyone was sniggering quietly. I opened the door and found him frantically scraping at the sausage with a napkin, trying to remove the hot sauce and render the sausage edible. He looked up at me, like a naughty schoolboy who had been caught smoking behind the bike sheds, and I couldn't resist a comment.

"Angel's piss, was it? I suppose that bin's a heavenly urinal."

"Fook off!" he retorted, and left.

I returned to the other customers, who were laughing and talking to each other about his performance.

There's more bad news for you too, pal, that chilli sauce is twice as hot coming out as it is going in!! I hope you keep your toilet paper in the fridge!

Things to be grateful for

1) That cocky people get their comeuppance one way or another.
2) Kleenex balm-infused toilet tissue, but I sincerely hope he hasn't got any.
3) I am wise enough to supply the chilli sauce to those who require it, but astute enough not to eat it myself!
4) FREEDOM!

JUNE 2000

Tuesday 6th June 2000

Word of the Day: Condolences…expressions of sympathy

7-30 p.m. On trailer in the village.

It has been quite quiet for a Tuesday evening, so far, although it is a bit early to say yet, whether it will pick up! I had been sitting, watching two jackdaws swooping down on to the grass outside, to pick up pieces of bread from the broken burger buns I had spread out there earlier. They were jumping at each other, feet first, like two cocks in a cockfight, each trying to protect its captured "prey". I had been playing "Guess Their Job," to amuse myself, as each customer arrived. Some I already knew, but my customer base has been broadening, and new ones are turning up all the time. One arrived, wearing a polo shirt with a Pickford's logo on it. I made a stab in the dark that he may have been a removal man. This amazing insight was borne out, when two of his colleagues arrived, and we had a chat about their activities in the village, moving a couple, from Essex, into a new 5 bedroomed house. The next guy was very interesting, as we talked incessantly about football, which ranks extremely highly in the Ben Arnold top 10 of infinitely interesting conversation topics. I got reasonably close to guessing his occupation, before our discussion, which revealed what his job was. He was very well spoken, dressed in an expensive suit and wore half spectacles. He looked like a banker or a solicitor. As the conversation developed, I found him to be very intelligent and personable, so I ruled out the bank manager idea, as in my experience, bank managers are usually outscored in IQ tests by bacteria, and most have had personality bypasses! In fact, if there were a tax on brainpower, my bank manager would be due a rebate! The customer turned out to be a doctor.

Well…it is a profession, and in the same realm of income, so I was not far out!

Interestingly enough, he was team doctor for a fairly local non-league professional football club. I enjoyed our chat and he left to go and meet his girlfriend.

That reminds me I really must try to see Louise soon.

The piece de resistance of the evening, up to now, however, was the guy who has just left, after ordering two kebabs and chips, for himself and his wife. He was a young moustachioed gentleman, (and I use the word gentleman deliberately), around my age, I would guess, and of not more than 5 foot 6 inches in height. He had what you might call "sensible" hair and a very well cut, three-piece suit, in very dark charcoal grey. He spoke with excellent diction, in a very calm and assured manner, and came across as very reassuring.

"Hello, we've just moved into the village, down Tinker's Bottom…"

I love that road name… conjures up thoughts of being a naughty boy and having your bottom spanked by a sexy lady, or is that just me?

"…our neighbour tells us that this is the establishment in this village, where we should eat."

"I won't argue with you there!" I replied. "May I compliment your neighbour on the measure of his astuteness?"

"I'd like a Cajun chicken kebab, please… and a lemon pepper one for my wife."

"Sounds like a good swap!" I used one of my standard ice-breaking jokes!

He laughed immediately and replied, "You haven't seen my wife!"

I like him already!

"Would you like chips with those?"

" Yes please! One large portion."

"Nine forty please!" He proffered the correct money and began to speak about his wife, who was a nurse. He was standing with both hands loosely held, palm downwards; one hand was resting on the other, at about the height of his waistband, and the tone of his voice was somehow deferential. I was ready to guess. This guy would not be out of place in the parlour of a bereaved family, offering condolences (hurrah! *for the word of the day not the situation!*), to the widow, while his colleagues were upstairs bagging up the body of her recently departed husband! The hand gestures were the clues, which led me to that conclusion. Our conversation turned to work and, as I cooked his food, I asked him how his day had been.

"Quite stressful, actually," he began. "But mainly due to internal wrangling at work, rather than the job itself."

"What do you do?"

He looked a little sheepishly then said, "Well, actually, I am an undertaker."

I really am quite good at this game!

He then revealed that he worked for a large family business of undertakers in Town.

I smiled to myself at my own astuteness. "Really? That must be an interesting occupation?" I replied questioningly.

"Yes, funnily enough. It is. You would probably be surprised."

I began to detect a twinkle in his eye, which betrayed a very dry sense of humour, and I knew at that moment that we were destined to be friends. I can't say why, but I will be surprised if we aren't.

"I'll bet there's a great deal of humour in it?" I said provocatively, "Black humour... Or it'd drive you mad, surely?"

"You know, you are absolutely right. There has to be. You find yourself in so many sad situations, that you have to see the funny side of things to survive in the industry. Not many people outside the industry would understand that, though!"

"Oh, I do. I'd like to think that I am a bit of a student of people and personality, and I see strange goings on, all the time, on here. We will have to exchange anecdotes!"

"Yes we will… I don't want to be rude, but how long will the kebabs be?"

(I wanted to say, "about six inches," but managed not to!)

"About another 10 minutes."

"That's fine. I just need to pop home for a few moments, is that OK?"

"Of course it is, no problem!"

I continued to prepare his food and, when it was ready, I placed it in the Bain Marie to keep hot. After about 15 minutes, a car pulled up in the lay-by behind me. A woman in a nurse's uniform approached the hatch. She began to speak in a loud outgoing voice. Her accent was southern English, very broad and probably from Essex or South London, and she gave the impression of being very at ease with the world.

"My husband ordered two kebabs and some chips?" she began. I was stunned at the news that this was the wife of the undertaker.

"Er… yes!" was about all I could muster.

"Don't tell me," she roared, " you would never have picked us as a couple, right?"

"No, you're right. You seem so different." This disclosure set her off on the most raucous laugh. I couldn't help but like her, too. There was a forthrightness about her, which made you believe that she would definitely call a 'spade' a 'fucking shovel!'"

"I could tell you a thousand stories," she said. I didn't disbelieve her!

"I'll bet!" I was becoming confident in her sense of humour. "So you try and save them, and if you can't, he plants them for you? Nice potential there for a family business!" I laughed confidently, but she stared at me, with her mouth open, in obvious horror. I swallowed hard and felt absolutely awful, suddenly knowing how Jamie had felt in his tumbleweed moment in the pub.

After what seemed a very long while, I opened my mouth, with the words of apology nestling on my lips, when she burst out laughing and said, "Had you going there, didn't I?"

Not many people are able to wind me up like that. I like this woman! I bet she is the perfect foil for her husband.

"If only it were a family business! His bosses drive him mad, and I am as frustrated as a nun in a nudist colony. The NHS pay is crap, they work you to death and I have to do agency work, on top, to survive. He wants to leave but we can't afford to let him, what do you do?"

We had a quick discussion on the pay structure of NHS nurses and the scale of pay for agency nurses and concluded that, maybe, full time agency working was the way forward. I hope they sort it out, because they are two really nice people. I guess it is true what they say, that opposites attract.

Things to be grateful for

1) The compassion and dedication of our nurses working in the NHS.
2) My judgement of a person's sense of humour and occupation is still second to none.
3) I have at least 2 new customers

Saturday 10th June 2000

Word of the day: antisocial... opposed or contrary to accepted social practices

9 a.m. On the sofa in the flat.

I have just woken up and found myself in a totally convoluted and unnatural position on the sofa. The last thing I knew, I laid down on the sofa, with a cup of tea, to watch a little MTV, while I unwound from the night's trading. It was about 1 a.m. Next thing I know, it is light, MTV is still blaring out of the TV, the cup of tea is still standing on the coffee table and I am unable to move, due to aches and pains in places where I did not even know I HAD places. It really is fatal for me to lay down, "for a few moments," I must stop doing it. Last night was extremely busy, and I am delighted at the level of business I achieved.

Oh! Good! I didn't count the takings. That is something to look forward to! I lurve counting the money that is the fruit of my labours).

I am not surprised that my muscles are aching, even acknowledging the unscheduled, involuntary sleeping arrangements. All evening, I was hopping around like a scalded ninja. I was never without a customer, from about six until past ten o' clock and, even then, it was quite steady up to pub closing time. My poor ankle was throbbing all night, inside its cast, but I didn't have time to sit down. I am going to have to get a part timer to help me at weekends; it is getting too much for one to cope with. I got quite panicky at pub closing time, when all hell broke loose. I was about to steal my first sit down of the evening, at 11-15, on my little storage stool. It is a bit low with my leg in plaster, but I had just managed to ease myself slowly down into the seated position and picked up my newspaper, but they were having none of that! I looked up to see a number of people approaching the trailer, noisily, like a cloud of locusts. I began to serve, take money and cook, as quickly as I could, but it was getting out of hand. This had happened before and had cost me a few bob, but it was a small price to pay for the lesson learned. Some of the local youths were a bit fly and took full advantage, when I was busy to the extent of not coping. One would come up and order a burger, for example, then 5 or 10 minutes later, when it was ready, I would call out, "quarter cheeseburger," and a youth would approach and claim the food. Then after a further 10 minutes and, usually when the busy period was under control, the youth who ordered it would come and say, "Where's my burger? I paid for one!" I would be left with little choice but to give one to him. It was impossible to keep track, in my head, of who had ordered what, so I was relying on their honesty. This proved to be an optimistic notion, so I developed a system of taking the cash with the order and giving a numbered ticket with each order at busy times, somewhat akin to the deli counter at Tesco. Their little scam no longer works. One tried it and I merely said, "no ticket, no food," and I stick to that and they now know I am on their case!

At the height of the rush, when I needed it like a hole in the head, my worst nightmare happened. The Doncaster builders were out on the rampage and had had several skinfuls of beer between them. To make matters considerably worse, the "angel's piss" guy from last week was with them, and he was totally rat-arsed. I had the greatest of difficulty in deciphering his slurred demand for a kebab, and he had completely lost the art of comprehension. He is not the sharpest tool in the shed at the best of times, when he is sober, but drunk, he was absolutely hard of thinking and communication impaired. Last night was the worst I had seen him. He was so dense, the light was bending around him! He could not grasp the concept of queuing, or that of being served in the sequence that orders were received. He had ticket number 22 and, when I took his order, the griddle was full and several orders were backed up, waiting their turn to get on the griddle. Chicken is, potentially, very dangerous meat, if not cooked thoroughly, so there is no short cut to making chicken kebabs. They are done when they are done, and not before! I had just completed the order of ticket number 8, and orders 9 to 14 were cooking. Everyone else was waiting patiently, seeing that I was working to capacity and making every effort to fulfil orders as quickly as possible, but not him! He kept staggering up to the counter, pushing people aside and being abusive, both to them and to me.

"Where's me fookin' kebab? I ordered the bastard three fookin' week ago!"

I forced myself not to give in, allow him to jump the queue and get his food out of sequence, just to get rid of him, so the abuse was intermittent over a period of about 30 minutes. Once his food was on the griddle and he came up, yet again, to ask the same question, in a similarly objectionable manner, I pointed it out to him.

"That one is yours, OK? Now - please be patient."

"Fookin patient, you're 'avin' a laff, matey!" He looked at the half cooked chicken, which had sealed and browned on the outside, but was still raw on the inside. "Giz it nah, cock.... tha's done enough fer me!" How tempted I was to let him have his way, but I just couldn't do it! He passed another foul, (no pun intended!) comment and walked away again and engaged in a few slight altercations with other customers, catalysed by his antisocial (hurrah!) behaviour. Eventually, when his food was ready, I called out "Number 22!" There was a loud cheer from the other customers.

Adjacent to the trailer's site, there is an old-fashioned bench, made up of three parallel planks for the seat and three for the backrest, on a cast iron frame. The centre plank of the seat was loose, because the local brain-dead had been at work, removing bolts for some amusing purpose that escapes me. However, there were three young girls of, maybe, 15 or 16 years of age, sitting on the bench, and these were the subject of this obnoxious man's unwanted attentions, so he did not hear me calling his number. I was standing there, like a spare part, with his food in my hand, getting more agitated by the second.

"Hey mate, number 22, it's ready!" He ignored me. "Oi! I thought you were in a tear-arsing hurry for this kebab?"

He approached, summoning up his most aggressive, intimidatory facial expression and said, "Are you talking to me, ya twat?"

I ignored him and spoke over his head to his friends, as though he were an annoying child.

"Take him home before someone gives him a good slap. If he speaks to me like that again, it'll be me!"

His friend, who was unexpectedly the master of understatement, said, "Yeah, sorry, cocker, he's had a bit too much."

The offending moron, who was depriving his own village of an idiot by being here in mine, took the kebab out of my grasp, then spun the rotating sauce dispenser round like a roulette wheel, and with such force that the chilli sauce was caused to spill over the counter.

"You are beginning to piss me off now.... **not** a good thing to do", I told him, "If you don't start behaving yourself, I'll come out there and sort you out!"

He was either too drunk to hear me, or chose not to.

"All these are free, ain't they?" He had removed all the lids from the rotary server and was ladling mayonnaise and garlic sauce all over his kebab. It looked a mess. I was getting to the end of my tether and grabbed the server and placed it out of reach on the work surface behind me. He was not to be beaten.

"All these free an' all? Ha! Ha!" He was laughing almost hysterically and squirting tomato ketchup, salad cream, barbecue sauce, brown sauce and mustard into the overflowing pitta bread. To make matters worse, I did not get his money when I took the order, and he was in no mood to part with his cash now. I asked him for payment, to no avail.

"O.K. That's it! I've had enough!" I stormed in a loud voice and began to move towards the door. One of his less inebriated friends detected that I was about to disembark my perambulator and throw my rattle.

"It's O.K. cocker, I'll gerrit fer yer! Hey, Macker! Give the guy his fookin' money and stop being a wanker!"

"Let him come and get it!" Macker was enjoying his little game, but was struggling with the overfilled pitta, trying not to spill it on himself, and the friend saw his opportunity and lunged at him, removing his wallet from his back pocket, where it was foolishly and blatantly vulnerable.

"Fook off, ya traitor!" yelled Macker to his mate, who handed me what appeared to be Macker's last £20 note.

"Thanks, mate," I began, "That's £3-95." I put the note in my cash box and attempted to hand the change to Macker.

"Put it in there!" he tilted his hip towards me, and I put the change in the pocket of the lightweight jacket he was wearing. He had not finished being loathsome yet.

He went over to where the three girls were sitting, placed his foot on the seat beside them and began to display the full measure of his attractive charm and seduction technique.

"Nice pair o' tits, darlin'!" he ventured to the girl nearest the end he was leaning upon.

The girl, whose mother had obviously trained her in the subtler skills of discouraging unwanted attention, replied, "Fuck off, you poxy creep!" and got up and walked to the other side of the trailer. He staggered backwards, greatly amused by her remark and was laughing inanely. The other two girls followed their friend, and they stood together, discussing what a nasty piece of work he was. Macker tottered back to the bench and replaced his foot on the seat, where it had previously been resting. However, as the girls were no longer sitting on it and the centre plank was not bolted down, as he transferred his weight onto it, it came up rapidly towards his face, as if he had stood on the teeth of a garden rake. It really was a scene straight from "Tom & Jerry". Had he not been holding the pitta to his mouth, when the plank arrived, I am certain it would have broken his nose and rendered him senseless. Instead, it thundered into the back of his hands, at some speed, rapping his knuckles with a resounding "thwack!" and forcing the pitta into his face. Owing to his very clever and inventive use of the sauces, there was an explosion of food and liquid, which left him covered in a Technicolor mess. Pieces of shredded lettuce and onion were hanging from his shoulder, and chicken was stuck to his face by the cloying mayonnaise. He could have found work as an exhibit in the Tate Modern – "Dickhead with Salad – A self-portrait". His face bore an expression of confused embarrassment, and the audience of some 25 people, still remaining, were immensely amused at his rapid degeneration from self confident arsehole to devastated fuckwit, not least his own bunch of friends, who were literally rolling on the grass with laughter, until I thought they were going to wet themselves! So the local vandals turned out to be the karma police! He was acutely embarrassed and, after picking the plank up from the floor and hurling it into the bushes in temper, he trooped off with his head bowed muttering to himself, "Pack of fookin' bastards!"

As the customers began to thin out, the last to be served were the girls and, as I was dressing the kebabs with salad, one said, "It's not funny for you, though, is it? All that stuff he put on his kebab! Must have cost you more than you made on his kebab."

"Oh, well," I said with an air of acceptance, "You win some, you lose some. At least, he kept my customers entertained at the end!"

As they bade me goodnight, and I began to clear up the mess on the counter, I smiled to myself, secure in the knowledge that I had only given him change for a tenner! It is a shame that he will probably never know it, but he paid £13-95 for a kebab that he ended up wearing instead of eating! Summary justice, I think!

Things to be grateful for

1) My customers were very supportive when the trouble looked like getting out of hand.
2) There was a positive outcome to the stupidity of the kids who removed the bolts from the seat.
3) No innocent party was hurt by their actions.
4) God moves in a mysterious way, his wonders to perform!

Sunday June 11th 2000

Word of the Day: Sanity... the state of being sane or mentally sound.

7-45 a.m. In bed

The telephone was ringing off its cradle! A bleary-eyed shadow of my former self sent forth a shaking hesitant hand to answer it ...
" Hello?"
Do I need to guess who this might be?
" Hi Mother! What time is it on the planet Zarg?"
"How the Hell should I know? I'm not a whatsit!... Astrology... Astronomy thingy! Patrick Moore or someone!"
"You wouldn't need to be... it doesn't exist!"
"What doesn't?"
"The planet bloody Zarg!" I said laughing.
"Why did you ask me what the time on it was, then?"
My brain is screaming, "surrender!"
"Doesn't matter!"
" I worry about you sometimes, you're talking gibberish! I should never have left you yet, you're not right in the head!"
"What can I do for you, Mother, now that I am awake?"
"Were you asleep? I'm sorry, shall I ring later?"
Change the bloody record someone!

"No I'm fine, How are you?"

"All right, now listen. You remember Mr Gillies, who used to be in your Dad's darts team?"

"When?"

" I don't know when!... When he used to play darts... before!"

(Totally bemused) "Before what? Before the war?... Before the watershed?... Before Christ?..."

"What **ARE** you talking about?"

"I was just being witty, Mother."

"No you weren't... and stop it, it doesn't suit you!"

"I don't know Mr Gillies."

"Yes you do!"

"Aaaaarghhhhh! Why do we always have this, when I don't know people that you think I do? I promise you, Mother, I do not know him! OK?"

"OK keep your shirt on; if say you don't know him, you don't know him.... But I'm sure you do.... Scotsman... lives down Exeter Avenue?"

(Speechless) "................!"

"Anyway, he's dead! Dad's going to the funeral on Wednesday, I thought you might like to go with him."

"Of course, Mother, I'll drive 60 miles with my leg in plaster, to attend the funeral of a man I don't know. It's one of the consuming passions of my life, you know, random dead stranger planting!"

"Stoppit! Show a little respect for the dead! Sometimes, you have the most disgraceful mouth on you, young man! I forgot you can't drive far, but I'm sure Dad would pick you up if you wanted to go."

"Mother, get a grip on reality. Please! I don't know the man, and I wouldn't come all that way for his funeral if I did.... **and** didn't have a broken ankle... and I am sure Dad could do without a 120 mile round trip in any event! He's not as young as he used to be, you know? Stop making arrangements for him. Give him a break!"

"OK There's no need to be rude, we're not ready for the knacker's yard yet! ... and another thing, I thought you were going to ring **me** for a change."

Maybe I would get the chance if you waited until daybreak before you rang me! You silly woman!

It went through my head but, as usual, I couldn't bring myself to say it aloud!

"I was going to ring you, as soon as I got up, but you beat me to it."

"That's easy for you to say now, isn't it?"

I managed to endure another twenty minutes of her advice, whilst retaining, (just), my sanity (hurrah!), before finally being allowed to say goodbye. It tired me out, so I decided I would slip down to the pub at 12, to see if Louise was about, and, in the meantime, went back to sleep for another hour.

Things to be grateful for

1) Louise is once more a free agent.
2) She did not blow me out completely when I saw her.
3) It's Sunday and I don't have to work!

Monday June 12th 2000

Word of the day: Despondency.... low spirits, despair.

9 a.m.

I went to the pub yesterday, and Louise was there with her younger sister. I bought them both a drink, and she described me to her sister as a good friend. I was even more confused than I was before and didn't know quite what to make of this. I was not altogether sure I liked being called a good friend, as it seemed as though the comment was for my benefit as much as her sister's! However, when her sister went to the ladies' room, Louise told me that she had given the boyfriend the red card and brazenly asked me whether I was still interested in taking her out. I said that I most certainly was and had always been. Nonetheless!

The path of true love is rarely smooth, as she told me that she had to go to Chichester with her sister as soon as possible, because her mother had to go to hospital for an emergency hysterectomy…

Eeeuw! Information overload!

…and she was needed to look after her father, until her mother was well again. We agreed to put it on hold, as she could not say with any accuracy how long she would be away. Did I show despondency (hurrah!)? No! Well, look on the bright side; Euro 2000 starts today, so I have a couple of weeks' serious football watching to do!!

7-45 p.m.

Well this is it! The start of England's victorious campaign to European, nay, World soccer domination. Kevin Keegan assures us they are up for it and are very confident of progressing to at least the latter stages of the Euro 2000. I should hope so, too. The new millennium and a resurgence of our once powerful nation to the pinnacle of soccer's international elite, is the minimum requirement.

I am open for trade on the trailer and, as I had expected, trade has gone dead as the nation expects… Kick off is imminent and everyone is in front of the TV, where they belong, and I am sitting close to my radio. Excitement unbearable.

7-51 p.m.

England 1 Portugal 0 YESYES YESSSSSSSSSSSSSSSSSSSS! What a dream start!

7-55 p.m.

A customer arrives!

Are you completely mad? Do you know what day it is? Are you aware that there is a SERIOUS football match in progress? Do you realize you are a worthless scumbag, who has the audacity to disturb me at this crucial moment?

" Good evening sir."
How do I do it!!?
"What would you like?"
How about an arsenic sandwich!
" Kebab, please."
"Do you want chips with that?"
"Yes, please."
"Four ninety five then, thanks"

8-05 p.m.

2-0. ...... This is unbelievable. The commentators are full of England's remarkable performance, the crowd is going mad, and I am cooking a kebab for someone who is living in a parallel universe!

"Not watching the football then?" I try to make him feel guilty at the interruption.

"Nah! I can't stand football, never could."

That's obvious, so you thought that, as your life is so miserable, you'd come and make mine miserable too?

"I can understand that."

Trust me, I can, but only because you are a boring little shit! Now go away, you horrible little man!

I serve his food as quickly as possible and return to the match.

8-25 p.m.

2-1….. Silly goal to give away but not terminal! We must pick up the pace in the second half.

9-50 p.m.

I do not believe it. We have lost 3-2! How can a team, that is supposed to be International class, lose an important match like this from a 2-0 lead? That's it, then. We are as good as out of it. Words fail me.

10 p.m.

The expected customers, full of pride, euphoria and lager, do not arrive throwing their wads of cash at me. Most have sloped off home in disgust and despondency. (Too sick to joke about it with hurrahs). Not only am I as sick as a parrot over the result, but it has probably cost me 50 quid, in lost takings, as well.

I wonder if I could sue Kevin Keegan and the England team for loss of business?

Things to be grateful for

1) I do not have a shotgun and the England team are not lined up against the wall in front of me.
2) There are another 2 games in the group stages, which, if won, will still allow us to qualify.
3) Germany didn't win either!
4) Southern Comfort in large doses does ease pain.

Saturday 17<u>th</u> June 2000

Word of the Day: Optimism... inclination towards hopefulness and confidence. (Yeah right!)

7-00 p.m. On trailer.

I cannot believe I am here working. I remember the days when I would not stray 10 yards away from the television, if England were playing against Germany at football, yet here I am! My radio is poised, though, and I am full of optimism, (hurrah!), more from the fact that Germany is looking even worse than England at the moment, than that England is looking very good.

On a more positive note, a young lady, who used to work in a cafeteria in a factory at Peterborough and, who has left the job after having a baby, approached me. The baby is now six months old, and she is looking for some part time work locally. She heard in the pub that I might be looking for someone, so I have decided to give her a try. Her name is Kirstie, and it turns out that her husband plays football for The Waysiders, in the Sunday Football League, and I know him.... vaguely. I've asked her to work Friday and Saturday nights between 7 p.m. and closing time.

Things to be grateful for

1) The German football team is very poor at the moment.
2) If we can beat them we can still qualify for the next stage of the competition.
3) Romania don't look very good either so there is every chance for us.

Monday 19th June 2000

Word of the Day: Exasperation... intense irritation and frustration

9 a.m. In my flat.

Yesterday was a day of big celebration, after the annihilation of the Germans by one goal to nil! All we need to do, now, is get a draw with Romania tomorrow, and the debacle of last week's defeat against Portugal will be long forgotten, and we can get back on the road to world beating! I was totally useless at the quiz, because I had far too much to drink at lunchtime, with all the other football revellers and, although I was sober upon my arrival at the Queen's, it only took one sniff of the barmaid's apron to render me pissed again.

Due to the remarkable victory over Germany, I was inundated with drunken football fans, when the pub kicked them out at closing time. Thankfully, this more than made up for the fact that, for all the business I did on Saturday night, while the match was in progress, I may as well have joined them in the pub and watched the game on TV!

12 noon

I have just got off the phone from talking to a woman at the company I am dealing with to go onto the airbase, who appears to have fallen out of an ape's family tree and landed on her head. I could get no sense out of her at all, regarding the progress of my application. The person I need to speak to is apparently a Frank Dykstra, who is "not in the office right now". I tried to elicit some semblance of intelligence from the woman, but she appeared to be on autopilot and would only deliver standard responses to my questions! In fact, I would guess that, if I were to put her ear against mine, I would probably be able to hear the sea! I gave up in exasperation (hurrah!), and I am beginning to lose hope of ever getting permission to trade on base. I need to try to develop business where I am and not hold my breath about the base.

Things to be grateful for

1) England is still in with a great chance of qualifying for the next stage of Euro 2000.
2) My hangover has begun to subside in time for me to get rat-arsed again when we murder Romania tomorrow.

Tuesday 20th June 2000

Word of the Day: Expectation... confidence in a particular outcome.

9-00 a.m. In my flat.

I'm feeling full of confidence, in expectation (hurrah!) of a professional performance from England tonight. We only need to draw, and we will be on our way!

11-00 p.m. On trailer.

I do not believe it! Yet again, the England team has managed to snatch defeat from the jaws of victory. Having recovered from going behind to a freakish, lucky goal to lead 2-1 at half time, they managed to concede an equaliser, after only 3 minutes of the second half! Even then, everything would have been all right, as a draw was all that was required; but I am amazed how the police did not arrest Phil Neville in the last minute of the match, because tackling a Romanian in the penalty area, at that stage of the game, is a criminal act! Everyone knows that they fall down, as though they have been shot by a sniper, at the mildest of contacts. It wasn't even as though there was any need to tackle him. Single-handedly, he has removed England from the tournament some 50 seconds before the end of the match. Everyone was already celebrating, because there was more chance of the entire Romanian team being struck by lightning than of their scoring a goal in normal play, at that time. Then along comes Phil Neville, with a lapse of judgement, worse than anything that has been seen since Mr and Mrs Neville decided not to use birth control on that fateful day, nine months before his birth! If he were any more stupid, you'd have to water him twice a week! I am going home to drink myself to sleep!

Things to be grateful for

1) Germany is also out of the competition.
2) Southern Comfort (again!)
3) Just one week to go before this bloody plaster comes off my leg!

Saturday 24th June 2000

Word of the Day: deflation… loss of confidence or conceit

9-00 a.m. In my flat.

Last night was very busy and I feel, this morning, as though someone left a concrete block on my legs overnight. Kirstie started working with me, and I cannot believe how well the evening went. She seemed to take it all in her stride, and she was a real help, so I hope it didn't put her off. She is about 28, and has a very pleasing personality, and she works very well with the customers. Best of all, I don't need to keep telling her what to do. Everything was going well until, at about 9-00 p.m., when Robin Stevenson, a sixteen-year-old, who is a very good advertisement for why the legal age for drinking in the USA is twenty one, turned up in a state of extreme intoxication. Although there were several young girls around the trailer, eating their purchases, or waiting for food to be served and, despite the presence of the tardis toilet at a distance of some ten yards from him, Robin decided to drop his tracksuit bottoms and urinate into the air for all to see. One or two of his friends, who had arrived with him, were laughing and goading him on to further indiscretions, so he finally decided to remove all his clothing and dance naked in front of the assembled throng. His dance involved much waving of arms and legs and, eventually, he took hold of his male appendage and waved it in the direction of a teenage girl, who had been laughing, more out of embarrassment than being impressed by his behaviour.

"What do you think of that, Lorna? Impressive eh?"

"Not really, Robin. We've all seen it before! It's just like a dick, only smaller!"

Exit one Robin Stevenson with acute (if not quite terminal) deflation (hurrah) of the ego.

Once more, the exponent of unacceptable behaviour gets his comeuppance. The things that go on in the real world never cease to surprise me. Just when you think you've seen everything, some pillock turns up and proves otherwise.

1-00 p.m.

I am so excited. Louise rang, "just to say hi!" and we had quite a long chat. I playfully chided her for not contacting me for two weeks, but she said that things had been really busy and that her mum had developed complications, which warranted her staying in hospital longer than anticipated. I felt a little ashamed to be joking, when I did not know how bad her mum was, but we got on to various other topics including football, and it turns out she likes football. That is a definite plus! I have invited her to come to a football match with me, and she said she would like that. Yes! Yes! Yes! Things are moving in the right direction at last

Things to be grateful for

1) If Robin thought that his was impressive, then mine is enormous!
2) The wit and wisdom of my customers.
3) Three more days until I can run again!!!!
4) Louise is a football fan
5) She agreed to go out with me again…to football!!! (There **IS** a God!)

<u>Tuesday 27th June 2000</u>

Word of the Day: Presumptuous…unduly confident

9-00 a.m. Waiting room of Fracture Clinic

At last, the moment arrives when I can reclaim overall control of my errant limb! Six weeks of discomfort and inconvenience has passed, and today it comes off! (The cast that is… not the leg!) I cannot wait. I may go for a celebratory jog this afternoon… just because I **CAN**! I ought to, really, as no time can be lost, if I am to get fit in time for the new season!

10-00 a.m.

A very attractive…n*ot that I noticed!*

… nurse has removed my cast with a very scary implement, which resembled an out of control electric pizza cutter! Better still, she remembered me from when the cast was put on six weeks ago.

"Hello. You're the chicken kebab man, aren't you? Wow! I can't believe it is six weeks since you were here!"

"Didn't think I was that memorable!"

"Anything to do with food sticks in my mind, trust me! My husband says I could eat my way out of anything, as long as it was made of chocolate." She let out a laugh, which seemed somehow incongruous with her appearance. It had a deep masculine sound, whereas she was quite petite and almost frail in appearance

.*Husband? Bugger! There goes another cunning plan down the tubes! You know what they say about nurses?*

"Think I might go for a little run tonight, see how it feels."

"Really? Very interesting…sounds like a plan!" She had an impish sparkle in her eyes, as she smiled, whilst removing the two severed halves of resinous material, which had been my ankle's prison for one and a half months. She laughed again and called her colleague over.

"Look at this Helen!" A ballpoint pen top and a drinking straw were lying accusingly inside the bottom half of the cast.

"I wondered what happened to that pen top!" I laughed along with them. "…But I know nothing about any straws!!"

"That's what they all say! Anyway… where are you going running tonight, then?"

"Oh, just up the hills at the back of the village."

"I'd love to see that!" She still had that amused expression on her face, which was becoming more worrying by the minute.

"Right! Now… place your foot on the floor…**gently now!**" She raised her voice as I made to jump off the couch. Startled by her concern, I placed it gingerly on the floor.

"Ouch!"

Holy fucking shit that is sooooooo painful!!!

"A little bit sore still!"

Such macho bravery! (**Dawning reality**…*Arse! There is no way I am going to be running on this tonight. I was a bit presumptuous (hurrah!), believing that it would be back to normal this quickly!*)

10-10 a.m. Consultant's office.

A very jovial Asian consultant examined my ankle and informed me that soft tissue injuries take even longer to heal than fractures.

This is not what I am waiting to hear!

"This may be waahnting six more weeks to be healing itself to be feeling strong!"

I get the gist!

"Now Mistah Arno, only exercising fraahrm here to here." (Passively moving my foot to move my toes directly away from me and back again, opening the ankle joint in its normal manner.) "This will be helping restaahr the muscle and naahrt caahrz you to be getting pain! Naahrt moving fraahrm side to side please!"

At this point, he noticed my frustration and reticence to accept his advice, and immediately discerned the obstinacy and stubbornness, with which I am endowed by my mother!

"You are waahnting to be trying dis? Please to go ahead!"

I flexed the ankle, gently, a fraction of a degree off centre in the prohibited direction, towards the other leg, and instantly felt searing pain flood into the joint.

"OK, den… dis is vaahrt I am telling you!"

"OK I'm convinced!"

After a nurse has put a double length of tubigrip bandage around it, I am ushered through the door to reception, where I am relieved of my walking aids and left to hobble off, unaided, to find breakfast.

10-50 a.m. Hospital Complaints Dept

I am shocked! Six weeks ago I was refused breakfast and today, despite being in the queue at 9-45, I was refused again! Don't these people know who I am? It was only 9-48 when I tried to order. I have registered my displeasure...
What a total waste of time!
.... but at least I feel purged of my anger.

4-30 p.m. in flat

My ankle has swollen up again and is giving me great pain! There is no way I can stand on this all night, so it looks like another night off, even though I cannot afford it. That settles it...I am definitely suing the council!

Things to be Grateful For

1) Solicitors who instil greed in their clients!
2) Doctors who encourage the same.
3) Southern Comfort to ease pain!

JULY 2000

Monday 3rd July 2000

Word of the day: Effeminate... feminine appearance or manner in a man, unmasculine.

9-00 a.m.

I am getting truly pissed off about the base. I am convinced that they simply do not want me on there. I don't take it personally, I don't think they want anyone else selling food on there. Why would they, when they have their own cafeteria there, which is the only food supply available? They've got everyone by the short and curlies! It's a captive customer base…a total monopoly!

Tech sergeant James Christie, who lives in the village, has been helping me, by keeping up the pressure from within. James and his lovely wife, Monica, have been regular customers for about a year now. She is English, and they have settled in the village and have two of the sweetest little girls you will ever see. They also have a German Shepherd dog called Nala, who thinks I am some kind of hero, as I give her odd pieces of cooked chicken, which I have dropped, every time she comes to the trailer with James. I think she believes my name is Pavlov, as James says she begins salivating whenever he walks her near the trailer's site, even if it is during the hours that the trailer is not there! James's job is something to do with morale and welfare, and he says that word is getting around the base that I am trying to get a concession and that the reaction by the "inmates" is very positive. Apparently, they are lobbying their superiors to try to get those responsible to stop dragging their feet.

I wonder where they got the information from, James?

James has told me that the company concerned is a very large and powerful corporate company, who like to exercise their power, and operate accordingly. He also said that they are about to find out that the military are **still** their bosses and, when I asked what he meant, he said, "It's need-to-know-basis information, and you don't need-to-know!" I admit to being somewhat intrigued, but I didn't press him. However, he did say I was to ring Frank Dykstra today, but not mention the conversation between James and me so here goes.

9-30 a.m.

I have just got off the phone to Frank Dykstra, who James had told me was the POC (Point of contact – the military always talk in letters and acronyms), dealing (allegedly!), with my application. I had to keep pinching myself to prevent laughing out loud! I don't know what he looks like, but he sounded just like a man pretending to be a woman. He spoke in an affected effeminate (hurrah!) manner and, as such, came across as being a bit offhand. Then again, if he is getting his arse kicked from within the base, maybe he **was** just being offhand. Anyway, the upshot is that I have an interview to discuss contract details. Tomorrow! Hmmm! There's nothing like being given plenty of notice, is there? Their office is at RAF Allingham, and I must meet him there at 10 a.m. James certainly seems to have some clout or, at least, has the ear of some people who do. Things have only started to move since he became involved.

Things to be Grateful For

1) Tech sergeant James Randolph Christie, fine gentleman that he is!
2) Dyksra does have to toe the line when the military says so.
3) It looks as though I can get a contract after all.

Tuesday 4th July 2000

Word of the Day: Disconcert… put off… disturb the composure of… spoil or hinder the plans of.

9 a.m. in flat

I am just preparing to go to the interview on base. I have been on my computer, since dawn, compiling some ridiculous lists that they require. They rang me back yesterday and insisted that I bring copies of my insurance certificates for Public, Product and Employers' Liability cover. Also, I have to write out my full menu, together with relative weights of each item, and its supplier, as all my suppliers have to be approved by the military, and no foodstuffs can be utilised from other sources… e.g. 4 ounce Beef burger… source JS FOODS …Beef 4oz; salad… source TESCO… 2 oz; sesame seeded 5" bun… Source Fletchers or KARA 4 oz; price £1-75 or US$ 2-80. FOR EVERYTHING I WANT TO SELL!!! AAAARGGGGH! Just when I think I have negotiated all the obstacles on the course, they move the goalposts. I am determined that they will not succeed in their plans to disconcert (hurrah!) me! I will do this inane, unnecessary task and arrive in my only suit, with my maroon leather, (almost), briefcase and present myself in the most professional manner possible. Auntie Marie bought me the shiny leather-look briefcase, when I started the business. It is quite revolting but marginally better than a carrier bag.

Noon RAF Allingham

Just left the office. What a little drama queen Frank Dykstra is! I was so right! He **is** trying to be a woman. He not only has the voice, but the mannerisms as well. He would never be allowed in the military!! I am surprised he is allowed **near** the military! I am being unfair. I don't know that he is homosexual; he may just aspire to being a woman and even be in the process of becoming one, for all I know. However, when you add pedantry and self-importance to effeminacy, you have Frank Dykstra, and (if you are me) the urge and desire to slap him. Having complied with their request for lists of product and weight and supplier and so on, they then described their standard contract to me.

Firstly, they want 20% of all takings! That amounts to nearly 50% of end profit. All they are supplying is the right to trade there and a power point to run my three strip lights, a kettle and toaster. They also promised to print some menus and fliers but not at first. Since all my cooking equipment uses gas, which I have to supply myself, they want a lot for very little in return.

Next, I will have to get every customer to sign for their food, so they know how much I am taking and then, every night, drive 10 miles out of my way, from Newton Molecliffe Base to Allingham Base, to deposit 100% of all takings, dollars and pounds, which they then keep for four weeks. After four weeks, they will draw me a cheque for 80% of all the money I have deposited and then there is another twist. It takes two weeks for their cheque to get to me and another ten days to clear, as it will be in US dollars. So they expect me to live for almost eight weeks with no income, whilst buying all the stock to trade for those eight weeks, pay all my bills and smile sweetly at them for being kind enough to allow me on base?

IT AIN'T GONNA HAPPEN!

I give up! They obviously do not want me on there and are making things as difficult as possible, so that I refuse to accept their contract. Even if I accepted the contract, they will probably give me such a bad time that I will leave anyway. I refused their contract point blank! They now know I am a man of few words, most of them abusive!

Things to be Grateful for

1) Finding out about about these people before I got tied up in a contract.
2) I still have a very good business in the village.
3) I created a few fireworks in their office, which is appropriate for them as it is 4th July!

Wednesday 12th July 2000

Word of the day: Multifarious.... Many and various, having great variety.

Lunchtime on Trailer

The lunchtime "rush" had subsided and I had just awarded myself a cup of tea, when a car pulled up in the lay-by. Bemoaning the advent of yet another customer, when I would much rather have had a few moments of solitude and sustenance, I laboriously hauled myself to the vertical, from the small storage stool upon which I was sitting, to greet the two prior occupants of the car. They were two black males with very well-tailored, expensive-looking suits who spoke in mumbled voices, which displayed strong accents. Using my multifarious (hurrah!) and well-proven accent detecting talents, I immediately recognised this as a broad West Indian dialect, but I was not that impressed with myself, as it was quite easy bearing in mind their skin colour. After about ten minutes of cooking and talking, the conversation ground to a halt so, bearing in mind their nationality and the current Tri-Nation One-Day International cricket series between England, Zimbabwe and The West Indies, I ventured forth on the safest conversation know to man, and that is to ask a West Indian about cricket!

"How did the match finish yesterday?"

"What match is dat?"

"The One dayer...? I watched Zimbabwe's innings...they got about 256. I thought your boys might struggle to get that many. I had to work so I missed their innings, how did it finish?"

"We watch football! We don' know fock abote crickette! We are from Nigeria!"

Oops! Ben strikes again. Another severe case of Foot in Mouth Syndrome!

7 p.m. Flat

My uncle Ben has just rung and offered me the chance to go on holiday in his caravan. I was named after him, while he, apparently, was named after boil-in-the-bag rice! He has booked for three days, at a site near Skipton, in Yorkshire, and then four days in The Lake District. Unfortunately, his wife, the aforementioned briefcase purchasing Auntie Maria, has had glandular fever and is not up to the trip. Having never before had a caravan holiday, I am dubious about the prospect, but he said that he would like me to go, as I might really get into caravanning!

I think not!

However, I am not likely to get a chance for a holiday if I ever I get on base, so I have agreed to give it a shot. Towing the caravan will be a piece of pudding compared to towing my trailer and, as Uncle Ben pointed out, it is a cheap way of seeing some countryside and, as I pointed out to myself, I will have my own shaggin' wagon following behind me! It is about time I broke my duck in the shagging stakes. I am sure I saw a cobweb on my trouser python this morning!!!

Things to be grateful for

1) The Nigerians were just passing through so I will not have to relive the embarrassment continually forever.
2) There were no witnesses!
3) It looks like I am going to get a cheap holiday this year.

Sunday 16th July 2000

Word of the day: Debacle... utter defeat or failure...sudden collapse of fortune.

3 p.m. Hard Shoulder of A1 (M) North of Doncaster

I am sitting here, like a shag on a rock, on the hard shoulder of the motorway, my Land Rover has burst a rear tyre, and the Automobile Association doesn't want to know! I can't believe how stupid I am! Ever since I bought this Land Rover, five years ago, I have never driven it, even a mile, without the spare wheel either inside, or bolted onto its housing on the rear door. When I was cleaning out the rear compartment, removing the debris and washing the rubber floor mat ready for this holiday, I removed it, intending to fill the compartment with luggage and other paraphernalia. My second task in the loading of the vehicle was to secure the spare wheel to that housing, so that the best possible use of space would have been employed. Having done the former, I obviously forgot the latter, and Sod's Law decreed that the very first time I have EVER had a puncture in my entire life, should coincide with the first time in my life that I have ever driven anywhere without a spare wheel!

Why me? Why now?

I set off at about 12-15, and you don't go anywhere very quickly in a 1981 Long Wheelbase 2.3 litre diesel brick, but I was making very good progress, when I felt it go. At first, I thought that it was just cross winds, but alas no! I rang the AA…

That's the Automobile Association not *Alcoholics Anonymous, although the way things are going I might need to join them too!

… and I was politely informed that, as I had no serviceable spare on board, I was not covered for breakdowns due to tyre failure. They could "arrange" for a tyre company to come out to me and repair it; at my own expense, they hastened to add; so I had little or no choice but to accept this. I have now been waiting an hour and am getting more and more frustrated and stressed out by the minute. My ankle is throbbing like hell, and my temper is doing likewise! This is going to ruin the holiday before it has even begun as, by all accounts, this little debacle, (hurrah!), is going to cost me the best part of my spending money. The AA said I should expect to have to pay £35 call out fee…doubled to £70, as it is Sunday and, before the tyre company would repair it, they would have to tow the vehicle off the motorway, at a cost of £65, but doubled to £130 as it is **still** Sunday and, then add the cost of a tyre and inner tube. So I am looking down the barrel of about £300, just for a flat fucking tyre!!

How much do I not like that? I am not amused!

I pray, (as it **is** Sunday!), that everything turns out better than it currently appears that it will, because, at this rate, I will have no money at all to spend on holiday. I am so stressed out, and I am not looking forward to sleeping in this glorified tin can either. I have never slept in a caravan, or ever felt the urge to do so, but needs must, I suppose. I couldn't have afforded a regular holiday, and now it seems I am destined, not only to sleep in one, but also be a financial prisoner for a whole week. It's a damned shame that Uncle Ben didn't leave his wallet in the caravan!

* Why are they called Alcoholics Anonymous when they have to get up and say "Hello, my name's Ben and I'm an alcoholic? Doesn't sound very anonymous to me!

Things to be grateful for

1) I am a member of the Automobile Association so at least I can get some help.

2) The tyre company are working on Sunday even if they will profiteer from my misfortune.

3) I have a caravan so even if I have not much money left I can still chill out in it, very economically.

4) Baked beans, as it seems I will be living on them for a week. (Might make the ambience of the caravan interesting!)

Monday 17th July 2000

Word of the Day: Seductively… enticingly, alluringly,

7-45 a.m. In the caravan.

I have **still** never slept in a caravan! (Hurrah for me!) In addition, I am not destitute, (at least for the moment), and can look forward to a reasonably financed holiday. The tyre man decided not to tow the offending vehicle and caravan off the motorway and replaced the tyre on the spot.

Result number one! No towage charge.

He then only charged the regular £35 call out fee, without doubling it because it was Sunday.

Result number two! What a Gentleman!

The tyre was a bit expensive, but I was in no position to haggle, so the total bill was only £126 (If you can say "only" about a £126 bill!). Seeing that I was on holiday, he said, "Where are you off to?"

"The Lake District, if this blasted piece of shit will get me there!"

"Well, you won't want to be paying me cash out of your holiday money then, will you?"

"Er, do I have a choice?"

"Yeah! I'll bill the AA and give you a docket with the address to send the money to. You get two weeks to pay. Worry about it after you've had a nice break in the Lakes!"

Result number three! Maybe things are not going to be so bad after all?

The remainder of the journey was slow and arduous, as expected, and I am seriously considering getting rid of this Land Rover and trading up to something a bit more modern. I love it to death, but it is costing me a fortune to keep on the road, and never a day seems to go by that I don't get one bill or another from it. The journey ended well though, as I arrived at the site just before 8 p.m., just in time to be able to go through registration and be allocated my appointed 'pitch'.

Whoa! Scary! I am talking in "caravanner-speak" already!

Ten minutes later and I would have had to park in the late arrivals area, just for the night, then move to the appointed pitch in the morning. Altogether too much hassle, so I was pleased to have avoided that. The caravan has two seats, with a removable table between them, which Uncle Ben showed me how to dismantle, even if I did have to suffer nearly an hour's patronisation in the process! The tabletop is then used to form a bridge between the wooden seat bases, and the cushions are rearranged to form a sort of jigsaw puzzle mattress affair. I performed this miraculous feat and was not impressed with the resultant "bed", which looked about as comfortable as haemorrhoids! Having laid out my sleeping bag over this contrived apparatus, I drove off in search of sustenance. I found a very nice pub, with a restaurant area, to which, had I known about it, I could have walked and had a few drinks to, perhaps, give me a chance of some sleep on the pile of foam rubber, which was to be my resting place for the night.

I arrived at about 9-20 p.m. and noticed a large sign, which read, "last food orders - 9-15 p.m." I was gobsmacked. Why do I always find myself wanting to order food five minutes after they stop serving?

I am sometimes kept working till an hour after my preferred closing time, because I don't turn people away, unless the griddles have gone cold, and I am about to hitch up. Why can't I be treated the same way?

I pretended I hadn't seen the notice, (albeit, one would have had to be blind to have missed it!), and said to the barman, "Do I order food here, or over the other side of the counter?" I pointed to the area where there was a refrigerated counter with desserts displayed within it.

"Um, I think the restaurant is closed, sir, I'll just check if the chef has gone home."

There was a very attractive young woman serving behind the bar, and she looked over at me and laughed knowingly. I placed an extended finger over my lips, made a "shhh" sound, and winked at her. She smiled back at me. The barman came back and had a list of unavailable items, but said the chef was still cooking a previous order and would be pleased to allow me to order from the abridged menu. I ordered a steak, which turned out to be superb and waited until the barman had gone to inform the chef, before approaching the barmaid, to order a pint of local bitter. She was about 5'2" tall and had long dark hair, which was swept back in a ponytail and had a ruched band keeping it in place. Her dark eyes were almond shaped, and she narrowed them when she smiled. Her girlish laugh was very appealing. She spoke with a soft Norfolk accent and was flirtatiously attentive. I sat down and waited for my steak to arrive and found myself focussing on the bar area, watching this barmaid moving about. Our eyes met on several occasions and we exchanged smiles. After I had eaten, I returned to the bar and ordered another half pint, which I didn't really want, just so that I could speak to her again. This time, I stayed at the bar and, as it was not busy, she stayed talking to me for some time. Her name was Stella. Good name for a barmaid, I thought but, luckily, I kept it to myself, because she said that I was the first stranger in the bar not to try that as a opening chat up line for a long time, and she found it refreshing!

She was from Sheringham, a very picturesque town on the northern coast of Norfolk, and I was pleased that I had been there and could converse about it with her. I placed her at about 19 or 20 years of age and found myself wishing I were ten years younger, as I was obviously too old for her. However, that did not stop my eyes popping out like organ stops, when she bent forward to get a bag of crisps from their container under the counter, to serve a young man of about 22 years, who had arrived at the bar to my right. The view down the front of her low-necked top was not entirely wasted on him either, and he gave me a knowing look and a manufactured pained look, together with a sucking in of air though pursed lips, as though he had just touched a very hot surface! He shook his head in feigned disbelief and went back to his table, armed with his crisps, which he proffered to his girlfriend. She snatched them and administered an immediate admonishment to him. He looked over her shoulder at me and shrugged his shoulders in a gesture, which said, "What did I do to deserve this? I'll never understand women!" I responded in like manner, by smiling and raising my eyebrows, widening my eyes and cocking my head slightly to one side, conveying, unspoken, "Me neither! You're wasting your time trying!" We men have an understanding, which doesn't require words. We are issued with a 'chip' in the brain, which puts us all on the same wavelength, I think! Obviously, a totally different wavelength to women, I'll grant you!

I must say the sight of the roundness of her breasts, as she bent down, had a profound effect on me. The bar area became busy, so I sat at the table next to the young couple, to drink my beer. I could now see that his girlfriend was not in a forgiving frame of mind and was presenting him with a face like a smacked arse! She caught me looking at her and, in defence of the expected scowl, I smiled my winning smile, and she smiled back in spite of herself but, just as I was feeling pleased with myself, for softening her mood, she seemed to wish she hadn't smiled, and frowned at me. I got up and went to the gents!

A few moments later, the young man in question joined me.

"G'day mate. 'Ow're ya goin'?" His accent was obviously Australian. "Nice country up here!"

Why do Australians abroad turn into caricatures of themselves?

"Yeah! It's my first time in this area, but it seemed quite pretty driving up."

"Yeah! Like that barmaid's pretty mountain range, eh?" He laughed. "My bird's dirty with me, just fer lookin'! Fuck knows how she'd go on if I touched 'em! I wouldn't mind, but that little show wasn't even for my benefit! Was it?"

"Wasn't it?"

"Nah! Are you blind, mate? It's you she's got the hots for! Top bird, too!"

"Are you serious?"

"A blind beggar could see it, mate."

"She'd be a bit young for me, though.... Hey! You're having me on!"

"Maybe she goes for the older bloke. Maybe she "goes" full stop!" He laughed loudly and was obviously amusing himself greatly. "Are you saying you wouldn't, 'cos I fuckin' well would, if my little bunch of trouble wasn't out there! If you get my drift!" (More enthused laughter!) "Anyway mate, better get back, or she'll think we're plotting against her. She's like that. Don't be long in here, mate, if you shake it more than twice, you're playin' with it!" He departed with even more raucous laughter. Although a little on the coarse side, you couldn't help liking him, but I was unsure whether he was genuine in seeing signals from the barmaid that my radar had not picked up, or whether he was just trying to prime me to go in feet first and make a fool of myself, to have a laugh at my expense. I thought I had better play it a bit cool and sauntered back into the bar. As I passed his table, the Aussie's girlfriend, who was also Australian, was still berating him, and I heard him say, "Jeez, hun, I didn't bring youse halfway round the bloody world to watch me get off with another woman!! Give it a bone!"

I ordered a Coke, as I had had enough beer for one night. A pint and a half? That's waterlogging country for me!

"Had enough? Very wise. Too easy to lose your licence these days." Stella opened a conversation.

"Yes, you're right. Do you drive?"

"Well I do, but I haven't got a car at the moment. The car went with the last boyfriend! It was a really stressful split."

I felt a pang of sorrow for her losing her boyfriend, but was quietly pleased that she seemed to be free.

"Oh I'm really sorry, must have been a bit of a wrench?"

Oh you moron. What a dumb thing to say! Of course it was a bloody wrench!

"Yes it was. I really miss that car!"

"Yes, the old ones are the best, and that one was older than your grannie!" I teased.

She laughed and flounced away to serve another customer. Unless I was very much mistaken, **that was definitely** showing out for my benefit!

She returned quickly, (another good sign!), "Are you just passing or on holiday?"

"On holiday, just drove up today. I'm staying in the caravan park just down the road, that way." I pointed towards it.

"You don't strike me as the caravan type!"

"I'm not! Believe me, I am not looking forward to this. My uncle lent it to me. Said it would be a good way to see the country without spending a fortune. I'm not so sure, though! The prices at these Caravan sites are not that cheap! I think I'd rather be in an 'otel. Mind you the facilities look quite good at the site I'm on."

"That's good, because my aunt and her boyfriend run that site. Caroline and Dave, did you meet them?"

"Yes, they seem a really nice couple. Didn't have much time to chat though, I only just made it. I think they were about ready to leave."

"Well, they didn't have far to go home! They live in the big static caravan next to the site office, so I doubt they were too bothered by you arriving late. Are you up with your family?"

Hah! Fishing, eh? Good!

"No I'm single." I smiled at her. "Never been married."

"OK! What's wrong with you, then? Gorgeous bloke like you? Why haven't you been snapped up by now?" (The laugh, which followed, was surplus to requirements! I was quite happy with just the "gorgeous bloke" comment!)

"Never found the right one, I suppose. Maybe I'm just an old romantic and set my standards too high. I've had enough girlfriends, but they either turn into ogres, or get snatched away by other blokes."

Oh my God! Did I really say that out loud? What a sad bastard she must be thinking that I am? Quick change of subject required!

"How long have you been up here?"

"Five years!"

"You haven't lost your accent." I paused, but she did not fill the gap in the conversation. "You must've still been in school when you moved, then? Did your parents move here?"

"You're a bit of a charmer, aren't you? I'm twenty three, thank you very much!"

"Really? You honestly do look younger!"

"I don't want to look younger!"

"You will when you're thirty three, trust me!" We both laughed.

"Are you thirty three then?"

"Just turned thirty four, actually! Recent birthday."

"I thought so. Men of your age are so much more mature. I'm not keen on twenty-three year-old blokes. They are too full of themselves and immature.

Correct response, if a bit strong on the generalisations! Could be in with a chance here!

I could feel the adrenalin flowing.

"What time do they close up here?"

"10-30 on Sundays." I looked at my watch, and it was gone twenty-five past.

Damn! Just when it was getting interesting!

"I guess that's about it, then?" I tried to show disappointment, without overkill!

"Almost, but you've a few minutes yet. It's not my turn to wash the glasses tonight, though, so I'm finished as soon as I've collected them in for Nigel, and the last customer is out of here. I hate washing the glasses, it takes forever!"

(Resignedly,) "Oh well! I suppose I'd better be off then? Before I get thrown out!"

"You won't get thrown out for twenty minutes or so!"

"Right then, let me help you collect them in."

She didn't say not to, so I moved quickly around the bar area, collecting the empty glasses and stacking them carefully on the bar. I suddenly felt numerous pairs of eyes following my every move. I felt like a monkey in a cage, but fortunately resisted the temptation to jump on a table and start scratching my armpits! She went from table to table emptying the ashtrays and polishing them with a yellow duster.

Mother would be impressed!

By 10-45, there was not a customer left in the bar, apart from me. Nigel, who had taken my food order, began washing the glasses on an automatic bottlebrush, prior to loading them into a glass-washing machine. She said her goodbyes and made for the exit where I was standing.

"I'll walk down with you, if you like." She offered. "It's on my way."

"I'm in my old Land Rover. I know it looks daft, but I didn't know how far I'd have to go to find somewhere nice for dinner."
"I love Land Rovers! What sort is it?"

"Only an old one. Nothing special."

"But the old ones are so full of character!"

"Same as blokes, eh?" I laughed.

She ignored the comment, we walked across the car park, and she looked over my old truck with an enthusiasm, which appeared quite genuine. However, there followed an interlude of some awkwardness, as I was unsure what to do next. Should I ask her if I could drive her home and risk rejection? Or should I say, "Goodnight," and go back to a cold caravan, wondering what might have been? We talked for about fifteen minutes, about absolutely nothing, and she made no attempt to draw the inane chatter to a halt, so I plucked up courage and asked her if she would like a lift home.

"I thought you were never going to ask!" She giggled, and jumped in excitedly. "I'd love a ride in this, it's fantastic!" She said, as she settled into its less than sumptuous passenger seat. I avoided the obvious sexist joke, although it took an immense amount of willpower, as I reminded myself that she seemed to be attracted to maturity and intelligence! Her flat is above a little gift shop in the village, adjacent to the caravan site, so it was a very short journey, before the next potentially awkward moment ensued. She immediately removed that potential by saying, "Is that all I get?" and pushing her bottom lip out like a spoiled child. I assumed that she meant that the joy ride was too short, so I offered more.

"Where would you like to go then?"

"Head out towards Skipton. I love riding in this. It is so beautiful. So… sort of primitive."

She was not wrong! It is about as primitive as you can get! We drove into Skipton and she directed me to a bar, which was open until 12-30 a.m., and we went in for a drink. Sitting opposite her at a small table, in seductive lighting, I found myself enchanted by her dark, dreamy eyes. She noticed my obsessive gaze and smiled, narrowing her eyes sexily as she did so. I began to feel stirrings, which had been unfamiliar to **that** region for many a month! The extra drinking time seemed to be over in a flash, and we were soon heading back. I drove slowly, wanting to extend the evening; I was enjoying her company so much. Eventually, I pulled up outside her flat again and turned off the engine. I moved slowly towards her, hoping for a goodnight kiss, but she smiled, again, that alluring smile and pulled away, opening her door and jumping out onto the footpath.

"Aren't you coming in for coffee, then?" She said coquettishly and scampered down the side of the shop, into the dark recesses of the alley. I followed nervously, as it was pitch black, and I did not know where she had gone. As I found the gate at the bottom of the alleyway, she jumped out and shouted. "Gotcha!"

I clutched at her and drew her towards me and kissed her warmly on the lips then hugged her to me tightly.

"Got **you**!" I whispered huskily.

She led me through her front door and up the stairs into her living area. She did not put on the lights, but led me seductively, (Hurrah and big time hurrah!!), by the hand, into her bedroom, and shut the door.

No Coffee, then!

"You are not going to rush off are you?"

"No". I responded, allowing myself to be led all the way to her bed. The very pleasant interlude, which followed, would have been depicted, in old black and white films, by the sea rushing in, onto the beach, and then crashing foamingly onto rocks, or by a train disappearing into a tunnel. I will say no more.

As we sat opposite one another at breakfast this morning, Stella was most complimentary about my performance, and was particularly impressed with the way I teased her, by bringing her almost to a climax, then stopping, kissing and touching, and starting to make love again. This happened four times, until, finally, she reached her climax with an earth-shattering groan. She said it was a most explosive orgasm and then said that she had heard that older men really knew how to please a woman, but didn't really believe it until now! I basked in the kudos and accepted, modestly, the praise she was so generously heaping upon me, elevating me to the realms of sex god. I did not however, own up to the fact that the real reason for my stopping and waiting and starting again, was that this was my first shag of the new millennium, and I was so gagging for it, that I was afraid of embarrassing myself by losing it in ten seconds flat! I felt really excited at the prospect of a lovely week with her and was going to cancel my four days in the Lake District to stay here, but Stella informed me at breakfast, that she was going to Kos for ten days, with three girl friends from Skipton, and was flying out tonight, from Manchester, at 6 p.m. I find it hard to understand why so much misfortune befalls me in the nookie department, all the bloody time! Has this enchanting goddess just been using me?

If so, it was worth it! May I often be thus used!

Well, perhaps we will get in touch at some point. We have each other's phone numbers.

Things to be Grateful for

1) My first shag of the new millennium!!
2) A fantastic evening with a very sexy woman.
3) Stella thinks I am a fantastic shag even though I cheated.
4) She did not notice the cobwebs on my private equipment!
5) The Australian bloke giving me the confidence to talk to her.

Tuesday 18th July 2000

Word of the day: **Ancestral...** Belonging to or inherited from one's ancestors

9-30 a.m. In a café in Ripon

I am just enjoying a very pleasant cappuccino, in a very small café, about one hundred yards from Ripon Cathedral. After yesterday's discoveries in Harrogate, I am surprised to find that Ripon Cathedral has not been turned into a shelter for the homeless, or a Health and Fitness Studio!

I feel a warmth and homeliness about this city. I am feeling very nostalgic in my ancestral (hurrah!) home. My paternal Grandfather was born here and several generations before him. I have researched my family history in a small way; in fact, I was allowed to enter the record room at the Cathedral, on a previous visit, to peruse the actual registers, which are still held there. I would love to know more, but for today, I just want to absorb this sense of belonging.

Yesterday, I went into Skipton and found a lovely café called 'Hatters.' As "the hatters" is the nickname of my football team, Luton Town, I was drawn to it, and found the food to be of very good quality. I enjoyed a full English breakfast there, as I was too lazy to get to grips with the primitive cooking equipment on the caravan. I noticed that they had a home-made shepherd's pie on the menu, so I made a mental note to return for lunch, at some point, and avail myself of a portion! However, I intended to turn the clock back to when I was that travelling salesman, and visit Harrogate. Every year, for about five years, I had to attend the Harrogate Toy Fair, which takes place in the first or second week of January each year, usually to the accompaniment of snowstorms and icy roads. I arrived in Harrogate at about midday, after having had a wander around Skipton market first, and made straight for Betty's tearooms, to sample the most wonderful Darjeeling tea. It tasted just as good as I remembered it, and I took a little trip down "Memory Lane," looking around this most familiar town and looking forward to the acme of my day's plans, a visit to the best Indian restaurant I have ever found, "The Shebab." After wandering around the town and visiting the Royal Baths, where I used to be situated during the Toy Fair, I had a coffee in The Old Swan Hotel, where Agatha Christie is reputed to have stayed, when she disappeared in 1926. Its olde world splendour is looking a little more olde and a little less splendorous nowadays, but its ambience is still quite special. I then set off in search of "The Shebab". I could only remember that it was situated in a very narrow street, somewhere off the town centre and, that previously, I had mostly gone by taxi from the hotel where I used to stay, "The Granby Hotel." After almost an hour of wanderings, I came across the familiar location and was horrified to find a large redeveloped wine bar complex in the building which housed "The Shebab"! I enquired the fate of the famous Indian restaurant and found out that the owner had retired and sold the freehold about three years ago. Arse! I had fantasised about eating there for about five years! I was so disappointed! I decided that I would have a quick look at the old Granby Hotel, before going back to the caravan. Rats, arse and double arse!

Even the Granby has been redeveloped into retirement homes; I don't believe it! Is nothing sacred?

I returned to the caravan, feeling a little deflated that progress had robbed me of a little nostalgia, and went out to find somewhere to eat. I am ashamed to say that I first paid a quick visit to the pub where I met Stella, to check if she was working and had just shot me a line about going abroad, to escape having to see me again. She was telling the truth, and I felt a little stupid in my distrust of her. I guess that this says more about me than it does about her!! I moved on to the Old Hall Hotel at Threshfield, in torrential rain, and got soaked running from the truck to the restaurant. It was worth it. I was very impressed with the roast lamb on the bone, which I ate with some relish. (Relish as in enjoyment, that is, not as in the condiment!).

Things to be Grateful for

1) That Harrogate is still there at all, as so much seems to have changed.
2) Betty's Tea Rooms which hasn't changed at all and whose staff is among the politest I have ever come across.
3) A very good meal, even if I was robbed of my Indian meal.

Wednesday 19th July 2000

Word of the Day: Stipulate... demand or insist as part of an agreement

9-30 a.m. Looking out of caravan window.

It is absolutely pissing down with rain, yet again. Funny how each day seems to begin and end with rain, yet at some point of the day it becomes quite warm and sunny. Must be something to do with the hills and dales. It is very refreshing looking at undulating countryside, though. You don't get many mountains in the Cambridgeshire fens! I spent a lovely day at Ripon yesterday, exploring the City of my father's birth. My Grandfather left Ripon to find work at the Vauxhall Motors factory at Luton, when my father was a teenager, (which is how come I find myself born there), but his roots were always here in Ripon, and I could feel it, walking the streets and visiting the locations that my father has often described to me. Many generations of my father's side of my genealogy were born and lived in and around this beautiful City. My great grandfather was a driver for the local bus service, before moving to Durham, where he drove the Civic Limousine, chauffeuring the mayor and his wife, and more infamously, the Lord High Executioner, (and the wooden crate containing the noose,) when he came to Durham jail to hang murderers. I can remember him telling me a story, when I was very young, about driving a psychiatrist to the jail to assess the sanity of a condemned man, which assessment would decide whether he was executed or sent to a high security mental hospital. The whole country was hooked on this case and was waiting with bated breath for the decision. Everyone had an opinion based on the information about the case, which had been rife in the newspapers of the day. Being before the advent of television, news travelled much more slowly than today, and many wagers had been made on the outcome of the case. My great-grandfather, having driven the psychiatrist to the jail, had to wait to take him back to the station to catch the train back to London. On the way back, he asked the psychiatrist how it had gone, and he replied, "His attempts at feigning insanity were puerile. He'll hang!" My great-grandfather, armed with this very valuable information, went back to the council garage and accepted bets from anyone and everyone who believed that the criminal would be reprieved and won several pounds, and even more pints of beer, on the strength of it! His father was a master painter, who specialised in gold leaf relief and restoration of old buildings with ornate architecture. I saw some gold leaf work that he did at Ripon Cathedral, over 100 years ago, and a lump came to my throat to think that I was standing in the very spot that my ancestor had stood, some 110 years earlier. I am not the world's most religious man, but I lit five candles to my forebears, who had been pillars of this community all those years ago, and found myself feeling quite moved;

so moved, that I bought a pork pie for my lunch from Appleton's, the pork butcher's, in the market square. This shop is one, which my father swears, makes the best pork pies in the universe. I also liked the look of the large home roasted ham and bought some for later consumption, and upon the recommendation of the butcher in charge, also bought a pound of very high quality pork sausages, (some of which I have just eaten, today, for breakfast). I struck lucky at the local Army Stores, where I purchased a wind and waterproof jacket and a fleece at seriously reduced prices, and then made for the car to eat my pie.

On the way back to the caravan, I stopped at a tourist information centre and learned that there were some attractive waterfalls, at nearby Linton, and took a walk of about two miles from the centre, to where the falls were located, before spending a relaxing half hour watching the animated water crashing over the rocks. The weather, by this time, had become hot and sunny and, by the time I had taken some fish and chips from the local village back to the caravan, my nose and forehead were glowing, having caught the sun, down at the falls. I may stay here today, and read, if this weather doesn't brighten. I feel I have missed out on a potentially fantastic week, had Stella not been booked to go on holiday this week. I wonder if she is thinking of me, too. I am leaving later today to head for the Lake District. There is nothing to keep me here now. If she had been here it may have been different.

Oh God, I sound like a slushy movie.

On the bright side, I have always wanted to see the lakes.

Damn! I forgot! Word of the day 1: Ben 0

Things to be Grateful for

1) After sun lotion, because my facial skin was tight as a drum this morning and burning from yesterday's sunshine.

2) A wonderful day, feeling a sense of belonging and of empathy with the surroundings at Ripon.

3) Appleton's very fine pork pies, ham and sausages!

4) Managing to buy my protective winter clothing at the summer sales! **Goddamn, so financially astute!**

Thursday 20th July 2000

Word of the Day: Accentuate... Emphasise...make prominent

9-30 a.m. In caravan at site in South Lakes Area

I am sited in a beautifully wooded area in the Lake District, south of Kendal and, although a heavy mist is laying over the site, it has refrained from raining at last! I have just been down to the site office and cadged some sugar for my morning tea and, as soon as the female site warden heard that I was single, and had barely lost my caravanning virginity, she commenced to mother me with a capital "M". She was a very pleasant lady in her early 50's, I would guess, and she provided me with milk and sugar and tea bags. She was so friendly and helpful I was almost embarrassed. Just then, a very large and obviously new caravan, being towed by a brand new Toyota Land Cruiser, pulled up outside. The driver, a "Hooray Henry" type, alighted and walked into the office and attempted to demand attention. The lady warden put him firmly in his place and made him wait, while she concluded mothering me, by selecting and handing me a series of tourist information leaflets. He stood impatiently, as though she had failed to realise just how important he (thought he) was and gave me a look that would have melted ice. I gave him a smirk of satisfaction and left. I had noticed, as he pulled up, that he had actually allowed two of his children to travel inside the caravan, which is decidedly dangerous as well as slightly illegal!

Ha! Ha! Slightly illegal! That's like saying you're slightly pregnant!

So, no matter how important he thinks he is, it appears from his intelligent interpretation of what constitutes child travel safety, that it is only will power that is preventing his ears from collapsing inwards and meeting in the middle of his head! I will have a look at the leaflets before deciding how to plan my remaining days away from the real world!

Yesterday, with the weather being a bit suspect early on, I went into Skipton again and went back to Hatters for the shepherd's pie lunch. It was good but I was amazed to find green peppers in it.

Peppers! What the hell are peppers doing in a shepherd's pie? Very traditional…not! I can just see those shepherds tending their sheep in fields of capsicums.

In truth, I did enjoy it, but I would have preferred it to have the more traditional flavours I was hoping for.

I next went down by the Leeds and Liverpool Canal and decided to have a touristy ride on a narrow boat, to kill a couple of hours in a pleasantly lazy way. I sat and watched the other passengers getting on after me. It was like a cackers convention! On the other side of the aisle, was an elderly grey-haired woman from Leeds, who had brought her three grandchildren on an outing. She had a big aggressive vocal capacity and graciously gave the entire assembled masses a running commentary on the activities of the moorhens, ducks and swans, and later the swallows.

I have just encountered my first Northern cackers!

Mrs Loud spent every other moment of non-commentary, barking safety instructions to her grandchildren, who, to be fair, did not require such direction and would have been better left to enjoy their trip without her constant attention.

"Mind your head, Shanice."

"You'll fall off your seat in a minute, Billy."

Then …" I won't tell you again!" (Although I KNEW she would!). I could feel the assembled throng mentally shouting, "For God's sake, SHUT UP!!!!!!" She reminded me of a character in a game of Cluedo.

The murder was committed by Mrs Loud in the Narrow boat with her booming voice.

Behind that family was another family, The Weirds. These were my second northern cacker family. The mother had lank dirty blonde hair and large ears, which stuck out. "Why, then," I asked myself, "did she keep scraping her hair back behind them to accentuate, (hurrah!), them?" The father had a peculiarly shaped head, which he also accentuated, (hurrah again!), by having shaved it to grade one. The two children were sitting with vague, unintelligent faces, gazing vacantly into space. If he ever decided to leave her, a paternity test would not have been required to decide if he should be responsible for child support! Both children had inherited his weirdly shaped skull, as well as the mother's prominent ears, and therefore accentuated, (Hurrah a third time!), perpetuated and exacerbated the family traits! I winced at some of the comments these two were making, misdirecting their children's education, with guesswork as to the varieties of waterfowl on display. The father pointed out a male mallard, and erroneously explained that it was an eider, the feathers of which are used to make eiderdowns. The mother showed them a female mallard and suggested it was probably a moorhen. Between them, they certainly gave proof to my cacker theory! Anyone is entitled to make a silly remark or two, but these two were definitely abusing the privilege. Behind me was a Scotsman, who had the brightest ginger hair I have ever seen, and he looked large enough whilst seated, but when he got up to go for a cup of coffee, he had to bend nearly double to avoid the roof. The lady in his company was a pretty, if all-too-thin, woman who had a very soft Scottish lilt to her voice. She made a few humorous remarks, engaging me in conversation, until the big man returned. He joined in the conversation, and I was embarrassed to be totally unable to understand a word he said. After I had asked him to repeat a sentence for the third time, the woman laughed and began to translate for me. We talked about our holidays, and I remarked that everywhere I looked, there were couples: on this boat, in the restaurants, in the caravan sites, everywhere. I would have enjoyed being a tourist a lot more, if I had someone to share it with. She said that her sister was joining them the next day, and she was also going to feel a bit of a spare part, but it was the only chance she would get for a holiday this year. I remarked that I had, more or less, come for a similar reason. It dawned on me that this woman might have been hinting that I should consider meeting her sister, but I couldn't be sure and, in any case, I had booked to move on to the lakes, so I did not pick up on that aspect of the conversation.

Later I went into the market.

Why do people who want to walk at 0.5 miles per hour always seem to be three abreast in front of me?

I had another coffee, which had the same strange taste that pervaded all water-based drinks in this region. The water here has a musty quality, which taints the flavour of tea and coffee or cordials. The rain eased off, as I set off for the lakes at about 3-30. I had read a leaflet about a waterfall walk at Ingleton, which is said to be one of the most spectacular in England, so I decided to stop off on the way to walk it. It was said to be about 4 miles around, so I thought it shouldn't take too long. As I arrived at Ingleton, the sun was shining, but there was a small valley down which the road ran, and in this valley, it was raining, On the other side, it was as sunny as the side from which I was approaching. A rain sandwich! I smiled at my inventive sense of humour and felt lucky that no one could hear what goes on in my head sometimes, for fear that the men in white coats might come and take me away! The waterfall walk was absolutely breathtaking in every sense of the word. The falls were indeed spectacular, but the terrain that had to be negotiated, to get around each of the five major falls, was incredibly tough and certainly left me with my breath having been taken! It may have been 4 miles, "as the crow flies," but after climbing up the hills and down the dales and so on, it must have at least added another mile and a half to the distance actually walked. After two and a half hours of pain and agony, I emerged with great satisfaction at having completed the ordeal and with pleasant memories of some beautiful sights.

I arrived at the new site and set off to collect a take away Indian meal at Kendal and, as one always seems to do, ordered far too much and ate only about half of what I had bought. I put the rest away in the fridge for future reference. I made a cup of tea, but it was still standing on the shelf this morning, without having been touched, as I must have crashed out immediately after the exertions of the day.

Things to be Grateful for

1) More picturesque countryside, especially the waterfalls.

2) My personal CD player as there is no television in this caravan, and no entertainment in this site.

3) The nice warden who put Hooray Henry in his place!

4) Word of the day 0: Ben 3!

Friday 21ˢᵗ July 2000

Word of the Day: Judicious… Of sound judgement… prudent and sensible

9-30 a.m. In caravan at site in South Lakes area

Only two days to go, and I haven't even been on the lakes yet! I guess I had better do that today, since the weather is bright and may not be tomorrow!

Yesterday, I decided to do the full Wordsworth experience and visited Grasmere, where his most famous residence, and ultimate resting place, was situated. I set off expectantly and, after about ten minutes, passed a signpost, which indicated that I had inadvertently driven on the correct road, but in totally the wrong direction, and I found myself near Grange-over-Sands. I thought that I would be unlikely to get another chance on this holiday to see the sea, so I detoured off the main road and ventured forth into Grange, from where I could take a scenic, if slightly circuitous route, all along the east side of Lake Windermere to Bowness, then on to Grasmere. Wrong again! Apparently, Grange-over-Sands was so named because there are miles of sands when the tide goes out. When I had paid £2 to park and wandered towards the coast to get a lungful of bracing sea air, I got a full view of the most boring coastline I have ever seen. The sea was not only out - it was on holiday! There was sand as far as the eye could see. I thought, "Is this the sort of day this is going to be?" I pushed on to Newby Bridge, and then followed the Lakeside to Bowness. This is a really pleasant town. I made a note to visit properly before going home. I passed through Ambleside, where one of the Bronte sisters used to visit and drove on to Grasmere.

I found Dove Cottage, William Wordsworth's former residence, parked and went straight to the adjoining restaurant, as it was already lunchtime. I availed myself of their Cumberland Sausage, which was served with designer vegetables and red wine onion gravy and a very tart apple and sage sauce, which turned out to be a very judicious, (hurrah!) choice. I could really get used to all this high-class food!

Although you can keep the apple sauce, which nearly turned my mouth inside out, it was so sharp!

I was feeling very intellectual, in such academic company, and took the guided tour around Dove Cottage. The guide was very humorous, and I enjoyed her talk enormously. I am already a mine of useless information, but this woman added to my store greatly. I learned about Wordsworth's sister and her journals and about his friendships with Sir Walter Scott, Coleridge, Lamb and Southey and, how the dinginess of the rooms was down to the government taxing property by the size of the windows; so houses were often built with inadequate windows, in order to avoid taxation. The witty Lamb was outraged at the dinginess of the house, for someone to write in, and coined the immortal phrase, "It is daylight robbery," on the strength of it. On display was, what in those times was called a candle, consisting of a piece of split and stripped rush, which was dipped in tallow and attached to a pivot at its centre. This was aligned vertically and lit for average light, but for more bright illumination, it was placed horizontally and both ends were lit. Hence the saying, "burning the candle at both ends" was born.

The house was originally the "Dove and Olive Branch" public house, so it has a very good cold room at the back. It really was a very pleasant afternoon. I wanted to buy a complete works of William Wordsworth, obviously to read at some point, but I do need a work of some sort to fill an empty space on my bookshelf. In my quest to find a 'good woman', I've taken a couple of books, ('Toilet Jokes' * and 'The Joy of Sex,) off the shelf. To replace them with Wordsworth will, (surely?), put any thinking woman within my grasp. Unfortunately, I am running a little thin in the pecuniary department and had to forgo the pleasure, for the time being. I did however walk into Grasmere and saw the river, which has the most crystal clear water I have ever seen in a river. I could see the fish in it, as clearly as if the water were not there.

* Written by Alex Comfort (!). I didn't really want it but it was one of those, which arrived from a book club when I forgot to send in the declination form. I thought it would add to my appeal but that was in the 80's. Perhaps I should get a copy of 'Tantric Sex' to replace it with?

Things to be Grateful for

1) Getting a trivia fix, which will stand me in good stead in the pub quizzes!
2) Getting a very adept guide and feeling close to history.
3) Seeing even more remarkable scenery and sights.

Saturday 22nd July 2000

Word of the Day: frugal… sparing or economical, especially of food.

9-30 a.m. In the caravan.

Can't see me beating the word of the day today, as I don't do frugal very well!!! I love my food. Today, I am going to go to the Kendal shoe factory, as I have just been told by my "caravan mother", who has only today told me that her name is Mary, that many bargains may be had there. I guess that means it will be full to the rafters with cackers, but I am a sucker for a bargain, hence my Army and Navy purchases in Ripon, so I will have a walk round Kendal itself, and then have a look for myself. I decided to eat the remainder of Monday's Indian last night. It was still very nice and tasted exactly as it had when I bought it. Very economical, but there was plenty of it, so frugal is probably the wrong word! Damn! However, this morning, I have serious heartburn and a further problem, which would be too much information for this journal, but suffice it to say, is not as big a problem in the open air as it is in a confined space, such as a caravan! I have been supplied, (by Mary), with some "Rennies" for the indigestion.

I went into Bowness yesterday, as planned. I arrived at about 11 a.m. and took a quiet walk around the town. I could have spent a fortune there. One shop in particular could have kept me interested all day, with its mystical objets d'art. I love crystals, marble and ethnic objects. I could really get into Feng Shui if I thought about it. Maybe there is bad Feng Shui in my love life.

Mental note: Investigate how Feng Shui works.

I went to the quayside and had a quick cup of tea, which was the colour and flavour of dishwater, while I awaited the arrival of the Motor Vessel Tern. I had bought a double ticket allowing me to cruise the Lake Windermere southwards down to another quay, where I got off and took a return steam train journey of about twenty minutes, which was so cool. I really enjoyed it. It really seemed weird to think that when I was a baby, they were still in service. While I was in the queue to get on the boat at Bowness, I noticed a tall woman of about thirty to thirty-two years, with shoulder-length, white-blonde hair. She was thin, almost to the point of emaciation, and was wearing a luminous bright yellow Lycra jacket, which appeared to have been designed either for sailing or for cycling. It clung to her skinny frame as though it had been sprayed on. She was also wearing a pair of cropped leggings, (clam diggers?), which ended just below her knees and the highest-heeled pair of sandals that I have ever seen in my life. She looked like a highlighter pen! I was so amazed by this woman's appearance, that I continued to watch her, as she stood impatiently in the line, with a small child of about five years of age, whom, I guessed, was her daughter or niece. As I continued to watch the woman, I came to the conclusion that there cannot be any mirrors at the place she is staying, as just about everything about her was wrong. She turned to face me and smiled, showing very uneven teeth. She appeared, at first glance, to have very full lips, but the brightly glowing pale pink lipstick was applied in a cupid's bow, both on and around her lips, to give that impression, when her lips were really rather thin. At a distance, the effect had been quite successful, but upon closer inspection, had the look of a cacker about it. Her face was bright orange in colour and had obviously had the benefit, (if benefit is the right word), of a liberal dose of fake tanning lotion and clashed horribly with the colour of her lips. She had a pointed nose and chin, and I smiled, when the thought crossed my mind, that she looked like "Witchypoo" in H.R.Pufnstuf, which I remembered from my childhood. Her lank, dirty blonde hair, (dirty blonde as in colour, not necessarily cleanliness), showed black roots and had a feathered appearance, which I thought was accidental rather than planned, and probably as a result of bleach damage. She unzipped the jacket, to gain access to the inside pocket, revealing a crop-top with the name of an Italian designer, of whom I had never heard, emblazoned across it. As we embarked, I noticed that the same lotion had been applied to her legs, which showed very marked streaks, pointing, accusingly, at the stilt-like sandals. I found a seat in the lower cabin with a window view and watched the water lapping at the boats on the quayside. When I looked back, she was sitting directly opposite me, at a table, and opened her bag, to produce a flask of hot coffee and a Tupperware container, with an orange drink in it. This she gave to the small girl. The elfin-faced child was wearing a very pretty floral dress and was sporting a trendy, Victorian-style brimmed hat, with the front turned up, severely. I chastised myself for observing that the child had similar features now that I was closer, and for having the thought that she looked like an apprentice "Witchypoo". This was obviously the woman's daughter. She began talking to the child in a husky Lancashire accent, and I pondered on the child's name for a few moments…Chelsea? Daisy? Rhiannon? Then my daydream was broken when the mother said, "Shall we look at our shopping, Portia?" I just knew it would be something pretentious!

She proceeded to disembowel the bag she had been carrying, and a procession of recently purchased items were soon exhibited on the table in front of the child, who looked on with a vacant expression on her face. An American Indian dream catcher, (Oops! I should say native American dream catcher!), a child's novelty watch, several items of trendy children's clothing, a pair of excessively large ornate earrings, two pairs of trainers and two pairs of sandals, (one each of child's and adult's), were pored over in turn, as she tried to enthuse the child with babying tones. Finally, she produced a Raymond Weil watch catalogue, which she perused with a covetous expression. She looked up and caught me staring at her, (in disbelief,) which she apparently mistook for attraction, and as an invitation to speak to me.

"My husband doesn't know it yet, but he is buying me **this** for my birthday next week!" She handed me the catalogue and pointed to a very expensive-looking watch, with an obscene amount of gemstones on it. I fear that, whether out of shock or embarrassment at having been caught staring, I took it and mumbled approval at her choice.

"Are you married?"

Oh God she is going to talk me to death, now. What was I thinking of?

"No. Never seem to have much luck with women. I'm a pretty sad individual really."

That should put paid to any further conversation! She thinks I am a sad bastard! I'll move away to the coffee bar and not come back.

I joined the queue for coffee, ordered a Cappuccino, and presented a five-pound note in payment. The sudden sound, over my shoulder, of the voice of the woman I had just left, startled me sufficiently to spill a small quantity of coffee over my hand and wrist. The shock of the scalding pain almost made me drop it.

"Aren't you going to buy me one of those?"

I winced in pain and gave out a gasp.

What do I do now? This is too scary!

"Ouch! ….Er… sorry I didn't know you were there. Would you like one?"

Damn! What am I saying? Am I completely mad?

"Same as you then, please." She smiled, what I guess was, her equivalent of my winning smile, though it was not in the same league as mine!

"Er… Is your daughter OK?" I tried to invoke enough guilt in her to get her to return to the child.

Alas, to no avail.

"She's fine. She's very good, she won't move. Anyway, I asked the lady opposite to keep an eye on her for me." She looked back to where the child was sitting and waved with a wiggle of her fingers, up next to her face.

God, you've got a damned cheek!

She sat at the table nearest to the bar and patted the seat next to her. In the absence of the remotest clue what to do next, I tamely obliged.

"Where are the toilets?" I asked in a moment of inspiration.

Panic has obviously set in! Why do I always head for the loo in moments of crisis?

"I'll show you, we take this trip quite regularly, in the summer."

She got up to lead the way. I fought the temptation to ask why they took the trip so often, even though I admit to being inquisitive. As if to read my mind, she pointed out of the window as we moved along.

"See that big white house…. just through those trees?"

I observed the palatial residence that she was indicating.

"That's ours. My husband owns a record label. He's got more money than he knows what to do with. Trouble is, he spends most of his time in London and leaves us up here to fend for ourselves. So we get very bored"

I'll bet you're very good at fending for yourself, darling!

"Really? That's a shame."

She led me to the toilets and, as I moved towards the gentlemen's, she gestured to me to wait.

"Hang on a minute!" She entered the ladies, peered round the door and came out again. "Quickly! In here!"

She grabbed my hand and pulled me behind her, into the ladies' room, opened a cubicle door and pushed me into it ahead of her. In an instant, she had pushed her cropped leggings and panties to her ankles in one movement, pulled me to her and was trying to manipulate the fly on my trousers. I panicked, opened the door and ran, hyperventilating, across the hall and into the gents'! I was terrified! It all happened so quickly. One minute I am going to the gents', and the next, I am standing in shock, in a ladies' cubicle, with a semi-naked woman trying to have her way with me. A woman, it should be said, whose appearance and demeanour is, at best, scary and, at worst, horrifying, and whom I had only met some ten minutes before the event. I imagine that many men would have been in seventh heaven in that situation, but it was just bizarre and surreal. I just couldn't do it. Even if I had have fancied her, I would have struggled with that sort of approach!

I hid in the gents' for about ten minutes, until I regained my composure. She must have been embarrassed enough to have moved somewhere else, surely? I ventured forth gingerly, but to my horror, she was sitting back in the original seat with her child and had a look like thunder on her face.

"Look... I'm... er, sorry about that...it's just that...er..."

"Fuck off!" She said, with no deference to the child's ears. "Who the fuck do you think you are? ... Eh?"

I assumed that the question was probably rhetorical and left with much alacrity and without comment. I went up the stairs onto the upper deck and took a lungful of cool air, which I released in a long hissing blow of relief.

At the other side of the Lake, the train journey was marred by a family with seven fighting children, which the parents seemed unwilling, or unable to control, who were in the same carriage. It was more of a carnage than a carriage! I began to reconsider the efficacy of wanting children. This was supposed to have been a relaxing exercise, but was rapidly turning into a nightmare. At the station at the end of the line, I went to the restaurant and ate a meat and potato pie, which was extremely good, then came out to catch the return train. However, after watching them alight, I allowed the train to depart with Mr and Mrs Fertile and their offspring, but without me, waiting the thirty-five minutes or so for the next train. This was a very wise move, as it allowed me to relax in solitude on the return journey and catch the later boat back across the lake, minus the blonde trouser burglar, who must have taken the very next boat back. This was an altogether more enjoyable cruise and the scenery was wonderful. There were a large number of privately owned cabin cruisers on the lake, mostly being steered by pompous looking elderly gentlemen in seafaring captain's caps. I don't know what they thought they looked like, but the words pretentious and dickhead spring to mind.

Damn! I should have had pretentious for my word of the day!

The highlight of the trip was, however, when a young girl with Down's syndrome came over and began talking to me. I seem to have an affinity with Down's sufferers, they are always so warm and outgoing, and their innocence moves me greatly. Her name was Charlotte and she told me, excitedly, all about her full day trip over all the lake. Suddenly, she threw her arms around my neck and gave me the most wonderful hug, and planted a kiss on my cheek. She had a strength, which belied her stature, and it took some strength, on my part, to withstand the power of the hug around my neck. Her horrified mother apologised, most profusely, for Charlotte's behaviour, but I explained to her, that I thought it was beautiful and that there was no need for an apology. Jane, the mother, about 40 or so years old, sat next to me for the rest of my trip across to Bowness, and we had an interesting chat about Charlotte's young life and the trials of being a single mother, in such circumstances, after Charlotte's father baled out, when Jane decided to keep her, rather than abandon her at birth. I feel quite ashamed to be a man sometimes.

Word of the Day 0 Ben 0 (I could argue that I used it in context in describing my dislike of frugality!)

Things to be grateful for

1) The childlike innocence of people with Down's syndrome.
2) The beauty of the lakes.
3) My honour remaining intact after repelling boarders!
4) Charlotte's father was not available to receive the smack in the mouth that he deserves.

Sunday 23rd July 2000

Word of the Day: Abstemious… Moderate, not self-indulgent, (usually relating to intake of food or drink)

7 p.m. Back in flat in the real world.

I arrived back at about 5 p.m. after a very lengthy and tiring journey to find that my answering machine is full of messages. One was from Frank Dykstra, at the base, asking me to contact him, as I might find out something "to my advantage."

Still a little drama queen, then Frank? Ha! Ha! I wonder what that is all about, better ring tomorrow.

Most of the messages were from suppliers, whom I had told not to ring me this week, as I was on holiday, but English is obviously **not** the first language of these people. Then we come to Mother. She knew I was away, but still found it necessary to ring, God knows how many times, and still be surprised that I was not here. I even sent her a post card from Ripon. I will have to ring her tonight, or I will never hear the last of it. First, I am going to soak in a nice hot bath until my skin goes crinkly. I deserve it after that drive. I was very disappointed not to have any messages from Louise. Maybe she just isn't interested.

I spent yesterday walking around Kendal and winding down ready to come home and face the real world again. Just up the road from the Indian take away, I found the strangest shop. It was called "Nutshell" and had a selection of antiques or bric-a-brac, which could be seen from through the window, but what amused me most was the sign in the window, which read, "From 4th July to August 30th this shop will open on Saturdays only."

What a good idea! Let's stay closed during the busiest holiday period, when we would take the most money in the year! This is a LOCAL shop for LOCAL people! I thought this was Kendal not Royston Vasey!

I also visited the Kay's shoe warehouse and found, to my surprise, that it was not full of cackers. Indeed, the majority of patrons seemed to be quite well to do and 'countrified'. The green welly and wax jacket brigade were very well represented and looking at the prices, I could see why. I bought a pair of expensive sandals and a likewise expensive pair of trainers, which combined to give me savings of about £60, so I was very impressed. However, I think frugal is going to be the word of the **WEEK,** now that I am home almost penniless!

10 p.m. asleep in front of television.
(Telephone rings)

"Hello? Benjamin?"
Oh no! I fell asleep and she rang me first! I'm in the shit now!
"Hello Mother. I was going to ring you earlier, but I fell asleep."
"That's easy to say now that I've rung **you** isn't it?"
"Well it is true, so I guess it is easy to say."
"Hmmm!"
"So… how are you Mother?"
Arghhh! No! Tell me I didn't ask that!
"Not so good. I've had all sorts of pain with my jaw."

Try resting it for a few minutes…He! He!
"Really?" I said, trying not to let the mental laugh escape.
"The doctor said it was due to not chewing properly. I've put something out of line, or something. Just gave me painkillers. They don't seem to be much good… and I've had terrible diarrhoea."

Eeuuw! Too much information!
"Did you get something for it?"
Like a bucket? Ha! Ha!
"Just some kaolin and morphine."
"That should sort it out, then, shouldn't it?"
"It stopped the pain and the squits, but I've got terrible wind now!"
"You know what you need for that, don't you?"

"No, what?"

"A kite!"

"Very funny, Benjamin. I'm being serious. It isn't funny when you are filling the room with bad smells."

"It is from 65 miles away!" I couldn't resist laughing.

"Well, you enjoy your little joke while your mother suffers."

As if that was not sufficient information overload, a further forty-five minutes worth of saved up ailments and complaints were paraded before me in a total barrage, before she decided that she had need to draw breath, and I was finally able to escape the tirade.

I attempted an effort to change the subject and get a word in about my holiday and the abstemious (Hurrah!) nature of my holiday existence. However, my words floated away on the ether and she got second wind, (the other sort!), and related all the news about her neighbours and relatives, until I was falling asleep on the phone! Time to go to bed I think!

Word of the day 0 Ben 1

Things to be grateful for

1) Safe journey home
2) I feel much less stressed after a week out of the rat race.
3) A lovely bath and snooze in front of the telly.
4) The sixty-five miles barrier between me and the ambient odour of Mother's living room! *Poor Dad!*
5) The warm bed I am about to disappear into.

Monday 24th July 2000

Word of the Day: Suspicion... the act of suspecting, tendency to believe without full knowledge or proof

3 a.m. on sofa in front of television.

The warm bed was inviting but, alas, the short sleep I had before Mother's phone call took the edge off my tiredness, and I tossed and turned and could not doze off, so I am snuggled up on the sofa with my duvet. I was just mulling over the events of the holiday in my mind and nibbling on a piece of Kendal Mint Cake. It reminded me of a girl I once dated, who had said that, at every opportunity, she wanted to sample whatever was named after the place she was in, at the correct place. I don't know if she was serious, but she said she would eat Kendal Mint Cake in Kendal, Bath buns in Bath, Chelsea buns in Chelsea, and so on. I did the Kendal thing and I ate Cumberland sausage in Cumbria, which is as close as you can get, now that Cumberland doesn't exist in the minds of the Government Department Of Nothing To Do Except Piss Off The Paying Customers.

I also remember that I once had a tart in Bakewell, but that is another story altogether!

10 a.m. Flat

I have just rung Frank Dykstra, (bless her!), and he informed me that I can go on to the base for a temporary contract, paying only the commission due on a daily basis, while I get things going, and I can go into Allington today, to fill in the application form, ready to commence next Monday. Also, I have negotiated a lower commission rate than their first offer. I cannot help but view this amazing turn around with suspicion, (hurrah!). It will also give me numerous stock problems.

Holy shit! I can't do it on my own. I need help. I wonder if Kirstie would do it.

3 p.m. back in flat

I decided that I have nothing to lose by giving the Air Base a try. The military inmates seem to want me there, which is good enough for me. I have contracted to be there from 7 a.m. till 2 p.m., which I think will be long enough. I am sure I can cope up until about 11 o'clock, so

I rang Kirstie and suggested she might drive down to the base for the 11 a.m. to 2 p.m. session. She said that, subject to her sister's earlier offer, to baby-sit for a few hours a day if Kirstie got part-time work, still being open, she would love to give it a try, as she enjoyed working with me, and the hours would be quite convenient.

Things to be Grateful for

1) An opportunity to improve business.
2) I have found someone to help who seems enthusiastic.
3) Word of the day 0 Ben 1.

Tuesday 25th July 2000

Word of the Day: Pragmatic... dealing with matters with regard to their practical requirements or consequences

10 a.m. Front door

The Post lady has just been and there was a letter addressed in delicate handwriting, which was postmarked "Chichester". Louise is coming home. I felt butterflies in my stomach as I read that she was arriving on Friday, and she would like to see me and maybe go for a drink, on Saturday.

Damn. She has forgotten that I have to work on Saturday nights. Never mind, taking the pragmatic, (hurrah!), view, perhaps we can do something on Sunday. I am really excited at the prospect of seeing her again. It seems like months since she went to her mother's.

Oh shit! I could have asked Louise if she wanted to work with me. She hasn't got a job at the moment. Oh well. Too late. I have already arranged for Kirstie to do it and working with Louise might spoil our embryonic relationship before it even has a chance.

Things to be Grateful for
1) Obviously! Louise is coming home.
2) She wants to see me.
3) She wants to go out with me.
4) My pulse is racing with excitement.
5) Word of the day 0 Ben 1

Thursday 27th July 2000

Word of the Day: Tentative… hesitant, not definite

10-45 p.m. In flat

Another boring evening in the lay-by. I guess half the village is on holiday. I rang Louise's mobile to try to rearrange the weekend, so we can go out on Sunday, but just got her voicemail. I left a message for her to ring me when she got my message, but nothing yet. It is very stressful, because I am dying to see her again. Absence really does make the heart grow fonder…. or does it just make you forget about bad things and fill your mind with what you want to be true? We'll see!

Things to be Grateful for

Not a lot today. I'm feeling too depressed and frustrated to be grateful for anything.

1) I am not dead.
2) My flat didn't burn down.
3) My tentative (hurrah!) plans for bonding with Louise.

Saturday 29th July 2000

Word of the Day: Reappraise... assess again, take a new look at (circumstances).

8 a.m. In flat

Depression is setting in. Louise said she was coming home on Friday and would see me on Saturday, but she did not call at the trailer last night as I had hoped. Neither has she answered my messages, on her mobile, to organize anything for Sunday. I am totally confused now...
Not a difficult state for me to achieve I know!
... as it really felt like she was warming to the idea of going out with me. I guess I am destined to be a workaholic, single, sad bastard for life. Reluctantly, it looks as though I need to reappraise, (hurrah!), the situation. I have to go to the bank and the Cash & Carry this morning. I may drop into the Lion for a quick one afterwards and ask if she has been about.

3 p.m. In flat

I have been out all morning, taking care of my banking and picking up a bit of stock for Monday. I got back at 12 o' clock and called in at the Red Lion for a swift half, but no one has seen or heard from Louise. I forgot to take my mobile with me, and when I got back and switched it on, the Voicemail rang and melodiously informed me that I have 3 new messages. That is just so typical of me. I wait in anguish for a call and don't get one and, as soon as I forget the bloody mobile, the entire world and his dog rings!

Hi Ben! It's Louise. Sorry I haven't rung you. I got your message but I had to work Friday night... oh I'll tell you all about it later. Anyway! I'm driving up on Saturday and will see you when I get there. Stay in for me, won't you? I'll be round about 4.

Hello Benjamin. It's that strange woman again. Remember? The one who carried you for nine months and had the Devil's own bad time delivering you into the world? Where have you been? I have been ringing your house phone all morning and now this thing is taking messages too. Are you avoiding me? Perhaps I should make an appointment in writing. Your dad isn't well and I am fed up of the sight of four walls and never seeing or hearing from anyone. If it does not put you out too much, is there any chance you might ring?

Hi Ben, This is Stella…remember me from your holiday in Yorkshire? I thought you were going to stay in contact… or was it just another notch (laughing) on your bedpost. Well, it was my bedpost actually! (laughing again). Oh… I hate these things. Anyway, if you want to speak, give me a ring soon? I am coming down to Sheringham soon. I think I pass quite close by you. Maybe we could have a drink or something. I don't want to be a pain. If you don't call I'll get the message. OK? Kisses………. 'Bye.

Wow, one minute my love life is about as exciting as trainspotting, and the next, I am a babe magnet! Hang on… Louise will be here in a moment. Better clean up a bit. Shit! Louise in my flat! My heart is pounding already. No time to do things to be grateful for, but I hope tomorrow will be a bonus edition!

Sunday 30th July 2000

Word of the Day: Plethora… an over subscription or excess.

7-45 a.m. In bed… alone!

Yet again, I awake to the sound of ringing and initially try to turn it off by manhandling my alarm clock. Reality bites, and I realize it is the phone and that can only be one person. I pick it up…

"Hello Mother, how are you?"

"How did you know it was me?"

"I'm psychic, Mother. Who else is up at sparrow's fart on a Sunday morning?"

"Don't use expressions like that, Benjamin, you know I hate it."

"Thank you for telling me what I know. If it weren't for you I'd never know what I thought about anything."

"If you are in that sort of mood, I don't know why I am bothering to talk to you at all. Did you get my message?"

"Yes, but at the time…"

"Well why didn't you ring? Your father could be dead by now and you wouldn't care."

"Is he?"

"No…"

"Well then, what is your point?"

"My point is… that he could have been."

"If he was, you'd have called me…anyway, to continue where I was before I was so rudely interrupted…"

"Don't tell me I'm rude. You are the one who ignored me, when I asked you to ring."

"No I didn't… will you listen a minute?"

"Yes you did……………" (click!)

Oh shit! Now the effluent is definitely going to make contact with the rotary ventilation apparatus! I dropped the phone and it landed on the talk button and cut her off. There is no way she is going to believe that.

I rang back immediately and had ten minutes of advice on how to treat mothers, particularly my own, on how downright rude I was to cut her off and sundry other matters. I could not get a word in edgeways. Finally, I was able to explain that I had three messages including hers and that Louise was due to arrive at any second as I listened to the messages, so I did not have time to ring her or the other message leaver, before Louise actually turned up. It turns out that Dad had a virus of the lower abdomen, which resulted in Mother giving me a lot more information than I needed about the state of his bowel movements. I enquired whether he was likely to shit himself to death and was again in receipt of the short end of her tongue. I don't know what was wrong with me this morning, I felt as though the filter, between my brain and my mouth, was malfunctioning, and my words were coming out unedited. She rang off and I felt ashamed of myself. She has the ability to make me feel guilty; always has and always will have! I guess that is what mothers are for!

Regrettably, about the visit of Louise, I have no major reason to be grateful. She came to the flat, and we had coffee and played some music, then got chatting about what had been happening in our lives, since we last met. She told me that she had got a job down in Chichester and was thinking about putting her flat on the market and staying there permanently. I pointed out to her that she had said she would like us to go out together, and that such a distance would place a very large obstacle in the way of such an enterprise. She agreed that it would, but that she hasn't made up her mind entirely. The job, at a solicitor's office, is going well and she wants to keep it, for a while at least, to see how things progress. We went to the Lion for a drink and then back to my flat to watch a video. I turned all the lights off except the standard lamp, and we snuggled down on the sofa to watch it All things appeared to be going well. I put my arm round her and cradled her as I moved towards her. I kissed her and she responded, kissing me back with a fervour, which excited me (and, I think, her too,) and we continued to kiss quite passionately for several minutes. Just as we were getting carried away, and I was ready to start investigating parts of her anatomy that I had been fantasizing over for weeks, she suddenly pulled away, and I could see she was quite flushed.

"This is all a bit intense," she began. "All a bit quick, I don't want to give you the wrong impression."

Oh, no! That's female emotional blackmail language designed to make me feel guilty about hitting on her!

"I'm sorry. I just think you are so beautiful. I have fancied you for ages. I can't help being attracted to you."

Touché! Now I'll give her my hurt expression.

"I'd better go before things get out of hand."

So my hurt expression was wasted. I can't understand it! It ALWAYS works!

I was torn between begging her to stay and risking rejection and allowing her to leave and thereby living to fight another day.

"I really like you, Ben. This has come as a bit of a shock. Give me time. I'll ring you tomorrow."
Promising!

We kissed goodnight in the doorway, and she was gone. My bed was a lonely place to be last night. I took comfort, (as one would!) in ringing Stella. Seriously, though, I felt weird about ringing her so soon after Louise left, but I am in a bit of a cleft stick at the moment. It seems rude not to reply to Stella's message. She appeared to be very nostalgic about our evening together and told me that she was really sorry that the timing of her holiday had cut short a very promising situation. She asked me if I had missed her and whether I would have wanted to see her again, if she hadn't been jetting off to the Greek Islands. I said that I was really disappointed that she had to go and that I would have loved to see her again. I told her that I had thought that she didn't seem too bothered, and I had assumed she wasn't interested. She assured me that she was and that she would like me to visit her any time that I wanted. We agreed to meet when she visits her family in Sheringham, and she is going to ring and let me know as soon as she has tied up the arrangements with her parents.

So, once again, I am in a quandary. How do these things happen to me? One minute I am desperate to find a girlfriend and can't, then, when I think I am in with a chance of getting one, I seem to lose her. Then, when I think I may have found another, the first resurfaces and I have two on the scene. A veritable plethora (hurrah!) of women fighting over me.

Things to be Grateful for

1) My love life seems to be advancing in the right direction.
2) My business seems to be doing likewise.
3) My father didn't die due to my neglect of him.

Monday 31st July 2000

Word of the Day: Frantic… frenzied, wildly stressful.

7-45 p.m. Collapsed in a heap on the sofa!

First day on base. What a day that was. Thank God for Kirstie. She was absolutely fantastic, a real trooper. I would never have coped with that lot if she hadn't been there. I cannot believe how frantic, (hurrah!), it was from 11 till nearly 3 o'clock. The Americans really love their food! I just hope that they liked what I served them, as much as the Americans in the village do. Maybe I am paranoid. They certainly seem to like Kirstie too, although I have to say, she was not wearing her wedding ring. Whenever she was asked if she was my wife, she was quick to say, "No I am just an employee."

The day was interrupted at 10 o' clock by a visit from the military environmental health officer. He seemed like a nice guy, and we hit it off quite well. He gave me a few pieces of advice, which I will follow to the letter. I don't want to antagonize him unnecessarily. He wanted me to take off my watch, which is fair enough, but I was surprised that he required that my inside bin should NOT have a lid on it. Out in the village, the British environmental health officer insists on the lid being in place. Oh well, whatever! The military environmental health officer is known by all on the base as "the vet", since he vets the food-selling establishments. He handed me a report form with about 60 boxes on it, none of which were ticked, (which is good, because if they are ticked it means something is wrong,) and he wrote "very good job" across the inspector's comments box. That is a very good start, and I intend to ensure that I continue to remain on his good side. His arrival did nothing to aid my preparation for the onslaught that was to follow. Some of them had to wait nearly an hour for their food. They won't wear that for too long, but I am not sure what I can do to speed it up. I did have some very good banter with some of them though. They seem to find my sense of humour a little difficult, but they will just have to learn!!

Things to be Grateful for

1) A very good start on base.
2) A real find in Kirstie. She worked so hard today.
3) A good start with the vet on base. He could make things very difficult if I cause him any problems.

AUGUST 2000

Wednesday 2nd August 2000

Word of the Day: Impracticable... impossible in practice, unmanageable

5 p.m. at flat

Another good day on base. This looks like being a very good contract. It is a shame about having to pay such a high percentage of takings for the priviege, but it appears that a good income is pretty well guaranteed here. Kirstie is still working hard, but it is difficult trying to get to know her, as we are always under pressure. It is also very difficult trying to maintain stocks of everything. I have just been to the cash and carry again and called in at Tesco, in the new township of Hampton Hargate, for some salad items, as their prices are better than the wholesale prices at the cash and carry, AND you don't have to buy whole boxes.

What were the town planners thinking about when naming the new township Hampton? It seems that everyone except them knows that Hampton (Wick) is Cockney rhyming slang for a male appendage! What are they on?

I wish I knew what to do about the two women of my affections, Louise and Stella. I really like them both, but I feel funny about going out with them both. Stringing them both along is not really fair to either of them, not to mention being impracticable (Hurrah!). On the other hand, if I blow one of them out and then the other blows me out, I am left in my usual state of total 'womanlessness' and any further blowing won't come into the equation! I enjoyed the short time I spent with Stella and the private encounter was very exciting, but on the other hand I fancy the pants off Louise.

Hmmmmmm, Louise with no pants on conjures a very pretty picture.

I wish I had a sister to talk to. I haven't committed to either of them and neither has committed to me, so I guess I have no choice but to go with the flow and see what happens over the next few weeks. But what the hell I do, if one, (or, heaven forbid, both), of them does want commitment, God only knows! *

* It's obvious that I am desperate; three references to religion. Perhaps I should hedge my bets and call for assistance from all deities?

Things to be Grateful for

1) I have at least two women who find me passably attractive.
2) My financial situation is on the up.
3) The picture, still in my mind, of Louise with no pants on, (and nothing else on, either, in the revised version).

Thursday 3rd August 2000

Word of the Day: Mysterious… inexplicable, secret, hidden, in a manner of mystery.

9-55 a.m. on base

A little while ago, I noticed an American walking towards the trailer and immediately recognised the hat he was wearing was a Greenbay Packers American Football Team hat. As he got nearer, I also noticed that the puffer jacket he had on, unzipped, was also sporting the Packers logo, as was the polo shirt underneath. He was not about to stop and buy food, but was walking towards the Post Office. Even so, he turned to greet me as he passed, as is the wont of most Americans here on base. I said to him, "Hi how're you doing?"

"Just great, and you?" He replied.

"Fine! You must be the other Packers fan!"

"How do you mean?"

"I've been following their fortunes for years."

"Really? Jeez I thought you Brits hated our football?"

"Well they are a bit poofy with all that padding!" I said, with a laugh.

"They need it with the force they hit one another!"

He was laughing too. I instantly liked this person; he had a warmth about him.

"So how come you like Greenbay?" He ventured.

"When they first showed American football on TV about 10 or so years ago, they showed a potted history of the game, and it seemed to me that Greenbay had a good heritage, even if they hadn't won anything for about 25 years. I figured it was about their time. So, I started watching their results and I have stuck with them. Didn't have a clue what they were trying to do, though!"

"And so it proved eh? Superbowl winners a coupla years back!"

"Yeah, but even with all that year's success you could still only buy Washington Redskins, Dallas Cowboys and San Francisco 49'ers hats in this country. No Packers hats at all!"

"You don't have a Packers hat? Whoa!! We'll soon sort that one out for yer! I'll bring you one by!"

Sorry if I am cynical, but I won't be holding my breath!

"Hey you better give me some of those fries! That smell is making me hungry! Is that your marketing strategy? Stop innocent passers-by and keep 'em talking till the smell makes 'em buy something?"

"No, but now you mention it, maybe I'll adopt it!"

He held out his hand for a handshake and crushed my fingers, enthusiastically, when I accepted it.

"Craig Steel! Are you Arnold?"

"Ben.... Ben Arnold!"

"Great to meet you Ben, welcome aboard. We need a few more Cheeseheads in this place!" (This is a reference to the strange hats worn by Packers fans up in Greenbay with enormous plastic cheese wedges on them). "Most of the guys in my office are Raiders fans, I am so pleased to find another Packers fan!"

I am an absolute addict when it comes to sport, and I will tune in to anything competitive, even sheep dog trials, but I have to say that American Football is a difficult game to fathom, (as is the question why the sheep dogs are never found guilty!) I began watching American Football when Channel 4 started showing it, over 10 years ago, but they failed to describe the rules, or even the concept, and left the viewer to just get on with it. My first attempt at an understanding of the game was feeble, to say the least. It seemed to me, that violence was the main intention. First, they appeared to form a huddle and discuss the next move, apparently getting advice from the team coach by means of a radio in the quarterback's helmet. They then form a line facing the opposing team's line, on, what I now know to be called, the line of scrimmage. Someone shouts, the ball is whipped back to the quarterback, and 95% of the players on the field commence to knock seven shades of shit out of one another. Then there are just two players who have any interest in the progress of the ball, the guy holding it, and the guy to whom he intends throwing it. I quickly got the idea about touchdowns, field goals and kicking between the goalposts for an extra point, but I took weeks to work out what they were trying to achieve in other "plays". Now that I understand the rules, and the intention, I am quite hooked on the game. One thing I still can't understand, though, is that they have over forty players to a team, and only the punter and the kicker ever kick the ball, and the other 95% of the players either throw it, carry it or have nothing to do with it, so why the hell do they call it football? I feel that the good citizens of Harvard, who drew up the rules, should have called the game "American legalised thuggery," as the ball is, for the most part, incidental to the physical contact! In fact, I wonder if anyone would really notice if the ball had been left in the dressing room. Another thing, which takes a great deal of skill and organisation, is to be able to pan out a game of 60 minutes to last nearly

6 hours, and yet the game can mysteriously, (hurrah!) end, before the full 60 minutes has elapsed, because one team get possession and then cheat, by adopting time wasting tactics, known as running the clock down. Most games would penalise such blatant abuse of potential playing time! I won a bet with a guy yesterday, when he said that a game never lasts longer than 4 hours. I bet him $10 they do and, after he took the bet, in front of his friends, I pointed out that the Superbowl programme, on TV last January, lasted over 6 hours, from the time the players were introduced one by one, until the final whistle! He was forced by his peers to pay up and look big! I must say, though, that I really enjoy the game. **Come on you Packers!**

The 'World Series' of baseball is currently taking place. Strange only one country is in it!

Things to be Grateful for

1) Another incredible days takings
2) Making a potential friend with Greenbay connections.
3) A bonus $10 from an unsuspecting Marine. I wonder if they will learn that I never bet on anything unless it is a certainty!

Friday 4th August 2000

Word of the Day: Quiescent... dormant, motionless, inert.

4p.m. in flat

Trade today was still good, but has fallen off a little bit. I guess there is a novelty value when you first start. Kirstie is a real natural at this game. Can I pick them, or what? She is also very attractive, which I am sure will stand the business in good stead, as the guys vie with one another for her attention.

Craig came by this morning and brought me two different styles of Packers football hat, both brand new with the NFL official label attached and, a Packers official newspaper, together with stationery and a folder to keep it in. I asked him how much I owed him for these very desirable items and he said, "Don't insult me, man, it's a gift. You just wear 'em with pride and hang in there and support them Packers!"

I admit to feeling somewhat humbled and guilty about doubting him, when he said he would bring me by a hat!

The England cricket team beat the West Indies again, to secure a 3-1 series win. That is the first time since 1957 that England has won a five test match series over the West Indies. I am so proud of them. I was also moved to see the England team form a guard of honour, on the field of play, when Curtly Ambrose came in to bat for the last time before retiring, and then did it again for Courtney Walsh, who is retiring soon, so was taking his last innings in England.

It was the Queen Mother's one-hundredth birthday today. She has done well to survive this world for such a long time through war, pestilence and adversity. Mind you, she and her family are not short of a bob or two, so they have been able to afford the best medical care in the world, especially through her nineties, when she seemed predisposed to throw herself on the floor at any given opportunity. She's had more breaks than Steve Davis. There is a rumour that she is not the real Queen Mum at all and was replaced by an android in 1989!

I wonder if she got a telegram from the Queen?

Damn I forgot the word of the day! No time now have to get ready for the Friday night session.

Word of the day 1, Ben 0

Things to be grateful for

1) Greenbay Packers!
2) My new Packers hats.
3) The restoration of my faith in human nature, by the England cricket team and Craig Steel.

4) Kirstie told me today that she is really enjoying working with me which is very good news as I would struggle to find anyone else as good.

Sunday 6th August 2000

Word of the day: acrimonious…. bitter in manner or temper

7-30 a.m. In bed
(Telephone rings)

I am in a state of coma and find myself strangely unable to operate my right arm. As I slowly achieve the state of consciousness, I become aware that I cannot even locate my right arm, due to the lack of feeling in it. I realize that I must have been lying on it and have prevented the blood from circulating within it and, as the painful 'pins and needles' sensation of the returning blood flow slowly increases, I find it is still attached, where I left it, hanging from my shoulder. I am reminded that I did not answer the phone, when after some four rings, the answering facility self operates.

"Hello?… Benjamin?… I know you are there!… This is not funny!… Pick up the phone right now!"

I am in a difficult situation now. If I answer, I will get a verbal pasting for not answering straight away. If I don't answer, she will, sooner or later, want to know all the ins and outs of a cat's anatomy, regarding where I spent the night. The safest bet to avoid an acrimonious, (hurrah!), conversation, would be to wait five minutes, then ring her back, giving me five minutes to think of an excuse.

Why am I apologizing for living my life? It's none of her business what I am doing, anyway!

However, it is a bit galling to get the grief, when I didn't have the pleasure of what she will accuse me of!

How does she manage to make me feel guilty, even when I have done nothing to feel guilty about?

(I'll still ring though.)

(Telephone rings again)

Oh no! Too late! It will be her again! (I pick up the receiver)

"Hello?"

"Hi Ben, it's Stella. How're you doing?"

"Fine thanks, except that I smell like a burger and chips!" (We both laugh).

Still laughing, Stella said, "Yes you do! I can smell it down the phone!"

"Cut me some slack, Stella, I'm still in bed. I haven't had time to have a shower yet."

"OK! I know it's early. I'm only up this early myself because I'm going to visit my Uncle Maurice, in Kendal. He's not very well and he hasn't been coping very well on his own. He's been useless since Auntie May died. I've been meaning to ring you, but I've had a lot on at work. I've arranged to go to Mum's next weekend and stay for the week, so we could get together if you'd like to."

"Of course I'd like to! What day are you coming?"

"Well I told Mum I would be there on Sunday. Would it be too presumptuous to ask if I could stay over with you on Saturday night? No pressure, but I just thought that if I came down early on Saturday, we could have the day together and maybe meet up again on my way back?"

"That would be fantastic! Of course you can stay here."

"Great, I'll see you Saturday then. I'll ring in the week to check directions, OK?"

"OK, I'll look forward to seeing you then. 'Bye"

Yes! Yes!! Yes!!! *That is brilliant news; I can't wait to see her again.*

(Telephone rings again)

"Hello?"

"I knew you were there, Benjamin! What are you doing? You couldn't answer it for me, but you were soon on the phone to someone else."

"She…er…**they** rang **me**, mother."

"So did I, but you didn't answer it."

"I didn't know it was you did I? I thought the second call was you ringing back. Mother.... it was about half past seven in the morning, anyway. What's the matter? Can't you sleep or something? I was in the shower when it rang the first time."

"Aha! So you don't always sleep in on a Sunday then, like you say you do?"

"It'd be all the same if I did. You still bloody rang... and you didn't know if I was asleep or in the shower!"

Wait a minute... I haven't had a shower! I'm beginning to believe my own tall stories! Ha! Ha!

"Don't use that sort of language to me, Benjamin, anyway...what was a young lady doing, ringing you at this early hour?"

You don't miss a thing do you? I'll bet they called you "sniffer" at school! You can always sniff out a bit of gossip.

"No one you know, Mother! Just a friend I met on holiday. There's no need to get your wedding hat out...And who said it was a young lady?"

"You didn't need to! I know what you're like. It's about time you stopped gallivanting around and settled down with one woman. And it seems to me, it would be more than a friend to ring this early?"

"Well it seems to you wrong, then... And if I ever find a woman that I could settle down with, I'll let you be the first to know. Anyway, Mother, what can I do for you?"

"I just rang to see how you were, seeing as how you haven't rung me all week."

"I have been really busy with the new contract on base, I'm sorry."

No I'm not!

"Don't worry about us, I don't even know anything about this contract, you keep talking about."

Is it me or is she talking in riddles?

"If I 'keep talking about it,' then you must know something about it. That is just logic!"

"Don't start bandying words with me, my lad. I'm still your mother, you know!"

Don't I know it? Anyway when you resort to reminding me that you're my mother, I know that I have won the argument!

"Yes Mummy! I know you are!"

"Don't take the Michael out of me, Benjamin!"

"As if I would, Mother!"

Another fifteen minutes of saying nothing ensue, and she rings off, with me none the wiser as to the purpose of the call. I almost dropped myself in it, though, when I was trying to wind the conversation up so that I could leave. The words 'I'll have to go, I've got to shower and shave' had formulated in my brain and were heading at breakneck speed towards my mouth, when my speech censoring mechanism kicked in, and I choked on them before they were uttered.

6-15 p.m. in the kitchen

I have just eaten a take-away Indian meal from a new place in Peterborough, which delivers to your door. I asked for a chicken madras 'but not too hot.' I am hiccupping like crazy. It nearly took my head off it was so hot. I tried to drink a cup of tea, but my tongue is so raw from the food that it hurt when the tea touched it.

(Telephone rings again)

I am popular today! That'll be Jamie, or one of the lads about the quiz tonight.

"Good evening, Marston St Andrews Home for Wayward Girls, Would you like to order one?"

"Oh, is it, indeed? (fortunate laughter!). Is there a space for me?"

"Louise! How are you? … There will always be a space for you, sweet one!"

"Sorry I haven't rung all week. Simon, my boss, is involved with a **massive** divorce case, and I have been working all hours with the word processing, filing and unfiling. I bet you thought I wasn't going to ring again after last week?"

"It's OK. I've been busy myself, with the base and that."

"Oh yes. How's it been going?"

"Really good. A bit more than I can handle to tell the truth, but it'll probably die down a bit, once they get used to me being there. Kirstie is brilliant. I couldn't have begun to cope without her help."

"Oh yes. I'd forgotten about her."

Do I detect a slight note of jealously there? I hope I did! There was definitely a little emphasis on the word "her"! Ha! Ha!

"She's very good with the punters. Do you know her?"

"No. Wouldn't know her from Adam. Well, Eve anyway!" She broke the slightly strained atmosphere with a little laugh.

"So… er… I…er…" I stuttered.

For God's sake get on with it, man!

"I …erm… I'm sorry if I overstepped the mark last weekend." I finally managed to say it.

"No… It's all right. It was my fault as much as yours. I shouldn't have let it get like that."

"Oh!… Do you mean you didn't want me to kiss you?"

"No, no…I didn't mean that! I mean… Oh God, I don't know what I mean. Yes, I wanted us to get… you know!"

"No… that's just it. I don't know. One minute we're all over each other, and the next, you seem spooked and fly out of the room like a ferret up a flue!" She laughed loud and long at my perceptive simile. "I really like you…and I thought you liked me. I would never do anything like that if you didn't want me to."

"I do. I like you a lot. It's just that… well… after my last... you know… relationship… I am a bit nervous. It was just a bit soon to be getting so… well… intimate. But…thank you for being such a gentleman and not trying to get heavy with me."

"I told you. I'm not like that. I would never get heavy with a woman. I'm just an old softy!"

"I think I knew that, really. Anyhow… thanks for not forcing the issue and making a scene. As I said, I shouldn't have let it get that far."

"You mean you don't fancy me?"

"I never said that! Stop fishing for compliments!"

"Argghh!! Busted!" We both laughed again.

"I hope you didn't think I was just hitting on you?" I continued.

"No. I wanted to get close as much as you did…but… oh I'll tell you about Mick next time I see you. The guy I was with before? He was very physical at times... and I don't mean "cuddly physical". It isn't a pleasant story. It's over a year ago, and I'm still not over it."

"I see…"

Now I don't feel so bad about the rejection.

"…I'm a good listener… when you are ready to talk to me about it."

"You really are so sweet. Thanks for being so understanding."

"So… would you like to go out again sometime?"

Getting brave again Ben! Risking rejection! Not like you at all!

"Don't say it like that! Sometime…as though it won't happen. What about next weekend? I could come up?"

Oh shit! Why do these things always happen to me? What do I say now?

"Um…"

Oh, that was really good. You have such a way with words!

"No pressure…you don't have to if you don't want to." She sounded disappointed at my reaction. ***That's the second time today that a female has said "No pressure" to me. Why do they say that at just the moment they are applying the pressure?***

"Of course I want to. It's just that I half agreed to go to the football match with a few guys in the village, on Saturday, and have a few beers afterwards."

"Never mind, then."

Whoa! She sounds really deflated. I feel like a right bastard now. What do I do?

"How about I come down to you on Sunday?" I offered a compromise.

"OK. That'd be nice. You know I am still staying at my parents' though, don't you?"

"That doesn't matter, does it? We can go out somewhere and get to know each other a bit."

"OK, then. Oh… but you won't know Chichester, will you?"

"No. Perhaps we could meet at a Little Chef, or something, and you could guide me in?"
I'd like you to guide me into more than a Little Chef!
"That'd be good."
"OK, leave it with me, and I'll look up the nearest one to you, and ring you later."
OK, Ben. Speak soon, then…'bye."
"'Bye."
How do I get into these situations? I feel even worse now. They are both really nice, and I fancy both of them. I am really uncomfortable about this situation, but I don't see what I can do about it. Well, I may have more of a clue after this weekend.

Things to be grateful for

1) I haven't got Louise and Stella both arriving on the same day. (More luck than judgement, perhaps!)
2) I restrained myself from alienating Mother, (even if she deserved it!)
3) My finances have received a very welcome boost this week.
4) My bank manager is impressed that I have not eaten so far into my overdraft this week.

Wednesday 9th August 2000

Word of the Day: Querulous… complaining, peevish

4 p.m. flaked out on the sofa

I have been so tired this week. The pressure of working on the base is far greater than I had imagined. During the busiest time each day, we are working at capacity for two and a half hours, solidly. I was just thinking how much my finances were benefiting from the increased turnover, when I arrived home to find a 'snot-o-gram' from the cretin who manages my business account at the bank. He had the nerve to bounce a cheque for £21-50, due to lack of funds, over a week ago, and the letter has only just arrived today. The cost for bouncing the cheque is £25, so whereas if he had paid the cheque, (knowing that I was due to bank cash anyway), it would have left me £11 over my overdraft limit, (for about 2 hours). By bouncing the cheque, he has left the account £14-50 over the limit, and I still have to recompense the supplier for the invoice that the cheque was supposed to clear. That pissed me off so much that I telephoned this mental giant.

Having taken almost six minutes to locate the department, and person, to whom I wished to speak, my demeanour had not been improved.

"Hello, Ben Arnold here, Arnold's Kebab Shack. Are you the person who sent this moronic letter?"

"Which letter is that, sir?"

"Don't piss me off even more than I am already. You are my personal banker? You should be aware of my account and know what is what."

"We each deal with a number of accounts, Mr Arnold."

"Are you sure it is personal **banker?**"

"There is no need to be abusive!"

"I wasn't, you obviously have a self esteem problem. Not that I am surprised!"

"Pardon?"

"Nothing! So…What kind of genius makes a decision that says, "It is unacceptable for you to be £11 over limit, so we'll make you £14-50 over limit instead?"

"We cannot condone writing cheques that take you over your limit, sir."

"But you are my personal…banker, so you know my banking habits, and therefore know that I bank most money on a Monday each week, and I did bank a large amount last Monday, when you bounced the cheque. The money was in there by lunchtime."

"But the contra entry was made before the money was in the account. It will be paid when represented, provided there are sufficient funds when it arrives. If your overdraft limit is insufficient, you should have applied to have it increased, before you wrote cheques, which would exceed your current limit."

"But the money was there on the same day! And I thought you didn't know what I was talking about when I came on the phone?"

"I have been getting your account on screen, while we have been talking. Yes…I'm sorry, I cannot waive the fee, because it is a clear breach of your overdraft facility and outside my authority to do anything else."

"I don't keep writing to you when I am in credit, do I?"

"I'm sorry?"

"OK, I am sorry I can't make you understand. Can I speak to someone with a brain, please? Or do you have a communal brain? When is your turn to use it?"

"I think we had better terminate this conversation, Mr Arnold."

"I thought I had, when I asked to speak to someone with a brain. Do you have anyone who fits that description?"

(Following a silence and a few clicks, I hear a new voice on the line)

"Hello, Mr Arnold. Nice to speak to you again." The bank manager! "I have been meaning to make an appointment to review your account. I notice that you have banked rather more than usual this past week."

"Yes, and you are still bouncing my cheques. I did tell you I was negotiating a new contract with the US air base. It was successful and trade is very good. The potential is extremely good."

"I am very pleased to hear that. Now, is there anything I can do for you to help in this new venture?"

"Yes, you could start by appointing me a personal banker who has an IQ which exceeds his shoe size."

He laughed. "Ah! Mr Broughton. He is very young and a little inexperienced, but he has operated correctly according to bank regulations…"

"Yes but…" I began, but he cut me short.

"BUT… in view of the circumstances, and the current level of cash being banked, I will, on this occasion, arrange for the fee to be repaid to your account. However, Mr Arnold, please endeavour to operate within the facility and ensure that you have banked sufficiently to cover cheques written in the future. Now… shall I make an appointment for us to get together and discuss the developments in your business and your future banking requirements?"

"OK. I would like to update some of the equipment on the trailer because, at the moment, I am too slow and they won't tolerate that forever. They like their food fast!"

"If I can help, Mr Arnold, I will, but let us have a full review first. I could pop out to you tomorrow around 3-30 p.m. I am in the village for lunch with a client. How would that suit you?"

"Great!"

"I'll look forward to seeing you. Goodbye!"

Having terminated my querulous (hurrah!) phone call to the bank, I still cannot understand their logic in doing it in the first place and then, when I shout about it, cancel the charge as though it didn't matter in the second place. Why don't they just do the right thing to start with? They are all the same. If you desperately need help, they suck in their breath and say that they cannot justify assistance at the moment, yet when you are doing fine and don't need credit, they are falling over themselves to throw money at you. You'd think it was their own bloody money!

Irony rules again!

Things to be grateful for

1) The comeuppance of the brainless personal wanker.
2) The bank manager seems quite positive about my situation, and didn't shoot me down in flames when I spoke of new equipment.

Thursday 10th August 2000

Word of the Day: Sanctimonious... Displaying a show of piety, being holier-than-thou

9 p.m. on trailer

The Bank manager came and went quite rapidly this afternoon…

Sanctimonious (hurrah*!*) ***bastard.***

… and gave me another lecture on keeping within the agreed overdraft limits. I suppose he never let himself go over his limit! He did agree to lend me the money to replace my slow one-burner griddle and non-functional char griddle, with two new state-of-the-art ones. However, he won't run to a doner machine, until I pay back the loan for the griddles. I suppose he isn't all bad… just most of him! I must now arrange some quotes to get them supplied and fitted. It is a bit slow tonight; I guess that many of my regulars are still on holiday. How I wish I were back on holiday. It is amazing how you forget about work and the troubles of the real world, when you are in that surreal world for just a few short days.

I have duly replaced my regulation black baseball cap with one of my new green and gold Greenbay Packers hats, as supplied by Craig. As he requested, I have worn it today on base, with pride, and I am surprised how much of a talking point it has proved to be. Comments like: -

"Bunch o' cheeseheads!" "Whadda loada losers!" and "You wanna get behind a team that can cut it!" have abounded, but all in good humour. One customer was wearing an Atlanta Braves baseball team hat.

"Land sakes! Y'all wearing a football hat! Wrong sport, dude!" He was laughing and had the most infectious smile, which radiated happiness and friendliness and continued, in a southern accent that you could cut with a knife, "Y'all oughta get into baseball, much more civilised. Y'all don't play baseball over here, though?"

"We do play it, but we stop when we are about 7," I began teasing him. "We call it rounders!"

"Hey! No, man! That's a whole nother ball game!"

Aaarghh! I wish he hadn't said that! It really grates on me!

"I know I was just winding you up?"

"What's that?"

"Winding you up… teasing?"

"Oh! Yeah! Whatchoo got here, then? Lemme see! Gimme a Cajun style Keebarb."

"Do you want chips with that?"

"Fries? Yeah, lemme have a side order of regular fries."

Obviously a star pupil at manners school!

"Anyway, how come they call Atlanta "the Braves"? You don't get many Indians in Georgia, do you?"

"Oh! No yuh don't… but I think there used to be."

"What… before the Atlantans shot 'em all?"

"Yuh knows…I guess that ain't far from the truth."

OOPS! More foot in mouth disease, Ben!

"Hey! Y'all cain't call 'em Injuns no more, though. They's Native Americans now, or eye noowits. All kindsa trouble callin' 'em Injuns, don't even go there."

"Eye noowits? I've never heard that term before. How do you spell that?"

" I..n..u..i..t……..I think. I seem to recall that they's related to the Eskimos."

I surmised that his southern pronunciation of the word inuit was probably not general and that it is probably pronounced inn-you-it everywhere else!

"Anyway, if it's a matter of political correctness, how come the Washington Football team are called "the redskins"? Surely that's **the** most derogatory term for an Ind… sorry, Native American?"

"Shit! I never thought o' that! Y'all quite correct!"

Spotting immediately that this guy was, in fact, highly pigmented in the skin department himself and, that a high proportion of my new American clientele are of widely ranging degrees of pigmentation and, not wishing to offend anyone, I was interested in developing this theme of Political Correctness with him.

"Mind if I ask you a question?"

"Not at all, axe away!"

Argghh! Another squirming moment. Why do some Americans insist in transposing the sounds in the word ask to say aks?

"Over here, it is Politically Correct to refer to, say, a West Indian, as "black", if you needed to refer to his race at all, of course! How do American "black" guys like to be referred to?"

"Black works for me, man, but y'all safer with "African American," 'cos that's the current buzz in the big cities."

"But surely, most of them were born in the United States? So why do they hark back to their ancestors' countries? Seems odd!"

"Yeah, but it's all about roots, man... and feelin' good about yosself after years of bein' under, know what ah'm sayin'? Used to be "Afro American", but brothers said, "we don't need to get called like no haircut!" He was laughing loudly and I laughed with him. "Ain't so many Afros on too many brothers these days, huh?" He was very amused by his own observation and the fact that his head was shaven.

"I guess not, but the English are a mixed race of German, French, Scandinavian and allsorts else, but you never hear someone say, "I am a German Englishman", or "a Scandinavian Englishman"... and I'd rather DIE than be a French Englishman!!" I am now laughing, but he doesn't quite see the humour, so I feel the need to explain. "It's a rivalry thing! We've been fighting the French for centuries, you know…? 1066, Agincourt, Waterloo and all that... and now we're great sporting enemies. They also hate **us** with a passion. Then there's the Common Market ……we have a history!!"

He begins to laugh as the humour of the whole P.C. thing came into perspective.

"Whoa! Great food and philosophy all in one shack!"

I turned to continue cooking his food and another black guy in uniform walked up. At this point a very complicated hand dance took place, with each banging the others knuckles and grasping each other's fingers and thumbs in an obviously practised sequence, before ending up in a strange handshake.

If they were policemen I would swear they were freemasons!

The Braves fan greeted the new arrival with, "Hey there, yuh ugly nigger, Whaassup?"

I admit to being a little taken aback by this, but the recipient of the greeting reacted, quite surprisingly to me, by hugging him. I smiled my winning smile and asked the new arrival if I could help him with some food.

"No, man… just ate. Ah'm juss sayin' "hi" to this ugly ole mountain goat."

They passed a few words like two friends catching up on lost time, and I glanced at Kirstie and displayed, in a strained look, that I did not understand the Political Correctness in the exchange of the two guys out front. She responded with a dismissive shrug of her shoulders. The "visitor" left to call at the Pass and ID building alongside my site.

"Wow! I thought that THAT word was strictly off-limits. In all these American chat shows they always say "the 'n' word" rather than even utter it!" I said to the remaining customer.

"Ah guess it is hard fur an English guy to unnerstand it. S'OK comin' from a brother, but you's right! Y'all don't wanna be usin' it!"

He laughed loudly, presumably at the notion of my using the word. I served his food and he stood for a few more minutes, chatting to another colleague who had walked up to order. This was a white guy, and I heard him recounting the discussion we had just had about the 'n' word, and the punishments that white military guys would get for using the term, then he said, "Great talking to y'all! Have a good one!" He left with the other black guy, who had now returned from Pass and ID.

I am a little concerned about Kirstie. When she took off her cardigan today, there was a bruise on her right bicep and a row of bruises along her right triceps, as though someone had gripped her arm really tightly. I hope I am wrong, but it would explain a lot about her reluctance to discuss her husband, when we are in conversation. It also appears that Louise had a similar problem with her last relationship.

Is woman-beating rife in the village? Oh God! I am starting to cluck like a mother hen. If I show Kirstie I care too much about her, she'll probably fall in love with me the way things are going at the moment!

I seem to be irresistible to women currently, and I certainly don't need to start a craze for Ben-beating!

Things to be grateful for

1) Not being of French descent.
2) Another really good day's takings
3) My diplomacy, tact and sensitivity in International relations.
4) Only 3 days to go to see Louise.
5) Stella is coming on Saturday.
6) My animal magnetism! (For the record, when I read this diary in 20 years time, I WAS only joking)

Saturday 12th August 2000

Word of the Day: Approbation… Approval or consent

9 a.m. watching Sky Sports Soccer a.m. and sucking on a Trebor extra strong mint.
(Telephone rings)

I assume, (wrongly), that it will be Stella ringing for final directions and pick up the phone excitedly and enthusiastically greet the caller.
"Hi! How are you?"
"My, we **ARE** in a good mood this morning! Did you take a lot of money last night?"
"Hello, Mother! You're looking very nice this morning!"

"Thank you. I do try to………..Oh yes! Very funny! I seem to be the butt of all your jokes. One day you will be sorry. I'll get my own back…you wait and see."

"Since you asked, it was quite busy. Kirstie is a great help, though."

"I've been saying for ages that you needed some help on there."

"I know you have, Mother…"

I'm going to choke on this.

"…. and you were right. But seriously for a moment…"

"Are you eating sweets?"

"OK, Mrs Marple, I confess! It's a mint. You want me to have nice breath down the phone don't you?"

"Hmm."

"I was trying to tell you…I have a bit of a problem relating to Kirstie."

"Oh my God…You haven't? Not with a married woman?"

"Of course not…"

Of course not? As if it hadn't entered my mind!

"And you don't want to start, either. You'd be asking for trouble!"

"I know! That isn't the issue. Listen to me for a minute. The other day she took off her cardigan and had bruises on her arm that would match a thumb and four fingers gripping her arm really tightly. I only saw one arm, but she is always very cagey about talking about her husband. I reckon he knocks her about. Problem is…what do I do about it?"

"Stay out of it and mind your business, if you've got any sense."

"But what if he really hurt her, and I could have stopped it?"

"The only thing you're likely to stop is her husband's fist, if you go poking your nose into their marriage business. Take my advice and keep out of it. He'll only think you want her for yourself."

"What if she mentions it?"

"What if, what if! I've told you my opinion!"

"OK, thanks."

Well I wasn't holding my breath for Mother's approbation! (hurrah!)

"Now **you** listen. I'm going with your dad to Devon for a week. It's a late break we saw in the paper. God forbid you should actually ring me and find me not at home and worry yourself to death about it. So… I thought I'd ring to let you know."

"OK. Mother, thanks for that. Have a good time. I must get on, I have a thousand things to do."

Well at least two things!

"Do you want the number of the hotel? It's the Regency at Teignmouth…"

"No, you're all right. Ring me when you get there, so I know you arrived safely."

"OK, we will!"

"Have a nice holiday."

"Thanks… now you take care of yourself."

"OK. Bye."

I am still at a loss as to what to do about Kirstie. Anyway, I could be totally wrong. I missed my chance to mention it, when I saw the marks. If I say anything now, it will seem intrusive. I'd better leave it for the time being. I have told her I won't need her to work tonight, as I am hoping to have a pleasant evening with Stella. If she ever arrives! Funny! I have butterflies anticipating her arrival.

Things to be grateful for

1) The anticipation of Stella's arrival.
2) The anticipation of my trip tomorrow to see Louise.
3) Fate kept the two of them apart this weekend!
4) Mother and Dad are away, so no interruptions to my weekend plans

Sunday 13th August 2000

Word of the Day: Immaculate… Spotless, perfectly clean, faultless.

4p.m. A1 southbound lay-by near Biggleswade

I seem to be making too much of a habit of this. I am waiting for the AA to arrive and tow me back home. My poor old Renault 21 is just about fit for the scrap heap. It inexplicably decided to eject its entire store of coolant from the hole on the side of the engine, which once contained a core plug! The result was a very rapid rise in temperature and steam and water everywhere. Most embarrassing. The visit to Louise is now obviously not going to happen. I have rung her to explain the situation, and she has suggested that we try again next weekend. This has jammed a spanner firmly in the works, because Stella is arranging to come next Saturday and stay overnight and is planning to stay most of Sunday too. How I get out of this one I do not know, but I am stressed enough with the car breakdown and cannot think too much about that for the time being.

Yesterday was the start of the new football season, and Luton began with their customary flair and defeat at home at the hands of a very ordinary looking Notts County. Not the anticipated glory start for Ricky Hill as new manager! Oh well he needs time to get things going.

Stella did not arrive until 4 pm, by which time I was almost exploding with anticipation. I put on some romantic music, (20 Greatest Love Songs Album), and I had prepared a salad and some assorted cheeses. We sat at the table, eating the food and drinking some coffee, and chatted for a while about what had occurred in our respective lives since we were together. I looked at her attentively and could not help but be impressed by her. I had forgotten how beautiful she was, but had previously given no thought to the fact that, when I met her, she was at work and therefore in her working attire. We had gone straight from her work for a drink and then back to her flat, so she had had no time to prepare for our "date". Her hair had been tied back when we met and, when it was finally let down, I did not appreciate, in the subdued lighting, how luxuriant it was. She had obviously made an effort to be at her best for this visit. Her make-up was immaculate, (hurrah! <in more ways than one!>). Her deep, dark eyes sparkled, and she had long curling eyelashes, through which she looked at me with a passion, which was compelling, if a little unnerving. Her hair, which cascaded down her back, was the darkest brown, had a remarkable smooth shine, and begged to be touched. Her lips bore a very dark, glistening, red lipgloss, giving an overall Spanish, even gypsy-like appearance. She was wearing a very colourful, cotton print skirt, which covered her knees, and a reddish 'v' necked top that allowed a fairly liberal view of her ample breasts, since they were showing a marked degree of cleavage.

How I wanted to be reintroduced to those wonderful breasts!

The overall appearance was absolutely stunning, and I could hardly wait to take her out in the village. It would raise my street credibility immensely!

That said - being seen with any woman would have done so!

I was really smitten by this beautiful woman and began to feel my confidence draining away, her beauty was so intimidating. However, she restored it in an instant, when she leaned over and whispered, "Don't you want to kiss me?", and then slowly pressed her glossy lips to mine, placed her hand behind my head and pulled me to her, exerting a delicious pressure to the kiss. As she drew slightly away, allowing us to breathe again, and my lower body status dramatically altered, I found myself replying.

"Oh Stella, I'd like to do more than kiss you!"

She stood up, provocatively drawing her hand across my lap and smiling appreciatively, and very seductively, upon finding physical evidence of my obvious excitement.

"Well you had better direct me to the bathroom, then."

Her words were soft and full of invitation. I looked at the clock and saw that it was approaching 6 pm. She came out of the bathroom, some five minutes later, wearing only the sexiest, matching bra, panties and suspender belt, which were black with deep red lace adorning them, together with silky, black stockings, with matching red lace tops. My mouth fell open in disbelief that this most beautiful woman had gone to these lengths to impress me. If our previous encounter had pictorially involved waves rushing up to the shore, and a train disappearing into a tunnel, this night of passion would have had to be represented by a whole coastline of rushing waves and a five engine train set!

I was greedy for her, and she seemed equally hungry for me. All hope of taking her out, to show her off, evaporated, as we did not emerge from the bedroom until it was light and after very little sleep indeed. My not even knowing the Saturday football results, until after she had left for home, this morning, showed the full measure of my infatuation with her.

Before she left, she told me that she had had a wonderful night, and that she had not slept with anyone since we were together at her flat. I admitted that the same applied to me, provoking the obvious question, as to whether I was involved with anyone. I was reluctant to admit to Louise's existence, but after an awkward silence, I finally explained the whole sequence of events; from the broken ankle to the current situation, including how I had thought that Stella had only wanted to see me the once, and that, when I didn't hear from her, I had continued to pursue Louise. However, I could not bring myself to mention the fact that I was travelling down to see Louise this very afternoon. I expected her to throw a scene at the very mention of another woman, and tell me she didn't want to see me again, but she was surprisingly understanding. She said that she realised I would not be living a monk-like existence…

Oh no? I wish!

…and she told me, (in her very provocative way), that she would love it if we could get together again and that she thought that we might become a little more serious, given time. We arranged for her to visit again, next weekend, on her return journey from Sheringham.

As she was leaving, she said, "We might have something really good going on here!"

Scary! Am I really ready for this? Stella is very attractive but we have hardly had time to discuss the weather, let alone a future together. A relationship is about more than just sex, even if it is fantastic sex! The Lorraine dalliance proved that much!

Hence my latest quandary!

Things to be grateful for

1) The most exciting and fulfilling night of passion in my entire life (to date!)
2) Membership of the AA.
3) Whoever it was who invented stockings and suspenders!
4) A proposed repeat performance next weekend.

Tuesday 15th August 2000

Word of the Day: Machination... plot, devious plan.

11-30 p.m. in flat

I have heard nothing from Stella since she left on Sunday. I have to say it is a bit of a surprise, after the way she sounded as she was saying goodbye. I have also left several messages on Louise's voicemail, but she hasn't responded. I hope she isn't mad with me. She seemed OK on Sunday, when I rang from the lay-by, and when I rang on Sunday night, to tell her I had got home safely, even though it was only a brief call. It feels as though they have some hidden agenda and, if I didn't know better, I would swear they are talking to one another. Argghh! Paranoia strikes again. In some ways, I am disappointed, but in others, I am relieved, because I do not have a clue what to do about my situation with these two women. They are both very nice in different ways. I will have to decide between them very soon, or else I am going to get into some very hot water. I feel very uncomfortable, yet my ego has been thoroughly massaged at the same time. It is a very odd feeling. It has to be said that I am ill equipped to deal with the machinations (hurrah!) of these women.

Things to be grateful for

1) Not having to deal with any relationship issues, while ill-equipped to do so.

2) My cat Jason still loves me if no one else does and is sitting on my lap attacking my pen as I am writing!

Thursday 17<u>th</u> August 2000

Word of the Day: Asinine... stupid, like an ass.

4 p.m. in flat

Yesterday afternoon, I decided that I should ring Mother to see how she has been. As I reached for the receiver, I noticed that it was slightly askew on the cradle, and my heart sank. If it had been like that for long, then no one could have got through, even to leave a message, so it would be giving an engaged tone. I rang Mother, expecting a barrage of abuse for being constantly engaged, but got no reply. I left a very sarcastic voice message for her, telling her how she always moans if I don't ring and that when I do, she is never there! I had just cut off after leaving the message, when I suddenly remembered that they are in Devon or Cornwall, on a week's break. Damn and blast! I'll never hear the last of it when she gets home and listens to that. I can hear it now.

"You never listen to a word I say! Blah blah blah!"

I rang the hotel, and she had obviously not rung me, as she did not mention it at all. We enjoyed a pleasant, if unusual, conversation. Unusual, in that she never passed judgement, nor talked of ailments, nor of people of whom I had never heard. She just described some places that I have actually been to myself and told me how much they are enjoying themselves.

Yes it <u>was</u> a short conversation!

I did my duty, and then rang off. I called Louise first and got her mother.

"Aha! The famous missing Ben!" She began. "Louise was trying to get an answer from you all night!"

"Yes, I guessed. I think my cat knocked the 'phone off the cradle slightly, so it never rang. She could have rung my mobile, though."

"She doesn't have the number for some reason. She thought you might have been camped on the Internet!"

"No I haven't been on there, for any great length of time, for weeks. That reminds me, I ought to check it in case there is e-mail."

"There will be, because she e-mailed you from work when she couldn't get through on the 'phone."

"Is she at work now?"

"Yes... and we're not expecting her home until about 7 tonight."

"I'll be at work then. Let me give you my mobile number."

She took it down religiously and then passed the time of day quite pleasantly and I rang off. Next, I rang Stella's mobile, but it just rang. As it did so, I could hear a strange echo, like a faint ringing sound, which I put down to some sort of fault on the line. After about fifteen rings, it switched to voicemail, and I left a message saying that I was upset she hadn't rung, and that I hoped everything was all right. After I had disconnected, I thought about the message I had left and decided that it might come across as a bit brusque, so I rang again. This time I was sitting on the sofa and, as it rang, the "echo" ring was louder, and I became aware that it was coming from between my legs! I pushed my hand down between the cushions and found, much to my horror, Stella's mobile phone, still switched on. Since she had entered my number into her mobile 'phone's memory when I gave it to her, I will bet she hasn't got it written down anywhere, so she couldn't 'phone me if she wanted to. Why do these chains of events always happen to me? What happens now? Is Stella coming this weekend or not? I suppose I'll just have to wait and see, since I have no number for her in Sheringham. Then I thought, *"Wait a minute... her parents' name will be the same as hers, since she is not married. I could try Directory Enquiries, perhaps unlike me, they are not ex-directory."* However, after three calls to Directory Enquiries and trying six different Harveys, I was about to give up, but gave it one last effort. I rang the 7th number furnished by Directory Enquiries and a voice answered.

"Norfolk Hotel, Rob Harvey. Hello?"

"Hello, Mr Harvey, sorry to bother you… I am trying to locate a friend whose name is Harvey. She is staying with her parents. Her name is Stella. I don't suppose you are her father?"

"No…"

"Oh…It was just a long shot…Sorry to bother y…"

"But I **am** her uncle!" He was laughing. "And she didn't stay with her mum and dad, she's here, staying at the hotel. Do you want to speak to her?"

No, of course not. I have rung half the Harveys in Norfolk NOT to speak to her, you pillock!

"If it's not too much trouble." My sincerity training came to the fore just when I needed it!

Stella and I had a long conversation, during which we both laughed about the telephone mix up and the asinine (hurrah!) behaviour of my intellectually challenged Birman cat, and also about how much we had missed each other. The plans were confirmed that she was to come and stay over on Saturday and return on Sunday morning, to North Yorkshire. She also told me that she had something exciting to tell me, but wanted to tell me in person. I am now going to be intrigued until she arrives.

Things to be grateful for

1) I have made contact with Stella and Louise so things are not as bad as I thought they might be.

2) Mother and Dad are enjoying a well-earned break in the sun.

3) I am two days away from seeing Stella again.

Saturday 19th August 2000

Word of the Day: Interject... interrupt with, insert comment.
10 a.m. Preparing for the arrival of Stella

I have booked the trailer into a local gas fitter, for Monday, to supply and fit two new griddles. One is twice the size of the other, and they will fit perfectly into the space left after the removal of the old griddle, and the old flame grill, which have become surplus to requirements. I will be £1200 down on the deal and will lose a day's trade, but it should speed up the throughput of kebabs quite considerably.

Yesterday was exceptionally busy on base and, as a result, customers had to wait up to fifty minutes for their food. I cannot let this state of affairs continue any longer, or I will lose the confidence of my customers.

I am becoming more concerned about Kirstie. She had a fierce looking bruise on her cheekbone yesterday morning, which she maintains was caused by leaving a kitchen cabinet door open and then walking into it. I told her that I might look stupid, but that appearance does not necessarily prove that I am. She became very defensive but we were so busy, we did not have the chance to discuss it further. I am sure her husband has given her a smack in the face. The question is: what do I do about it?

On base yesterday, one of my most regular and prolific customers, Robbie Haskins, came by, having placed an order by 'phone, for seven kebabs of various types and enough chips to clear the Euro chip mountain. As normal, he was accompanied by an entourage of one other male and three females. They are all Naval personnel and very personable. There is often some hilarious banter among them, as well as with me, and today was no exception. Their order was ready and keeping warm in the Bain Marie. As usual, I added up the order in pounds and announced the total order value upon their arrival. Also as usual, there was a large number of people who had ordered at the counter, waiting for their food and Robbie and co were totally disorganised in their mode of payment. Kirstie served their food, while I tried, resolutely, to decipher the convoluted manner in which they approached the task.

"OK! I wanna pay for two kebabs and two fries in dollars…" He handed me a twenty-dollar bill, and I furnished his change. "…Then I need to pay for another two in pounds." Again I took his proffered cash.

One of the ladies interjected, (hurrah!), "But I need a Cajun and fries."

"I know that, " replied Robbie, " Let me deal with it."

"But you haven't paid for it yet," she continued.

"That's because you didn't give me the money for it. Christie's getting it right now… you can pay Ben for it yourself!"

By the look on her face, Kirstie was not impressed that he got her name wrong.

They were all laughing by this point, as another of the females joined in the harassment of the beleaguered Robbie. She looked a little formal in her battle dress uniform, but her face was very attractive. Her complexion was dark and smooth and her very dark hair was tied up at the back, but the size of the bun led me to believe that it must have been quite long.

"Have you got my lemon spice kebab there?" She asked him.

"Yes, and your fries."

"I didn't order fries."

"Yeah you did, we all ordered fries."

"No, I got a fries for Sergeant White."

"Well it pretty much amounts to the same thing, doesn't it?"

"Not really, the fries are not for me."

" Jenni! They're with your order! Who cares who they are for?"

"I guess no one…and Ben, I need an order of large chips for another guy in the shop, extra to the order Robbie 'phoned in."

Strange how some Americans ask for "an order of large chips" instead of a "large order of chips." Makes it sound like each chip is large rather than the portion.

"Hey, Ben. What she really needs is a large order of 'shut the fuck up'… then a side of 'stay the fuck shut up!'

"That's really mean, Robbie."

Funny, but really mean!

"Thank you, Ben," she continued. "Can I get those extra chips and extra, extra garlic sauce on my kebab?"

These Americans are really good at extra extra!

"You can get anything you want on it, when you smile like that…"

Jenni smiled warmly at my flirtatious remark.

"…anyway, I cook your lunch **every** day, it's about time you cooked mine for a change."

"Don't go there," said Robbie, "I've tasted her cooking! The US government make her put a health warning on **her** cooking!" They were all laughing again, and I laughed along with them.

Finally, I sorted out all the payment, much to the relief of the assembled crowd, and they were on their way again. The episode was, however, the source of much amusement to the amassed throng and myself, although Kirstie was shaking her head in disbelief that I had laughed at his sarcasm. However, their long-windedness created pressure from which we were destined not to recover until almost 2 p.m.

I am looking forward to seeing Stella again. She is quite late. She was supposed to arrive at about 10. I guess she'll get here when she can.

Things to be grateful for

1) The patience of my customers with each other!
2) My ability to make ladies smile!

Sunday 20th August 2000

Word of the Day: Delinquent… neglectful of duty.

7 a.m. In bed
(telephone rings)

I wake up just as the answering machine fields the call, and I sense Stella stirring next to me. It is a strange feeling, but also somehow reassuring and secure. She snuggles up to me and whispers in a husky, first-thing-in-the-morning voice, "Hello you." She presses her mouth against mine and her hand begins meandering beneath the duvet and a sexy smile plays on her lips as she encounters confirmation of my arousal. This evidence surprises as much as it pleases me, because we had spent most of the evening and the early part of the morning in passionate oblivion, but we greeted the day in the same way that we had bid the night farewell, in lustful abandon. However, this morning it was accompanied by the sound of the telephone ringing and the answering machine clicking on and off, but since I had switched off the speaker, no messages were heard. As we rolled gently apart, quite breathless, she smiled and said, "I wonder who wanted you this early in the morning…apart from me that is!"

"Almost certainly my mother."

"You could have answered it."

"No I couldn't. You had your hand over my ears!"

"That was NOT your ear, Ben."

"Well whatever it was, it definitely made me deaf to the phone ringing!"

We both laughed and I said that I would ring Mother as soon as Stella had gone.

We got up and, in my most courteous fashion, I offered her first use of the shower. Once she was in the shower, I went into the bathroom to brush my teeth.

"Is that you?" She called.

"It had better be!"

Come to think of it, whoever it was the answer would have to be "Yes!"

"Well what are you doing out there? Get yourself in here, it's lovely!"

She slid back the shower screen door and held out an inviting hand and ushered me in beside her. This morning's was the most interesting shower I have **ever** taken! Stella is such a lustful, adventurous girl. It was the most erotic experience I can remember, without actually making love. The heat of the water and the soft caress of the foamy shower gel being administered by her very adept hands, while I returned the compliment, were from the realms of fantasies, which I had harboured since puberty! Reluctantly, Stella got out first, while I continued to enjoy the hot water playing on my chest, and she put on a towelling dressing gown and wrapped a towel around her, still-damp, hair.

"I'll make some tea," she offered, as I was getting out of the shower.

This was an offer that I simply could not refuse. I thought to myself that she looked very contented in a domestic sort of way, walking across the room, wearing the robe and with the towel piled up on top of her head. Scary or what?

We had breakfast and discussed what a fulfilling night and morning it had been. She kissed me warmly on the doorstep….

No, it was on the lips!

… then made a very worrying parting remark before she set off for home, promising to ring me in the week, to let me know when arrangements had been made for her to move to Sheringham. She said that she really feels part of a proper couple!!!!

Things to be grateful for

1) I think I am in lust with Stella!
2) The best sex I have ever experienced. It seems to get better all the time.
3) She will be close enough to see her more regularly.

Things to be worried about

1) Things seem to be moving very quickly in the Stella scenario.
2) Stella looking domesticated and feeling 'couply' already. (I know. I invented the word 'couply', how clever am I?)
3) The sex is great, but I am not sure that there is any real substance to the relationship other than that.

4) If I get in too deep with Stella, any potential relationship I might have with Louise may be out of the window and I don't want that.

Monday 21st August 2000

Word of the Day: Filial… of or due from a son or daughter.

10 a.m. In flat.

Luton managed to lose again on Saturday. This is not the ideal start to a season. Having said that, Wigan are a very good team and have spent big money on their team, and they will probably feature in the promotion race at the end of the season, so no need to panic just yet. The new manager will need time to get the team sorted out.

The trailer is in for the new griddles to be fitted, so I am having a welcome day off. Mum and Dad are back from their holiday, and I am going to drive down to Luton to do my filial (hurrah!) duty. God knows when I will get the time to go and see them, if I don't take this opportunity. I also have a cast iron reason for not staying too long, as I have to get back to pick up the trailer by 6 p.m., so I have it ready for tomorrow's trading.

10 p.m. Back home

Mother was in fine form as always. I rang the doorbell and she opened it gingerly.

"Oh! It's you. You remembered where we live? Why didn't you answer your phone yesterday? You could have rung me back."

"Hello Ben. Nice to see you. How are you?" I said aloud to myself.

My sarcasm earned her famous unimpressed stare.

"I didn't bring you up to talk to your mother like that."

"I'm sure you didn't… and I'm sure that Nan didn't bring you up to talk to your child like that, either."

We had walked into the lounge, where Dad was standing with a stifled smile at my comment.

Mother detected it at ten paces. "And you can wipe that grin off **YOUR** face as well. You're both as bad as one another…like a couple of kids!"

"Hi Dad, how're you doing?"

"Not too well by all accounts!" He raised his shoulders like a naughty schoolboy and we shared a mutual subdued giggle.

"So…to what do we owe this rare pleasure?" Mother regained centre stage.

"Well… I fancied a cup of tea, and I couldn't be bothered to make one, so I thought I'd come over and let you make it."

"That would be funny if it wasn't probably the truth. Go on… sit down… I've already got the kettle on."

"I can't stop too long…I've got to pick up my trailer by six."

"Charming! We don't see you for weeks then, when we do, you're in and out like a fiddler's elbow."

"I don't get much time off… and the first free day I have, I drive sixty odd miles to pay you a quick visit, and you are not even pleased to see me." I put on my best, devastated expression.

"Of course we are pleased to see you, even if it is only for a little while…aren't we George?…"

HA! GOTCHA! The old hurt expression never fails.

"Of course we are, Ben…you know we are." Dad agreed with her, though looked a bit nonplussed by my antics.

"…And don't think I was born yesterday, with your sarcasm and your "little boy lost", "look how hurt I am", expressions. You forget I can read your theatricals a mile away!"

One day I am going to win one with her…one day!

"Your Auntie Joy had the bug man in last week."

"The what?"

"You know… the man from the council. To kill some bugs in her kitchen. She had some pasta in a plastic box…well you know she never eats anything exotic like that…and apparently it's been there for years. Well… I didn't know this, but it turns out that some sort of beetle things get into pasta if you keep it too long."

"They're only weevils, Mother. Hardly a cause for fumigating the house!"

"Well she wasn't too pleased. Especially when he poked a stick down between her cupboards. She said, "I was that embarrassed! He poked a stick down between the cupboards and, when he pulled it out, it had a big piece of fluff and two bits of pasta on it!"

By this time, I was laughing my socks off. The image of Auntie Joy, in total horror at having the exterminator in her house, and then having him find a bit of fluff…let alone two bits of pasta. She is so house-proud. That would have been worse to her than having the weevils. I am surprised she didn't have a coronary. Mother spent the rest of my one hour visit, trying to explain to me that weevils only like clean places… and so on…and so on…

Smile and nod, Ben. Smile and nod.

Things to be grateful for

1) A cunning plan to visit the parental units without having to stay too long.
2) Auntie Joy has survived her invasion of the pasta snatchers!
3) I should be much quicker in producing kebabs on the new griddles.

Wednesday 23rd August 2000

Word of the day: Ameliorate… improve, make better

4 p.m. in flat.

Luton managed to get a 0-0 draw against Peterborough, in the Worthington Cup first round first leg. Maybe they can take heart from that and get their first league win on Saturday against Bournemouth.

At the height of business today, the very attractive, dusky skinned, young woman from the US Navy came up to the hatch. She told me she wasn't ordering today, but she smiled in, what I have to say was, a very sexy manner, as she surreptitiously handed me a small envelope. It looked like a notelet. Kirstie was obviously unimpressed and frowned quizzically at me. I shrugged my shoulders in silent answer to her silent question and slipped the envelope into my back pocket.

As we finished for the day, and I had closed the hatch and switched off all the apparatus, we began the cleaning up process. I tentatively broached the subject of her recent run of "unfortunate physical mishaps."

"I am worried about you, Kirstie."

"Why…what do you mean?"

"You know what I mean… the kitchen cupboard incident. It's only one of a string of recent **"accidents"**, which seem to keep befalling you." I placed a dramatic emphasis on the word accident. "No one has that many accidents."

"I'm OK… really!"

"The way you said that does nothing to alleviate my fears. He's been hitting you, hasn't he?"

"No! Er…why do you say that?"

"It doesn't take a rocket scientist to add two and two and come up with four, Kirstie."

"I'm OK. He isn't hitting me. I'm just…clumsy… that's all."

"Yes and I'm the Queen of Sheba!"

"What do you want me to say?"

"I'd like to think you could be honest with me… in fact it would be a start to be honest with yourself."

She became ashen faced and withdrawn, so I didn't push the point, but after an uneasy silence, which lasted until we had finished cleaning, I tried once more.

"I'm a good listener, you know…. if you want to talk about it.

"You don't understand…"

"Damn right I don't. How can you let yourself be in danger like that? You've not long had a baby!"

"That's part of the problem. Ever since I had her, he's changed…. he seems to hate me."

"So he **has** been causing all the bruises?"

"You know he has…but I love him! I thought he loved me, but he can't do, can he?"

"You need to get help. You can't go on letting it keep happening to you. What if he turns on the baby? Or loses control completely and does you serious harm? And you're right…how can he love you if he keeps beating you up?"

"I can't do anything…."

She began to cry. Tears were streaming down her face, and she was gasping for breath between sobs. I held her gently by the upper arms and bent down to look into her, now puffy, eyes.

"Come on…it's not so bad. You can sort it out."

Unfortunately, this comment did nothing to ameliorate, (hurrah! For the word of the day not the fact that I made her cry again!), the situation, because it obviously **was** that bad. She continued crying, even more vigorously than before. I felt such sympathy for both her plight and her current demeanour. She reached out and put her arms around my waist and pulled herself towards me, resting her face on my chest. I had raised my arms, which now seemed surplus to requirements, as I held them uselessly in the air. It seemed more natural to bring them down and I wrapped them around her shoulders and held her tightly to me, in a gesture of support. I found myself stroking her hair and its silky texture was rather sensuous, even though I realised that it was a very inappropriate time for me to notice the fact! I almost succumbed to the moment and, for a split second, considered kissing her, but my conscience insisted that I resist the temptation, just in time.

"OK that's enough of that crying and stuff…" I attempted to come over all macho and in control.

I had really enjoyed the hug, despite the knowledge that the feelings were improper. I am sure she was only needing to be liked…loved…

well… supported or whatever… and I am sure we would have both been embarrassed later, if I had have kissed her. I didn't even realise that I found her that attractive. In any case, I think my love life is quite complicated enough, without adding married women to the equation!

She smiled a smile of resignation, which told me that she understood. However, I still couldn't help wondering to myself, on the very unusually quiet journey home, what it would have been like to kiss her. Well, I **am** a red blooded male! I dropped her off at The Green and came inside. I got undressed to take a shower and the envelope fell out of my chef's trousers and fluttered to the floor. I opened it inquisitively. I read the exquisitely scripted handwriting.

Dear Ben, (if I can call you Ben.) (?)

I just wondered if you was joking when you said it was time I cooked you some food the other day? I think you are real cute and I would love to cook you dinner one night if you wasn't joking. Don't take no notice of Robbie… I can cook real good, but cooking for one isn't much fun. I live on RAF Allington and your ID pass is good for there as well as Newton Molecliffe. My number is written below so please give me a call if you were really interested. I hope you will.

Love from Jenni xx

I didn't know whether this was a set-up or for real. The dot over the 'i' in Jenni was a small heart and the grammar was appalling. The last time I received a note like this was when I was about 13! I do find her attractive though. She must be about 25, and she has a very pretty face, I would almost say baby-faced. It is difficult to assess her more basic physical attributes, as they have always been hidden under a battledress uniform when she has called at the trailer. I still think this is a joke, though, maybe down to that Robbie character, he's always winding me up, so I'd better play it cool.

Things to be grateful for

1) Finally getting through to Kirstie, problem is… to whom do I recommend she talk?
2) Resisting the temptation to kiss her. God knows what complications that would have caused.
3) I seem to have inadvertently pulled one of the military women, (or have I?).
4) I managed to use the word ameliorate. Word of the day 0 Ben 1.(hurrah!)

Thursday 24<u>th</u> August 2000

Word of the day: Derogatory… involving or implying discredit, insulting

Midnight after shower.

I am buzzing at the moment. I feel that high you get after serious exercise, when the endorphins kick in. It is a long time since I have had a sporty workout. I have just put the trailer away, after Kirstie worked the evening session on her own for the first time, while I skived off! Luckily it was fairly quiet for her, but I thought it would be. Wednesdays are usually the quietest evenings. It did mean, however, that there was very little profit for me, after I allow for her wages. By all accounts, she coped very well, so maybe I can delegate a bit more and free up some time for a little more leisure. I feel, sometimes, that all my life consists of is work and sleep!

I played football tonight on the Astroturf, with Jamie, Gordon and Brian, the other members of the Far Canal quiz team. We have been trying to get together socially, in a 'non-quiz' environment, for ages. We joined in with some members of the village football team. They treated it as a training exercise, but still ran us ragged. I thought I was fairly fit, but not compared to these blokes. I stood the pace better than the other three though. After the game, we showered and went down the Red Lion for a few drinks, before I closed the business down for the evening. However, the strenuous exercise came as a bit of a shock to my system, as I was still glowing and perspiring after the shower, even when we got to the pub, hence the extra shower when I got home. It was great to have a 'blokey' night out. There was a lot of banter and piss-taking all evening, especially, for some reason, over my love life. As on quiz night, I held my own in that department.

"Maria is getting on my nerves lately. She can't cope with the kids at the moment, so she takes it out on me. She is as moody as hell! She never used to be like this. I remember our wedding day as if it were yesterday… If it were tomorrow I'd fucking cancel it!" Brian, the only married member of the group, was feeling very sorry for himself. If he thought he was about to receive any sympathy in this company, he was drastically mistaken, his comment invoking universal laughter.

"PMT can be fatal if you get in the way of it!" Gordon offered a helpful observation.

"She's got permanent fucking PMT lately. You two don't know when you're well off." Brian referred to the fact that Gordon and I were both still single. I laughed.

"Being single produces problems of its own, you know!" I said, and recounted the saga of the Ben Arnold love triangle, and how I wasn't sure if it was about to become a quadrilateral!

"I'd like to have a crack at coping with those sort of problems for a while, instead of my marital ones, you lucky bastard," Brian supplied the special kind of support, for which he is famous.

"You're just a tart, Ben!" Jamie observed.

"You can talk!" I retorted accusingly. "You've got a fiancée at home and a girlfriend at the office, so don't give me that 'tart' stuff! At least I'm free and single. That makes me legit, and you the bastard!"

Everyone laughed, including Jamie.

"You're all just jealous!" He said.

"So what are you going to do about this American bird, then?" Gordon voiced the question to which all present seemed to want to know the answer.

"I don't know. I am totally confused."

"No change there, then!" Jamie provoked some mild amusement.

"It's not like you to be funny!" I stole his thunder." Anyway… do you think it is a hoax, or not?"

"Probably," Jamie came back. "D'you want me to give her one for you and check out her credentials?"

"You are so coarse…No I don't. I am quite capable of doing it myself, if it needs doing at all, thank you very much! Anyway, she is much too nice for you. She has an IQ of at least 100, and the ones who go for you are usually somewhere between idiot and moron!"

In truth, his fiancée, Sam, is very intelligent and a stunning looker, and he has half the girls in the village lusting after him as well.

"Fuck off!" was his cultured reply.

"…And what about Louise?" Brian queried. "I thought it was her knickers you really wanted to get into."

"They'd probably suit him too!" Gordon caused a mild ripple of laughter.

" Shut up you tart! Anyway, to answer the question…I do like Louise a lot, but I don't really know her that well, and I don't seem to be able to **get** to know her either. It just doesn't seem to be happening somehow."

"Poor little lost Ben! It won't happen while you're shagging that **country** girl, will it?" Brian advised. His emphasis on the word 'country' displayed a derogatory (hurrah!) tone. "If you put the effort into seeing Louise, that you put into playing 'hide the sausage' with her, maybe it would happen."

"Yes, but with her down in Chichester, and me up here working silly hours of the day and night, we never seem to get it together… and Stella **is** coming on a bit heavy!"

"Eeeuw! Too much information!" Jamie made the obvious joke provoked by my ambiguous statement. I gave him an accusing look, and the others both looked at him in silence, creating another of those 'tumbleweed' moments, for which Jamie is rapidly becoming infamous. He looked suitably abashed.

"There's no need to lower the tone, " I compounded his embarrassment. "It's gutter level already."

I continued to explain my difficulties, but as the alcohol intervened, I got increasingly little sense out of any of them. In fact, by the time I mentioned Kirstie's situation, I regretted it instantly.

"She's old Mick Whatsisface's missus isn't she? Oh Christ, You're not giving her the benefit of the old trouser snake tango as well, are you?" Gordon, who had been sitting with a vacant expression on his face for the previous few minutes, suddenly re-entered the land of the semi comatose.

"No… I am not." I asserted with conviction.

"He reckons himself a bit of a hard case, doesn't he? Shame he has to hit women to prove it… If I see him, I'll fucking tell him to his face." Gordon's alcohol began to take over his conversation for him.

"Yeah right," said Jamie, "You're full of shit."

"And Budweiser," I assisted.

"I'd still have him, if I was sober!" Gordon was not to be discouraged.

"Anyhow… when are we going to see this Stella nympho?" Jamie came back at me. "I can always help out if she's too much for you."

This seemed to be the right moment to leave, as the conversation continued to degenerate. I swigged a larger quantity of beer than my mouth would hold and nearly choked on it, in an effort to drain my glass quickly, while the moment was still ripe to leave.

"OK, You pillocks! I'm knackered, and I've got to go and relieve Kirstie."

Jamie opened his mouth to speak, and I predicted that his intended comment was going to relate to the type of relief I may have been going to give her.

"Don't go there, Jamie. It's too obvious. Do you want to be known as 'tumbleweed' for the rest of your life?" Even as I said it, I realised that I **was** probably labelling him for life with the nickname. Oh well, serves him right!

Louise left me a message on the answering machine:

"Hi Ben! Where have you been hiding? I tried your mobile but it was switched off. Aren't you working? I thought you would have rung me. Anyway, if you are not too late in, give me a ring? I'm coming up next weekend... perhaps we could do something? Er... Sunday lunch out somewhere maybe? Look forward to hearing from you. Bye, Ben."

Does she mean the weekend coming, or the following one? Either way, it's something to look forward to.

I wanted to ring her, but it was 11-45, by the time I got in, and I know she would have been asleep by then. I'll try tomorrow.

Things to be grateful for

1) A good blokey night out.
2) Louise rang and it looks like a nice date on the horizon.
3) Kirstie looks capable of holding the fort on her own.

Monday 28th August 2000

Word of the Day: exacerbate... make worse (pain or anger), irritate (a person)

Just after 5 p.m. in flat

It was late summer bank holiday today, but the Americans don't have it as a day off, so I had to work. That put me into the wrong frame of mind to start with! It appears to have been the start of the wasp season again, too. It is so annoying when they keep coming into the trailer and buzzing round everything. There were several incidents where I had to execute offending insect invaders, by beating them to the floor with my Packers hat, then squashing them while they were dazed. It really is an art to flick the hat out, with expert timing, and I had mastered it very well, flicking the hat, flooring the wasp and returning the hat to my head in one movement. On one occasion, I performed the coup de grace with such lightning aplomb, that I appeared to have propelled the wasp right out of the trailer and into oblivion, as we were unable to find it. Two and a half hours later, after a very busy session, I finally closed the hatch, and we cleaned up ready to leave. Just as I locked the trailer, I was aware of an irritation on my head. I removed the hat to scratch it and a very bewildered wasp flew out. I must have flicked out the hat, missed the wasp on the way down, and scooped it up on the way back to my head and knocked it out in the process of pinning it to my head. I was very concerned that I might have been badly stung, with a wasp inside my hat for all that time. Kirstie, however, found the incident the source of great amusement and laughed so much that she almost wet herself and had to repair to the Ladies to prevent an unfortunate incident!

I received a call from Stella, who is anxious that we should meet again very soon. She is still making arrangements to move back to Sheringham, but she has agreed to work two weeks notice at her job in Yorkshire, to allow her manager to find a replacement for her.

I have just rung Louise, and she is coming up on the 2nd. We are having Sunday lunch together.

Things to be grateful for

1) Luton won their first match of the season 1-0 against Bournemouth on Saturday.

2) My head does not look like a scale model of the Himalayas as my incarcerated wasp was too bewildered to sting my head.

3) It was good to see Kirstie forgetting her problems for a while and having a really good laugh, even if it was at my expense!

SEPTEMBER 2000

Friday 1st September 2000

Word of the Day: Oxymoron... figure of speech where apparently contradictory terms appear together

11 p.m. Absolutely knackered!

Had a few good laughs on base today. A female customer rang in to order two portions of chips. There were five customers waiting for orders to be cooked as I answered it.

"I'd like to place an order for two things of chips? How long will it be?"

Things?

"How long?" I repeated so that the waiting people could get the gist of the call. "That's a very personal question to a relative stranger, isn't it?"

The laughter from the "audience" must have carried down the 'phone to her.

"Oh, no I'm sorry, I meant...Shit Arnie, You know what I meant!"

"Yes I know... and I can see you blushing down the 'phone! What name?"

"Sorry?"

"The order... What is your name?"

"Erm.........."

"Do you need to 'phone a friend?"

She laughed. "No, that's Ron."

"OK. About ten minutes…Thanks."

I disconnected.

"Now **that** is scary for an Intelligence Base! She couldn't remember who she was…and then thought she was called Ron!"

There was universal laughter and a few non - PC jokes about women, particularly women in the military, but these dried up instantaneously, when a female major arrived to place an order and, as she outranked all those males present, they all jumped to attention and saluted her. She responded with a salute of her own.

"I don't know what I want yet." She began, as she perused the menu.

"Well, you're a woman, what can I tell you?" There was a hissing sound as the enlisted men present made sharp intakes of breath.

She looked up at me. I was smiling my winning smile, in as impish a manner as I could muster, and she winced as she smiled back.

"It's OK. I'll be getting a slap, as soon as you've gone, from my able assistant here." I pointed to Kirstie, who turned a very dark shade of pink. She still hasn't got used to my sense of humour.

"I should hope so. I think you need an ass kicking!" The major responded with another wry smile.

"Well that's a very kind gesture, in fact, the best offer I've had all week!" The men behind her were screwing up their faces, trying not to laugh.

"I'll have a Cajun kebab and a regular fries…I'll be right back… I'm just going to check my mail at the Post Office." She said, and left.

"JEEEZUS H. CHRIST, Arnie. She's a major, dude!"

"…And your point is…?"

"Well she outranks all of us here."

"She doesn't outrank me! I don't need to kiss her arse, even if you do! She probably gets cheesed off with it anyway… Mind you it's quite a pretty arse, maybe she'd like me to kiss it!"

"Don't even, Ben! Not even in jest."

Just then the woman, who ordered chips under the name "Ron", arrived.

"I ordered two things of chips?"

"Have you remembered your name yet?"

"I'm sorry? Oh! No… I said Ron because a guy called Ron, in our shop, was going to pick them up, but he got busy, so I came myself."

"You had me worried for a moment… I was beginning to think that 'Military Intelligence' was an oxymoron." (hurrah!)

"I'm sorry?"

Pearls before swine! Some days you just have to accept that you are wasting your wit on an unappreciative audience!

"Nothing."

Later in the morning, Kirstie gave me a gently tentative telling off.

"You are so rude to some of those customers. It's a wonder they come back. You made me blush with embarrassment a few times today!"

She really is quite sweet.

"They love it! They think I'm a Great British eccentric. They never know quite what to expect from me. I like to keep them guessing."

"But what about that lady major?"

"What about her? She was laughing along with me. She knew I was only teasing." "I never know when to take you seriously!"

Long may it continue! Ha! Ha!

I haven't heard from Jenni all week, so I guess it was a joke. Robbie came on Wednesday, but only ordered for himself and he didn't mention it, so I couldn't say anything either, or I would have walked into his trap. Unless… it was genuine, and she is too embarrassed to visit the trailer, because I have not responded. Oh! Shit! I am no nearer knowing what is going on than I was before.

Things to be grateful for

1) Kirstie's concern for me!
2) The new griddles have speeded up service by a mile.
3) Great British eccentrics…me included!

Sunday 3rd September 2000

Word of the Day: Trepidation... feeling of deep fear or alarm

7 p.m. Getting ready for the pub quiz

Louise and I are doomed! Every conceivable effort to get to know her seems to be hexed. Am I destined never to get close to her? We had arranged to meet today, for lunch, as it was not viable to meet on Saturday. She went to the wedding of her close friend, Madeleine, which took place in Cambridge yesterday, and she was not due to arrive in the village until about 7 p.m. at the earliest. Of course, I was working from 6 p.m. and, by the time I finish on a Saturday, I am not good for anything apart from sleep, so it was a non-starter to meet last night. As it turned out, she didn't get back until gone nine and had had an adequate amount to drink to render her socially unavailable, anyway!

Today is her mother's birthday, and her father has organised a family get-together to celebrate it, so Louise has to be back in Chichester by 8 p.m. If we had have been proper boyfriend and girlfriend, I could probably have passed for 'family' and gone too, but we really have not yet even passed "go!" Therefore, our big chance to get 'off the ground' was Sunday lunch.

She arrived at the flat this morning at 11-30, looking a million dollars, in a very becoming navy blue jersey dress, which accentuated her busty substances! Very up-market. Her long hair was waved and shiny, and she was fully made-up. I could have ravished her then and there, and you could keep your Sunday lunch! However, being the gentleman that I am, (at least in her eyes), I retained my self-control and suddenly realised that I had thought I was ready to go out, wearing my best jeans and a maroon polo shirt. I now felt totally under-dressed, so I made her a cup of coffee and slipped away into the bedroom and quickly changed, emerging, some five minutes later, in an open necked shirt, black chinos and my best shoes. She complimented me on my appearance, which gave me an immense ego boost, and I realised that I had not complimented her on her appearance. It was now too late to do so, without appearing to have been prompted. I drank my coffee and we got up to leave. As she stood by the door, she waited for me to open it for her, and I stood back and looked at her.

"Wow!" Was all that came, incredulously, from my mouth.

"Well, thank you very much, kind sir," she replied sincerely. It appeared that I had redeemed myself from my earlier gaffe and she felt genuinely complimented.

I reached for the door latch and, as my fingers began to open the door, the doorbell rang. I continued to open it.

"Hello, Benjamin! We thought we'd surprise you!"

FUCK! You certainly did THAT!

Mother pushed past us both and let out a hiss of mock exhaustion, as she collapsed into an armchair.

"We came out for a Sunday drive and found ourselves at Sandy, so we decided to push on for here and treat you to lunch, didn't we, George?"

Dad nodded, shrugged his shoulders towards me, resignedly, and followed into the room.

"We were only half an hour or so away," she continued, " and you never eat properly."

"Yes I do, Mother…! I eat quite well…**Actually!**"

I winced, as I heard myself emphasise the word 'actually' in the manner of a petulant schoolboy, and in front of Louise, too! Whatever did she think? I was horrified and could have cheerfully strangled my mother on the spot.

"Louise and I were going to the Admiral Nelson for lunch… oh! Sorry… Louise, this is my mum and dad… Mum and Dad… this is Louise… a close friend of mine."

"Oh? Really? Well, I've been saying for a long time that it's about time you found someone and settled down! You're nearly thirty-five, for goodness sake!"

"Mother! You're embarrassing Louise."

"No I'm not…am I Louise?

Talk about a loaded question. How could she answer, other than "No"?

"Er?... No, of course not..."

"Well, you are certainly embarrassing me!"

"I'm your mother! That's my job!"

"Erm...Well, if you like, Ben, we can do this some other time."

Louise tried to escape gracefully, but Mother was not letting her get away that easily.

"Don't be silly!" She began, in sugar sweet tones. "We're the intruders..."

YES YOU ARE!

I had, for just one second, thought that Mother was about to do the right thing, for once in her life, but that hope was short lived.

"...you are **more** than welcome to come with us!"

Louise made a further polite effort to get out of coming, but was met with absolute adamance on Mother's part, that she should join us. Louise looked at me with trepidation, (hurrah!), in her eyes. I was in a cleft stick. I really wanted to say that Louise and I had a 'date' and that, as they had inconsiderately arrived without prior warning, they should excuse us. However, I knew that I would be made to suffer for weeks, if I did! Louise went to the bathroom, so I tried the watered-down version. Through clenched teeth and full of innuendo, I said, "Mother! We were going on a **date**!"

"That's OK, we can have lunch on our own." Dad, the voice of reason and sanity, made the obviously correct observation.

"Don't be daft! We don't come over **that** often. If anything, Ben can arrange another date, I'm sure."

Mother was not to be dissuaded. As we were about to leave, she dealt another potentially fatal blow to my credibility with Louise.

"Aren't you going to put a tie on, dear?"

DEAR? Argghh!

There followed an insufferable lunch, where Louise was interrogated about her background, her working life, even her intention to bear children. I am only surprised that Mother failed to inspect her teeth, like a horse in an auction. Louise seemed to find the whole episode very amusing and, I have to say, she held her own with Mother, only answering questions that she wanted to answer and deftly sidestepping those, which she did not! She declined to return to the flat afterwards though, and made her excuses and ran! I could hardly blame her. We had no opportunity to spend any time together, so I know very little more about her now, than I did before lunch. The problem is that the skeleton in my closet that is my mother is now well and truly out. Now that Louise knows about her, I doubt she'll ever want to see me again. Maybe I ought to lock my maniacal mother away in the loft like Rochester did his wife, in "Jane Eyre".

Mother and Father left at about four, leaving me a gibbering wreck. Louise rang to say goodbye before she left… which was nice.

"So that's what we are, is it? Very close friends?" She laughed, as she rang off.

Things to be grateful for

1) I did not strangle Mother
2) I did not strangle Mother
3) I did not strangle Mother!

Tuesday 5th September 2000

Word of the Day: Ominous… of evil omen, indicating disaster or difficulty

9 p.m. working on trailer.

Louise just rang.
"Hiya! How are you today?" She began breezily.
"I'm fine…what about you?" I added with an ominous (hurrah!) voice.
"She laughed, "Why do you say it like that? Are you afraid of me?"

"I'm not afraid of **you**…just scared that you might have run a mile after Mother's performance."

"It'd take more than that to put me off you! She's quite sweet **really**…"

No one's ever accused her of that before! Ah… but the sting was in the "really".

"…she only behaves like that because she cares about you! …"

God preserve me from caring women, then!

"Anyway…"

She seemed to be reading my thoughts!

"…it was still very nice to go out together, even if we were chaperoned! Can we do it again sometime? Perhaps on our own, though, next time…eh?"

"I'd **really** like that. When are you coming up again? Or should I try to come down to you again?"

We both laughed at the memory of my previous aborted attempt to visit her.

"I'm busy this weekend…what about the one after?" She suggested.

"Sounds good to me," I enthused. "Oh yes…" I suddenly remembered her mother's party. "How did the party go?"

"Well it wasn't what I would call a **party**, more of a family reunion. It was OK seeing a few relatives that I hadn't met in ages, but not really my scene."

We talked for a while about her job. I was hoping that she might be getting bored with it, and with living down there, away from her friends, but it appears that she is very highly thought of at work and has made some new friends. I guess that means she will be staying. Shame, because I really like her, and it would be nice to be able to see her regularly. A customer interrupted our conversation, so we said a hasty 'goodbye'.

A few minutes later, Stella called.

Have these women got radar?

She is staying another week in the Lake District, as her replacement cannot start work until 18th September.

Things to be grateful for

1) Louise is made of sterner stuff than I gave her credit for.
2) Business is still steady.
3) I haven't noticed any new marks on Kirstie.

Sunday 10th September 2000

Word of the Day: Exacerbate… make pain, anger or distress worse

5 p.m. in flat

That has to rank as one of the weirdest nights of my life. The lads at the pub would never believe it.

Saturday began, as normally as any day should. After Luton's first home win, two weeks ago, they followed up with two creditable away draws, at Wycombe and Rotherham, and I was full of hope for another home win against Northampton. I went into town and paid some cash into the bank, then returned home to take up my Saturday afternoon position on the sofa, to watch the afternoon's football unfold on Sky Sports channel. Naturally, I promptly fell asleep and woke up to find Luton were trailing 2-0, with about fifteen minutes to go. I left the flat full of disappointment and sited up the trailer, then stocked it up ready for the evening and opened. Kirstie arrived punctually at 7 p.m., and we spent an average evening, closing at about midnight. I drove her home, as I always do, (it is a condition of working late that I leave her at her door. I don't want rape and mugging on my conscience!), dropping her off at about 12-15, and went home, ready to collapse into bed. I was awakened by the sound of frantic ringing on the doorbell and groggily looked at the clock. It was 2-15 a.m.

"Who the hell is that at this time of the night? " I said aloud, as I struggled to my feet. I did not get an answer. Thoughts of disaster ran through my mind. Something had happened to Mum or to Dad? The trailer! Did I leave the fryer on? God it's on fire! Or it's been stolen.

I rushed to the door and opened it, very slightly, and peered gingerly through the crack. Kirstie was standing there, with no coat on, crying hysterically and holding her terrified baby in her arms.

"Whatever has happened?" I asked, and then noticed that her sweater was covered in blood. Her face was a mess, with cuts and grazes, and her nose was bleeding. I opened the door wider and let her in. She ran inside. She was obviously terrified herself and the baby was screaming at this point. I took the baby from her and sat Kirstie in an armchair. I took the baby into the bedroom and laid her on the bed between two pillows and covered her with the duvet. I began to stroke her head and whisper to her and she calmed down, a little, to a quiet whimper. I returned to the other room, to find Kirstie pacing up and down in a confused state. I was at a loss as to what to do, but put my arms around her and she went limp, as she relaxed, while I held her. I cannot remember what I said to her, but I remember trying to reassure her and get her to calm down. She regained her composure and sat down, while I knelt down in front of her, telling her that she was safe now. She began laughing softly through the tears, and the irregular sucking in of breath, as she continued to sob. Her gentle laughter seemed a little out of character with the situation; until it slowly dawned on me that I was totally naked! In my panic to get to the door quickly, I had not dressed, intending to assess the situation, with the door slightly ajar, then close it, dress and then deal with the problem if need be. The shock of seeing Kirstie in that state had driven my 'lack of apparel' status completely out of my mind.

I quickly pulled on a tracksuit and returned to her. Mike had certainly excelled himself this time. She had taken quite a beating by the look of her. She said that he had accused her of sleeping with me instead of being at work and, when she showed him her wages, he went ballistic and said, "And he's paying you for it. That makes you a whore!" Then he started to hit her. My first instinct was to go round there and punch his lights out, but when I said so, it merely exacerbated (Wow! Good one!) the situation. Kirstie became hysterical again and begged me not to go. I bathed her face and cleaned up the cuts, which thankfully were only superficial, then helped her to pinch her nose to stop it bleeding. It seemed that it was the nosebleed, which had been responsible for drenching the sweater with blood.

I fetched her one of my jumpers, so she could change out of the soiled one she was wearing, expecting her to leave the room to change, but she merely whisked her sweater over her head and dropped it on the floor, revealing the fact that she was not wearing a bra! At this point, I would like to be able to report that I averted my gaze in deference to her semi-nakedness, but I confess that I cannot, since I stood transfixed, staring at her breasts for what seemed like an eternity, while she aligned the jumper, then slipped it on. In noticing my stare, she smiled and said, "Haven't you ever seen a pair of breasts before?"

I could feel my face colouring up in shame and embarrassment.

"Yes…er…Oh Christ! I'm so sorry Kirstie… I was a bit shocked… I erm… I didn't mean to…"

She had had her moment of amusement.

"It's all right…I'm only teasing you! There's no need to be embarrassed. I wasn't! Thanks for helping me; I don't know what I would have done without you. I didn't know where to turn."

"Shhhh! It's OK. You're safe here."

"I know. I couldn't take any more. He was so angry… and for no reason."

"So what are you going to do now?"

"I daren't go back, I thought he was going to kill me."

"I'm going to call the Police." I said.

"No!" She shouted, then realising she had startled me, apologised. "Sorry…no don't…please. It won't help."

"I feel so useless. I haven't got a clue where you should go for help. Maybe your doctor?"

"You're not useless. You're lovely. You're so dependant!"

I hoped that she meant dependable, but I was not about to correct her!

I made us both some coffee, and we sat talking about what had happened to her since the birth of the baby, and I could not understand how she could have endured the abuse that had been levelled at her. It made me so angry that he could be so callous towards someone he professes to love. The baby had fallen asleep by the time we had finished talking, some time after 4 a.m. I showed her into the bedroom and left her to sleep and curled up on the sofa. My eyes could not have been shut for more than a minute, when the doorbell was ringing again, constantly. I answered it and Mike forced his way past me into the room.

"Where the fuck is she? I'll break her fucking neck!"

"Hey calm down," I interposed myself between him and the bedroom door. "I think you should go home."

"I'm going nowhere without my wife and kid! Now where is she?"

"She is lying down with the baby."

"Oh yeah? Very cosy! I suppose you were lying down with her!"

"I won't even dignify that with an answer, you foul minded moron."

"Do you want some then? Come on!" He invited me to fight him.

"Mike, you do **not** want to do that. You are not big enough to frighten me…and **I'm** not wearing a dress!"

He came at me, fists flying, but I sidestepped him and, as his fist whistled, futilely, past my cheek and he lost his balance, I lashed out and my fist made a satisfying crunching noise, as it hit him squarely on the nose. Kirstie came out of the bedroom and screamed out, "Stop it, you two!" I sat down and Mike stayed on the floor, where he had fallen, looking very sorry for himself. He looked at Kirstie and began to whimper.

"I'm sorry, my sweetheart!" He said.

"Well, sorry doesn't really cut it, does it?" I intervened.

"Ben…please…don't…" Kirstie pleaded. "Come on Mike, let's go home."

"You don't have to do this, you know." I told her.

I could not believe that she actually wanted to go with him.

She went to the bedroom to pick up the baby. I walked up to Mike and stood face to face with him and said, "… and YOU…! You **ever** lay a hand on her again, and I'll rip your fucking head off!"

They left, with his apologising to her and promising that it would never happen again. As Mike went ahead of her, she looked back and mouthed the words, "Thank you," silently, then kissed her finger and pointed it towards me before, finally, following him out on to the walkway.

I will never understand women if I live to be a hundred!

Things to be grateful for

1) Mum and Dad are OK.
2) I didn't set fire to the trailer.
3) The trailer was not stolen.
4) Mike got the punch on the nose that he had coming to him for a long time!

Tuesday 12th September 2000

Word of the Day: Elaborate… go into detail to explain

5 p.m. in flat, preparing for night's trade

Kirstie was in a rather buoyant mood today, despite the weekend's wrangling. I asked her how things were at home, but she merely shrugged and said a less-than-convincing, "OK", and did not seem to want to elaborate. (hurrah!)

Robbie and Jenni, together with the usual mob, came for food today. I was performing rather well, with my customary attempts at wit and humour and, when Robbie's order included a Jumbo Sausage in a roll, I could not resist the temptation.

"I modelled for these, you know! Be impressed!"

Robbie said, "See Jenni, see what you are missing?"

Jenni had seemed to be very bashful, prior to this turn in the conversation, and not at all as gregarious as usual. At Robbie's remark, she gave a sheepish grin and looked directly at me, inquiringly. I wondered whether she had indeed been genuine in her invitation, so I decided to 'bite the bullet' and ask her. I indicated to her, to go to the door and leaned out to speak to her.

"I read your note, but I didn't know if it was one of Robbie's jokes, or if you meant it."

"It was nothing to do with him, I meant it. I thought you weren't interested. I felt such a fool when you didn't ring." She whispered.

"I'm sorry, really sorry. But you know what Robbie's like. It's just the sort of set up he would engineer. Just to have a laugh at my expense. Is the offer still open?"

"Of course it is… but only as long as it ain't a mercy date!"

I laughed. I had heard American men talking about sleeping with women that they (allegedly!) didn't find attractive, then excusing themselves, by pretending that they were doing the woman a favour. They tell their buddies, "It was just a mercy fuck!" I knew from this what she meant, but I hadn't heard the watered down version before.

Robbie began shouting at the front hatch.

"Hey you two, I hope you ain't doing anything unhygienic back there!" much to the amusement of the others.

"Ring me tonight, " she continued. "We can talk then, without all these ears listenin' in. They're gonna give me so much B.S."

"OK. Will do."

As soon as trade slowed down, Kirstie was onto the case like a dog with a bone.

"I heard that!" She almost sang the words tauntingly.

"Heard what?" I knew she wasn't going to release the bone just yet.

"You…sniffing around that Jenni woman!"

"And your point is?"

"Nothing. I was just making the observation!"

"Thank you for your concern! I'm touched."

"I'm not concerned for you…more for her!"

"Charming! Murder my self esteem, why don't you?"

"I was thinking of what you said about the Jumbo Sausages. She thought you were joking. But I know you weren't, don't I? I could have vouched for you." She was highly amused by her comment and the fact that it made my face colour up again.

Why do I keep blushing lately? Especially as I was secretly flattered by her remark.

"I was very impressed." She continued. "I wish Mike was built like that!"

"So was I… impressed with what I saw, I mean." I retaliated.

"You shouldn't have been looking," she responded. "I thought you were a gentleman."

"And I thought you were a lady. So it was just tit for tat." I said innocently, and as the pun hit home we both collapsed into laughter.

Quite honestly, though, I am pleased we can deal with it humorously like this. I was worried that it might have spoiled our working relationship.

"So…are you going to go out with her, then?"

"I don't know yet. I may do…depends."

"On what?"

"If I have a vacant date in my busy calendar."

She responded by putting on a high-pitched, mock upper class voice.

"Pardon me, your Lordship, shall I consult your diary to see if we have a window to allocate to her?"

"No thanks. I'll survive!"

11-30 p.m. on sofa, watching Drop the Dead Donkey

I rang Jenni during work tonight, and she asked if I would like to have dinner at her place, tomorrow evening. I said that I would love to, provided Kirstie would work to give me the time off. Also, it will relieve me of the pressure of knowing when to leave, as it is predetermined by the fact that I have to close up and let Kirstie go home.

Things to be grateful for

1) It appears that Jenni was serious in her invitation.

2) Kirstie and I can laugh about having seen each other's naughty bits.

3) Kirstie seems to be OK. (I hope she really is.)

Thursday 14th September 2000

Word of the Day: Tentative… hesitant, not definite

3 p.m. in flat…where else do I get to go?

I am worried about Kirstie again. She did not show up for work today, after working last night to allow me to visit Jenni. I am surprised she hasn't left me a message of explanation. Yesterday, I parked the trailer in the village lay-by at 2-30 p.m. after the air base session and wheel clamped it, to avoid it going walkabout by itself. Kirstie went home for a shower and returned promptly at 5-30 p.m. I helped her get started and then left at 6, to take a shower and get ready, then headed for Jenni's. I arrived at the base housing on time at 7, and she met me with a smile and a glass of wine. I sipped at this, while standing with her in her kitchen, as she put the finishing touches to the meal. She had prepared a steak chasseur style casserole, with jacket potatoes, and I was very impressed when it tasted every bit as good as it had smelled when I arrived. I teased her a little, by saying that I didn't want to put her to any trouble, but I was vegetarian, as she announced what we would be eating, and she was temporarily horrified.

"I thought, with you selling chicken, that you couldn't be vegetarian…" Then she noticed my wry smile and realised my mischief.

I have to say, that I enjoyed her company and the meal and, although not of a highly intellectual nature, the conversation flowed nicely and was quite natural. Her sense of humour was also very pleasant. The appalling grammar of her note did cross my mind as we talked, and it appears that she just writes letters, as she speaks, without recourse to grammatical correctness. Americans are not noted for their grammatically correct speech, after all, and she is from the South, where I imagine 'grammar' is someone who is married to 'grandpa'! The conversation did, however, reveal that this potential relationship was about to go the way of all my relationships, to date, (nowhere), as she is being posted back to Texas in about two weeks. I assisted with the washing up…

Millennium man or what?

…and noticed that she was flexing her neck and shoulders as she dried the dishes.

"You need a shoulder rub, the way you are flexing those muscles!"

How many times have I used that line?

"I sure do…they're really tense…are you volunteering?"

Still works though!!

"Certainly am. I am an honorary citizen of Tennessee, you know…. The Volunteer State!"

"Are you really?"

"No!"

One thing led to another and, before I knew it, she was lying on her bed, face down, in just a flimsy top and matching panties, and I was massaging her back and shoulders. Unlike the other evening, when Kirstie was in my flat, however, Jenni had disrobed modestly in her bedroom and placed herself discreetly, face down, before calling me into her bedroom. As my hands encroached under the silky top, it was immediately a very sensuous experience for me, and from the nature of her sighs and gentle moans, it was for her too. My hands were gently caressing her beautiful, soft, coffee-coloured skin, and I asked if she had any oil. She produced a small bottle of Ylang Ylang massage oil…

How the hell do you pronounce that?

…from an aromatherapy company. It had never been opened.

"Perhaps you should take off your top," I suggested, helpfully, "to stop oil getting on it."

Oh, you smooth seducer of women!

She looked coyly over her shoulder and smiled. She indicated with her hand for me to turn away, and then quickly removed it. I returned to my ministrations and began gently rubbing the oil into her back. This was now moving from the realms of sensuality, to the erotic for me, especially when she gave a contented sigh. I slipped my hand under her shoulder and gently turned her over. She did not resist, so I leaned over her and kissed her softly on her lips. She began to unbutton my shirt and stroked my bare chest with the palms of both hands. I slipped the shirt off and continued to kiss her. My hand still bore a coating of the oil and, as it found the softness of her breasts, she gave a gasp of pleasure. I continued to gently squeeze and stroke her breasts, then moved slowly southwards like a gentle zephyr and, while still prolonging the sweet kiss, my fingers found the waistband of her panties and slid slowly down inside them, encouraging a sharp intake of breath, as she was startled by the sensitivity of her own skin. My fingers reached down, until they encountered some very interesting places! As she responded to my touch, I increased the pressure and rhythm, and she began to make the most delightful sounds of contentment, and climaxed at my very fingertips. As her breathing began to slow down again, her hand gently brushed against my lap, and she smiled shyly, as she felt my reaction to the moment. I opened the button on my jeans and her hand wandered slowly and seductively inside. There was no turning back. It was time, once again, to cut to pictures of a rocket launch at Cape Canaveral!

Time seemed to fly by, and when I next looked at the clock, I was shocked to see it was 10-30 p.m. I had to let Kirstie get home and put away the trailer, but when I voiced this intention, Jenni pouted like a little girl, and said in a pleading tone, "You're not going to leave me now? I was kind of hoping you might want to stay all night."

I was torn between taking her up on that, and going back to the trailer, but weighing the two options was a very short exercise. I asked to use her phone and called the mobile on the trailer.

"Hi, Kirstie. I'm sort of tied up at the moment. Could you be an angel and take your wages out of the cash box, then lock up and pop the keys through my letter box for me? I'd really appreciate it."

"I'm sure you would," she began. I knew I was going to get some ribbing for this. "Hmmm! Tied up are we? Hope the handcuffs aren't too tight!"

"Stop that! You know what I meant!"

"Do I? We'll see about that tomorrow. I might have to tell that Robbie what you two have been up to!"

"Don't even think about it!" I laughed. "You don't mind do you?"

"Of course I don't mind. Have a nice time. I will want to hear all the juicy details tomorrow!"

"You will **NOT!**" She was still laughing as I put down the phone.

I stayed with Jenni all night and enjoyed the remaining playful time immensely, before we fell asleep in the early hours.

This morning, as we were drinking coffee, she said that she hoped we could spend a little more time together before she left, and then mentioned that it was her birthday, on Sunday. Her friends were throwing a combined birthday cum leaving party for her, and she invited me to go with her.

"Ha! Ha!" I began. "Are you twenty-one?"

"Not yet, thank you!" she replied.

I had thought I was joking when I said it but, after a few moments, the penny dropped that she may have been serious, and that she really is not yet twenty-one.

"Which birthday is it then?" I asked tentatively (Hurrah!).

"Technically, I'm still a teenager till Sunday!"

How I managed to keep the gulp of coffee in my mouth and prevent myself from spraying it all over her in shock, I do not know!

OH MY GOD! I have just seduced a teenager! I am old enough to be her father! (OK! Only just!) Now I know why I felt like a teenager last night.

She detected the horror in my eyes, instantly.

"What's the matter?"

"Are you really only nineteen?"

"Only till Sunday. Why? What's wrong with that?

"I… er… thought you were …older. That's all. I er… I mean…"

"You mean… you thought I was older. I got it the first time!" she laughed. "Well? So what? What's wrong with that? I'm legal! You won't be arrested!"

"I know but…"

"But nothing! You must have known I've had a crush on you since I first saw you?"

"No. Why didn't you say something?"

"You know why. Robbie would have given me hell, especially if you blew me off."

"Whoa. Steady. That sounds like something I wouldn't want to do in front of Robbie!"

"Anyhow… How old are you?" She ignored my attempt to divert the conversation by the use of humour.

"Thirty-four."

"That's not so old. Back home, there are sixteen-year-olds hooking up with fifty-year-olds!"

"OK. OK! I was just surprised, that's all!"

When I left this morning and picked up the trailer, I noticed that it had a large dent in the front panel.

If I find out who did that, they're dead!

I towed it to the base, but when Kirstie failed to show, I feared the worst. I opened up and was inundated with customers baying and howling for food. I struggled on manfully, but I simply could not cope on my own. Tomorrow, thank God, is a down day, so I don't have to work on base. I hope Kirstie will be OK by Monday. I rang the house, but got no reply, so I still don't know if she is all right. I am so stressed out and tired that I have decided not to work tonight, so I have put the trailer away.

6 p.m.

I have just had an irate call from Kirstie's husband.

"Is that you, Ben?"

"Yes, Who's that?"

"Mike…where's Kirstie?"

"How the Hell should I know…She didn't show up for work today, I know that much. I was flat out on my own all day."

"She's not here."

"Well she's certainly not **here**!"

"You expect me to believe that?"

"Believe what you like, but she's not."

"You fucking home wrecker! I know you were fucking her last night."

"No...you don't! As it happens, I was fucking someone else last night."

"I saw her coming out of your flat last night. All the lights were off and you hadn't even put your poxy trailer away. Couldn't wait, could you? You're busted...both of you. **Now** tell me you weren't sleeping together."

"We weren't. We haven't and we don't. How plainly do you want me to say it? I wasn't even home last night. You're off your head. Listen...have you been hitting her again? I warned you what will happen if you do."

"Fuck off!" He slammed down the receiver.

I'll bet a penny to a pound he has been beating her up again, and she has run off... and I'll bet it was him who damaged the trailer. I think it is time my fist had another word or two with his nose!

Things to be grateful for

1) A very pleasant evening at Jenni's
2) Waking up this morning in a strange bed with a beautiful woman.

Things to be pissed off about

1) Kirstie's been hit again
2) It looks as though I have lost a good helper
3) My trailer is damaged
4) I've lost a night's trade
5) Shall I go on?

Saturday 16th September 2000

Word of the Day: Obnoxious... offensive, objectionable, disliked

4 p.m. preparing for Saturday night

Stella rang this morning, to tell me she is coming to visit on Monday, on her way through to Sheringham. All her goods and chattels have been sent to her uncle's hotel and are safely stored in his cellar. She begins her new job in a week's time, so she may be staying a few days. If she does, I may have to put her to work!

4 p.m. (telephone rings)

"Ben?"
"Yes?" It was Kirstie.
"It's me… I'm sorry I let you down but I had no choice."
"Don't worry…What's happened?"
"I've left him. I'm at Mum's… he did it again. When you were with that American woman. I can't take any more!"
"I'll kill him!"
"No, Ben. Please don't…it's not fair…it isn't your problem, you might get hurt."
"I'll make it my problem…I warned him."
"That'd just make things worse! He's convinced we are having an affair. He came out at about eleven and found the trailer locked up and closed. Then he saw me coming away from your flat, after I put your keys in, put two and two together and came up with five."
"I've already told him I wasn't even in."
"You've spoken to him?"
"Yes. I rang to see where you were and got no reply, and then he rang me back to ask **me** where you were. He was an arse and we ended

up having a row…. Anyway I'm glad you're safe. I guess you didn't leave him a goodbye note, then?"

"No, I just took the baby and ran, as soon as he had left for work. I didn't even stop to pack my clothes."

"That was daft. You'll have to go back and get them now."

"I don't care. I just wanted out!"

"Where is your mum and dad's place?"

"Nottingham. I expect he's worked it out by now. I'm not going back unless he sees a psychiatrist."

"You'd be mad to go back at all."

I'll bet you do, though!

"But I was really happy with him. You know, before the baby came."

"That's probably the problem. He can't handle sharing you with the baby….

God I'm a chat-show psychologist now!

…in any case, it's too dangerous an environment for you and the baby. And you deserve better…" There was a silent pause as my words sank in.

"…So what **are** you going to do?" I broke the silence.

"I'm not sure yet. Dad says I can stay as long as I want. Permanently, if I need to…The house is certainly big enough."

"That's a relief. Anyway, I am glad you're safe…keep smiling sweetie…and stay in touch!"

"I will…and thanks for everything. 'Bye."

"'Bye."

It is a relief to know she is away from that obnoxious (hurrah!) toe rag! I hope she leaves him for good. He doesn't deserve her. It leaves me in the lurch a bit, though. Even if she comes back to him, I doubt she'll ever be able to work for me again. He'd never wear it. I'll have to advertise, maybe on base. Perhaps an Air Force wife might like to earn a little pin money.

Things to be grateful for

1) Kirstie is safe.
2) I have a party to go to tomorrow.
3) Maybe I can look forward to a few après-party antics.

Monday 18th September 2000

Word of the Day: Consequence... result or effect of an action

9 a.m. Just arrived home with a headache.

I love Mondays! No work today and nothing to rush about for. I do have to clean up a bit, though, as Stella is arriving later.

Last night was interesting, if a little strange. I escorted Jenni to her party, and I was the only non-American male there. There were a couple of Jenni's English female friends there, and neither they, nor I, was allowed to purchase alcohol, due to VAT regs or something. There was no shortage of my customers there, who were queuing up to buy me drinks all evening. The consequence, (hurrah!), of that was that I was totally wrecked, by the time we left the club, and unable to drive home. Jenni was quick to offer me half of her bed, which I gratefully accepted. We drank copious quantities of black coffee and eventually the room stopped spinning.

Well, at least it slowed to a manageable few revolutions per minute!

We became a little amorous, and, by the time we went to sleep, it was almost time to get up! My head is now pounding, and I imagine poor Jenni is having the same problem at work right now. She wants to get together again before she leaves next weekend so, selfish bastard that I am, I hope Stella doesn't stay too long and put a spanner in the works.

I wonder what Louise is doing this weekend. She said she was "busy", but didn't say why. That's unlike her. No doubt she will tell me, when we talk. As it turned out, I was pretty busy myself, one way and another. (and another and another!)

Things to be grateful for

1) My head has reduced its rage to a dull throb, thanks to the Excedrin caplets that Jenni gave me to bring home.
2) One hell of a night out.
3) One hell of an overnight afterwards.

Tuesday 19th September 2000

Word of the Day: Obnoxious... offensive, objectionable, disliked

9 p.m. on trailer.

It has finally gone quiet. Stella arrived yesterday at 1 p.m. and almost dislocated my shoulder in her urgency to drag me into the bedroom. The sound of the door shutting behind her was still echoing in the hallway as my arse hit the bed! We re-emerged briefly, at about six, for some food and drink, after which, I promptly fell asleep on the sofa, to be rudely awakened by Stella biting my manhood, which was battle-weary enough as it was!

"Ow! What did you do that for?" I whined, covering my assets protectively with my hands.

"Poor baby! Does you want Stella to kiss it better, den?" she mocked, in a baby talk voice.

"No thanks, I'll manage."

"What? To kiss it better yourself? That'd be a good trick. I'd pay to see that! Mind you don't break your neck, though."

"If we men could suck our own cocks we wouldn't need women at all!" I teased, being deliberately provocative. I knew that I was taking my life into my own hands, but I was not ready for the speed of the aggressive charge she made at me. Too quickly for me to defend myself, she flattened me to the floor and sat astride me, pinning my arms above my head.

"Now I've got you where I want you." she said. "What are you going to do now?"

I jerked my hips upwards, causing her to rise into the air like a bronco rider. However, big mistake! It did not cause her to unbalance and fall off, as intended, and she came crashing back down onto me, her (rather attractive) bottom slapping forcefully into my lower abdomen, driving the wind out of me.

"I don't think so, do you?" she murmured smugly, but also curiously seductively.

She reached back behind her and began stroking the top of the insides of my thighs, and my adjacent apparatus. When she had succeeded in encouraging the required response, she gripped my appendage with her hand, and then slid herself backwards, until she had achieved the requisite alignment, then bore down, impaling herself on it, giving a gasp as she did so.

"Now you can play bucking broncos as much as you like! In fact, I insist!" she barked, and pinched my nipples, causing a sharp pain. "Or there will be consequences!"

I admit to having been pleasantly, if a little surprisedly, aroused by this display of dominance from her. However, I was tiring rapidly and, fortunately, so was she. We slept, but I don't know what time it was that we succumbed. I do know that I did not want to wake up this morning.

During the interval when we had eaten dinner, we talked about what had been happening in the Kirstie household, causing me to be struggling to cope with the demand on base. Stella insisted upon helping me out and said she would work with me until I found someone, or until Friday at the latest, as she had to get to Sheringham to start work. I offered to pay her the going rate and she accepted readily.

In all fairness, she was a great help on base today, but what a flirt she is! She has already got half the US military drooling over her. She was exhibiting stereotypical 'tarty barmaid' behaviour, though, and was quite coarse at times. She even made **me** wince at a few of her remarks. Not lady-like at all. It crossed my mind at this point…

As if I didn't already know!

…that she is not the sort of girl to take home to meet your mother. GOD! **MY** Mother would freak out. The sex is brilliant with Stella, but I have had enough sex, this last week, to last me a month. When I popped into the Chemist, for another pack of twelve appropriate gentlemen's requisites, the pharmacist asked me if I had been buying them for the entire local football team, for the last few weeks! Regrettably though, if you take away the sex, I think Stella just gets on my nerves.

I put up notices today, on the trailer and also in the Post Office on base, advertising the vacancy. Let's hope there is a response.

Stella has gone to the Red Lion tonight, for a drink and, no doubt, to flaunt herself at the local blokes. She brought me a pint to the trailer earlier and said she was having a great laugh. I hope she wears herself out and needs some sleep! Damn! I forgot the word of the day!

Things to be grateful for

1) Too much sex (This time last year I would have killed to be able to say that!)
2) Stella helping me out on base.
3) The pharmacist thinks I am a superstud, which of course I am. (But not tonight, pleeease!)

Friday 22nd September 2000

Word of the Day: Implication… act of implying or suggesting

12-10 a.m. Just in from working

That was the first Friday I have worked alone, in a long time. I'd forgotten how stressful they are when the pub turns out. I had to use my "display-signs-of-being-wound-up-before-you-are" strategy, to avoid allowing myself to really get wound up, as several guys, in various degrees of inebriation, seemed to think it was Ben Arnold piss-taking open season. One in particular, who seemed to be in practice for the "Village Idiot of the Year" competition, was particularly disagreeable.

"You should be grateful to me," I told him. "I saved you from getting into a hell of a mess."

"Oh Yeah? How did you manage that then?" He slurred with a smirk on his face.

"By controlling myself and not smacking your kebab in your face!"

His friends completed his humiliation with laughter and much more piss taking.

Stella left yesterday and starts work at her uncle's place on Saturday. When I got home on Tuesday night, she was lying on the bed, naked and spread-eagled, as though she had been frozen in the middle of a horizontal star jump!

"OK Big boy!" She began. "Tonight, YOU are in charge! Take me any way you want me! I'm all yours. Do with me whatever you will!"

I was tempted to tie her hands to the headboard, tape up her mouth and leave her there, while I went for a sleep on the sofa! If I'd had some handcuffs, I just may have done it. However, once I got into the spirit of things and rose to the occasion, I enjoyed being in total control, just as much as I had enjoyed being controlled the night before.

On Wednesday, she worked very hard on base. It was so busy. She was, again, a bit too suggestive with the customers, for my liking, and too free with the implication, (hurrah!), that there were plenty of extra-curricular perks to the job. Two women applied for the vacant post of assistant, (not for the aforementioned reason I hasten to add). One was fairly young and quite attractive in an obvious, Barbie-doll sort of way. She would certainly be "eye candy" for the customers, as the Americans say. She is the girlfriend of a young US Army guy. The other applicant was an older woman, rather plain looking by comparison, but with a bubbly personality. She is married to a Naval officer. Stella was quick to voice her opinion that the older woman was the obvious choice and that the younger one was clearly unsuitable. I have never needed to interview before, and I found it impossible to choose between them, and I would not have a clue how to tell one of them that she had been rejected. I overcame this problem by offering them both the opportunity of sharing the available hours. If they agreed, then, if either was unavailable at a certain time, the other would probably be available, and vice versa. If they did not agree with the shared hours idea, one of them would probably withdraw, relieving me of the burden of rejecting her!

Clever or what?

'Or what,' as it turned out, when I announced my decision to Stella. She was singularly unimpressed! So unimpressed, that she went into the bathroom, ran a bath, and stayed in there for ages. When she came out and got into bed, she merely said, "Goodnight," and turned away from me. There is a first! How relieved was I, though? I don't think I could have performed, if called upon!

I asked the elder one, Stacey, to work on Thursday, and she was fine. It took her a little while to get into my working pattern, but once she did, we worked well together. Today Ashley, the younger, worked, and took to the job like a duck to water. The guys gave Ashley and me some stick, in the wake of Stella's comments earlier in the week.

"Hey Ben. You old son of a gun! Is it true that all your assistants have to sleep with the boss? That's what Stella said!" I thought this guy was going to choke himself on his laughter.

"Yes it's true. Why? Are you looking for work?"

It got a laugh, but did I really say that? To a bloke?

Ashley was looking concerned.

"It's OK Ashley, don't look so scared. He's only joking." I reassured, and then hit her with the punch line. "It's optional, not compulsory."

More appreciative laughter ensued, I was labelled a 'dog,' and several of the waiting throng began to howl like dogs to great mutual amusement. Ashley had turned red and looked somewhat abashed. I thought, perhaps, I had overstepped the mark on her first day and apologised to her later. She said she understood that it was just banter and was OK about it.

"Hey, you guys, you'd better not give Stacey this kind of shit. Her old man's a Lieutenant Commander, and he'll bust your arse if you get out of order." I warned them. Much bravado was shown but we'll see how brave they are when she's working!

Things to be grateful for

1) Both new workers seem to be suitable.
2) I've had a couple of sexless nights to recuperate.
3) I am feeling fit and vibrant again.

Sunday 24th September 2000

Word of the Day: Emphatically... forcibly, significantly

9 p.m. in flat

Louise rang on Saturday, to cancel our plans to meet today. Her sister, Emily, had decided to visit and made arrangements to go out with her parents and Louise for the day. Yet another opportunity slips away.

I went to Mum and Dad's instead. Mother seems to have launched a "marry Ben off" campaign.

"What's wrong with that Louise, Ben? She seemed like a really sweet girl. She obviously thinks the world of you. What's up with you?"

"Mother. We hardly know each other. I like her a lot, but we are just friends at the moment." She did not look convinced. "Anyway, there's no point in trying to find me a wife. I'm gay!"

"YOU... ARE... NOT!" She spouted the words emphatically, (hurrah!), and individually. "Don't even joke about it."

"Have you got something against gay people, then?"

"Stop it! Whatever would people think? You're not gay... are you?"

"No! But it would be all the same if I were. You don't know all the circumstances of my personal life, so you shouldn't interfere… and why do you worry about what other people think, anyway? Would it be so bad if I were?"

I was really enjoying seeing the confused look on her face. Dad was reading his newspaper very intensely, but I could feel his amusement, without seeing his face.

"Anyway, what is the point of buying a book when you can join a library!"

"That's enough of that filthy talk. It doesn't become you!"

Maybe not! But it sure as hell stopped you talking about marriage! 1-0!

Things to be grateful for

1) I managed an unexpected visit to my parents.
2) I scuppered Mother's plans to interfere in my love life!

Monday 25th September 2000

Word of the Day: Ostracise… exclude from society or from common privileges

7-30 a. bloody m.
('phone rings, Ben wakes up !)

"Hello Mother!"
"How did you know it was me?"
"It's always you at this time of the morning, Mother."
"It's the only time I can bloody catch you in!"
"I saw you yesterday. I've only been home 12 hours!"
"Don't be facetious, Benjamin. It's **about** yesterday."
I knew it would get to her!

"Oh yes? What about yesterday?"

"What you said…you're not…are you?"

"Not what, Mother?"

"Don't mess about, you know what!"

"Do I? I'm still half asleep. What are you getting at?" She was squirming and I was enjoying every minute of it.

"You know…like, um… boys instead of girls." She blurted out the final phrase in a rush, as if she thought that speed of speech would prevent the words from sullying her mouth.

"You can say "gay", Mother. It's not a swear word."

"It is round here, they hate them. They beat them up." She was totally unaware of the comedy in her words and delivered them in all seriousness.

"Anyway, who says I like either better than the other? I might be bisexual for all you know. Am I to be ostracised (hurrah!) if I dare not to conform to family stereotypes?"

"Well…are you or not?" She ignored my provocative monologue.

"Hang on, I'll ask my friend…" I called out to the imaginary friend, "…Rodney? Would you say I was gay?"

I held the 'phone at arms length, put on an effeminate voice and answered myself. " Put the phone down and come back to bed, Ben."

I heard Mother try to muffle the sound of her voice, by putting her hand over the mouthpiece, but I could still hear her talking to Dad.

"Oh my God, George, I think he really is… you know … the other way. I think he's got a man there now."

I couldn't stop laughing, and she heard me try to stifle it.

"Are you playing about?"

"It serves you right, Mother. Fancy ringing someone up at half past seven in the morning to discuss their sexual preferences. My inclination on that subject should be a personal matter, but seeing that it's of such major importance to you, to wake me up in the middle of the night about!!… I am not gay, I do like girls. I sleep with dozens of women every week!"

"Well, that's a relief!" Then the penny dropped. "I mean that you like girls, not sleep with lots of them. Oh you KNOW what I mean."

Normally, she would have given me a roasting over the promiscuity comment, but she was so relieved that I was not about to bring the family into disrepute, nor bring the Arnold family lineage to a screeching halt by daring to be different, that she forgot. No doubt she will remember to do it at a later date!

Things to be Grateful for

1) I think I may just have permanently cured Mother of meddling with my private life! (Or perhaps not!)
2) She saved me from taking too much sleep on my day off!

Tuesday 26th September 2000

Word of the Day: Objurgate... chide or scold, verbally admonish

3 p.m. in agony on the bed

I am completely seized up. I have got pains where I didn't even know I had places! Jenni invited me to go to the gym with her, on my day off yesterday. One of her English friends, Angela, was there too. She was drop-dead gorgeous; absolutely stunning. The instructor worked out a few basic circuits for me, since I hadn't been in a gym for over 6 months, and I began to work each machine as instructed. An American guy came in, who looked like a professional, with all the gear with designer labels, including some expensive-looking weight lifting gloves. He was quite well defined, muscularly, and really looked the part. He ignored all the modern machinery and went straight to the free weights. I watched him put 240 kilograms on the bar, which was supported on a cradle.

"Very impressive," I thought to myself, "but I'd love to see him press that weight!"

He lifted the bar off the cradle and pressed it out to arms length, then began to lower it, whereupon his elbows collapsed under the strain, and the bar came down onto his chest, pinning him to the bench and removing the smug look from his face in an instant. I rushed over to try to help, but could only take part of the weight, at least assisting him to breath until the instructor came to his aid. After he had struggled free, the instructor objurgated (hurrah bigtime!) him. (I bet the instructor was unaware that what he was doing was objurgating, though!).

"What the fuck did you think you were doing? You could have killed yourself, you dickhead!"

"I can press 240 pounds easily," he said. "I don't know what went wrong."

The instructor looked at the weights. "So why are you trying to press 240 Kilos, then?"

The American guy looked bewildered. "Kilos? Say what?"

I fell about laughing! Most people in the States wouldn't know a Kilo from a cauliflower.

After the workout, which did not seem too physically strenuous…

Although seeing Jenni's lovely skin glistening with sweat did raise my blood pressure somewhat!

…I went for a shower. A young man, in his early twenties, I would say, came in, having just had a swim. He looked emaciated. He was so thin his chest was concave. He was also very strange in appearance. His facial features did not appear to match, as though a committee, working independently of each other, had designed him. I've said it before, anyone is entitled to be unattractive, but this guy was abusing the privilege! Matters went from bad to worse, when he opened his mouth to speak and sounded like he was auditioning for an English version of Forrest Gump.

"One of life's losers." I thought. "Only a mother could love a face and body like that!" When he took off his swimming costume, I felt my jaw hit my chest. I have never seen anything like it! He was hung like a horse. I have always been satisfied with my own endowment and, indeed, have even received compliments on its dimensions, but this guy made me feel inadequate. I went to the bar to meet Jenni and

Angela, the latter of whom was now sporting a very prominent engagement ring. I was just about to relate the story of "Forrest Gump" in the changing room, when he appeared, dressed in a tracksuit, and approached us at the bar.

"Hi baby," He said to Angela and kissed her very inviting lips. "Are you ready to go?"

"In a minute, I'll just finish this drink." His arm was now protectively encircling her shoulders, as if defending his territory. "Oh, Gary, you don't know Ben, do you?"

"We met briefly in the changing room." He announced.

"This is my fiancé, Gary," She told me. "Gary, this is Jenni's new friend, Ben."

Beam me up Scotty! Just try to tell me that size isn't important!

Jenni and I spent the evening locked in lustful embrace, but the whole episode was tinged with sadness, as she is leaving tomorrow. Her empty apartment echoed when we spoke, as all her belongings, apart from hand luggage, were shipped over the weekend. I left before midnight and was not looking forward to parting. I hate goodbyes; they always make me feel awkward. I was very touched when the time came to leave. Her eyes filled with tears, which seemed to be making a supreme effort not to fall, but finally gave in and spilled tenderly onto her cheeks. I didn't realise that she cared so much. I had treated our short time together as fun, and living for the moment, not allowing myself to become too attached. I guess it's a man/woman thing. We agreed to contact each other by e-mail when she gets back and, maybe, meet to talk online.

Things to be grateful for

1) Oh the warmth and tenderness of women!
2) The brief time I spent with Jenni was sweet yet invigorating.

Saturday 30th September 2000

Word of the Day: Encounter... meet as an adversary, a meeting in conflict

10 a.m. in flat

I spoke to Louise this morning. She asked if I could go to visit today, but Stella is coming to stay overnight, so I told Louise that I had some things to do, but would go down in the afternoon. I feel guilty about lying to her, even if only by bending the truth, but I really don't want to upset her. She was very understanding, as I had hoped she would be, and suggested that I stay here this weekend, and we could meet next weekend instead. Phew!

9 p.m. on trailer.

Business has been brisk again this evening, proving that I was right and Stella was wrong. She arrived at a little after 1 p.m. and, as seems to be par for the course lately, could not wait to get me into bed. At first, I was quite turned on by her urgency, but I'm getting a little bored with it now. A few minutes of "Hello, and how are you doing?" would not go amiss! She was also very angry when I got out of bed at 4-30 p.m. to shower and get prepared for work.

"Do you have to work?" she barked. "It's not as though we get to be together very often."

Often enough, the way things are going!

"I have to work. You know… that stuff we all hate doing, but which brings us the means to live?"

"Don't be fucking clever!" She continued, making me wince at her coarseness." I work too you know!"

"Yes you do…but you don't hear me telling you not to work, so that I can see you, do you?"

"That's different, you work for yourself. You can have as much time off as you want."

"Yes, if I don't want to eat or have a roof over my head."

"You probably wouldn't even do much business tonight."

"How can you possibly know that? It is Saturday night. People go out!"

"Exactly! We are people…people go out!"

I walked away in frustration at her attitude, and she shrieked after me, "Fuck you, then. I'll go to the pub on my own! AGAIN!"

WHATEVER! *No doubt you'll make an exhibition of yourself!*

I really do not need that sort of stress. She is begging to be dumped! She'll be organising my life for me soon. I wonder if she will want to tell my mother that she is redundant, because Mother certainly considers that running, (or attempting to run), my life, is part of her own job description! Now! That would be an interesting encounter. (Hurrah! Only just made it!)

Things to be grateful for

1) Having a mind of my own
2) Doing some good business and proving I was right to work!

OCTOBER 2000

Sunday 1ˢᵗ October 2000

Word of the Day: Bestow... to give as a gift

7 p.m. getting ready for the quiz

Stella was in an extremely odd mood today. I guess it was the hangover from our row last night. Right from the moment she got up this morning, she was odd, to say the least. She went to shower, and then arrived back in the bedroom with the announcement, "I've got bad news for you, if you were expecting a shag. The game's off… the pitch is unplayable!"

"Thank you Stella, for placing that wonderful image in my head!"

"I suppose I could give you a blow-job, though! If you want."

I winced at the graphic language she was using. I know that talking dirty in the throes of passion is supposed to be a turn-on, but somehow this was not the right moment, and it had the opposite effect. In any case, she showed no disappointment when I declined and went to shower instead. When I came back into the bedroom, to dry off, she was sitting on the bed, clipping her toenails. This is another habit, which I find intensely annoying, especially in someone else's bedroom! Why would you do that?

"Do you fancy a cup of tea?" I asked.

"Yes, but I'll get it. You're still soaking wet."

She left the room and, as she reached the kitchen, there was a light knock on the front door.

"I'll get it," she called, "You can't answer the door in your underpants!"

"I haven't got a door in my underpants!" I bestowed (Hurrah!) upon her, the full measure of my wit.

"Oh God! That is such a bad joke!" She laughed, in spite of her comment.

However, her grasp of the situation was quite correct. I could not go to the front door half naked. She closed the bedroom door, to protect my modesty, and went to answer the front door.

After a few moments of silence, I heard muffled voices through the closed door and made myself decent as quickly as I could. Obviously, whoever was at the door wanted to speak to me, so I came out of the bedroom, only half dried, in jeans and tea shirt, but with bare feet, just in time to hear the door close with a resounding slam.

"Who was it?"

"I don't know, some religious freaks or something." She said dismissively.

I wasn't sure if it was just me, or whether she was being evasive. Something about her manner seemed suddenly withdrawn.

"Well? Was it or wasn't it? You spoke to them… surely you must have asked what they wanted, before slamming the door in their faces?"

"OK! Yes! They were selling magazines and stuff. Jehovah's Witnesses…all right?" She was showing signs of distinct irritation with me. Very strange, but I didn't push it. I have to say, though, that I felt a measure of relief when she left at around one o'clock. Even saying goodbye was weird. She had been moody all morning; then suddenly, as we were parting, she embraced me warmly and sensuously, kissing me with immense enthusiasm and inserting her tongue halfway down my throat.

Am I missing something? Did I turn over two pages and arrive in a different scene? Was there a time warp I failed to notice? I will still never understand women. They are an alien race to me!

After she had left, I rang Louise, but there was no reply. I suppose that she is out with her parents again. It must be a real drag for her, living with her parents, all day every day, being on tap to be taxi driver and nursemaid all the time. I'll ring her after the quiz.

Things to be grateful for

1) I don't live with my parents.
2) No phone call at dawn from Mother. I switched the phone ringer off!
3) Being unable to fathom women. I enjoy the mystery!
4) It's quiz night!

Monday 2nd October 2000

Word of the Day: Badinage... playful ridicule

10 p.m. Just home from bowling with the lads

We performed well in the quiz yesterday. We won most of the rounds. However, we nearly got ourselves thrown out, at one point, because we couldn't stop laughing. One question was, "What is the collective noun for a group of beavers." I suggested a sniff of beavers, which started everyone off, and then Gordon topped it with a snatch of beavers. We had been asked to keep the noise down, when Jamie said, "what about a pube of beavers?"

This being singularly unfunny, we all gave him another tumbleweed moment, until I broke the silence and said, "Hey! Tumbleweed! That's so not funny that it's hilarious!"

The quizzical look on his face had us all in stitches again, much to the annoyance of the question master.

After the quiz had finished, the conversation turned to women and sex, as it nearly always does.

"So are you still shagging that Stella bird?" Jamie got the discourse off to a delicate start.

"What's it got to do with you, Tumble?" My use of the shortened form of Tumbleweed caused more silly alcohol assisted laughter.

"I bet she fucks like a rattlesnake! He persisted.

"OK, David fucking Attenborough, " Gordon came into the conversation. "Talk us through a rattlesnake fuck, then. How do they do it? You tell Ben, then he can compare and let you know the answer!" Gordon was more amused by his comment than the rest of us, although we did laugh, if only to embarrass Jamie.

"Why do you always have to pick on me?" Jamie whimpered. " I could have had her myself the other night. She was well 'up for it'. Half the pub fancied their chances."

"Watch your mouth, stupid." Brian warned.

"Well, it was true. She was sitting on blokes' laps and touching them up. I don't think she bought a drink all night!"

"Yes, but that is Ben's girlfriend you are talking about, you dickhead." Brian continued to try to prevent a situation developing.

"He must know what she's like… and she's hardly your girlfriend, is she Ben? He's just giving her the benefit of his old pork sword!" Jamie persisted. "She's not a bad looker, Ben, but you have to admit, she's a bit of a slapper."

"He's right about how she was flaunting herself in the pub, though, Ben. She was the same yesterday." Gordon confirmed my suspicions.

I didn't know whether to take offence or accept that they were right. I was not overjoyed at hearing all this, but I had a feeling she might have been like that when I wasn't around.

"She wouldn't have shagged you, anyway, Tumble," I teased him back. "She may be a slapper, but she knows when she's well off! She'd have to wriggle about to feel if your dick was in or not!"

"You don't know how big my dick is."

"No, but Sam does, and she told me, in bed the other day, that your nickname is needledick!"

This caused a renewed bout of mirth and lightened the moment.

"I also heard that you once went to the loo, pulled out a hair by mistake and pissed yourself!" Brian continued the badinage, (hurrah!).

"Fuck off, you lot!" Jamie concluded the discussion with his usual last word! We decided that we would go bowling on Monday night, at Peterborough, and had a great time. It turned out that Jamie has played in a proper competition before and trounced us all.

"That's for last night!" He said, as we each paid him a £5 note in prize money.

Next time, I must get them to play table tennis, so I can play the same trick on Jamie.

I have tried to ring Louise several times today, but got no reply. I hope everything is OK down there in Chichester.

Things to be grateful for

1) Good friends
2) A nice sociable night out.

Wednesday 4<u>th</u> October 2000

Word of the Day: Unthinkable… that which cannot be imagined.

10 p.m. on the trailer

I give up on Luton! They are having a nightmare season. If they don't soon get a grip of themselves, the unthinkable, (hurrah!), will happen, and they will find themselves relegated to division three. They have played ten games in the league now and only won one of them. On paper, they are a far better team than their results suggest, so they had better start proving it, or Ricky Hill will be losing his job!

Business has been slow tonight, so I have tried to ring Louise several times. I am getting paranoid again, as her mobile rings normally, then cuts off, as though she is refusing to accept the call.

Things to be grateful for

1) Good earnings on base today.
2) Ashley is a natural, and the guys all like her.

Friday 6th October 2000

Word of the Day: Exacerbate... make matters worse. Irritate (person).

Midnight back at the flat

I am a bit concerned that I was unable to contact Louise again, yesterday. Her mobile was off all day, and I got no answer from her parents' home either. Last night, I tried to ring her mobile again, it rang and the same thing happened as has been happening all week. I am convinced that she is refusing to take my calls. I don't understand it. What have I done? I got her mother yesterday but even she was terse.

"I'll give her your message, Ben, Goodbye."

What was **THAT** all about. I have an eerie feeling that I must have upset Louise in some way, but if I can't contact her, how can I find out how, or try to make amends?

Stella must have rung my mobile about five times tonight and then, finally, got arsey, because I was too busy to speak to her. How am I supposed to hold a 'phone conversation when I'm trying to cook kebabs? She then blurted out that she was working all weekend, so she won't be coming to see me. I'm a bit annoyed with her. I was going to ring her when I got in, but if I do I'll probably be rude to her, so I'll give it a miss.

I tried again, this evening, to contact Louise, but to no avail. Finally, in desperation, I rang her sister, who is now back in the village, and asked her how Louise was getting on, since I have been struggling to make contact with her. She was very friendly in the conversation, but seemed cagey.

"Hi Emily, it's Ben."

"Hi Ben, how are you?"

"I'm OK but I am worried about Louise. I haven't been able to get hold of her for ages. She seems to be avoiding me. I got your mum once, but she sounded a bit 'offish' as well. Have I upset her in some way?"

"You might say that!"

"I can't for the life of me understand how. Is there really a problem?"

"Seems to be, because she **is** avoiding you."

"Why? What did I do?"

"You really don't know?"

"Of course I don't, or I wouldn't be ringing now to find out!"

"Well… you deserve to know the truth of the matter. Last Sunday? Half naked female? Answering your door?"

"**WHAT?** Who to?"

"To Louise!"

"Louise didn't come on Sunday."

"Oh yes she did! She rang you a few times to let you know she was up for the weekend. She stayed with me, but she did want to see you while she was here. When you didn't answer the phone, she thought you were asleep, or in the shower or something, so she just popped round to surprise you."

"Oh shit!"

"Yes! I told her it wasn't a good idea. Anyway, a young woman in a dressing gown answered the door."

"Well… it could have been anyone. Might have been my sister or a cousin."

"Was it?"

"Well… no. I haven't got a sister, but she didn't know that. She was still jumping to conclusions…. And Louise and I are not exactly in a relationship yet, are we? So there's no need to avoid me."

"Maybe not, but when Louise asked where you were, this woman apparently said, *"He is still in bed and doesn't want to be disturbed."* And when Louise asked if she could leave a message, she said, *"What message would you like to leave?"* Or something like that."

"Well that's not unreasonable?"

"No… but when she said, *"Please ask him to ring me later, it's Louise,"* the woman asked her why. And when Louise said, *"Because we are friends,"* she was warned off in no uncertain terms! *"I don't think so, he doesn't need ex- girlfriends hanging round him, he's with me now! I suggest you fuck off and find your own man!"* I think Louise told me she said… then shut the door in her face. How could you let a stranger answer your door like that?"

"She's not exactly a stranger…"

"Obviously not, if she was half naked!"

"That isn't what I meant. I was in the shower. Come to think of it, she did answer the door, but she told me it was Jehovah's Witnesses. I didn't think any more about it."

"Well, Louise was not exactly pleased about it… and to answer your question…

Yes she is extremely upset!"

"I don't want to upset her, but we have been trying to get a date together for ages, and nothing seems to go right. This other girl, Stella, is someone I met on holiday, and I didn't expect to even see her again. A little while ago, she started contacting me and came down from Yorkshire to visit her family and stopped off to see me. I'm not exactly married to her!"

"She seems to be repelling all competition. Sounds like she's got big plans for you, matey! Anyway, shouldn't you be telling all this to Louise instead of me?"

"I would if I could get through to her!" I raised my voice in an attempt to illustrate my frustration. "Look, Emily… I don't want to exacerbate (hurrah!) the situation, could you ring her for me and tell her I am dying to talk to her?"

"I don't know. I don't want to get involved."

"You **ARE** involved. She has told you everything, from her point of view, and I have told you from mine. You have passed on hers to me, so you should pass on mine to her.... Point of view that is. Does that make sense? Only fair... yes?"

"I can see why she likes you. You have an uncanny knack of getting your own way don't you?"

If she had been here instead of on the 'phone, I would have backed up this convincing argument with my winning smile!

"Is that a 'yes', then?"

"OK, but I can't promise she'll listen."

"You are a real sweetheart!"

"I'll ring you when I've spoken to her."

"Thanks Emily, see you."

She hasn't rung me back, so it isn't looking too good.

Things to be grateful for

1) At least I know what has caused the problem with Louise.
2) Emily was good enough to explain the circumstances.
3) Emily is trying to explain enough to Louise to get her to (at least) speak to me.
4) I've got a weekend off from Stella, so I can get together with the lads.

Things to be concerned about

1) No news from Kirstie
2) Stella is taking too much for granted.
3) She has embarrassed Louise.
4) She has embarrassed me in front of my friends.
5) All my friends think she is a slapper.
6) She really pissed me off tonight with her attitude.
7) I really should have rung her tonight and given her a piece of my mind.

Sunday 8<u>th</u> October 2000

Word of the Day: Receptivity... able to accept stimuli, able or quick to receive ideas

7-30 a.m. in bed
(telephone rings!)

No!!! Not again!!!
"Hello Mother."
"How did you know it was me?"
"Haven't we had this conversation before?"
A million times!
"I've been up an hour and a half. Best part of the day."
Thank you for sharing that information! It might be, if you would only let me sleep through it, just one Sunday in a while!
"Not when you didn't go to bed until past one o'clock, Mother."
"I didn't. I was in bed at ten."
"I rest my case."
"What ARE you going on about?"
"Never mind, Mother. What can I do for you?"
"What do you mean by that?"
"You rang me? I know that I am no Sherlock Holmes, but I deduce that you have a reason for doing so, Watson? I realise it is a giant leap of faith, but I am sure…"
"OK, Mr. Sarkey! There's no need for rudeness."
"I apologise unreservedly for the use of sarcasm. It is, I admit, the lowest form of wit, but it is all I can muster when woken from a coma in the middle of the night."
"It's half past seven! Stop moaning. Now listen. It is our Crystal Wedding in three weeks time, and we are having a party at the Irish Club. I just wanted to let you know in plenty of time. You are quite welcome to bring a guest."

"And you couldn't have told me that at ten o'clock? Or five o'clock? Or next week?"

"Oh, we **are** in a mood this morning. Have we got out of the wrong side of the bed?"

"I haven't got out of any side of the damned bed yet!"

"Language! There's no need for that!"

As I slowly assimilated the gist of her words I ventured, "The Irish Club? Why the Irish club? You are not Irish, neither is Dad! Why on earth would you have a party there?"

"We went to a do there, last year. For a friend of your Dad's. Remember Mr Flynn?"

"Oh God, don't start that again. Please!"

"You remember him. Very short man. Irishman, married to that red headed woman."

"No hair? Just a red head?"

"Can I ever have a serious conversation with you, Benjamin?"

"Not at this time of day when I'm half asleep. You're lucky to get coherent. Serious is pushing your luck."

In order to prevent a long and frustrating argument, I wilfully lied to her.

"Of course I remember them. Lived at the bottom of our road?" I was guessing.

"Well, loosely. Just around the corner in Abbey Way."

"Of course they did."

In preventing the argument and pretending I remembered this couple, I had to endure an update on their entire life history over the last fifteen years, including all of their six children. It turned out that that was the sole reason for ringing and, now, she is in a mood, because of my lack of receptivity, (hurrah!), to her call. I am sure she does it deliberately. One of these days, I am going to ring her at 4-30 a.m. and tell her how lovely the weather is, and see how she likes being woken up two hours early.

I rang Stella twice yesterday, but her uncle said she wasn't available. She didn't ring me back. I have to laugh in the face of the irony that, the two women in my life that I am trying to talk to, are both avoiding me, yet the one to whom I didn't want talk, at the moment, rings me while I am still asleep!

7 p.m. Getting ready to go to the quiz.

Stella finally rang me, at about five this afternoon, and stole my thunder by launching into a tirade about my not talking to her on Friday night. I raised my voice to attract her attention, and then began a tirade of my own.

"Firstly, how the hell can I talk to you when I have got a queue of customers and a full griddle. Secondly, where do you get off verbally abusing my friends when they come to the door? Who the hell do you think you are? We haven't known each other two minutes, and you are trying to run my bloody life and screaming abuse and accusations at innocent parties, who are just good friends!"

"Only one party and a not-too-innocent one at that! I've heard all the crap about "just good friends" before. She is an ex-girlfriend for Christ's sake!"

"No she isn't! We have never been in a relationship." I found myself unnecessarily defensive. Before I realised it, I had explained the entire situation, about how I had been trying to take Louise out, without much success and that Stella "happened" in the middle of it all. Then how, when I thought she was **not** interested, Louise had suddenly said she **was** interested in going out with me, just as Stella came back on the scene. Then how nothing had ever happened between us.

But obviously not that it was not for the lack of trying!

Surprisingly, Stella seemed quite accepting of the explanation, but was quite forceful in ending the conversation, on her terms, about which, in retrospect, I am totally unhappy.

"Well, I can see how it happened, but if you and me are sleeping together, it is one on one. I am not going to be stood in a queue. There is no room for two-timing. **I'm** not two-timing **you**. It's your choice. I told her to fuck off, and you'd better see to it that she stays fucked off, or forget it. Now I have to go, I'm working. I'll speak to you later." On that note, she hung up and was gone.

She seems to have got it all planned, including repelling invaders! What chance does a mere man stand against such womanly wiles? <u>She</u> seems to think that my choice has been made for me! <u>I</u> think Stella's days are numbered! I doubt Louise will even talk to me again…ever! I feel really awful about what happened to her though. What a horrible situation to walk into. I would at least like the opportunity to apologise to her for what happened. I just hope that Emily is successful in persuading Louise to talk to me.

Things to be grateful for

1) It is Sunday, time for quiz night and the relatively sane world of the guys and me!

2) Stella is not here and yet again I do not have a shotgun to shoot her with!

<u>Monday 9th October 2000</u>

Word of the Day: Catalyse… cause or give rise to

7-00 p.m. in Red Lion

Had a good night out with the lads at the Queen's Head last night. Drank far too much beer and woke up with a real hangover. I've had a headache all day; so have just dropped in the Red Lion to see if another pint might chase it away. We didn't do very well in the quiz, either. The other teams were so pleased at our demise, that there were loud cheers when our losing scores were called out. Oh what it is to be famous! I think we had a surfeit of alcohol, which was not helpful to our performance, but we did have a few laughs.

"So… what's new, you old bastards?" Jamie enquired in his usual way with words.

"Not a lot." I said dismissively.

" Luton are fucking useless!" He continued.

"Fantastic observation there, Tumble. We were playing probably the best team in the league yesterday. Millwall will win that division."

"Fancy losing it in the last minute, I bet you were gutted." Gordon joined in.

"Let's talk about something different." I tried to change the conversation.

"OK! What about sex? Who's getting my share?" Brian caused a smile in all of us. "Maria is totally off it. If she's not careful, it'll heal up!"

"Don't look at me!" Gordon said. " I'm not even getting mine, let alone yours!"

"And you can wipe that grin off **your** face Jamie, we all know you're at it like a rabbit." Brian slapped him playfully on the back.

"I'm saying nothing," Jamie said, with a smirk of self-satisfaction.

"Yeah, rabbits take about ten seconds, so that sounds about right for Jamie," I interjected, catalysing (hurrah!) a confused look on his face, as our laughs echoed around the bar.

"I'll bet Ben's getting plenty as well, though," Brian rejoined.

"Yeah, that Stella must be draining him dry!" Jamie was happy to be relieved from being the subject of the conversation. "She only wears knickers to keep her ankles warm!"

"Very funny, Jamie... except I haven't seen her this week, she's working."

"Never mind, Ben, have a rest!" Brian suggested. "Who's for a pint?"

"Thanks mate, usual please." I replied.

Jamie said, "Is it your round, Brian?"

"What do **you** think?" Brian asked him. "Do you think I was asking what you want on behalf of someone else? You say some bloody daft things at times, for an intelligent bloke!"

"Stupid people should be made to wear a sign," I suggested. "So we don't waste our time asking them questions! I always pick a pillock to ask directions. You'd be able to just walk up to them and say, *"Excuse me, mate, do you know where...no it's OK, I just saw your sign!"* and save yourself the trouble. And when dickheads come up to the trailer when

I'm really busy, and say *"Are you still open?"* I could say *"Yes mate, what would you like...Oh by the way... put this sign on.""* We all laughed, and got stuck in to our fresh beers, as supplied by Brian.

"Yeah," Gordon came in. "Like when we moved to the new house. The removal lorry was outside fully loaded up and one of the neighbours came up and said, *"Hello Gordon. Are you moving?"* I should have said, *"No... we load all our stuff into a lorry once a month so my missus can vacuum the carpets."* Much mirth was shared by all at these observations, inducing half the pubs patrons to look at us disapprovingly.

"If Stella's been working all weekend, does that mean you've been giving Louise the benefit?" Jamie changed the subject back.

"Don't assume we are all like you, Tumble. I haven't seen her, either."

"Oh dear. Is Ben losing his touch?"

"If you say so. Are you as subtle as this when you are selling advertising?" I asked him.

"Yep. Had a fucking brilliant week. Did nearly the whole month's target in one week. I'll be into bonus by next Wednesday."

"Good for you!" Gordon seemed genuine in his praise.

We finished our drinks and got up to leave. As we did so, I couldn't resist it.

"Jamie..."

"What?"

"Don't forget your sign, mate!"

We all staggered out of the pub laughing.

"Fuck off, you lot." Jamie didn't find it as funny as the rest of us!

Things to be grateful for

1) A good night out with my mates.
2) A few good laughs, mostly at poor Jamie's expense.
3) Good mates. We give each other a hard time, but we are true friends who stick together.

Tuesday 10th October 2000

Word of the Day: Reciprocate... offer or give something in return

2-20 p.m. on trailer

Another interesting day on base. The Braves baseball fan came back duly adorned with a Braves baseball cap.

"Y'all wanna buy yosself a decent hat, Arnie!"

"No thanks, I'll stick with the Packers. I'm not a turncoat!"

"Y'all wanna get into baseball. 'T'sa far better game than football."

"You reckon? There's no better game than proper football. You call it soccer."

"Buncha prissy, prissy pansy boys."

"I'll tell Vinny Jones you said so..."

Well, it made **me** laugh, as it sailed with the burger and onion impregnated air, ten feet over his head. How would he know who Vinny Jones was?

"...anyway, what's all that crap about a World Series?"

"Yuh? Fantastic series o' games between the world's best. Y'all ready to watch it?"

"Behave yourself! How can it be the world series when only you lot are in it?"

"Ah! Well... ain't no one else good enough to beat the USA's best."

"How will you ever know, if no non-U.S. teams are ever invited? Sorry, no logic in that one."

"So what about cricket then? What the fuck's that all about."

"Now that **is** a fantastic game...and when we have the World Series, it really means it. All the top cricketing nations of the world compete."

"Jeezus H, man, Tha' has to be the most boring game in the world."

"Not when you understand what's going on. Unlike baseball, where a guy just slings the ball at the batsman on the full, and often the batsman isn't even good enough to hit it…"

He was laughing loudly at my observations on his favourite game.

"…in cricket the ball has a raised seam, it's kept polished on one side, so it swings in the air, like a baseball, but when it hits the ground at ninety miles an hour, it can bounce high, keep low, go straight on, or veer off to one side or the other. Some bowlers spin it, so it kicks up at you and turns off the wicket, and sometimes it swings in the opposite direction to what it's supposed to! The variables are almost infinite. You very rarely see two balls the same in any spell of bowling."

"Yuh know, I unnerstood Jack Shit o' whatchoo juss said, Arnie. Yer full of it man! Anyways, where d'you get off givvin yo' customers a bad time, man? We's yo' livin', dude."

"Doesn't mean you can come here and talk out of the top of yo' head."

Oops I am beginning to catch this guy's accent.

He laughed again and, as I handed him his order, he said his goodbyes, then offered his fist to me, which I guessed meant he wanted me to reciprocate (hurrah!) and as mine approached his he touched mine, and said, "Y'all crazy man. See yuh tomorrer!"

Things to be grateful for

1) Being able to decipher the gist of what the Braves fan was saying today.

2) We play cricket, a skilful and infinitely variable game of finesse.

3) We don't play baseball over here, a basic and repetitive game better suited to children!

Friday 13<u>th</u> October 2000

Word of the Day: Escapism… the tendency to seek distraction and relief from reality.

12-30 a.m. in kitchen

Argghh! Friday the thirteenth! Nightmare! Actually, I guess it is really Saturday the 14th already. I have finished a busy night, got home and, now, I can't sleep, so I have got up to get a drink and watch TV. Problem is, I can't find the damned remote control, and the TV won't switch on from standby without it. How did we ever manage without them? Just imagine having to get up out of your chair to manually change channels! This TV cost over £600 and won't work if there are no batteries in the remote control, (nor if you can't find the damned thing!). How ridiculous is that?

Still haven't heard from Louise or Emily. I may ring Emily over the weekend, just to find out what has been happening.

Stella has rung every day this week. She has been all lovey-dovey and trying to chip away at the cold shoulder I have been giving her. She has apologised, every day, about being abusive to Louise, and freely admits she was out of order. Her fawning has been like the Chinese water torture. Drip! Drip!! Drip!!! However, I'm still seething over it and have not yet forgiven her. She wanted to come down this weekend, but I told her I was busy, because I really don't need to see her at the moment. I can't just pretend that nothing is wrong.

I was invited to go to York for the day, this Sunday, by a customer on base, whose name is Paul. He was telling me that he'd always wanted to go to York and had got the weekend off, so had planned to take his wife on Sunday. I was just giving him a list of places to see and he suddenly cut me off.

"Hey, Ben! You know what? I'd like you to be our guest and come along. You could show us the attractions in person. Hey, do you have a partner to bring? We could make a foursome."

"No, I don't have a partner... and anyway, what about your wife? She may want a little time alone with you."

"No way! She'd be as happy as a clam!"

Are clams happy? How can you tell? What are the parameters for the measurement of clam happiness?

I was very flattered to have been asked, so I agreed to go. It will provide a little escapism, (hurrah!). I suppose I could have asked Stella to come, but I am still mad at her, and I am not sure yet, if I even want to see her again.

I must try to get some sleep.

Things to be grateful for

1) Another Stella-free weekend
2) A day out in York to look forward to

Monday 16th October 2000

Word of the day: Detrimental... harmful, causing loss

4 p.m. in flat

I'll bet that confused the hell out of Mother. She would have been witless all day! We left for York at 7 a.m., so if she rang after that, her mind would have been racing all day over why I wasn't there. If she did ring, she didn't leave a message.

Paul picked me up at the flat, and we drove down to the base to fill up with petrol. I could not believe the price of petrol on base. He filled up his Ford Expedition for just over £20. At our prices, it would have cost nearer £60. We set off and stopped for breakfast, after about an hour, then arrived in York at about half past 11. Paul and his wife, Hally, are extremely good company. They are very softly spoken and laid back, and so obviously in love. I felt like a gooseberry half the time. We started to walk around the city, admiring the remains of the city wall and came across a Starbucks Coffee House. Paul insisted on going in and having a Frappucchino and I joined him. I showed them around The Shambles, a very old narrow street, with many picturesque beamed buildings. The upstairs bay windows of some houses and shops, which are opposite one another, seem like they are almost touching. It really has charm and was just as beautiful as I remembered it. Coming out of the top end of The Shambles, we came upon a group of street entertainers, who were juggling, doing magic tricks and clowning, on a small square. One performer, a mime, was extremely talented and very funny. Being American, Paul and Hally were mesmerised by the olde worlde charm of the area, especially the entertainers. I began to direct them towards the Jorvik Centre, but Paul immediately became distracted, when we passed a branch of Yeoman's, when he noticed a pair of what he called "Zippy Pants", displayed in the window. They were a kind of hikers' trousers, which could be made into shorts by unzipping and removing the legs.

Of the trousers, not the occupants!

Hally, however, could not be persuaded as to the need for Paul to purchase said zippy pants! The funniest thing that happened was after we went away from Yeoman's. Paul was sulking gently over the zippy pants, but his eyes lit up when he saw a factory shoe shop. We went in and they were both in their element. We must have been in there an hour, while they, (Paul in particular), tried on pair after pair. I think they must have a shoe fetish!

Finally, we made it to the Jorvik Centre, with its "ride through the ages" attraction. The electric cars, take you back to a reproduction Viking village, with facsimiles of the houses and Tussaud like waxwork people and animals. It even comes complete with smells! Unfortunately, our car's commentary by Magnus Magnusson, was out of sync with the ride. It didn't matter much to me, as I have done it before, but Paul and Hally were not getting the best out of the experience, which was a shame, as we had queued for about forty minutes to get in. I summoned up the courage to report the fault to an operator, explaining that "my guests" were American. They took our car out of service immediately and asked us to select another, then invited us to go around again, so the problem was solved and was not detrimental, (hurrah!), to our enjoyment of the day. My companions were very impressed with the results of my low-key complaint, and also with the organisers for their customer service. It was remarkable, as Americans generally regard us as very backward when it comes to customer service, and for consumers accepting poor service without complaint. We later visited the York Dungeon, which was great fun, and then looked over York Minster Cathedral. Finally, we ate dinner, at a very pleasant restaurant, before returning, later in the evening. I missed the quiz, but it was worth it. I had a lovely day out, free from the stress of love-life matters.

Things to be grateful for

1) Meeting and enjoying the company of new friends.
2) I didn't have to deal with any acrimony relating to Stella

Wednesday 18th October 2000

Word of the day: Contretemps... Awkward or unfortunate occurrence

4 p.m. asleep on sofa
(' phone rings)

"Hello?"
"Hello, Benjamin, where have you been all week?"
Argghh! How the hell does she know when I'm asleep? I am sure she is psychic.
"Nowhere special. You know. Work, eat, sleep. Work, eat, sleep."
"I rang on Sunday. Why didn't you answer?"
"Maybe I wasn't there?"
"Well, were you?"
"No."
"So why did you say "maybe"?"

"I was being ironic, Mother!"

"Facetious more like! Anyway, I rang to see if you had marked our wedding anniversary on your calendar. You didn't ring me back to say that you were coming."

"Of course I'll be coming, you knew I'd be there, Mother. I've just been so busy with the base and bedding in new staff."

"That's a strange choice of words?"

"Mother! Wash your mouth out with soap!"

I knew that, one day, all the silly things she said to me, as a child, would surface! Things like, "if you fall out of that tree and break your leg, don't come running to me!" And, "do you want a good hiding?" (Oh yes please mother!) Another of her favourites was, "it is as broad as it is long!" (That makes it a square then, I guess?) She has a million of them. Aha! That reminds me of others, "I've told you 1000 times, don't exaggerate!" and "I won't tell you again!" (Promise?) Usually, ten seconds before she did tell me again.

"Well, are you coming or not? We need to know, for the caterers."

"I'm sure that the caterers' numbers will not be thrown a mile out by one person, one way or the other. Anyway, it's nearly two weeks away."

A small contretemps (hurrah!) followed, where I was accused of being selfish and uncaring. I was told how difficult it is to organise a function, especially when people don't respond to invitations. However, once she had unloaded all the displeasure she had been storing up, she handed the telephone to Dad, and we had the opportunity to talk a little. Mother was obviously hovering in the background and could not resist the temptation to interfere in the conversation between my father and me. I could hear her in the background, saying, *"tell him this... tell him that... tell him the other"*. As she could only hear him, and not me, I was making outrageous suggestions to Dad, such as, *"tell her to bite her arse,"* and, *"tell her to mind her own business",* causing him to laugh and her to ask, *"what're you laughing at?"* By the time our conversation was over, I would estimate that he was in deep trouble with her and left him to his fate!

Luton still haven't won any more games. They drew at Oxford last night, 0 – 0, although Oxford are probably the worst team in the second division. We really need to be beating teams like this.

Stella hasn't rung since before the weekend. She obviously has 'the hump' over my decision not to see her last weekend. The Americans have a saying for it, "Oh well!"

On base today, I got chatting with Randy Sparkes…

Yes, that really is his name. I remember when he first came up to the trailer, and introduced himself by saying "Hi, I'm Randy!" I told him that was not something you said to an Englishman. Not if you are a bloke, at least, and fancied keeping ALL your teeth!

…He was explaining to me how, last weekend, his girlfriend drove them both to Wales. It was the first time that she had driven such a long distance.

"Yeah, Ben. I'll tell you, I'm used to her being dumb, but this trip said it all. We left Friday at six o'clock in the evening… by the way, I should also tell you, at this point, that it is also the first time she's driven a long distance in the darkness… just before we reached Cardiff, she goes and says, *"This high beam stick is too damned far from the steering wheel for my small hands. It is making my hand muscles all cramp up."*"

"You mean that she didn't have the sense to let go of the steering wheel to change to main beam?"

"It's worse than that buddy, she'd spent the entire journey holding the high beam stick towards the steering wheel. You know, not on the regular high beam, but pulling against the spring on the flasher! She didn't even know that you could set high beam permanently… and she's been driving for years!"

"You made that up, Randy. No one could be that thick."

"I'm not joking, it really happened that way, I swear!"

Things to be grateful for

1) The opportunity to speak with Dad and have a laugh with him

2) Childhood memories of the laughs I had over Mother's pet sayings

Thursday 19<u>th</u> October 2000

Word of the day: Intricacy... perplexing detail

11 p.m. Finished early

I've been feeling a bit tired this week. Things went quiet about 10 o'clock, so I sloped off early.
So sue me! What is the point of being your own boss, if you can't skive off occasionally?
I rang Emily tonight, to see if she had any news about Louise. She told me that Louise is coming up on Sunday and wants to talk to me. That has got to be good news! (Or has it?) Maybe we could have a nice lunch together and get ourselves back on track?
I had a count up, last night, and I have enough cash put by now, to pay off the loan for the griddles. Then I can get a new loan to buy the doner machine. Hang on! What am I thinking of? What is the point of paying off one loan, then taking out another, when I could keep the existing one and use the cash to buy the doner machine outright and save all the paperwork and setting-up fees? Duh!

Things to be grateful for

1) My brain finally working out the intricacies (hurrah!) of high finance!
2) Louise is coming on Sunday.

Sunday 22nd October 2000

Word of the day: delectable... delightfully pleasant
11 a.m. just out of the shower

I was naughty this morning and switched the phone and Ansafone speaker off! I can see there is a message. It will be from Mother! For once, I just needed a lie in. I didn't get up until nine o'clock and, then, just sat around in my dressing gown, ate a leisurely and uninterrupted breakfast and have just had a bracing shower in preparation for meeting Louise for lunch. I feel like I'm about to go on a first date again. I have butterflies of excitement, and I can't wait to see her again. I feel bright and breezy, and all is right with my world. All this, and Luton beat Brentford 3-1 yesterday! No problems finding things to be grateful for today, I think!

Things to be grateful for

1) A Mother-free phone zone.
2) Luton are now ready to relaunch their season and start winning a few games!
3) A lazy lie in and leisurely breakfast.
4) The prospect of a romantic lunch with the delectable (hurrah!) Louise.
5) Quiz night, tonight – maybe! Unless Louise has other plans! (Mmmmmm!)

Monday 23rd October 2000

Word of the day: Inimitable... impossible to imitate

4 p.m. just back from base.
(The Ansafone light is flashing. It is a message from Gordon.)

"Hello, Bollock-brains! Where the fucking hell have you been hiding? Are you shagging yourself to death? That's two weeks running you have been missing from the quiz! Of course, we won two rounds last night without you – so don't feel guilty or anything! I'm at work 'til five tonight. Give me a ring and let me know what's going on? We thought we'd go bowling again tonight. Interested? We are leaving at about 7. Message timed at Monday 23rd of October… Year of Our Lord 2000… at 1300 hours. Over and out!"

I don't know if I can be bothered. I really am not feeling up to it. Mind you, why should I lock myself away? I'll give Gordon a ring. Maybe it would do me good to get out.

Yesterday was a horrible day. I met Louise for lunch, full of hope and anticipation that we could get over the small blip in our relationship and get back on track. We met at 12, for a quick drink in The Lion, and went off to the Admiral Nelson for lunch. All seemed to be progressing well. I apologised for the distressing episode with Stella and explained to her how Stella had appeared on the scene, while I was on holiday, and how she had suddenly turned up again, out of the blue, a few weeks later. Louise listened to my explanation intently and said that, while she wasn't happy at how she had been treated by Stella, she realised that it was not my fault and had now got over it.

We had an excellent lunch, during which I had an epiphany, (like Paul on the road to Damascus), and made the momentous decision, to dump Stella, once and for all, and to ask Louise to go out with me, on a steady basis, to give us a fair chance. However, before I even opened my mouth, she stopped me in my tracks.

"Ben, there's something you should know." She touched my wrist gently.

Ominous!

"No, wait. I wanted to say something…"

"No, Ben…let me get this off my chest first…One of the partners of the law firm I work for has been asking me out for months. Ever since I've been down there, in fact! I've been saying *"no"* to him and fending off his advances, because I really thought **we** would get together. But after what happened, I was really upset, and I assumed, from what she'd said, that you and she were an item… That you must only see **"us"** as friends. So, I agreed to go out with Simon… that's his name… and we really seem to have hit it off. You know I told you that I had a real problem with my ex? He wasn't violent exactly, but he used to scream at me, if he didn't know where I was, or if I did anything without telling him. He controlled everything I ever did. It was as though I didn't have a life of my own. He could do as he liked, of course, including going out with whoever he liked. He was always out with some tart or other, the bastard… And having had to deal with that and finally escaping from him, I don't ever want to be in that position again. When that nasty woman appeared, at your door, and told me, in no uncertain terms, that you were virtually her property, it set alarm bells ringing in my head. I can't deal with all that stuff again."

"But you wouldn't have to. I am not committed to anyone. I can be faithful to the right person. I think you could just be that person. **"We"** never had the chance together, yet. Can't you tell this "Simon" it was nice, but you aren't ready to be exclusive yet? It's not illegal to date two people at the same time, you know. Then you can see who you like most and decide who you want to be with, if either of us."

"No. I'm sorry Ben. I know it's an old-fashioned way of going on, but I only want to be with one person at a time… and Simon has done nothing wrong. He was a perfect gentleman, while I was telling him "no!" And he's been a perfect gentleman, while we've been dating. We're not even sleeping together."

"Are you saying, *"this is it,"* then? Don't do this, Louise, not yet… **please!**"

Fucking hell, what has come over me? I've never begged a woman like that before!

"I'm sorry, Ben. I like you a lot, too… and I think we would be good together. If I had known how you felt before, it may have been different, but I can't just abandon him, after he waited so patiently until I was ready to say *"yes"*… I need to let Simon have his chance."

FUCK SIMON! (Not literally!!)
"You mean I've blown mine?"

"I didn't say that…" She began to cry. "I'm sorry Ben…sorry… I have to go… goodbye."

She got up and left quickly. I felt like crying too! I went home and just laid on the sofa, staring blankly at the TV. I'm not sure if I fell asleep or not, but it was 6-30 before I shook myself out of my doldrums and made a cup of tea. I couldn't face the quiz and the guys' inquisitive banter. I just sat and watched TV, until I fell asleep for the night.

I still feel numb today, as though I have suffered a bereavement. I've had relationships break up before, but I've never felt like this in my life. The weird thing is, we were never really in a relationship, so why do I feel so upset? "Things to be grateful for" is going to be difficult again today!

11 p.m. back from bowling

The lads noticed right away that I was depressed and, in their inimitable (hurrah!) fashion, took it upon themselves to cheer me up. I guess that is why I am now pissed out of my head and can hardly see to write this entry. Sleep and oblivion beckons!

Things to be grateful for

1) My friends' caring approach to my disposition.
2) Alcohol anaesthetises not only the body but also the mind.

Wednesday 25<u>th</u> October 2000

Word of the day: reciprocal… bin return, expressing a mutual action

11-45 p.m. back at the flat

I just seemed to be going through the motions today. I was feeling very sorry for myself and everyone on base is noticing. I really must snap out of it.

Stella rang me on the mobile tonight, and I was quite sarcastic and aggressive towards her. I guess deep down, I blame her for the pain I am experiencing at the moment. She took it in her stride though and tried to appease me, rather than respond in a reciprocal (hurrah!) manner. I think I would have felt better if she had fought back, because now, on top of everything else, I feel guilty about that too! Anyway, she is not coming this weekend, yet again. She is working.

That'll make a change!

Under the circumstances, I am not bothered either way! Maybe I should finish with her anyway and have a total break from women… Altogether!

At least, Mrs. Hand and her five slim daughters don't answer back!

I was feeling bad enough tonight, so the last thing I needed was the apprentice Village Idiot, Brian Naylor, riding his motorbike round the village constantly. He must have ridden behind the trailer 15 or 20 times tonight. I felt like securing a throat wire across the road! His motorbike sounds like an angry wasp and makes a noise as though it was trying to do 120 mph, but in reality can only do about 20 mph downhill, flat as a strap, with a tailwind **and** with his arse on fire! Being in this trailer is like being in a speaker box; sound reverberates around the walls and can nearly deafen you. At about ten o'clock, he came to buy a burger, and I told him that if he continued to ride past, with his throttle wide open, making as much noise as he had been all night, I would come out and throttle him. He thought it was a matter of much amusement. Then he tried to ring his friend on his mobile phone, but unfortunately could not remember the number. He asked me what the number for directory enquiries was on Vodafone. I told him he was mad to use his Vodafone, when he could get the number for free, using the BT payphone, which was less than 10 yards away. By this time, two other motorcyclists had arrived, and Brian was in the phone box. They went over to him and were listening to his call. Suddenly, everyone was laughing, uncontrollably. One of them came back to me to tell me what had happened.

"God, Arnie… You won't believe that how thick Naylor is. He's just rung Directory Enquiries. Listen to this…

He says: *Naylor…..B…..Marston Ferrars…..High Street…..number 2….. What are you talking about? That's my number!*

What a twat!"

That is the second piece of ridiculous behaviour I have encountered today. On base today, there was a large box in my dustbin, which was taking up too much room and should have been placed in a skip. It had contained a parcel sent to an Army Lieutenant through the open mail! The address label said,

Lieut Joseph Smith (made up name to protect the guilty!)
Intelligence Specialist,
USAF Newton Molecliffe, Cambs.

I am sure that, since it is a very high security intelligence airbase, his superiors would have had kittens if they had seen that label. Why doesn't he just draw a target on his back?

Things to be grateful for

1) I feel intellectually superior after witnessing Brian Naylor's exhibitions of genius today and thinking about the sender of the package to the Lieutenant!

Saturday 28th October 2000

Word of the Day: Apposite... apt, well chosen

Midnight ready to commit ritual Hare Kari

I know Luton are having a bad season, but today takes the biscuit. Leading 3-0, with about 35 minutes to go, they managed to engineer a 4-3 home defeat against Wrexham. There is no hope for them. I will be very surprised if Ricky Hill lasts another week as manager. As much as I like him, I would probably sack him myself, if I were the chairman!

Stella rang yesterday. She is being extra loving and attentive, and she is still apologising over the Louise incident. She said that it was only out of fear of losing me that she behaved that way. She actually used those three little words for the first time, which threw me completely. I'm not sure I could ever love her in return, but I found myself softening my attitude towards her. She is working again this weekend, but then has two weekends off, so we made plans for her to come and stay. At least, it might help to get my own feelings straightened out, if we spend some time together.

Tomorrow is Mum and Dad's crystal wedding anniversary, so I have to go and find something apposite (hurrah!) today, to give them to commemorate completion of a 35-year sentence. Joking apart, that is some feat in this day and age.

Things to be grateful for

1) Mum and Dad's celebrations.
2) Maybe there is something worth resurrecting with Stella.

Monday 30th October 2000

Word of the Day: Reminisce... remember things past; mentally relive an earlier period of life

8 p.m. watching TV

The party was much more enjoyable than I had anticipated. Mother was dressed as though she were going to a wedding, and Dad looked like a fish out of water in a new pinstripe suit. I went over very early to help with the organisation and had some really enjoyable quality time with Dad. He was reminiscing (hurrah!) over the early years. He told me about their "courtship," and their engagement, and how proud he was when I was born. That was quite a moment. He has never said anything quite that emotional in his life before. He came from a line of males, who were strongly discouraged from showing their emotions. His father's lineage was from Yorkshire and his mother's from Durham, so, "real men just don't do that sort of thing!" Not like today, when all these self-help and spiritual publications suggest we all "get in touch with our feminine sides" and let our emotions out. Coming from that background, it is hardly surprising that I still find it difficult myself!

Big boys don't cry, do they?

I can remember some of the early days, myself. Dad (and Mum) really wanted me to get on in life and have opportunities that they didn't have. He was a stickler for my manners being perfect, even though he couldn't live up to his own standards. I remember one such incident. In my normal Lutonian vernacular, pronouncing the letter 't' in a guttural fashion rather than sounding it fully, I asked him to "pass the bu-ugh" (butter). He immediately picked me up on it and made me repeat, "butter," emphasising the 'tt'. I dutifully repeated, "butter," eliciting the response from him, "Tha's be-ugh!" (better). When I laughed, he did not understand what was funny and clipped me round the ear, for being disrespectful!

Happy Days!

It was good to see all the aunts and uncles again, and I did enjoy being part of the centre of attention. As an only child, I was coerced into making a speech, which I did, and made Mother cry. Unless I was very much mistaken, I would swear that Dad had a little tear in his eye too, although he would rather die a horrible death, than ever admit it!

Things to be grateful for

1) Meeting all my relatives again.
2) An emotionally gratifying time with my parents.
3) I think my parents and I learned how much we are mutually loved today.

Tuesday 31ˢᵗ October 2000

Word of the day: Confrontational... showing hostility and defiance

3-50 p.m. just in from base

Frank Dykstra rang today. He said that he was getting flak from his superiors about my being on a temporary contract and only paying 15 %. If I want to continue to trade on base, I have to sign a new permanent contract. It would have to be a standard contract, which means paying all my takings to them daily and not seeing any income for two months **and** paying 20 % commission. This I am not keen to do. However, I feel I have no choice. I now know how much this contract is worth to me and, while it goes against the grain to back down from my original stance, I'm not about to cut off my nose to spite my face!

"I'm sorry Ben. It's out of my hands," said Pontius Pilate...oops! I mean Frank. As I had told him, when we met at the beginning, that there was no way I would accept that contract, I guess he was expecting me to refuse it.

"I'm not very happy about that." I responded.

"Didn't for one minute think that you would be!" He continued.

"However, I don't have a lot of choice, so OK."

(Silence)

"............................Er...Oh, um I'll have to get back to you!"

They want me out of here! He was expecting me to tell him to stick it!

"What for?"

"Um...to meet up to sign a new contract. I'll have to get it drawn up and I'll ring you."

"OK, whatever."

I felt uneasy, as though all was not above board.

Several customers came by after Frank rang and, as I was feeling very downtrodden, I was telling them all how I reckoned I was being ripped off.

One guy gave his opinion.

"Jeez, Ben! They sure are shafting you. Why don't you tell them to blow it up their ass?"

"Why do you think? Because they are holding all the cards. If I don't accept their terms, I lose my livelihood. There is nothing I can do about it. And, of course, you'd lose your food, too!"

A discussion on the relative merits of the system, which ended with his saying:

"They's just a bunch o' bastards man!"

"Don't let them hear you say that. They may have you shot!"

"You don't shoot the military, man. They shoot you!"

He left, chuckling to himself at this 'in' joke.

Things to be grateful for

1) The opportunity to confirm the contract on base, and therefore gain security of tenure.

2) The support, (however confrontational (hurrah!) and disrespectful!) of my customers.

NOVEMBER 2000

Thursday 2<u>nd</u> November 2000

Word of the Day: Demonstratively... actively demonstrating or expressing a point

6-15 p.m.

I am sitting quietly reading my newspaper, when a mad rush of one customer breaks my concentration.

"Mega with chips please, how're you doing Arnie?"

(I smile sweetly).

"Fine thanks. You?"

"Not bad"

This riveting exchange is interrupted by an argument between two youths over on the footpath about 15 yards away. They part and one rides off on his bicycle. I put the chips into the basket and lower them into the oil, place the burger on the griddle and commence cooking. The customer decides to utilise his waiting time as efficiently as possible!

"Is it OK if I pop into the Red Lion, for a quick pint, while you are cooking that?"

"Of course it is!"

"Don't worry, Arnie," he starts to smirk at the "original" joke, which is evolving in his head. It spews forth in a bad impression of The Terminator.

"I'll be back!"

He sidles off to the pub repeating the line to himself, as though he cannot believe he thought of it. I am left, lost in my own world, turning his burger over and contemplating the universe, when there is a large and very sudden explosion, just the other side of the front wall of the trailer. It has come from the cupboard attached to the trailer, which contains two 19-kilogram bottles of Propane Liquid Petroleum Gas and, in that split second, my life flashed before my eyes. My underwear is immediately in danger of being assaulted with heavily soiling matter, and I am confused as to why I am not dead! After a further few seconds, with my heart pounding and my lungs hyperventilating, I become aware of the remaining youth, laughing uncontrollably, while sitting on the adjacent bench. The realization dawns that he has thrown a seriously loud explosive firework under the trailer, and it has gone off under the gas box. There being enough fuel in 38 Kilograms to blow all of us, within a 20-yard radius, into the next Kingdom and beyond, the joke is lost on me, and I find myself having run out of the door and standing right in front of him. Involuntarily, the flat of my hand caresses the side of his head, with a resounding "thwack", and I become aware that I have committed an assault.

"I'll fetch my dad down to sort you out"

"Fetch him and I'll slap **him** as well… for having you!"

7-17 p.m.

A Police Officer arrives in a car, with blue lights flashing. I am rather disappointed that he does not commence with "'allo, 'allo 'allo, wot's goin' on 'ere then?", but he doesn't.

"Good evening, sir. I have had a report of an assault on a 15-year-old boy. Do you know anything about it?"

"Who reported it, his dad?"

"No, sir. I believe it was the victim himself."

"As it happens, I do know about it… and if he comes back, I might just slap him again!"

"That might not be a very good course of action, sir! Would you like to explain what happened?"

I recounted the story, with absolute truth and accuracy, and the policeman shook his head in disbelief, as I described the "air-bomb" exploding, and my panic that only a small leak would have been necessary in there, for a very large explosion to have been caused.

" So, did you actually strike him?"

"Yes I did, but I would do it again in the same circumstances."

"I said, "Did...you... strike him?"" He repeated, slowly and deliberately.

"Yes?" I replied quizzically, mentally questioning the status of his hearing apparatus.

He shook his head demonstratively (hurrah!) and negatively, from side to side, as he spoke again…"I will ask you one final time before I **arrest** you sir! Did you strike him?"

(Falling in with a big splash)…"Er … No!"

"Well, that's OK, then, sir, it is his word against yours. We get a lot of unsubstantiated allegations nowadays." He winked at me. "Take care now. Good evening, sir."

With that, he left, somewhat less conspicuously than he had arrived, leaving me to fend off questions by the local "lads" as to why "the pigs" were here.

I rang Stella, shortly after the policeman left, and recounted the story. Far from supporting me and giving me sympathy, she said that I had overreacted and should lighten up.

"Boys will be boys!" She said.

She was a little under the weather and sounded as though she was about to have a cold. Consequently, she said she would wait and see how she felt at the weekend, before deciding whether to come or not.

Things to be grateful for

1) I have not been spread thinly over the surrounding countryside.
2) I did not kill or maim the moron who nearly blew us up.
3) Aren't our policemen wonderful?

Sunday 5th November 2000

Word of the Day: Summarily... in a manner causing curtailment or cutting off.

7-15 a.m.
(telephone rings)

"Hello, Mother!"
"Why do you always say it like that?"
"Like what?"
"Like it's a burden to answer the phone."
"Because, until two minutes ago I was in a deep sleep, Mother!"
"Well, I'm sorry if I woke you." She said, unapologetically.
"That's OK, the phone was ringing, anyway."
"Very amusing, Benjamin... But hardly original. You've said that before."
"So you **do** listen to what I say, then?"
"More than you listen to me, apparently. Nowthen..."
What the hell does that mean? It is neither one thing nor the other!
"... did you keep that cat of yours in last night? It was bonfire night, you know."
"No it wasn't, bonfire night is tonight."
"Split hairs, why don't you? You know what I mean. The organised firework displays are always on the Friday or Saturday nearest to the fifth."
"I see! So that was what all those coloured lights and explosions were in the sky last night!"
"Very funny! Anyway... Did you?"
"Did I what?"
"Keep the cat in."
"Let me get this straight, Mother. You rang me on a Sunday morning..."

Again!
"... at the sound of the dawn chorus..."
Again!
"... to advise me, **after the event**, to keep my cat in... To avoid him being frightened? Of **yesterday's** fireworks? Doesn't that smack of stable doors and bolting horses?"

"Oh! Sometimes there is just no talking to you!"

"How's Dad?" I attempted to change the subject.

"He's not awake yet."

"Lucky Dad!"

"Well, it is about time he was up!"

If I'm up, everyone must be up, eh, Mother?

"How are you both?"

Argghh! I did it again! When will I learn, that she is the one person in the entire universe who, if you ask how she is, will actually tell you... In graphic detail... For three quarters of an hour.

When she finally noticed that Dad had got up, showered, shaved, and dressed and was now sitting in his armchair, all in the time she took to disseminate the gory details of the malfunctions of her grisly bits, he must have been smiling.

Mistake!

"What are you smirking at?" She barked, (obviously at Dad.)

"How can you tell I'm smirking from down the phone?" I pretended that I thought she was talking to me." Have you got one of those videophones? Where's the camera?"

"Don't be silly, Benjamin, of course I haven't, I was talking to your father. Anyway, I haven't got time to stay on the phone all day, I'd better get his breakfast."

I was summarily, (Hurrah!) albeit willingly, dismissed.

Stella's cold has developed into something nasty. She sounded awful on the phone last night. She has decided to postpone her visit for another week, until she feels better. So, once I was off the phone to Mother, I got up and looked forward to a restful day off.

Things to be grateful for

1) A pleasant day in my own company.
2) A live football match to watch this afternoon.
3) Quiz night with the lads.

Monday 6th November 2000

Word of the Day: Inconspicuous... not easily noticed.

There were strange people on base today, who seemed to be watching me. Am I paranoid, or are they really out to get me!!! Every time I caught their eye, they looked away. Weird or what? The really funny thing was that the wind was extremely forceful today, and it rained quite hard at one point. Yet these two plonkers stayed out there, trying to look inconspicuous (hurrah!)

Quiz night was quite enjoyable last night. We were on reasonable form, won one fun round and the drinks round. No one won the jackpot. Again!

Things to be grateful for

1) If they were spies, they got weather-beaten all day!

Tuesday 7th November 2000

9-30 a.m. on base

Everyone on base is full of election fever. By this time tomorrow, we will all know who is to be the new president of the U.S.A. It seems that the military guys mainly favour George W Bush, as he is pro-military and is likely to do more for servicemen than Al Gore, but it could be one of the closest run presidential elections for years. It is now all-quiet until the rush at 11-00 a.m.

Wednesday 8<u>th</u> November 2000

Word of the Day : Emanate... originate from, issue from

7-30 a.m. In flat

I stayed up half the night watching news of the election and, finally, fell asleep at about 2 a.m. Have just heard the news that Bush won by a very narrow margin and Gore has rung him to congratulate him and concede defeat. That should please most of the guys on base.

9-30 a.m. On base

A very tall naval officer arrives for breakfast. In the distance, I can hear gunfire emanating from the shooting range.
" Hi, how are you?"
"Outstanding, thank you. Are you having a good day?"
"Fine thanks. Is that the sound of Democrats shooting themselves, I can hear?" I smiled.
"Not just yet. News is breaking that it was so close in Florida that Gore has withdrawn his congratulations and wants a recount. Overall victory depends upon Florida, so it is not all over yet! We will have to see what happens. This baby could run and run!"
"Yeah, but I've never heard of a recount changing the result at any election. Usually, there are only a few votes difference in a recount."
"Yeah, I guess. It don't matter much to me who wins, one's a liar and the other is a pathological liar."
"I don't know which one is which to you, but one of them had a damn good teacher!"
He laughed. "I guess the world will get a good laugh out of this one."

11 p.m. flat

The news is full of recount mania over the US elections. It appears to have been a monumental cock up on the counting front. We shall see what ensues next!

Stella is still, (allegedly,) coming this Sunday. I will be pleased to see her, (I think!). I've forgotten what a shag is like, and I am sure the cobwebs have reformed over my private equipment!

Things to be grateful for

1) Stella is coming this weekend.
2) I have a feather duster to remove the cobwebs before she arrives!
3) I have got some wonderful material from the US presidential elections to taunt my customers with!

Sunday 11th November 2000

Word of the Day: Culminate... reach the highest or final point

5 p.m. in flat in shock!

Stella arrived at about 9 a.m. and, for the first time ever, she suggested a coffee rather than hurtling recklessly into the bedroom.
Irony rules again!
For once, due to my enforced celibacy for as long as I can remember, I was rampant and ready to shag her brains out, an hour before she arrived; and she wanted coffee! The sex, which ensued, was of a rather urgent nature, (on my part at least), so assumed a rather animal quality. It culminated (hurrah!) in an extreme climax, and I have to say that trains and tunnels, or waves rushing to shore, would have been totally inadequate pictorial images to portray it! A nuclear explosion

with commensurate mushroom cloud was more appropriate. We lay side by side, exhausted form our exertions, and she said, "My God, someone needed a fuck this morning!" This detracted somewhat from the pleasurable relaxation in the wake of a powerful orgasm! Then she became suddenly quiet and softly began to speak.

"Ben?" She began. "Have you ever thought about having kids?"

Whoa! She's getting broody! Not with you I haven't, sweetheart!

I could feel the adrenaline rush, as I feared she was going to ask me to have a child with her.

"Yes, I guess so…at some point" I emphasised the words to convey the lack of urgency I felt to embark on parenthood.

"What would you say if I told you that, "at some point", was now?"

Jump off a bridge?

"I don't know, why?"

"Because I am pregnant." She said in a matter-of-fact monotone.

"Are you sure?"

God, why do we men always say that? She would hardly be telling me if she wasn't sure!

"Of course I'm sure, I did a home test. Trust me, there is absolutely no doubt!"

My mind raced from the thought of marrying her, through nappies and prams and on to my mother's delight at becoming a grandmother. I then began to mentally question how the hell this could have happened.

How could I have been so stupid? But I always used condoms, and I don't remember any accidents. However it happened, it still happened. If she says she is pregnant, I guess she is pregnant. It's not something you can get away with lying about, after all, because, sooner or later, if you don't produce a child, everyone knows you were lying! What the hell am I rambling on about? My head is in a whirl!

"You've gone very quiet. Is it such bad news?"

"I didn't say that."

"You didn't have to! You have been dumbstruck for ten minutes! I thought we felt that we make a good couple? Can't you see us as a family unit?"

Holy shit! What have I done?

"I guess I always wanted to have kids one day…"

She interrupted. "Well then! It looks as if your wish has been granted, doesn't it? You're not getting any younger, you know. We all have to settle down sooner or later."

"I suppose we do…I just assumed it would be later." I smiled at her and wondered if motherhood would make her any more refined. Then I remembered the intensity of our recent lovemaking.

"Oh my God, should we have been going at it, hammer and tongs like that. We could have damaged the baby."

"Don't be silly, of course we couldn't. Babies are well protected, no harm will come to it."

I realised that I did not know anything about parenthood…

Other than how not to do it, courtesy of my mother!

…but I was going to have to do some very quick learning now!

We spent the rest of the day in a reflective mood and didn't speak much at all. We watched a little TV, and she just sat beside me, snuggling up to me, as if trying to show how 'couply' we could be. She left at about four, to get back to the hotel, to work the evening shift. After she had gone, I continued to mull over the situation in my mind and pondered how dramatically this would affect my life. I wondered what Mother would make of Stella as a potential daughter-in-law and shuddered at the prospect. I decided that the time was not right to reveal this news to anyone. We had not yet had time to assimilate the information, let alone decide what our future plans would be. Strangely, I thought about Louise and how different it might have been, if fate had not intervened in out attempts to get properly acquainted. I wished that it could have been her, instead of Stella, then felt guilty for wishing it. I concluded that I had made my bed and would now have to lie on it. How many times did my mother tell me **that** over the years! Suddenly, as if a large coin had suddenly dropped into the tray of a slot machine, my mind began to race along previously uncharted territory.

Wait a minute! I haven't even seen Stella for over a month, let alone slept with her!

In fact, I counted back, and it is five or six weeks since we were together, and I can also remember that the last time she was here, she had offered me oral sex, because she was starting a period. How the hell could she be pregnant? She must be lying...

BIG SPLASH!

How could I have been so stupid? It's so obvious. She must have been sleeping with someone else! Maybe it was a one-night stand, and the bloke was long gone before she knew she was pregnant and that is why she is so keen to make me believe it is mine. Either way, there is something rotten in the state of Denmark. What do I do now?

I decided to sleep on it, and I can't face the quiz tonight, in this frame of mind.

Things to be grateful for

Can't be thinking positively tonight.

Monday 12th November 2000

Word of the Day: idiosyncrasy... peculiarity, unconventional behaviour, eccentricity

2 p.m. in flat

I had to ring Stella last night. I couldn't contain myself any longer. I found her out in another lie, when her uncle answered.

"Hi! Can I speak to Stella please?"

"I'm sorry she is not in right now. Can I take a message?"

"I thought she was working tonight?"

"No, she has gone to see her boyfriend for the weekend. I'm not expecting her back until tomorrow lunchtime."

I see. Can you tell her Ben rang, please?"

"OK. 'Bye."

I was extremely angry and some very unkind thoughts permeated my mind.

I was awake early this morning, in fact I hardly slept at all, and the 'phone rang at 7-30 a.m.

"Hello? Stella?"

"Who the devil is Stella?"

"Oh, it's you, Mother!"

"Thank you for your enthusiasm. I thought you said that I was the only one who calls you so early in the morning?"

It doesn't stop you doing it though, does it?

"And there's me thinking that you never listen to a word I say!"

"So? Who is Stella…and why were you expecting her to call so early? Is something wrong?"

"No. Nothing is wrong."

"I know that tone. It's your sulky tone. Has this Stella upset you? Something's up!"

You don't know how true that is! Something is most definitely "UP". The point is "Who put it up!"

"No really, I'm fine, Mother."

"You know you can always talk to me. I am your mother!"

"If I needed to, I would. I promise."

Like hell I would!

My mind was in a turmoil, and I endured a further ten minutes of Mother's idiosyncrasies, (hurrah!) feeling my lifeblood slowly ebb away, as only the elderly, and one specimen in particular, seem able to provoke. It was about 11-30 a.m. when Stella rang. She was overdoing the chirpy personality, in an obvious attempt to pretend that nothing was wrong.

"So where have you been staying? You said you were working."

"I got the rosters wrong. It wasn't my shift at all, so I went to my mum's."

"No you didn't. You have been gone for the whole weekend. You only spent about half of Sunday with me, so who did you spend Saturday and Sunday night with?"

"What do you care?"

"You're a free agent. You can do what you like. Just don't keep lying to me about it."

She tried to get a word in, but I cut her short. "Yes, but…"

"Just let me finish! You said the other week, on the 'phone, that it was supposed to be one to one… and you made damned sure that Louise doesn't want to give me the time of day…and you are sleeping with someone else yourself!"

"I'm not sleeping with anyone else. No one could match up to you…"

I cut her off again.

"Don't feed me a load of bullshit! I can count you know. You say you are pregnant?"

"You know I am!"

"What was it then, the immaculate fucking conception? Or am I firing superhuman sperms, which fight their way out of condoms, then hide somewhere inside you for a couple of weeks, while you have a period, then miraculously manage to get you pregnant?"

"What are you talking about? I haven't had a period for two months."

"Oh. So you were lying then? About the period you were having last time you stayed?"

"No! I thought I was having one, but I wasn't."

"Like you thought you were working the last five or six weekends, then were working on Saturday, and then again on Sunday night? I know you're lying."

"Oh, what is the point of arguing with you in this mood. I'll talk to you tomorrow."

Now I am totally confused and don't know what to believe any more. If she is lying about work schedules, she could be lying about anything. I don't think I want to work this hard at a relationship.

Things to be Grateful for

Still can't think of anything

Tuesday 14th November 2000

Word of the Day: Irreproachable... blameless, faultless, impossible to disapprove of

4 p.m. in flat

I have just spent what is probably the worst night of my life. I have been wrestling with all the information, with which I was bombarded yesterday, and I am suffering from information overload! I can't make head or tail of it. Working on base today, with Stacey, was quite difficult, especially for her. It did not need a mental athlete to work out that I was in a state, even though I tried very hard not to communicate it to the customers. I did have a little banter with one of the customers, which served to take my mind off my problems, a little. Ironically, the main topic of discussion was TV chat shows, which mainly deal with dysfunctional relationships.

"Hi, what can I get you?"
"I need two Cajun kebabs and two regular fries."
Bit of a southern drawl there.
"Nine-ninety, thanks."
I still can't get used to some Americans' style of demanding instead of asking and never saying please.
"How you doing, Arnie?"
"Fine, how about you?"
"Outstanding!"
"What part of the States are you from?"
"Texas!"

"Thought so! I was listening to Oprah the other day, about how the old Texan cattle dealers were taking her through the courts, because she had said something about beef on her show."

"That'd be correct. Them cattle barons got a loada power back there... and they know how to use it!"

"They didn't win though, did they?"

"No, that Oprah has a loada power of her own. You watch a lot of American shows?"

"Yeah, I'm a bit of an American talk show addict!"

I find myself fighting to avoid copying his Texan accent.

"What about that Jerry Springer?"

"Shit, that's a whole nuther story!"

Americans' propensity to split infinitives jars me enough, but when they split words like "another whole" into "a whole nuther", it drives me to distraction! Every time Startrek opens with the words, "to boldly go, I find myself mentally..."

And not always just mentally!

"... shouting, "to go boldly, you moron!""

Another mystery, to me, is why the audience members on most American talk shows pronounce the word whore as though it were a garden implement, by shouting "Hoe!" at any female remotely accused, by another guest, of daring to sleep with more than one person... usually having heard only one side of any story. If the errant party is male, they are satisfied with just booing him. It is a moot point, indeed, about the quality of humanity in the audience, that they think it is appropriate behaviour in a decent human being, to verbally abuse another human being in such a coarse and vulgar manner, regardless of their personal life's foibles. When invited to comment, on mike, from the audience, people either try to be pseudo psychologists, or try to be clever and gain their ten seconds of fame on national TV, making moronic jibes, little realising that they often come over to the viewer as no better and, often worse, than the guests. I guess that chat show producers are very careful to choose audience members who have led blameless and irreproachable (hurrah!) existences!

Pots and kettles maybe?

Perhaps I have misunderstood and the audience are really communicating that they feel that a spell of gardening, would do the errant guest some good? Most chat show hosts seem to really wind the guests up, try to get them at each other's throats and then castigate them for their behaviour. The worst of these is definitely Jerry Springer. He is a master at provoking the confrontational violence, and then takes cheap shots at them, making them look stupid...

And for the most part they need no such assistance!

... while his heavies stop the guests from ripping each other's heads off. The thing which amuses me most though, is how Jerry Springer can do a show which has people admitting to being prostitutes and strippers; sleeping with the partners of their best friends, of either sex; with all members of their own family from siblings to parents; having rampant sex at the age of 12; being secretly gay, bisexual and any other variation you can think of; where grown men wear nappies and actually have women changing them, after crapping and peeing in them; but God forbid they should ever show a nipple on TV! Even more ironic is that, more often than not, the most outrageous behaviour seems to come from people in the South, in the "bible belt". Maybe I might have to draw this one by the chaplain, next time he drops by for a kebab! The worst part of all is the "final thought" segment. Having created problems which didn't exist, exacerbated the problems which may have existed, encouraged the mayhem on stage and even, in many cases, provoked couples to split up, he then has the gall to thank them and hope that they can work out their problems! He then finishes with a "piece to camera", taking the moral high ground, and stating how morally reprehensible the guests behaviour seems to have been. Then he gives advice, in retrospect, on how they should have behaved or lived their lives.

What a sanctimonious bastard!

That said, if the people on the likes of "The Jerry Springer Show" are remotely real or genuine, or are in any way representative of the rank-and-file American, then it is an entire nation of cackers! I don't believe it is representative. It has to be rigged. I imagine it is about as genuine as the aggression on WWF wrestling.

WWF? What is the World Wildlife Fund doing getting involved with violence, real or faked? (Joke...! Just in case, when I read this journal in about 20 years time, I am horrified that I didn't know the difference!)

Talking of the World Wildlife Fund, I wonder if Prince Philip is still patron. I also wonder if he has yet managed to fathom the irony of a person in that position, spending their spare time shooting anything that moves and employing peasants to disturb the undergrowth to ensure that anything not moving does move! I think it is about time our royal family set an example and stopped terrorising the country's wildlife just for fun!

At the end of lunchtime trade, Stacey was very motherly and put her arm around my shoulder.

"Whatever is wrong, Ben? You haven't been yourself for a few days."

"Oh? And who have I been then?"

My attempt to divert her with humour was an abject failure.

"I mean it, something's wrong."

"You don't want to know, Stacey! My life was complicated enough, but it is now the mother of all complicated lives!"

"Well, you strike me as a pretty well-balanced kind of guy. What is so complicated that it is weighing on your mind so heavily? I know I haven't known you long, but I'm a pretty good judge of character, and you deal with problems so well, usually."

"Well, it's not every day that you are told you going to be a father!"

Oh my God, what the hell made me tell her that?

"Promise me you won't say anything to anyone about this!"

"Of course I won't...Wow! Isn't that normally grounds for congratulations? Why do you say things are complicated?"

Oh well, in for a penny in for a pound!

"Are you sure you want to know?"

"As long as you don't think that I'm poking my nose in your business."

"OK! It's a long story, but the crux of the matter is whether or not I could be the father."

"O-oh!" She intoned in the manner of a tellytubby.

"O-oh, indeed. We haven't been together, not even in each other's company, let alone bed, for five or six weeks."

"Well, that doesn't mean you are not the father. Maybe she's six weeks gone."

"Ah yes...but...the last time we were together, she was... how can I say this tactfully?   She was at that time of the month."

"You can say, *"having a period"*. You won't shock me."

"OK, she was having a period. Or, at least, that's what she said. But, when I pointed out to her that we had not slept together since, she claimed that she only thought that she was having a period, but actually wasn't! Call me old-fashioned, but I thought it is pretty obvious to a woman if she is or isn't."

"Not necessarily, it is possible when a woman is pregnant, to have spotting. That could lead her to believe she is having a period. "

"Oh God, so I could still be the father?"

"I don't know her, but it is possible. Would it be good news if you were the father?"

"I don't know. It wasn't something I'd planned on...not yet... and probably not with her."

"Then why have unprotected sex with her? HELLO!!"

I hate that American habit of saying 'hello' when they are not actually greeting someone!

" That is one of the problems! I'm not stupid! I did use protection... every time!"

"They are not 100% reliable, Ben. You could still be the father."

This conversation was supposed to have helped. I am now more confused than I was before. I don't know if I believe that Stella has been faithful to me, or not; whether she is pregnant, or not; whether she had a period that weekend or not; whether I am the father, or not, if she is pregnant. I think we need to talk.

Things to be grateful for

Is very difficult, to define gratitude at this point in time! Until I know, once and for all, the answers to the questions above, I can't say if I'm grateful or not, about being a father or about not being one! My mind is in a whirl!

Wednesday 15th November 2000

Word of the Day: encapsulate... summarise, express the essential features of

9 a.m. in flat

Last night, at about 9 p.m., the telephone rang.
"Hello." I recognised Stella's voice immediately. It sounded extremely tentative.
"Hello Stella! To what do I owe this pleasure?"
"I see. You are still in **that** sort of mood!"
"What did you expect? You drop a bombshell like that, after the recent history we've had and, when I question it, you go off on one!"
"I think you'll find it was you who went off on one, Ben!"
"**You** hung up on **me**!"
"You didn't ring me back though, did you?"
"I'm not into mind games like you are. I just want to know, am I the father or not?"
"I thought you said you couldn't be?"
"Stop fucking about and tell me."
"Of course you are!"
"So what about all these mysterious disappearances? Are you telling me there is absolutely no chance it is anyone else's?"
There was a short silence, which spoke volumes.
"I'll take that as a "no" then, shall I? I thought something was going on!"

"You didn't wait for me to answer, did you? There is no one else. I just want us to be together, to be a family. I know it's a shock for you, it was for me too, but I know that once you get used to it, you will be as happy about it as I am."

You know an awful lot then, Stella! More than me in fact!

I was convinced of only one thing. She was lying. I've come to the conclusion that it's easy to tell when Stella is lying. Her lips will be moving, and you can hear her voice!

"So, you want me to believe that the period you had was just a figment of your imagination?"

"I noticed blood and thought it was one, but it couldn't have been, could it? I wish I'd never told you, and all this wouldn't have happened."

"I wish I knew. We were using condoms, for Christ's sake, and I thought you were on the pill anyway."

"I haven't been on the pill for months. Until I met you, I haven't been out with anyone for months."

Believe that if you like!

I left the conversation less than convinced, and she is going to ring me on Thursday. It is so difficult to encapsulate (hurrah!) your thoughts over the phone. I think we need to be face-to-face to discuss an important issue like this. You can tell a lot from body language.

Things to be grateful for

Not much at the moment!

Thursday 16th November 2000

Word of the day: re-establish... consolidate anew

Ricky Hill has been sacked. I'll bet he is gutted. He is a genuinely nice guy and a great coach, but his inexperience as a manager seems to have been his Achilles heel. Obviously, the board see it that way. Lil

Fucillo only came to the club about six weeks ago as a scout; next thing you know he's coaching and then he's assistant manager; now he's manager. I should think that at this rate of progress he'll be chairman by Friday week! I know one thing. He has got a right banana skin for his first match in charge. Rushden and Diamonds in the FA Cup on Friday night. They have nothing to lose and Luton have everything. It's live on Sky TV and I have to work! Damn it! Rushden and Diamonds are near the top of the Conference, so if we get relegated and they get promoted, we could meet on level terms next season. It doesn't bear thinking about!

Frank Dykstra called today and has made an appointment for me to go, next Wednesday to Allington, to sign the new contract. Thank God for that. A little security in the making.

Things to be grateful for

1) A new contract and the security that comes with it.
2) Maybe a change of manager might help Luton to re-establish (hurrah!) themselves.

Saturday 18th November 2000

Word of the day: Perplex... puzzle, bewilder, disconcert

9 a.m. just stirring.

Luton managed to scrape home 1-0 last night. I recorded the game and watched it when I got in. They were very fortunate, but a win is a win, especially in the cup. We have had plenty of defeats this season, when we have been unfortunate to lose, so maybe this will redress the balance a little.

I have no clue what is going on with Stella. She was supposed to ring me on Thursday, but didn't bother and when I rang the hotel, on Friday, her uncle said she had gone out with her boyfriend, and he was not expecting her back until Saturday morning. This is so perplexing (hurrah!). Is her uncle winding me up, or is she playing me for a fool?

4 p.m.

I have just had a long telephone conversation with Stella, and I am now in shock!

"Hi, Ben, how are you?"

"Fine. I thought you were ringing me on Thursday to discuss coming over here this weekend, to talk about things?"

"Yes sorry, I got called on to work."

"You could have let me know! It wouldn't have hurt you."

"Yeah! Sorry. What's up? You sound so distant."

"Your uncle told me you were out with your boyfriend last night... all night. D'you take me for an idiot?"

"Oh!"

"Yes! **"Oh!"** Why have you been lying to me? What is the point?"

"Er...I...er...what can I say? I... Well... I didn't know what was going on."

"Well if you don't know what's going on, how the hell can anybody else?"

"Well I've sort of been seeing someone..."

"You don't "sort of" see someone, you either do or you don't. That's like "sort of" being pregnant...? Hmmm.... now that you mention it...."

She made a noise, which showed she disliked the comment, while I continued unabated.

"There's you giving me all that crap about wanting to be a family and being one on one; giving poor Louise all that verbal and, all the time, you were seeing someone else yourself. How can you justify that? How could I ever trust you again?"

"You remember I told you I was engaged? Then when we broke up... I went up to Skipton to work... To sort of... Get a fresh start?"

"You seem to "sort of" do lots of "things". What's this particular "thing" got to do with anything?"

"Well... It's him I have been seeing."

"Oh great. So why didn't you tell me?"

"Because I love you."

"Yeah right! You love me, so you start going out with your ex-fiancé and lie to me about it, just to show how much you do? That's a fantastic basis for a permanent relationship!"

"We just bumped into each other in town and it just happened. I'm sorry."

"You just bumped into each other? So hard that you landed on your back; minus your knickers; with your legs apart? I suppose he fell forward, penis erect from the shock of the collision; his pants fell down, and he landed cock first, so far up you that you got pregnant? I'd like to see that on an insurance claim form!"

"Very funny! It wasn't like that."

"I would hope not! It would have frightened the shit out of anyone walking along the same piece of pavement! I was being facetious. So.... I guess it **is** his baby?"

"It.... could be, I suppose. Anyway, he still wants to marry me, he asked me again last night."

"Well, you'd better do it then."

"I already said *"yes"*." She said petulantly.

"In which case, there's not much more to say is there?"

"I'd rather marry you, Ben. Really I would. You know I would. We still could, you know."

"It's a bit late for that now, isn't it? You'd have more chance of being struck by lightning!"

"Well, thanks a fucking bunch! I didn't think you could be this much of a bastard!"

Am I missing something? Or is she really in "Cloud Cuckoo Land"? It seems to me that I am the injured party here!

I hung up, my mouth so wide open with incredulity, that it took me ten minutes to get it to shut!

Things to be grateful for

1) I'm not lumbered with a sham marriage.
2) I'm not the father of her child (or am I?)
3) Stella is out of my life for good!
4) I can now get on with my life.

Monday 20<u>th</u> November 2000

Word of the day: Vitriolic... caustic, hostile speech

3 p.m. just home from shopping!

I awoke this morning, with a thousand little men, with pneumatic drills, apparently trying to repair roads inside my head. However, I forced myself to drink some water, eat some dry toast and get my backside into town. I had decided to spend some money to cheer myself up. There is nothing like a little retail therapy for restoring one's confidence and generating a little feel-good factor!

I have just returned home, having purchased a new pair of black loafers, some cool black trousers and a black button-down collar shirt. I will look like a warlock! Black and mysterious. OK, babes, come and get me!

Last night, I phoned Jamie and told him the latest news about Stella and me. I also explained more fully why Louise is not still an option.

"Fuck me!" He replied, after listening intently to my confession.

"It's a kind offer, Jamie, but I will have to decline!" I replied.

"Ha! Ha! You haven't lost your sense of humour, then? Hey! Why don't we give the quiz a miss and go down the club instead. We could have a game of snooker and get totally rat-arsed. That would liven you up, a bit. I'll ring the others and see if they fancy it. We can still go, even if they don't. What do you say?"

"OK! I didn't fancy the quiz much anyway."

We met at the club, and the lads took it upon themselves to cheer me up, in the time-honoured fashion. This, of course, involved in the utilisation of copious quantities of alcohol and volumes of "verbal support."

"Well, she was an old slapper anyway!" Jamie tried to help in his own inimitable way.

"Plenty more fish in the sea!" Said Gordon.

"You could try my missus if you are desperate," Brian offered. "You might have more luck with her than me! You might even get her jump-started and remind her what it's for!"

This induced the first ripple in an evening full of laughter. We played a few games of snooker, which Jamie won quite easily. He really has an eye for skill sports. I pushed him quite close on one game, though. Eventually, however, coordination lost its battle with the alcohol, and we sat down to talk, (truth to tell, before we fell down!)

"I could have been a pro snooker player," Jamie boasted. "When I was young, I had my own little cue, a frilly shirt, the bow tie and everything. I only needed the waistcoat. I asked for one for my birthday, but my mum said I was growing too quickly, so it wouldn't last me very long, and they were quite expensive. She liked to get value for money!"

"So, just because you had a frilly shirt and tie left over from some poxy wedding, you reckon you could have been a pro snooker player?" I enquired. "Then your mum fucked up your career by not buying you the waistcoat? What an evil cow!" I said sarcastically. Everyone laughed.

"Very funny, Benny boy!" Jamie responded, not amused.

Gordon tried to lighten the mood with a joke.

"What's the definition of Australian foreplay?" He began.

"I've fuckin' heard this!" Jamie interjected.

"Well! Not everyone has, so shut the fuck up for a minute!" Gordon advised tenderly.

"Go on then, tell us." Said Brian.

Gordon continued, in a poor attempt at an Aussie accent.

"Brace yourself, Raeleen!"

"Very good! I got one," Brian came in.

"This bloke tells his mate that he is divorcing his wife. His mate says, "Why would you want to do that after ten happy years of marriage?" He says, "It gets so boring poking in the same hole, day in, day out. I fancy something different." His mate says, "Why don't you try turning her over and poke her other hole, for a change?" He says, "What? And have a house full of kids?""

Everyone laughed; in fact we had a really good laugh all night, which is probably the reason I woke up this morning feeling like I had a 200 lb head on top of a 100 lb body.

I chose the word of the day as I was sure something vitriolic would come up but it didn't, dammit!

Things to be grateful for

1) Another good night out with the lads.
2) I didn't think much about anything last night, not even women.
3) I'm looking forward to the rest of today off!

Wednesday 22nd November 2000

Word of the day: Malevolent... wishing evil to others

4-30 p.m. returned from war!

I arrived on base earlier this morning and had reluctantly got both Stacey and Ashley to work, while I went over to RAF Allington to meet Frank Dykstra and sign the new contract. I was a little uncomfortable leaving them on their own for the first time, but I anticipated that it would only take about one hour, and I could be back before the rush began.

I sure as Hell wasn't ready for what transpired. They obviously don't like the competition I am providing on base and want me out of there so they concocted a web of intrigue which culminated in their saying that they can't make the contract permanent. I am so angry with them. I have been shafted bigtime! This has nothing whatsoever to do with the issues they raised and everything to do with their losing profit from their cafeteria. If they had had the balls to come to me and say, *"Arnie, we're really sorry, but this isn't working for us. We're losing more from our profits in the cafeteria than we are making in commission from you"*, I would have conceded the point, shaken their hand and left. I am a businessman. I could respect a commercially sound decision like that, but I believe this action is to cover their own arses, so that when the guys on base kick up over my being kicked out, they can say they were justified. Dykstra is a malevolent (Hurrah!) weasel. Oh well! I think I will set up outside the base and see what happens then. At least all profits from trading outside will be my own!

Things to be grateful for

1) I love it when I get the upper hand in a war of words!
2) I won't have to lose my income for two months by taking a standard contract.
3) Any business I can do outside the base will be totally commission-free!

Thursday 23rd November 2000

Word of the day: Drastically... pertaining to having strong or far reaching effect

3 p.m. just home from shopping again!

Today is Thanksgiving Day, so the base is virtually closed for five days. This has given me the opportunity to take back the trousers I bought on Monday to exchange them for the next size up. The original pair I purchased cramped my bits for space! This is the first time I've ever bought trousers with a 34-inch waist! I must cut down on the old alcohol, I think. While I was out, I had a coffee in Marks & Spencer's cafeteria. It was almost as expensive as the bloody trousers! How do they justify those sorts of prices? On my menu, it is only 60p for a coffee, and I am taking the piss charging that much! It is a long time since I was last hiking around the big stores, and they have obviously changed drastically, (hurrah!), in the meantime. One thing I did notice, which had eluded my observation previously, was a breast-feeding room! Now, that is a wonderful service to provide. I failed to understand why there wasn't a long queue of men at the door, waiting to avail themselves of such an opportunity, and thought about starting one! Seriously though, this must have been an idea, which was created by a man, trying to impress women. I mean, it was in the ladies toilets, for goodness sake! I wonder if the genius that came up with this idea would like to eat **his** lunch in the Gents?

I won £10 on the lottery last night. How have they got the nerve to advertise with the slogan, "It could be you!"? You have to be suspicious of an organisation, which is backed by the government and, which makes claims like that. Previous governments have said, "HIV - 32 million to one against - It isn't going to happen" - then they approve the National Lottery (odds against winning the jackpot 54 million to one?) saying, "It could be you!" Scary or what?

Things to be grateful for

1) £10 win on the lottery. (It wasn't me!)
2) My new trousers fit superbly.
3) I have a reduced workload due to Thanksgiving.

Sunday 26ᵗʰ November 2000

Word of the day: Sporadic... scattered, occurring only occasionally or in a few places.

6-45 a.m. unconscious!
(telephone rings!)

I reach instinctively to answer it, then realise that it is very early and decide to ignore it. Unfortunately, I have forgotten to turn off the answering machine and it cuts in.
"Hello, this is Ben Arnold, I am unable to take your call at the moment, please leave a message after the tone, and I'll ring you soon as I can...beep!"
"Benjamin Arnold, I know you're there. Pick up the phone, it's your mother!"
There is a long silence, as she waits for me to pick up the phone, but I am nothing if not obstinate and refuse to do so. I felt myself gently drifting back to sleep.

9-00 a.m. watching sky sports and having breakfast!
(Telephone rings again!)

This time I picked it up.
"Hello, Mother! How are you this bright and, until now, serene morning?"
Either my small injection of satire evaded her, or she chose to ignore it; probably the latter.
"I'm fine, thank you, Benjamin. Although the morning is half gone. I tried to ring you earlier. Were you asleep?"
"If I was, how would I know? Sleep is unconscious, so if I said, "yes", I would be lying."
"I see. We're in one of those moods, are we? Do I have to pay a fee to talk to you these days? Should I make an appointment next time?"

"That would be wonderful, Mother, but my appointment book does not begin at 6-45 a.m."

"So, you were awake, then?"

"What do you mean, Mother?"

"I didn't mention a time. I said "earlier." If you knew it was 6-45 a.m. you must have been awake and heard it ring."

Once again, I have been outwitted by Mrs Annoying of Luton! I guess I will have to come clean.

"OK, Mother, you win. I did hear it ring, but I was just too tired to answer it. After working Friday night and Saturday night, I am just not at my best on Sunday mornings before 8 a.m."

"I had something important to tell you, that would not wait."

"In that case, I'm sorry. It was morally reprehensible of me and I apologise unreservedly. What was it?"

"What was what?"

"The important something, that couldn't wait, that you rang to tell me, before the sun had woken up."

"I can't remember now!"

My mind turned instantly to blancmange! How I resisted the temptation to scream I'll never know! I am fighting a battle that I can never win.

Mental note: buy a white flag and wave it at Mother, the next time I see her!

Things to be grateful for

1) I am not at Mother's house, which has saved her from being shot!

2) It is Sunday. Mother's phone call has taken place already, meaning I have a peaceful day ahead.

3) Her telephone calls are only sporadic (Hurrah!) and hurrah for the fact also!

4) The Far Canal lads are meeting for lunch, then tonight is quiz night!

Monday 27th November 2000

Word of the day: Potatory... pertaining to drink

3-00 p.m. bored and hungry

There is nothing in the flat to eat, and I really should think about going to the supermarket. Having said that, I really can't be bothered. I'll get a piece of toast in a minute, provided the small quantity of bread, which has been cowering in the far corner of the refrigerator for over a week, has not come to life and walked away of its own accord. The word of the day is sponsored by last night's pub quiz. One of the questions was: "What does the word potatory mean?" There were several funny answers to that question, like "having the flavour of potatoes"; "potato-like"; "relating to potatoes"; and one team even thought it was a potato farm. Apparently, if the quizmaster is to be believed, it has nothing to do with potatoes at all. It derives from the Latin "potare" – to drink - and is the root for the words potion and potable. I love the way the teams moan and groan with trick questions like that one! How I am going to manage to use it in context, though, is still a mystery to me at the moment!

We had another good evening at the quiz, following on from a really "blokey" Sunday lunch at the same pub. Our waitress was a very pretty young lady, whose name was Pat. This fact was apparent, due to the badge bearing her name, which she was wearing on her blouse, just above her left breast.

Jamie could not resist asking her, "Is that your name, darling, or is it an invitation?" Brian, not to be outdone, pointed to her left breast and ventured, "If that one is called "Pat", what's the other one called?"

She smiled sweetly, pretending that she had not heard those remarks a hundred times before, but as I raised my eyebrows and gave her a look of resignation, she responded with a warm smile, opened her eyelids wide and rolled her eyes back in their sockets. This response adequately communicated the words, *"What a pair of dickheads!"* I felt constrained, mentally, to agree with that observation.

It is now common knowledge within the group that I am, once again, without a girlfriend, and this seemed to be the main topic of conversation for most of lunchtime.

"Maria's got a friend who is just divorced. Want me to fix you up with a blind date? She's not bad." Brian offered.

"I think I have been associated with enough neurotic women, lately, to last me a lifetime. I think I'll pass. She's probably got enough on her mind with the divorce."

"I don't know. You might be good for each other. Anyhow, it's your call. Let me know if you change your mind."

"Poor old Ben!" Jamie cut in. "He's been blown out more times than a nun's candle!"

For once, Jamie avoided one of his famous tumbleweed moments and managed to induce genuine laughter. Even I was forced to smile.

"What can I say? It's true."

"Why haven't you been in touch with the American bird you were shagging?" Gordon tried to be a little more constructive, in a very down-to-earth manner!

"How do you know I haven't?"

"You'd have said something, you pillock!"

"True enough! Anyway, what's the point? She's in Texas and I'm here. And in any case I've lost her e-mail address."

"You useless tosser! Sounds like an excuse to me." Brian added a helpful aside.

Meanwhile, Jamie had got another round in. Gordon had picked up his new pint and took a hearty swig. It was quickly obvious that this pint must have come from the bottom of the barrel, because he had already drunk two pints from the same pump and they were OK, but the head on this one was virtually non-existent. Having said that, the real clue was that Gordon spat it out and exclaimed, "Fucking hell, that beer is disgusting. It's flatter than a witch's tit!"

He took the pint back to the bar, to find that the landlord had just gone to change the barrel, so he was not surprised to hear Gordon's complaint when he returned. Gordon's potatory (hurrah! Bonus point I think!) problems sorted out, he returned to the table and we were able to continue with lunch, Brian had noticed a couple of young women who were eating lunch in the pub's restaurant annexe.

"How about the blonde one, Ben? She looks a bit of all right!"

"Nah!" said Jamie. "Ben likes 'em with big tits. She must be a witch! Her chest's like an ironing board!"

"What are you talking about, you moron?" I chided Jamie.

"Gordon said his beer was flatter than a..." I cut him off before he had finished, as I picked up the trail of crumbs that had led him to that comment.

"OK! OK! I get it. But it is not a very kind observation, is it? She is probably a very nice girl."

"Probably a lesbian! Look at the pair of them! Two girls having lunch together?" Brian said in a questioning tone, nodding his head "knowingly" as he did so.

"You think so? And they're probably looking at us and thinking, "Four blokes together...hmmm...I'll bet they're two pairs of uphill gardeners!" I replied mischievously.

"Of course they aren't! We're macho blokes...you couldn't mistake us for poofters." He responded.

I put on a stereotypical effeminate voice, put my hand out with a limp wrist and said, "Oh, I'm sorry! I forgot that gay guys walk around with a sign that says, "Look at me! Whoops! I'm a fairy!"" I finished by putting my other hand on my hip and ended up looking like a teapot!

"Hey, Ben! You're too fucking good at that. You want to be careful, mate!" Gordon was splitting his sides at his own appraisal of my stylised impersonation. Unfortunately, I don't think any of them realised I was being ironic and sarcastic and took my performance at face value. I decided I needed to be more direct to make my point.

"Not all homosexuals look like escapees from "The Village People", you know!"

"No? You can tell 'em a mile away!" Gordon persisted and received grunts of agreement from the others.

I give up! There is no hope for any of them!

This, then, was the tone of our lunchtime revels. I have to say, though, that it was good to get out. One of the two girls in the other part of the restaurant, ironically, not the one that Brian had suggested, did exchange eye contact with me on a few occasions, but there was no way on this Earth that I was going to speak to her, while this bunch was remotely within earshot! Yet another opportunity falls by the wayside.

On the subject of Jenny, I would like to contact her, but now I am off base, I can't even ask Robbie to get her e-mail address for me. My point about the distance is valid, though. When am I going to get the time to go to the USA? Maybe I could try going on the Internet and meet someone in a chat room. I've heard that relationships can be struck up quite easily in that way. There's not much to lose. It is not as though they can see you through the Internet and best of all, neither can the lads from the Far Canal!

Things to be grateful for

1) A peaceful day off.
2) We managed to eat lunch yesterday, without being thrown out!

Thursday 30th November 2000

Word of the day: Equitable... reasonable, impartial, just.

11-15 a.m. On trailer outside base

Robbie and his entourage came out to order food.
"Where have you lot been? I thought you had all died!"
"Nah! We just don't get the opportunity to get off base very often. And, when you move your car, you lose your space in the car park. Jeez... I hope you guys can get back on base pretty soon. We really miss your food, and you must do a lot more business inside?"

"Yes. A lot more. Anyway, how have you all been? Heard anything from Jenni?"

"Ah! Yes! You are in big trouble! I got an e-mail last week... and she said in it, that you have not made contact since she left. What's up, Ben? I thought you really liked her."

"Yes, I do. I just can't find the piece of paper with her phone number and e-mail address on it, and you guys haven't been here since I moved outside. So, I haven't had a chance."

"Well, let me ring you when I get back to the office. I got her e-mail. I'll let you have it."

"Thanks. I was worried that she would think the worst."

"You are right. She's one paranoid chick! Make sure you write her."

"So how's all the election buzz on base? With all my recent disasters, I haven't really kept up with the news."

"You are joking man! Everyone's bored out of their brains with the whole thing."

"I guess."

Oh my God! I'm sounding more like an American every day, with all this, "I guess," business and other stuff!

"Only in America could you have a one-day election that lasts a month!" I joked.

"Yeah! And it ain't over yet! They are still arguing over the Florida recounts. Whether they can have the time or not... whether it's constitutional... if the court needs to set a cut-off date. It's a whole big mess, and the world is laughing its ass off at us. Anyways... it looks like whoever wins Florida wins the election.

"Not that it will make much difference. They both seem to have had a personality bypass. I still reckon George Dubya will win. You can't let someone override the whole system."

"Yeah but... Gore won the popular vote."

"What the hell does that mean?"

"He got more votes than Bush."

"So what? You can't change the rules of an election halfway through, just because one of the candidates doesn't like the outcome!" I laughed.

"What do you mean?"

"Both candidates knew, before the election began, that the US system provided a winner based on the number of states won, not the total number of votes gained."

"Well yeah, I know that."

"Well it's a pity that Gore didn't! Our system could throw up the same thing, I would think. The country is broken up into constituencies, and each has an election to find a Member of Parliament. The party with the most seats wins the election, but I don't think that all constituencies have the same number of voters. So it is possible to win without having the majority of votes."

We chatted for a while about various arguments relating to their electoral debacle and the relative merits and drawbacks of our respective systems, but I felt I failed to convince him that the original result was fair and equitable, (hurrah!), under the rules which stood, prior to the commencement of the election. He telephoned as soon as he got back to his office and gave me Jenni's e-mail address. She is on AOL, the same as I am, so we should be able to make contact easily. However, this is not the e-mail address, which I had written down before she left, because I would have noticed that she was on AOL.

Things to be grateful for

1) I have an e-mail address for Jenni.
2) She is on AOL so we can talk in real time on Instant Messaging. (If I can work out how to do it!)
3) It was good to see Robbie and friends again.

December 2000

Sunday 3rd December 2000

Word of the day: Meander... wander, roam, amble

8-01 a.m. still asleep
(telephone rings)

Did my clock stop at 8-01 p.m. last night? I cannot believe that my mother actually listened to what I said and has called after 8-00 a.m. by choice!
"Hello Mother! Thank you for allowing me to sleep in!"
Sleep in? What am I saying? It's still the middle of the bloody night!
"I didn't know what time it was! I've been up half the night with your father. He's had stomach pains all night, again."
"I'm sorry to hear that. What's caused that, then? Have you been cooking again?"
"You cheeky little sod! You have been glad enough of my cooking, my lad!"
LAD? How rude!
"Anyway. Stop interrupting and let me tell you."
"All right, I'm trying."
"Yes you are...very trying!"
OUCH! Why do I end up playing her straight man, when it's me that is trying to be funny?
"I had to get the doctor out of bed at 7 o'clock, to examine him."
Couldn't resist it!

"Why did you want to examine the doctor, when it's Dad who has the problem?"

"Don't be stupid, Benjamin you know exactly what I mean...I got the doctor out of bed to examine your father."

"It was lucky the doctor was there!"

"What?"

"In bed. Anyway, what were you doing in bed with the doctor?"

And why am I in such a ridiculous mood?

"And why are you in such a bloody ridiculous mood?"

Whoa...that was scary!

"I don't know...Why am I in such a ridiculous mood?"

Why can't I control this mouth today?

(Click!)

Oops...now I have done it. I don't know what is wrong with me this morning. I'd better get showered and ring her back, or I'll never hear the last of it!

8-30 a.m. in the shower singing "Oh What a Beautiful Morning" at the top of my voice.

(telephone rings)

Two observations meander (hurrah!) aimlessly through my mind.

1) What the hell is going on in my head this morning!

2) Even though I am naked and soaking wet, I'd better answer that and make peace with Mother before it gets out of hand!

"Hello Mother! Look I'm really sor..."

"Hi Ben, do I sound like your mother?"

The soft, East Anglian accent of Stella was unmistakeable.

"What do **you** want?" I could not stop the venom in my mind overflowing into my voice.

"That's a nice way to greet a lover."

"What can I do for you?"

"I just rang to tell you I'm missing you. And to check that you are OK."

"I'm OK, apart from the fact that I am standing here dripping water all over the carpet. I was in the shower."

"Mmmmm! Thank you for putting that sexy picture in my mind! I wish I was there now! Kneeling at your feet...stroking and...."

"OK, OK, look... can we do this another time when I am a little less damp?"

"OK I'll ring you later. 'Bye"

"No, look I didn't mean..."

(Click.)

Argghh! Now she has taken it as an invitation to ring me again!

I was feeling a little shivery, by this point, and slipped back under the warm spray for a little longer.

(telephone rings yet again)

Bollocks! If that's her again, I'll kill her!

"Look... give me a chance to get dry.... Hi, Mummy!"

She began to laugh! "It's a long time since I heard you call me "Mummy.""

I know which buttons to press in an emergency!

"So, can we take your humble apologies for being so rude, as read, and avoid a blazing argument?" She said smilingly.

"I don't know what had got into me this morning. I think the Devil made me do it!"

"I'm sure he did! So...where was I? Oh Yes! The doctor...got out of his **OWN** bed and arrived at about half past seven. He began to push and poke at your father's tummy, and said, *"Ahhh! I can feel something there. I think it is probably just constipation or a wind lock..."* well, talk about timing... the doctor had only just got the words out, and your father let off the loudest noise you've ever heard! Talk about embarrassment. I went as red as a beetroot!"

"I'll bet Dad didn't. If he'd been in pain all night I should imagine he was glad to be rid of it!"

"Yes but wait on... that isn't the funniest bit! It wasn't our own doctor. Doctor Shah is on holiday, and this was a whatsit?"

"Locum?"

"Yes, that's it. He gave him a prescription for something minty. And guess what? The name on the bottom was Doctor Windass!" At which point, she began laughing, cackling on like a broody hen, for what seemed like ages. Due to my previous unacceptable behaviour, I found myself having to laugh patronisingly, until she stopped.

"Now Benjamin... what are you doing for Christmas?"

"I still don't know, Mother. I need to wait until I know what is happening at the base, before I can commit myself."

"You know you are always welcome here. I will not allow you to spend Christmas all alone!"

"OK. If I find myself alone at Christmas, I will come to you."
"You promise?"

"Cross my heart and hope to di..."

"Don't say that! It's horrible."

I resisted the extreme temptation to enter into a discussion on the topic, said my goodbyes and returned to the shower yet again, only to find that, because I had left it running during both phone calls, the water was now freezing cold.

Things to be grateful for

1) I still have a month to make alternative arrangements for Christmas!

2) I got out of the conversation with Stella very quickly, before I said something I would have been ashamed of.

3) Dad has managed to fill their residence with a brown haze, and Mother will be castigating him about it, even as I write this!

Monday 4th December 2000

Word of the day: Assertion... statement, claim, idea.

9 a.m. Fresh and squeaky clean from the shower!

I spent most of yesterday out of the house and, so, managed to avoid any further telephone calls. Once again, the lads decided to give the quiz a miss and go to the club instead. Also once again, Jamie took the rest of us to the cleaners on the snooker table. Copious quantities of alcohol were, as usual, imbibed, and plans for a future foray into the Peterborough club scene were made. I am not sure how it happened, but the conversation drifted towards my business and then on to what is ethical and non ethical.

"How come you always go wandering around the pub before closing time, on Friday night?" Gordon enquired.

"So that my usual clientele are aware that I am open for business and then, when the pub turns out, they come over to order. I call it my 'Pavlov's dog' walk."

"How does that work then?" As usual Brian was not paying attention.

"You've heard of Pavlov's dog experiments? Where he rings a bell and the dog eats. After a while, the dog associates the sound of the bell with food and its mouth waters. When the people in the pub see me, their mouths start to water, and they feel like they need a kebab. They don't know why, it's subliminal."

"Sub-fucking-normal if you ask me!" Jamie observed.

"No one did ask you though, did they?" I felt constrained to point out to him.

"Bollocks!" Was my response from Jamie.

The Wit and Wisdom of Jamie Ryecroft" is one of the shortest books known to man, even shorter than *"The Italian book of War Heroes"* and *"The Jewish Anthology of Athletics Record Holders"*!

"What about vegetarians, then?" Brian tried to get the conversation back to some kind of order.

"What about them?" I replied, wondering where this was leading.

"I notice you do vegetarian stuff, veggie burgers and sausages."

"Yes. What about it? Do you actually have a point?"

"Yeah! Why do you pander to a bunch of grass munchers?" It was obvious that the alcohol was once again taking charge of the conversation.

"Because, there's a lot of 'em about. And they eat, just the same as everyone else! I get a lot of business from vegetarians, because I take the trouble to stock vegetarian food."

"I'd have a lot more respect for vegetarians," Jamie rejoined, "if they had a bit more respect for the environment."

"You really are a knob, Jamie. People who are vegetarian are probably more likely to care about the environment than you do!"

"So why do they go around fucking eating it, then?" he rested his case.

I sat for a few seconds, waiting for him to laugh, but it did not happen! Neither did the others laugh, leaving me to believe that they actually thought he had a good point! I am not sure if it was the alcohol in me, but their lack of laughter at such a ridiculous assertion (Hurrah!) struck me as extremely funny, and I succumbed to a fit of giggles. Although they didn't realise what I was laughing at, they all began to laugh with me. The more I laughed, the more they did, and, the more they laughed, without knowing why, the funnier it seemed to me, causing an uncontrolled session of laughter, which left me with my ribs aching and the desire to throw up. Luckily, I avoided doing so. One thing I do know is that these three relatively intelligent human beings, become increasingly moronic, in direct proportion to the amount of alcohol they have consumed.

Things to be grateful for

1) A damn good laugh in times of adversity.
2) A new slant on the selfishness of vegetarians, as supplied by the inebriated viewpoint of James Ryecroft.
3) The realisation that I am a superior human being to all of them!

Tuesday 5th December 2000

Word of the day: Riposte... wisecrack, retort, reply.

3 p.m. Back home from outside the base

I am so tired today, I feel sick! As it is self-inflicted, I know I do not deserve any sympathy! I went online last night, to leave an e-mail message for Jenni, before getting waylaid, by going into a chat room, to see what they are all about. e-*mail to Jenni*

"Hi Jenni!

Remember me? I know I was supposed to e-mail you as soon as you got back to the States, but I lost the e-mail address that you gave me. I got kicked off base, (tell you about it later), and I am now working outside the main gates. It's not as good as inside, but better than nothing.

Robbie came out to get food yesterday, and he gave me this e-mail address, so I hope this reaches you OK. I'm sure this wasn't the address you gave me originally, as I am on AOL too, and I am sure I would have noticed. As we are both now on AOL, maybe we could meet online and chat real-time with instant messenger?

Please respond soon, to confirm that I have the right address.
Missing you
Love Ben. xxxxxxxxxxx"

After I had finished writing, I signed into a chat room, with the intention of watching what went on. It was quite fascinating, although in many ways shocking, but time seems to fly by. I ended up going to bed after 4-30 a.m.! At first, I did just watch. Some of the conversations were quite outrageous. I noticed that there were several options, while in the room, to get more details about people in the room. These details are listed on a profile, which you can access by clicking on the name and selecting "more details". I noticed that some of these profiles stated, "no profile/no chat". Being a chat room "virgin", I asked, in the room, what it was all about. The first problem I had, was convincing the occupants, that I really did not know what I was doing. Once they believed me, they were most helpful, and I posted a profile of my own.

Name: Benjamin Arnold.
City, state, country: Marston Ferrars, Cambridgeshire, UK
Birthday: 3 May
Sex: male (I wanted to say yes please!)
Marital status: you must be joking!
Hobbies: playing football and pub quizzes.
Computers used: yes they are!
Occupation: self-styled Kebab King.
Personal quote: do you want chips with that?

As I left my profile, a message came up telling me that my profile may take up to 24 hours to appear, but when I checked, it seemed to have been instantaneous.

Within minutes, I got my first instant message from a woman in Peterborough.

"Hi Ben, how are you?"

"I'm fine. Who are you?"

"Maddy. How old R U?"

"34. U?" I responded in what appeared to be the approved IM shorthand.

"29. blonde. 34C. 5'8". Med build. U?"

Whoa! They certainly cut to the chase quickly enough!

"6'1". Med build. Lt brown hair. Hazel eyes."

"Mmmmmm! You sound delicious. I see you play football."

"When I get the time. Why? Do you like football?"

"I prefer indoor sports!"

Wow, it gets personal very quickly on here!

"I see!"

"I guess you are really fit then? You need plenty of stamina for football."

"I do my best."

"How would you like to fuck me all night long?"

Holy shit. Did I read that correctly? Yes! That's what she wrote.

"Not really. I don't even know you. Isn't that a little premature?"

"Well it's your fucking loss!"

With that parting riposte (hurrah!) she was gone. I checked her profile, but there wasn't one under her name. I was quite shocked, but I deduced that if she asked me **that,** after only five minutes of talking, she must have been the town bike! I may not be getting any right now, but I don't want to join that queue! I'm not that desperate!

Things to be grateful for

1) A bit of fun online.
2) A new diversion, (if it doesn't become an obsession).

Thursday 7th December 2000

Word of the day: Commiserate... sympathise, pity, console

10 a.m. On trailer.

It was extremely cold this morning, and the Land Rover wouldn't start. I rang the AA, and they sent out a mechanic, who got it started.

"Your battery was just a bit flat." He said patronisingly.

"What shape is it supposed to be?" I asked 'innocently'.

This comment merely attracted a look of disbelief on the mechanic's face.

Hasn't anyone got a sense of humour any more?

"Sign here, please."

I am rapidly coming to the conclusion that I am wasting my time being here for breakfast. It is rare that I get more than a couple of customers. I think from next week, I will just work the busier lunch period from 10 until 2. Even that is not exactly busy, compared to being inside the base. I may have to rethink about Stacey and Ashley. They are expense I could do without, at the moment.

4 p.m. back home.

Craig Steel came out at lunchtime. We commiserated (hurrah!) with each other, over the poor showing of the Packers this year.
"It's gonna take a miracle to make the play-offs now." He said shaking his head resignedly. "Keep the faith, though, Ben. Don't desert them."
"You want a winner's hat, Ben!" Another regular suggested. "How about I get you an Eagles' hat?"
"No thanks. I'll stick with the Packers. If Brett Favre had have remembered that we play in green, we wouldn't be in this mess!" I laughed. "I may not be an expert, but when you are leading by 4 points with 50 seconds to go, and you're in possession with a first down, why the hell wouldn't you just throw the ball away four times, or at least play safe and run the clock down?"
"Good point!" They replied in unison.
"Well, in the first or second game of the season, with 50 seconds to go, Favre threw a long pass on first down, which was intercepted and the opponent ran about thirty yards with it, before they caught him. Then, with a few quick plays and using up their time-outs, they managed to get to first and goal, with just seconds left, threw a touchdown pass and we lost by three. That was the start of a bad run. We're going OK now, but I think it's too late to do anything."
"I'm afraid you're right." Craig agreed.
"The Philly Eagles looks set to make it, though," the other customer gloated. "I can still get you that hat, if you'll wear it!"
I changed the subject to the electoral fiasco, and they told me that they are still no nearer to declaring a winner. After the guys had gone, I

found a key on the floor outside, as I closed up. It had the Packers logo on the key ring, so I guess it could be Craig's. Unfortunately, I don't know where he works, so I will have to hold onto it, until I see, either him, or one of his colleagues.

Things to be grateful for

1) Greenbay Packers are playing much better and still have an outside chance of making the play-offs.
2) Luton are playing Darlington in the cup on Saturday and surely must win against lower division opposition.
3) Membership of the AA!

Friday 8th December 2000

Word of the Day: Depleted... at a lower level, reduced in strength.

11 a.m. on sofa in flat

The damned Land Rover would not start again, this morning. I was too embarrassed to call out the AA, two days running, for the same fault. Instead, I bought a new battery, which cost £70, and I lost the morning's trade, so I am not a happy bunny! The Land Rover dealer, from whom I bought the battery, seems to think that the problem lies in the fact that old diesels take a lot of charge from the battery in order to start the engine, especially in cold weather. It then takes a reasonably long journey to put that charge back into the battery. My journeys are fairly short and having to stop and start the engine several times, in order to hitch up and unhitch, means the battery gets a little more depleted (hurrah!) each day, until there is just not enough charge to start the engine. It seems that I will have to keep one battery on charge, and another on the vehicle. What a pain in the arse! He suggested that the alternative could be to get a more modern vehicle.

Well, he would, wouldn't he?

I must say, I am tempted. It seems that this Land Rover costs me money, every week, just to keep it on the road. If it isn't one thing, it is another. The new battery started it first time, though, so I'm OK for tonight.

Brian rang to say they are going out to a club on Saturday night, as planned last week, but I had to decline, as I need to work. It hasn't been a good week, and the battery was an expense I didn't need.

I have not heard from Jenni, but I got seven E-mails from my inaugural chat room appearance!

Things to be grateful for

1) The Internet seems like a good way to meet people.
2) Land Rover is operational again.

Things to be pissed off about

1) No word from Jenni.
2) I wish I dare make contact with Louise.
3) The lads are going out on the town and I can't go.
4) The Land Rover is costing me a fortune to run.

Sunday 10th December 2000

Word of the Day: Can't think of one

7-02 a.m. dead to the world!
(Telephone rings).

"Hello, Mother. I thought you were going to ring after eight on Sunday mornings?"

"Oh! Thanks a lot, Benjamin. What a loving greeting. You really know how to make a mother feel wanted."

"Don't be like that. You know I love you!"

Did I really say that? My paternal grandfather would spin in his grave, if he heard me say that!

"Really? You have a strange way of showing it."

"Mother!"

"Now. Are you coming here for Christmas or not? I need to plan my shopping."

"I expect so, but I'm still not 100 percent sure. One little one, more or less, isn't going to make a lot of difference on the catering front, surely... And it is three weeks away, so you don't need to start shopping just yet!"

"Well, thank you very much. If you decide to grace us with your presence, would you have the decency to let me know beforehand?"

"Don't be like tha..."

(Click!)

I can't do right, for doing wrong, with her lately! Is it me? I'm sure she has a "Blue Peter" badge for making something out of nothing at all! Well I'm not going to encourage her moodiness by ringing her back! When she's ready to apologise, she can ring me!

It was freezing cold last night. By the time I had wound up the stabilisers and put the trailer away, my hands were bluer than a baboon's arse! I still felt cold when I went online to check out that chat room again. I received another shock today. A woman from Cambridge, named Corinne, IM'd me today and told me she knew my address and telephone number and could stalk me if she wanted to. I was gobsmacked! As it turned out, she was not a nutcase, but simply pointing out to me how naive my profile was. Apparently, I have given much too much information, allowing anybody to work out who I am and where I am and, as she pointed out, there are enough weirdoes on the Internet to cause problems. I thanked her and made suitable adjustments to my profile, to be a little more vague. I also added her name to my buddy list, so that we can talk again at some point. I managed to get to bed by two o'clock, this time!

Things to be grateful for

1) Corinne, a friendly soul who put me wise on Internet weirdoes before too many of them found me!
2) Another peaceful day in prospect.
3) We are going to do the quiz tonight.

Monday 11th December 2000

Word of the Day: Petulance... peevishness, tantrums

Just after midday, just out of bed!

I cannot believe that it is past midday, and I have only just managed to prise myself out of bed and get showered. I obviously needed some sleep! Mind you, it would help if Mother did not feel the need to wake me, early, every damned Sunday morning! Quiz night was extremely average, but I had one of the biggest laughs ever.

It was supposed to be the lads' night out on Saturday, but I had to miss out because of work. As it turned out, Brian had to miss out too, because Maria wouldn't let him go and, even Jamie had to lie to Sam, that he had to go to a stag night for someone at work, in order for him to go with Gordon. As there were only two of them, they decided against going to a club and found a pub instead. The place they found had recently been refurbished. Gordon said it had a bit of a wine bar "feel" about it.

"We got settled in," Gordon began to narrate enthusiastically, whilst Jamie was at the bar getting in drinks. *"The place was heaving with birds, mostly on their own. There was also a lot of blokes, but not many with females. We noticed one pair of likely looking women in the corner, who kept returning our glances. So Jamie jumps in with both feet, doesn't he? He goes and asks them if we can buy them a drink, and before you know it, we've pulled. As he was the one who got us "in there", he insisted on having the first pick, and picks the blonde one. She has got the most*

beautiful pair of knockers and, to be fair, she doesn't look half bad, but the dark one with sort of reddish hair isn't bad either, so I agree."

Jamie returned from the bar, and Gordon chuckled to himself, causing Jamie to realise that Gordon is divulging the details of their Saturday night out.

"You couldn't wait to tell them, could you?"

Jamie seemed genuinely pissed off.

"You wanker!" He continued.

"Well, you've got to admit it, it was fucking funny!" Gordon tried to justify his apparent breaking of a confidence!

"I'm going for a piss!" Jamie used the age-old escape mechanism.

Gordon ignored Jamie's petulance, (hurrah!), and continued with the story.

"To cut a long story short, we get them back to Jackie's place... That's the redhead that I'm with... the other one's called Rhondda... and we have some coffee and chat some more. Jackie says to me, "Shall we leave these two lovebirds alone and go into the bedroom?"

"Yeah?" I must have sounded disbelieving, because Gordon responds very quickly.

"Don't say it like that. I do get my end away occasionally, I'm not a fucking alien!"

"OK OK!" I tried to appease him. "I just wanted to hear more."

"OK then! Well shut up and fucking listen... *We get into her bedroom and start to do the dirty deed and she is fantastic. I mean... fan-bloody-tastic! I'm just finished and lying there cuddling up to her, when there is a commotion like you've never heard, coming from the other room.* "Oh, for fuck's sake!" *Jamie's shouting.* "You dirty, evil bastard. What the fuck do you think you're doing?" *Rhondda is in tears, crying out,* "I thought you knew. What did you expect in a gay bar?"...

"What's up?" *I said, trying to defuse the situation.*

"**SHE** is only a fucking **bloke!**" *Jamie blurts out, lookin' horrified. Well... I could have pissed myself laughing, until I started thinking,* "Hang on a minute! If Rhondda is a geezer, what about Jackie?" *So I turned to speak to her, but before I can open my mouth, she says,* "Don't even think *about it! There's not a man in this universe with a pussy like mine, baby!"*

Jamie returned from the bar at this point of the story.

"OK, have a good fucking laugh at my expense... As usual."

"No... Really..." Brian was trying manfully to sound sincere, but unfortunately, not one of the three of us could stop ourselves from almost collapsing in laughter. So much so, that Jamie went a shade of puce and walked out in a fit of pique. I followed him into the pub car park and stopped him.

"Could have happened to anyone of us, mate. At least nothing much happened."

"Didn't it? She'd been shoving her tongue down my throat for starters... What am I saying? **HE** had! I'd had my hand inside her bra... and they were proper tits! I'm telling you! They **were** implants, like, but loads of birds have implants nowadays, so why would I suspect anything? Then she... Oh Fuck... **HE**... *went down on me.*" His voice tailed off to a whisper, as he finished the sentence.

"You mean..."

"Yes, you plonker! A blow job!"

"I'm a plonker? I'm not the one with his cock in another bloke's mouth, though, am I?"

He looked deflated and embarrassed, and I felt really guilty at my comment.

"Sorry Jamie, I couldn't resist that one. You mean the "full Monty" blow job?"

"I am afraid so. And what is worse, I fucking enjoyed it! But wait. This is the worst part! I slipped my hand up her skirt and inside her knicker leg, expecting to find a nice furry ferret, but instead I've got a fucking great handful of meat and two veg!"

"Couldn't you tell? I mean... just looking at the face?"

"Do you think I would have done all that, if I could have seen she was a bloke?"

"I guess not."

I persuaded him to come back into the pub, brave it out and laugh it off. Apparently, since its change of appearance, the pub has become a leading gay haunt, so "Rhondda" wasn't trying to trick him. He probably really thought Jamie was gay. I have to say that, to look at him, it is easy to make that mistake. He is very pretty for a bloke!! But Jamie did manage to get a laugh at Gordon's expense by saying, "Jackie thought Gordon was bisexual."

Things to be grateful for

1) I didn't go! It could have been me!
2) Another good laugh at Jamie's expense.

Wednesday 13th December 2000

Word of the Day: Ignominy... dishonour, infamy.

I am just home from work and checked my e-mail and there is, at last, a message from Jenni. It was very brief, just saying that she is at Fort Worth, and very busy. She has quite a difficult schedule, up until Christmas, and suggested that we make contact after that.

The Supreme Court has ruled that recounting must stop, so there should be a result to the presidential elections soon.

On Monday, England beat Pakistan in a test match. Apparently, they carried on batting almost in darkness, to gain victory, despite Pakistan using every means at their disposal, to slow down the over rate! Well played the lads!

Things to be grateful for

1) An end to the American election ignominy (hurrah! Bonus or what?) is in sight.
2) English cricket appears to be on the up.
3) A response from Jenni.

Friday 15th December 2000

Word of the Day: Galvanise... rouse forcefully

4 p.m.

At last, Gore has conceded defeat. What a waste of time that was! All that hassle and the original results stands. I could have told them that!

Craig came by, yesterday, and collected his key. He brought me a Packers quilted jacket. It was a genuine NFL approved, embroidered jacket and must have cost a fortune. He would not allow me to pay him a penny for it, and I was totally overwhelmed. What a generous man he is!

Today has been really quiet. One of the few customers, who did come out, told me that there were some potluck parties going on in many offices. Apparently, everyone brings in some food, and then they pool it and then share it. Whatever! I guess!

Stella rang again last night, but I told her I was just going out and had no time to talk. I can't go on like this, avoiding her calls, as she is not getting the message. I'm going to have to galvanise, (hurrah!), myself into action, face the music and just tell her!

Things to be grateful for

1) The incredible generosity of Craig.
2) Being the proud owner of an original Packers jacket.
3) They finally know who the President is going to be! As if it mattered!!

Monday 18th December 2000

Word of the Day: Countermand... make an order revoking a previous one, overrule.

Just after midday, freezing cold and seriously thinking about going back to bed!

Mother rang yesterday, but remarkably, not until about ten o'clock. She made no reference to our little argument of last week and was very sweet, so I didn't bring it up either. I have accepted her invitation to spend Christmas with them. I could hardly refuse; after all I'm not doing anything else exciting and, if left to my own devices, would probably have a cheese sandwich for my Christmas dinner!

I had just got off the phone after talking to her, when there was a knock at the door. I opened it and was shocked to find Stella standing there.

"Good grief! What are you doing here?"

"Nice welcome, Ben! What you think I'm doing here?"

"I thought you were engaged to your ex-fiancé now? "

"I am. So what? It's you I've come to see. Aren't you going to invite me in?"

"Er.... Yes, I suppose so. Sorry. I'm in shock!"

She was wearing a half-length coat, with a wrap-around belt, which she removed to reveal a very short skirt and a ribbed, sleeveless, polo-necked top. It was obvious that she was not wearing a bra, and she had a tiny bump, barely disclosing her pregnancy. I would be lying, if I said that she did not look very sexy, and, due to my recent enforced celibacy, it was not wasted on me! I made her coffee, and she told me that they had not made any formal plans to marry, yet. Not wishing to pursue that particular line, I told her how things had been since I was off base and asked her how her job was progressing. We avoided the subject of our former relationship, which suited me fine at this point, although I knew that I must make it quite clear to her, before she left, that there was no future for us as a couple and that it was not a good idea that she had come.

After about an hour, she said that she needed the bathroom, regular visits being a legacy of pregnancy, and said that she would give me my Christmas present, when she returned. I felt absolutely awful, as I've not bought a present for her. Hardly surprising, when I didn't even expect to see her again. She was gone for almost 15 minutes and, in view of her condition, I became worried. I knocked tentatively on the bathroom door and asked if she was OK.

"I'm fine, I'll be right there." She replied, so I returned to the living room and sat down on the sofa. A few moments later, she opened the living room door and made a grand entrance, taking up a position right in front of me, with her tongue sensuously licking her top lip. She was wearing high-heeled shoes, a black lace bra and panties and black fishnet stockings, held up by black suspenders. She had reapplied her make-up, but this time with scarlet lip-gloss. She looked stunning and overtly sexy. I was unable to find anything appropriate to say, but sat, transfixed.

"Well? How do you like your present?"

"It's beautiful, but I am not sure it will fit me!"

When you can't deal with a situation...make a joke!

"Very funny! Are you going to sit there all day making jokes...?"

She parted her legs seductively, dragged her hand between them up the front of her body to her breasts, which she cupped with her hands, as though presenting them to me. I sat there, bemused and confused.

"... Or are you going to take me into the bedroom and give me what I have been missing all these weeks?"

My head was trying to direct my mouth to say, "Get dressed! Don't be ridiculous and go home, but an irresistible, overriding force, prevented speech of any kind! I stood up, picked her up, cradling her in my arms like a baby and carried her silently to the bed. I confess that what transpired was a very pleasant afternoon, not unlike a mortar attack on a lone outpost! When she left at 4 p.m., I slept like a dead man. I woke up briefly, at around 7 p.m., fully intending to get up and go to the quiz, but fell asleep again as the resolve evaporated.

When I got up this morning, I felt terrible. I was ashamed that I had succumbed to her seduction. I know I should have sent her packing, but as Oscar Wilde once said, 'I can resist anything except temptation', and she is so bloody good. However, she is pregnant, and engaged to the father of the child. Even if she wasn't, I really wouldn't want to be with her long term, so I feel like I have just used her. It is not a feeling I am comfortable with, or proud of, although it may well be that she was just using me too, as she instigated it. I still shouldn't have done it, though. She might be thinking now, that "we" are "back on" again.

Why does the brain in my pants always countermand, (hurrah!), the one in my head? I guess, as the man proudly said, "I don't think with my cock, I let my cock think for me!"

Things to be grateful for

1) I did enjoy a very sensual and satisfying afternoon.
2) Mother seems to have finally grasped the idea that it is better to ring later on a Sunday morning.
3) It's nearly Christmas!

Things to be pissed off about

1) Stella seems to be trying to get round me. There may be a hidden agenda and, if so, I just fell for the first item!
2) I have agreed to spend Christmas with Mother and Father.
3) I hate Christmas anyway!

Friday 22nd December 2000

Word of the Day: Malediction... curse, evil spoken about someone.

Midnight, hurrah finished for Christmas!

I didn't bother at the base today. It has been quiet all week, so I didn't expect today would bring much business. I told Stacey and Ashley that I wouldn't be needing them after Christmas. I felt bad about it, but I only kept them on this long, because I didn't want to see them lose their jobs in the run-up to Christmas. Stacey has been teasing me all week about her New Year party. She has invited me, with the sole intention of setting me up with her friend. I'm getting sadder by the minute. Everyone seems to see me as a charity case.

It was extremely busy tonight. Everyone was saying that they didn't want to cook for themselves this evening. They are all getting in the party mood. I must go shopping tomorrow for Mum and Dad's Christmas presents, or Mother's malediction (hurrah!) will ensure that I will be dead meat! What the hell I will get them, though, I do not know!

Things to be grateful for

1) Work is over for Christmas.
2) I haven't got to cook for at least a week.
3) Stella has not rung since her visit. (Phew!).
4) Luton beat Darlington in the cup replay last night.

Saturday 23rd December 2000

6 p.m. home from shopping.

Now I remember why I hate bloody Christmas! The shops were packed; there was no parking and most of the goods I considered buying had been damaged by the seasonal morons! It has taken me about four hours looking for something different, but functional, but to no avail. What little inspiration I had was driven from me in the mad scramble of last minute shoppers. I had to settle for the mundane, as usual, and purchased a dressing gown for Mother and a cardigan for Dad. He has, after all, become "Cardigan Man" in his old age! Tomorrow, I head for Luton for the duration! Give me strength!

Sunday 24th December 2000

Word of the Day: Parody... distortion, lampoon, spoof.

7-30 a.m. in peaceful oblivion!
(Telephone rings!)

I know it's Mother. Perhaps she is calling to tell me Christmas has been cancelled! In my dreams!
"Hello, Mother."
"Yes, very clever Benjamin. No one's impressed, you know!"
"What can I do for you, my sweet?"
"I just wanted to remind you that we are going to Auntie Joy's today, so don't be late!"
"It's seven in the morning! Give me a break!"
"It's gone half past seven! It's time you were getting up and getting ready to come over."
Why don't I just resign myself to the fact that my life is not my own, from this moment forward, until next Sunday, and save myself the stress?
"We didn't even arrange a time that I would be arriving."
"Well, we have told Joy, now, that we're coming at 2 p.m. Are you going to make a liar of me?"
There is no answer to that! At least, not one that will avoid a week with an atmosphere you could cut with a knife!
What a strange parody (hurrah!) of a human being I am, reduced to spending Christmas with my parents, at my age. A few months ago, I thought I would be having my pick of women to spend Christmas with. How swiftly things change. I am no further forward now, on the woman front, than I was on my birthday eight months ago. Oh well, better bite the bullet and get my arse over there.

Things to be grateful for

1) Somewhere to go for Christmas.
2) I don't have a lot of people to buy Christmas presents for!
3) A few days rest. Mother always dotes on me when I stay with them.

Thursday 28th December 2000

Word of the Day: Conspiratorially... by way of a conspiracy, intended to conspire with another

1-15 p.m. in Mum and Dad's spare room.

At last, I have managed to get a few moments alone. Mother has managed to monopolise my life for the past five days. She has managed to force me to eat when I was not hungry, drink when I was not thirsty and get up when I was still tired and needed more sleep. It is driving me mad, and I'm counting down the days, hours and minutes, 1 day 12 hours and 40 minutes to be precise, before I escape from Colditz! Poor old Dad has been through the same regime. Christmas Eve was a hoot at Auntie Joy's. I told her about the breast-feeding room at Marks & Spencer's.

"I was shopping a few weeks ago, Auntie Joy, in Mark's? Do you know they now have a special room for breast-feeding? I nearly started a queue!"

Auntie Joy laughed like the proverbial drain, but Mother looked horrified.

"That's it! Show me up in front of my sister!" She began, and then a memory flickered in her mind. "I'm not surprised, though. You always did love the breast! I remember whenever I was breast-feeding you, if someone in the room spoke, you'd bite down with your gums on my nipple and turn your head to see where the sound had come from, without letting go. You stretched it out like a piece of elastic!"

Dad winced as he visualised the stretched nipple. I winked at him before my reply, and we exchanged a wry smile.

"Mother! That is just too much information, thank you. Are you drunk?"

"No I am not!"

I am sure she was!

We went back to their house and had egg and chips for dinner, which I absolutely loved. It brought back memories of my childhood, which made me smile fondly. It didn't matter how much food was in the house, especially bought for the festive season, not one scad of it could ever be touched until Christmas morning. Never mind that we'd be eating turkey until New Year and walnuts till March! I also reminisced how, in our house, you always knew what day it was, by what you were eating. Dad would buy the Sunday joint on Saturday, take some slices off and fry it with mashed potatoes for lunch. On Sunday, we would have the traditional roast beef dinner, with all the trimmings. Monday, the remainder of the beef would be eaten cold, with chips. Tuesday was minced beef pie and veg. Wednesday would be chops, pork or lamb; whichever was best value for money. Thursday was stew and Friday was fish and chips. There was hardly ever any variation. Maybe egg and chips on a Monday if the roast didn't stretch that far, but God forbid we should ever have the stew on a Monday, or the mince pie on a Wednesday! The beauty of it, though, was that every meal was totally home-cooked. We never had convenience foods in those days. In fact, to this day, my dad has never eaten rice as a vegetable, Chinese or Indian food, or even pasta (other than tinned spaghetti, which doesn't count!) Flexibility is not high on their list of watchwords, but the food was always of the highest standard. Since I now live out of Tesco's ready meal cabinet, I miss Mum's home cooked food tremendously.

Christmas day came and went, with its usual expectation and anticlimax. I have always thought that Christmas was overrated. All that preparation and the expense, then blink and it's gone. At very best, it is an excuse to get pissed! Christmas dinner was just how I remembered the Christmas dinners of yesteryear, and, although Dad could not be persuaded to partake, a bottle of red wine was opened, purely for my benefit. Mother drank one glass to be sociable, but I polished off the rest quite happily. Dad stuck to his Captain Morgan's rum with blackcurrant, and, by 3 p.m., both he and I were patently lacking in sobriety!

"You two don't know when to stop!" Mother castigated us. "You'll be sick in a minute!"

"What are you? The alcohol police?" I bit back.

"If I was, you'd be under arrest by now, both of you."

Dad smiled and rolled his eyes surreptitiously. Not surreptitiously enough though!

"I saw that!" Mother barked. Then looked at me and winked conspiratorially, (hurrah!).

This was enough to cause me to start giggling, which was the catalyst for Dad to do the same. Mother shook her head in mock disbelief, but I could see that secretly, she was in her element. Her family was together and having a good time. We sat in the living room during the evening, half watching television, but talking over it, about Christmases long past. I was again criticised for wearing my Packers hat in the house, and the conversation turned to various hats and indeed clothes, owned and worn by the three of us over the years.

"Do you remember when Ben went up from Wolf Cubs to Scouts, George? That beret he wore, which almost drowned him?"

Mother had been dubious of my staying power in Scouts and did not want to buy a brand new uniform, merely to have me drop out a month later. My cousin, Nick, had been a Scout and had left at the age of 15, so he had donated his old uniform to me. The problem was that it fitted him, when he was 15. I was only 11, at the time, and there was room to hold a Jamboree inside it, when I wore it! The shorts came past my knees, and the belt drew the waistband in, like curtains on a track! The shirt bore more resemblance to a marquee than an item of clothing and the beret would have buried my head, were it not for my protruding ears. Mother then felt the need to get out a photograph of me, setting off for that first meeting. Much mirth was created as these memories were shared.

"Look at him!" Mother had that loving look in her eyes that only mothers seem capable of. "He was so proud of that uniform!"

"He looks like an Oxfam reject!" Dad observed.

"I should prosecute the pair of you for child abuse! Imagine letting me go out in public looking like that. You told me I looked smart!"

The conversation meandered through different passages of my childhood, while various photographs were produced in support of the memories. Many more drinks were consumed during the process and, whilst on the subject of hats, I recounted the story of only a few years ago, when we were all watching the Wimbledon tennis championships. I couldn't recall the players concerned, but there was a match between two men, one of whom was seeded, and one of whom wasn't. Mother constantly made remarks about how the underdog was performing well, although Dad and I could see that the seeded player was winning easily.

"Are you sure you know which player is which, Mother?" I had asked her.

"Of course I do. Do you think I am stupid?"

"OK then, which one is the seeded player?"

"The one wearing the cap!" She announced confidently, though incorrectly.

"No it isn't! It's the other one!"

"Are you sure?"

"Of course I'm sure. You know I know my sport."

"Well why is the other one wearing the cap, then? She asked.

"Because the sun is in his eyes." I began to worry about her sanity.

"How are you supposed to know what is going on if they don't abide by the rules?"

"What rules?"

"About caps."

"Mother? What are you on?" I began to lose patience and so did she.

She said, "Oh forget it!" Then she walked out.

At the end of the match, they showed the revised draw, for the next round, on a caption. As is normal, the seeded players names were written in capital letters and the unseeded players in lower case.

"There you are! I knew I was right! You two trying to make me think I was going out of my head! What does that say at the bottom?" She asked defiantly.

"Seeded players in Caps!" I read from the bottom of the caption.

Dad and I collapsed in paroxysms of laughter, much to the annoyance of Mother, who did not see the joke. We were laughing so hard that we could not get enough breath to explain for several minutes. Eventually, we calmed ourselves, sides aching from the laughter.

"It means the seeds names are written in caps on the TV caption! That's 'caps', short for capital letters!" I tried not to sound as though I was belittling her.

"You silly bugger!" Dad chirped, causing her to turn beetroot red and leave the room.

Luckily, the years had mellowed the memory of the incident for her and, this time, she laughed along with us.

By the time it got around to midnight, and the announcement that Christmas day was officially over, both my dad and I were almost paralytic. As we went to bed, we negotiated the stairs on all fours, with me using my shoulder against his backside to propel him ahead of me up the stairs. We were both giggling like schoolgirls and Mother, bringing up the rear, tutted in disgust at the spectacle.

Things to be grateful for

1) Christmas wasn't so bad after all.
2) I had some really good moments with my Dad and Mum.
3) Mother through all her martyrdom, complaints and disgust, (mostly artificial!), had a really memorable Christmas.
4) It is nearly over and I can go home to some sanity!

Friday 29th December 2000

Word of the Day: Efficacy... effectiveness, efficiency, healthiness.

11-15 p.m. in Mum and Dad's spare room.

It snowed a heavily overnight, which really made it seem belatedly Christmassy. Dad recalled the winter of 1963, when it snowed in November, and there were massive snowdrifts. He said it had snowed, on and off, from November to the end of March, without a proper thaw. He and Mother had been engaged at the time, but were still living with their own parents, so it had been quite difficult for them to see each other. Those snowy Christmases almost never happen nowadays. I guess it is the legacy of the greenhouse effect. It's a shame it couldn't have snowed on Christmas Day. I queried the efficacy, (hurrah!), of living with one's parents when over 30 years old and they both reacted very defensively, explaining that things were different in the 50s and 60s.

"My mam and dad had very little money coming in," Dad began.

"Nor did mine!" Mother came in.

"So where is the sense in you each giving them another mouth to feed?" I enquired.

"We were both working and paying board to them." Dad announced proudly.

"So why didn't you live together, in place of your own? Surely that would have been more cost-effective."

Dad let out a gasp of incredulity.

"You didn't do that in those days! Wasn't the done thing at all. Apart from anything else, my mam and your mother's dad wouldn't have allowed it!"

"So why didn't you get married then? Mum told me that you were engaged to each other at 19."

"Yes!" Mother was enjoying this. "Why didn't we...? Mainly because he liked being single too much!" She answered her own question.

"It wasn't that. I wanted to save and have a good start when we got married."

" That's a good one!" She said. "We didn't have any money when we **did** get married. We probably **never** would have got married if... erm..." she seemed to hesitate. "... If we had have waited till you had saved up any money." She said, eventually.

"Well, if you didn't get married for over 10 years, until you had a wedge saved, how come you got married without any money saved?" I asked mischievously.

"Well, we just did!" He was obviously very uncomfortable with the conversation and Mother was enjoying his squirming just a little too much, so I let him off the hook.

"God, it's like a desert in here. A bloke could dry up like a leaf and blow away!" I put my tongue out to indicate thirst.

"OK. OK. I'll put the kettle on." Mother relented. "It works OK when other people put it on too, you know!"

Dad and I exchanged boyish grins. I really seem to have bonded with my parents this week, I am quite surprised! Maybe I am getting old myself!

Things to be grateful for

1) Getting on well with parents.
2) Having the opportunity to learn a bit more about them.

JANUARY 2001

Monday 1ˢᵗ January 2001

Word of the Day: Incompatibility... state of disharmony, state of being unsuitable

10 a.m. Back in the real world!

Although I enjoyed my week with my parents, it was really good to get back to my own space. Ironically, I didn't know what to do with myself over the weekend, as there was very little going on in the village. I therefore found myself attending, with some reservations, Stacey's New Year party. The vast majority of the assembled revellers were of the American persuasion, many of which were customers from the base and their families. I was introduced to Stacey's "spare" friend Jane, who turned out to be somewhat older than I had expected, at 44! She was obviously aware that I had been invited to be paired off with her, and she clung to me, all evening, like a limpet. She was a thoroughly pleasant woman, and not unattractive to look at, but I was not remotely attracted to her as a potential girlfriend. I felt almost guilty about it, especially as she linked my arm and dragged me from person to person, claiming that I was her toy boy. I was not put off by her age, in fact, she seemed considerably younger, but there was no chemistry there. As if to compound our incompatibility, (hurrah!), as the night wore on, she became increasingly drunk and sillier by the minute. By the time midnight struck, she hardly knew **who** she was let alone **where** she was! As the New Year was rung in, kisses were exchanged by all and sundry, in the traditional manner. This was the opportunity that she had been waiting for, and she kissed me with a great enthusiasm, like a demented Hoover. She was quite reluctant to detach herself. As the lack of oxygen began to take effect, I pulled away gasping for air! Jane was staying over at Stacey's and was quite upset when, at about 12-30 a.m., I announced that I must leave. Stacey had been aware of Jane's behaviour and, instinctively, knew that I was relieved to be leaving. At the door, she apologised profusely, assuring me that it had been out of character.

"She is really quite shy, and I had built you up so much that she was scared to death that you wouldn't like her. I really hope you will give her another chance?"

I smiled a non-committal smile, but had vowed to myself that it would never happen!

Things to be grateful for

1) I managed to escape from the party with my tonsils intact! Just!

2) Jane lives at Mildenhall, so it is unlikely we will cross paths again.

3) I hope that I have now exhausted all the charity introductions of my friends and am free to make my own acquaintances!

Tuesday 2nd January 2001

Word of the Day: Indictment... comment, condemnation, accusation.

4 p.m. Between work sessions

Back to work today, just as I was getting used to being a man of leisure! I spent most of the weekend watching TV, or at least channel hopping. It is a sad indictment, (hurrah!), of British TV that, with the Sky satellite service and the terrestrial stations, there are over 200 channels to choose from and, last night, I surfed them all and there was nothing remotely worth watching. I wonder if it is the diversity of choice that dilutes the quality. I remember, as a kid, having only the choice of BBC1, BBC2 or ITV. I also remember Mum and Dad saying that TV was all black and white, until just after I was born. I bet that made snooker compulsive viewing! (He's lining up the grey, to the bottom pocket. It is nestling just behind the grey to the left of the grey! Ha! Ha!).

It was quite busy outside base today, and, at one point, it was more like a United Nations Convention. On base, there is a European contingent, and the vast majority of them must have been out there today. There were two from the Italian navy, Ferruccio and Alessandro; Dag from the Norwegian navy; Franck from the German army and Francisco from the Spanish air force. There were also two Dutchman, but I didn't catch their names. It was really interesting, chatting to such a wide range of nationalities. I enjoyed teasing them about various national traits, like the Germans' propensity to leave towels on sun loungers, when on holiday, and the Italians' way with the ladies! Ferruccio smiled and said, "I am not going to disagree with you. I **LOVE** the ladies." I half expected to see him turn into Swiss Tony on The Fast Show. *("Eating Ben's kebabs is like-a making love to a beautiful laydee!")*

Franck also agreed that it is just as frustrating to other Germans, when his countrymen leave towels to reserve sun loungers while they go off to breakfast, or even shopping, for two hours. "I alvays move zem, when I need to. Vot are zey going to say to me?" He asked.

"Well you are a big bloke. I guess they wouldn't say anything!" I replied.

"Exactly!" He let out a very Teutonic guffaw.

Ferruccio and Alex have been a few times before, and they are both from Rome. However, Ferruccio supports Lazio, while Alex supports AS Roma. That's Rome's equivalent to Tottenham and Arsenal! They are always taunting each other, jokingly, about their respective allegiances.

"So Ferruccio, you are a Lieutenant Commander in the Italian navy! Have you ever seen a ship?" I jibed.

"Of course, I am on a ship, before I am coming to England. When I return in July, to Roma, I will be again with the ship. Why do you say this?"

"Almost all the American navy guys on base have never been posted to a ship. They are all intelligence workers and have always been stationed in offices."

"Oh! I see what you mean."

"I also tease them for wearing the same battledress camouflage, regardless of which service they are in. I see that you are the same." A look of confusion appeared on his face.

"Why do you wear army camouflage, when you are in the navy?" I asked.

"It's because we all wear the same mode of clothes here."

"Navy camouflage should be sea green, with little boats on, Ferruccio! And Francisco's should be sky blue, with little fluffy clouds! Trust me! If you wear that on a boat you will be seen easily. There are not many trees at sea, or in the air!"

They all laughed.

"I think that of Englishmen, you are a very different person." Ferruccio said carefully.

"You mean I am off my trolley?"

"Which trolley are you off?" Ferruccio enquired.

I indicated madness by twirling my index finger next to my temple.

"Off my head... Mad...?"

"Oh no! You are very smart. You speak very well politics and of other countries. And of course you are sportsman. We are all following the football here. Is very good." Francisco joined in the conversation.

"As long as none of you are French!" I joked. "How difficult do you think it is for an Englishman to know that France are football's world champions?"

"Ha! Ha! I will tell Marcel when we get back. We have a Frenchman in our office, and too, a Belgian!" Dag said.

"I sometimes joke about the Belgians. Can you name three famous Belgians?" I asked.

"I cannot even manage one!" Franck, the German, laughed.

"Me neither! But as long as we beat Germany in the World Cup, I will be happy!" I responded, the innuendo finding its target instantly.

"Yes. But it vill not heppen!" Frank suddenly developed a very German accent! "Ve are already vinning in your Vembley, how you sink to beat us in Munchen?"

"Seriously, I am looking forward to it. It seems both Germany and England are in a transitional period, rebuilding their teams. It will be very interesting, neither of us played well in the Euro 2000." I said with sincerity.

"No you are right." He agreed.

We continued to talk about a variety of subjects, and they seemed reluctant to leave. In fact, they ate their food, while talking to me, and must have been there for at the best part of an hour.

Things to be grateful for

1) It is good to be back at work and earning some money.
2) My wonderful work in cementing relations with our European visitors.
3) The World Cup has started again, and I hope that the French reign as World Champions is coming to an end!

Friday 5th January 2001

Word of the Day: Simultaneous... synchronised, at the same time, concurrent.

3-30 p.m. Knackered before I even begin Friday night!

Today, at the base, I was inundated with customers. I could hardly cope on my own. The cafeteria inside the base has been closed for refurbishment and will not reopen for at least three months, when it will be a pizza franchise. I am going to have to contact Stacey and Ashley, to see if they want to re-establish the previous arrangement. Looks as though business is on the up, though!

Jenni e-mailed me on Wednesday and asked me to meet her online last night, at midnight GMT, for an instant message chat, which I did. It was only 6 p.m. in Texas. It seemed weird being six hours ahead, in fact it was the early hours of Friday here, but still Thursday over there. How weird is that? She told me that she was enjoying the work there, but missing England and more especially missing me!

Understandable! Ha! Ha!

I filled her in on the antics of her former colleagues, and we had a good time reliving our "special" moments. While we were talking, I received several IM's from other women and quickly learned how to align several message windows on the screen and talk to more than one person at a time. I did very nearly send messages, intended for one recipient, to another, on a few occasions. Most of the incoming IM's were inane drivel, but at about 1-30 a.m., Corinne, from Cambridge, with whom I had the conversation about my profile, IM'd me. We spoke for an hour or so, while I was still connected to Jenni, and I blocked IM's from everyone else, as it was just too confusing to cope with more than two people at the same time and also made me feel like a two-timer! Corinne suggested meeting each other, but I felt it was a bit soon for that and, although she was disappointed, she seemed to understand. She said she would e-mail me and that she would like to chat again sometime and I agreed. If I had known what trade was going to be like at the base today, I wouldn't have stayed up so late, though!

Things to be grateful for

1) A very healthy increase in business today.
2) A couple of enjoyable simultaneous (hurrah!) conversations online.

3) I opened all the Christmas cards, today, which arrived while I was staying at my parents. One was from Louise and said she would like to hear from me.

Sunday 7th January 2001

Word of the Day: Apoplexy... sudden loss of consciousness, enragement, a stroke.

7-15 a.m. unconscious
(Telephone rings)

I wonder who that is – NOT!
"Hello, Mother!"
"Hello, Benjamin. I've got exciting news! Your Auntie Joy and your Auntie Paula are both going to be grandmothers! Deborah and Sarah are both pregnant."
Oh God! Beam me up! I know what is coming next.
"Really? How lovely? Haven't seen Sarah and Debs for ages. Not since your anniversary party." I tried to deflect her from her obvious purpose.
"Yes. We'll have to get another "family do" together."
"Maybe at their babies' christenings?"
"Crikey! Give them a chance. They're only just pregnant!"
"Nine months soon passes, though!" I winced as soon as I had said it, as I had set her up to deliver the killer blow!
"Yes it does! So does nine years...!"
Here it comes!
"... I'm so jealous, I could squeak! I'm older than both of them and...."
"I'm older than Sarah and Debs!" I cut in, finishing the inevitable comment.
"Well, now you come to mention it, yes you are. When are we going to have some grandchildren?"

305

"When I find someone who wants to have my children?" I answered sarcastically.

"You are not getting any younger, you know, and nor are we."

"Picasso fathered a child at 80, Mother. There is no rush!"

"Oh great! So I have to live to be 150 to see my grandchildren?"

"I've told you a million times, don't exaggerate!…"

I've been waiting years to boomerang that one back at her!

"…Anyway, not everyone has kids, you know. What if I marry someone who doesn't want a family, or can't even have kids?"

Silence reigned! God, a tumbleweed moment all of my own!

"I hardly think it is an issue, if you haven't even got a girlfriend." She said facetiously.

"Exactly, I rest my case! It is not easy producing children on your own. There's only been one recorded case of that in the last 2000 years!"

"Ooh! You can be so exasperating at times!"

"It's all part of my irresistible charm."

"Well, it's about time you started using it in the right direction, then, isn't it?"

"If you wanted to be sure of grandchildren, you should've had more kids yourself, to improve the odds."

"You were a big enough shock."

"Oh! So I wasn't planned, then? Poor old Ben. I'm an unwanted child." I whined with my tongue firmly in my cheek.

"Of course you were wanted. You just came a bit sooner than we had expected."

"You could have had more kids later. What if I had been gay? You'd never have had grandkids then."

"Don't start that **gay** business again. What are you trying to do? Give your father heart failure?"

I reckon that if I had been gay, my Dad would have taken in his stride much better than Mum. It would have been she who would have had apoplexy (hurrah!)!

"Well, fortunately for your desire to have grandchildren, I'm not. Talking of ancestry…" I changed the focus, if not the subject, on the conversation. "I was talking to a bloke on base who is looking up his English ancestry. I might be interested in doing a bit of that."

"I've often thought about doing some myself, but I never knew how to go about it." She replied.

"You start with the ones who are alive. Get them to tell you about their childhood and all they can remember about their parents, grandparents and stuff, then work from there. The Mormons have made a big index of many registers of baptism, marriage and death. You can access them at libraries. You can look at parish records as well. The Council have a department. You can even get copies of certificates of births, deaths and marriages, for your own records. Talking of that. Where's **my** birth certificate? I haven't got it."

"In my passport wallet, I think. Or maybe in your dad's old suitcase, along with our other paperwork. I'll get it out for you next time you are over."

Our conversation continued into even more mundane topics, but the end result was that it was 8-10 a.m. and I was wide awake, so I got up and eased myself into the day. I might just ring Louise today! Then again, maybe I won't.

Things to be grateful for

1) My ancestors – whoever they may be.
2) My cousins are having babies. Good for them!
3) Quiz night resumes after the Christmas break.

Monday 8th January 2001

Word of the Day: Diaphanous... light and delicate, almost transparent.

9-00 a.m. Only just back from Sunday night out!

It was back to normality last night at the quiz. We were in sparkling form and won every round, including the jackpot! A startling sum of £27 to share among us. The quizmaster was gutted, as he always intends the jackpot to remain intact until it reaches the maximum of £60. After the quiz, as we had not seen each other since before Christmas, we went back to Brian's with some "take out" beers. Maria was less than amused and stormed off to bed with the parting comment, "Don't make a lot of noise and wake the children. And you..." She pointed to Brian menacingly, "... Don't come to bed pissed and wake me up, or you will be in big trouble."

We all made faces at Brian, and he responded by making a bird's beak with his hand, pointing it after her, and mimicking a bird squawking, as if he was doing 'The Birdy Song'!

"You wouldn't dare do that to her face." I suggested helpfully.

"She gets on my tits, sometimes." He said with a depressed look.

"Well, be fair!" I continued. "You did bring yourself and three half drunk mates home on a Sunday night, without telling her."

"Well, I didn't know, did I? We only decided at closing time!" He replied, as if it were a viable excuse.

Gordon was already falling asleep, upright, in a chair.

"Oi! Pinder!" Jamie shouted. "Can't take the pace, you lightweight?"

"Fuck off!" Was Gordon's erudite response.

"What do you do if an elephant comes into your house?" Jamie asked.

"What the fuck are you talking about?" Brian petulantly enquired.

"Elephants! Don't you speak English?"

I realised that Jamie was trying to tell a joke and helped him out.

"What do you do?"

"Swim or drown!" He laughed.

"That's gross," the semi comatose Gordon suggested.

"But funny... for Jamie!" Brian observed.

A joke telling session ensued, with much loud alternating laughter and groaning, which eventually prompted an irate bang on the bedroom floor from Maria!

"Oops!" We said, almost in unison.

"So what sort of Christmas did you have?" I asked them.

"Usual crap! Spent a bloody fortune on her and the kids and still she isn't happy!" Brian complained.

"Sam and I had a fantastic Christmas. Spent most of it shagging!" Jamie boasted. "I think I'm in love!" He said with some affection.

"With yourself, maybe!" Gordon made another of his sporadic, yet strangely salient comments.

"What about you?" Jamie asked me.

"It was OK." I was reluctant to admit to having enjoyed a saddo Christmas with my parents.

"How many of your harem did you shag, then?" He continued.

"Mind your own business." I avoided the question. "Anyway what harem?"

"Ha! Ha!" Jamie began in a puerile tone. "Ben didn't get any!"

"Yes I did!" I lied. "I just don't have to boast about it!"

Gordon left at about 2-00 a.m. and Jamie went with him, muttering about the time and something about Sam cutting his balls off, which sounded a suitable punishment.

"Harsh, but fair!" I chuckled to myself.

I was some way past walking home and fell asleep on Brian's sofa.

At about 7 o'clock this morning, Maria got up and came downstairs, wearing a silky dressing gown, to check if Brian had gone to work. He was nowhere to be found, so we assumed he had. She didn't seem fazed by my presence. The children were running around upstairs and, as she made us a pot of coffee, she said, "It's a good job the children are here! I might just have jumped on you!"

Whoa! What was that all about?

"Only if you wanted Brian to kill you!" I defused the tension with my usual humour.

"I'm climbing the walls!" She continued. "We never do it any more."

"Would I be correct in placing that little snippet in the file marked 'too much information', Maria?"

"Maybe. He's just so bloody boring these days." She continued, oblivious to my discomfort.

Her dressing gown had slipped open, revealing a diaphanous (hurrah! <in more ways than one!>) nightdress underneath, which left little to the imagination. My bottle decidedly went and I took my traditional refuge at moments like these, in the bathroom. When I came out, she had adjusted her gown and all was once more proper. How much of what she had said was a friend confiding and joking, and how much was serious, I haven't a clue, but it was a bit scary there, for a while!

Things to be grateful for

1) A good night out with the boys.
2) Maria made me an Alka Selzer for breakfast!
3) I escaped without disgracing myself, maybe only thanks to the presence of the children!
4) I have all of today to get rid of this hangover!

<u>Thursday 11th January 2001</u>

8-00 p.m. On the trailer

It is very quiet tonight. It seems as though it has been pissing down with rain for weeks. It is getting beyond a joke. Fields are flooded and it does nothing for my evening trade. I don't know why, but I have been sitting here, this evening, thinking about having kids. It's funny, but I always picture myself with Louise in these mental ramblings. Mother must be getting to me, but it would be nice to have a little Ben or Benjamina at some point!

I was chatting online again last night, with Corinne and, somehow, I relented and agreed to meet her in the future, but we didn't set a time or place. I'm not sure I really want to do it, or why I agreed to it in the first place.

Things to be grateful for

I can't be arsed to think of any today. Too pissed off by the weather.

Sunday 14th January 2001

Word of the Day: Myopic... lacking foresight, short-sighted.

11-00 a.m. Just woken up!

I looked at the clock and realised it is 11 a.m. and Mother hasn't called.
Has God taken pity on my poor earholes and given her laryngitis?
I was so surprised, that I dialled 1471, to check if I had slept through her call, but there had been no calls. Now! Do I thank my lucky stars, or do I ring her to check that all is well? How ironic that I beg her to let me sleep in on a Sunday and, when she does, I am worried witless!

Friday was a down day on base, so I went to see the specialist, which my solicitor arranged, to examine my ankle, further to my claim against the highways department. He reckons it is about 70 percent normal and may not get much better than that. I am torn between hoping that he is wrong, as I am fed up with it aching towards the end of each session, and hoping he is right, to maximise my claim. On balance, I think I'd rather get it back to full fitness.

Dave Kingsley, the referee, called by again on Friday and gave me details of a referee's course being run by The Football Association, for eight weeks from the 29 January. I might go. I quite fancy having a go at refereeing. I couldn't be any worse than some of the myopic (hurrah!) Referees I have had to suffer in games that I have played in.

4-00 p.m. on my sofa

I went for a quick pint, in The Red Lion, at lunchtime. Louise's sister, Emily, was there. I bought her a drink and chatted with her for about an hour. She told me that Louise was unhappy in her relationship with Simon. Apparently, he is a bit of a control freak, and he wants to know where she is and what she is doing all the time.

I bet she's got deja vu!

She would dump him under normal circumstances, but she likes her job and doesn't want to lose it. She is convinced that Simon, as a partner of the firm, would get her sacked if she leaves him. I admit to a part of me feeling a little smug about it, after she chose to be with him rather than me, but the major part of me felt sad for her.

"She can't live like that and be held to ransom. She should dump him and sue the firm if they sack her." I said.

"She hasn't been there long enough." Emily replied. "They can sack her without any reason, and what solicitor is going to sue another, in any case?"

"I hadn't thought of that. She should still leave him and get another job, somewhere else." I ventured. "She sent me a Christmas card, but I only opened it this week, because I spent Christmas with my parents. She wrote me a little message in it, saying that she would like to hear from me."

"Well ring her, then!"

"She wasn't very happy with me over the Stella incident."

"Are you still seeing her?"

"No. It wasn't really that serious. I just got into a daft situation and, then, Louise walked into it, at the wrong moment."

I told her about the ex-fiancé and the baby and said that it was Louise that I had always wanted to go out with.

"I was really upset at the way things panned out. I guess we were never destined to have a relationship."

"If you want her, go and get her, you silly bugger! She really liked you."

"She didn't like me much, when she decided to go out with Simon the snake!"

"Yes. But she thought you were with that Stella. According to her, you were an item. That's what she told Louise. At least call her. She always asks me if I've seen you, and how you are."

"Really? Oh! Maybe I'll ring her later."

I came home to make some dinner, but couldn't be bothered and, now I'm lying here, I don't feel like moving. I may have an hour's sleep, have something light for tea and then go to the quiz later.

Things to be grateful for

1) Louise is getting fed up with Simon.
2) She still mentions me fondly.
3) Maybe all is not lost.

Thursday 18th January 2001

Word of the Day: Temerity... impertinence, audacity

11-30 p.m. Just home.

I do not believe the gall of Stella! She rang me, while I was working, to tell me that her fiancé wants to set a date for their wedding. She actually had the temerity (hurrah!), to tell me that this was my last chance. For once in my life, I was quite speechless. I don't know her fiancé, but I feel sorry for him. They are making plans to get married, and she's still trying to get off with somebody else. What a great basis for a marriage!

Things to be grateful for

1) I found out what she was like before it was too late!
2) I think she has finally got the message.

Sunday 21st January 2001

Word of the Day: Invariably... consistently, always.

7-15 a.m. On a sun drenched beach, palm trees swaying softly in the breeze. The cool, clear Hawaiian sea is lapping gently at my feet, and I am surrounded by a bevy of semi naked beauties, one of whom is about to rub some factor 15 lotion onto my expectant body...

(Telephone rings)

"Hello, Waikiki Beach Hotel."

"What are you talking about, Benjamin?"

"That's where I was until you just woke me, Mother."

"Where have you been for two weeks?"

"Here. Where else?"

"You didn't ring me. I could have been dead for all you knew."

"Well, if you were, you wouldn't have answered the phone, anyway, would you? So it would have been pointless ringing."

"Your smart mouth will get you into trouble one of these days!"

"Anyway, I'm not pregnant, if that's what you're ringing to find out."

"Very funny. Don't you want to know why I didn't ring you last week?" She was bursting to tell me something.

"Not really. If you wanted to speak at me, you'd have rung." I refused to ask her what she wanted me to ask!

"Don't think I didn't notice the 'at'. You make me sound like an ogre!"

"OK. I'll buy it. Why didn't you ring last week?" I relented.

"Well. You know we're on cable?"

"Yes."

"The water board were digging up the road, on Friday, and ripped up the cable! We didn't have a phone all weekend."

"Haven't you heard of call boxes, then?"

"I'm not going all that way, on a Sunday morning, in torrential rain, just to be verbally abused by my own son."

1-0 "Why? Where do you usually go?" o*r **what?***

"You **are** full of yourself this morning, for someone who is supposed to be half asleep."

"Yes I am, aren't I? How's Dad?"

"Oh, he's OK. You know. He doesn't change much."

"Can I speak to him?"

"No. He is still asleep. And it's 'may I' not 'can I'. "

"How come he can get a sleep in, on Sunday morning and I can't? Or should I say He may and I may not?

"Don't cheek your mother, Benjamin. You're not to big to get a clout, you know."

"I think you'll find that I am, and also about 65 miles too far away to get much force behind it!"

She laughed, in spite of herself, and we recalled how, when I was young, she used to chase me around the house, if I had been naughty, trying to hit me with a stick. I was always too quick for her and invariably, (hurrah!), got away, and we'd end up laughing. However, one day I tried to jump over the back of the settee, to escape, but was not quite as nimble as I had hoped. She caught me across the back with the stick. The shock made me lose balance and fall, unhurt, onto the carpeted floor. Thinking quickly, I writhed in simulated agony and worried the life out of her, until I could no longer keep a straight face and burst out laughing. Fortunately, because she **was** still holding the stick, she saw the funny side of it and laughed too! For once, when we had finished talking, I went back to sleep and did not wake up until midday!

5-00 p.m. just off the phone.

I called Louise about an hour ago. As it rang, I could feel the adrenalin surging in my midriff. Her mother answered.

"Hello, Mrs Burnham, is Louise there?"

"Er... yes...hang on.... Louise! It's for you! Take it in there!" She shouted through to the sitting room.

"Hello? Louise?"

"Yes...er... Hi."

"It's me, Ben."

"I know. How are you, Uncle Jim?"

"Oh shit! He's there, isn't he?"

"Yes! It's a shame isn't it?"

"Yes it is. Can I ring you when he is not there, or is he always there?"

"Mostly, but not always. How's Susan?"

"Who the hell is Susan?" I laughed, realising that she was inventing the situation for the benefit of Sime the slime!

"Oh, right... never mind, then. Call me when you have a little more time."

"Do you need me to say when, at this point?"

"It would help, a bit."

"OK! Thursday at about 7-30 p.m.?"

"Sounds great. I'll look forward to it. 'Bye then."

I hate weird calls like that, but I guess there wasn't much she could do. She sounded like she wanted to talk, though. That's a definite plus!

Things to be grateful for

1) A belated Sunday morning lie in.
2) I have made contact with Louise.
3) She sounded very friendly.

Monday 22<u>nd</u> January 2001

Word of the Day: Rhetoric... oratory, speech-making, dramatic speech

10-00 a.m. Eating breakfast

Bush was sworn in as President at the weekend, amidst a lot of rhetoric, (hurrah!), pomp and circumstance. After all the ridicule of recounts, I would have expected it to be a bit more low-key. I will be most surprised if he survives for the customary second term of office. The vote was so close, in fact, I think that Gore actually got more votes overall, that the next election will be very interesting.

The quiz night was as dull as ditchwater, yesterday. Only and Gordon and I turned up from our team, and there were only three teams in all. Each of the three teams won a round, but the jackpot of £3 remained intact. Thinking about it, the low jackpot, after we won it last week, is probably the reason for the poor turnout.

Things to be grateful for

1) I went home sober last night!
2) There was a message on the answering machine from Louise, confirming that she will try to be Simon-free on Thursday, and that she is looking forward to speaking with me.

Wednesday 24th January 2001

Word of the Day: Anathema... abhorrence, abomination.

3-30 p.m. Between sessions.

My friend Paul, with whom I went to York, came by today. He asked me if I would be interested in going back to trade inside the base.

"Not if I have to deal with the same mob, I wouldn't!" I declared adamantly.

"What if you contracted directly with the military?" He said, in an attempt at an enticing manner.

"It won't happen though, will it? "

"But the cafeteria is closed now. There is no food on base. If they are not able to provide a service that is needed, the base Commander can make his own arrangements."

"Well! In that case, I would be interested."

"OK. Nothing will happen for a while, but Colonel Draper may drop by just to have a word. He wanted me to sound you out, in private, before he gets involved. The guys on base are really not happy, with nowhere to eat lunch. You'll be the only show in town, you could make big bucks here!"

I guess he's right. It'd be too good an opportunity to miss, depending on the cost, of course! I wonder how much they will want in commission. Well, nothing ventured! It won't hurt to speak to the Colonel. I'll bet he sent Paul out, to avoid the embarrassment of my saying 'no', outright! It is good that he understands that accusations about my integrity are anathema (hurrah!) to me, and that he obviously has some devious plan to get me on base without the hassle of last time.

Things to be grateful for

1) There is a possibility of a new base contract.
2) It was nice to see Paul again. We must get together again soon.

Friday 26th January 2001

Word of the Day: Antagonistic... hostile, unreceptive.

3-45 p.m. On sofa.

I rang Louise last night, as arranged, but regrettably her guard dog was there again. We had another of those ridiculous "Uncle Jim" conversations, which made me want to scream. It wasn't her fault, but I still felt antagonistic, (hurrah!), towards her, quite unfairly. Once I was off the phone, I felt really bad about my attitude and hoped that she did not pick up on it. However, at about 12-30 a.m. the phone rang and it was her.

"Hello, you!" She said sexily.

"Hello, yourself!" I replied, quite taken aback to find her calling out of the blue.

"I'm sorry about earlier," she began. "He has only just left."

"Are you still staying with your parents, then?"

"Yes. There's no point incurring unnecessary costs, if you are not setting down roots."

"Oh! So you don't see Chichester as your future home, then?"

"Not really. No."

"And you haven't moved in with him... Simon... Yet?"

"Good heavens, no! He wanted me to, about two weeks after I went out with him, but I'm so glad I didn't even think about it. It would have been an even bigger disaster than Mick. I can't move without him being there, wanting to know what I'm doing, where I'm going. If I so much as breathe a word of complaint or resistance, he gets really grumpy."

"So, sack him. The man's a 24 carat plonker."

"It's not as straightforward as that, is it? My job is at stake."

"But, if you don't see yourself with him, or in Chichester, why worry? Come back to Marston Ferrars, get another job up here."

"I'm scared of him, though. He is a powerful man..."

"What, physically powerful...? "

"No!" She let out a hushed laugh. "He's a wimp! I mean that he's got a lot of influence in legal circles, and he's not going to give me a glowing reference, is he?"

"So get a different job in a different field. You really need to break away from him."

"I know you're right, but the time is not right to do it."

"You can really pick them, can't you?"

"He seemed really nice, at first. But now he thinks I'm his property. Just like Mick did."

"I guess you must go for controlling men, then!"

"Not by choice! Especially after seeing my dad behaving like that with my mum."

"That's the cycle of abuse thing going on. You subconsciously pick men who are like your dad!"

"Thank you, Benjamin Freud!" She laughed. "Mind you, there could be something in that!"

We continued talking for nearly two hours, but I don't think I managed to persuade her to dump him; at least, not yet. But she is talking to me, now. Maybe, given time, she will realise she can't live her life like that. She is like a vulnerable little bird, and I feel the need to protect her and hold her. I want to make everything all right for her.

God! I am getting all gooey!

Things to be grateful for

1) I really enjoyed talking to Louise tonight.
2) She rang me, late, after he had gone, so she must be seriously thinking about her situation.
3) It's me that she is confiding in!

<u>Sunday 28th January 2001</u>

Word of the Day: Indignant... offended, resentful

8-30 a.m. In bed
(Telephone rings...)

No prizes for guessing who this is!

"Ben Arnold's Massage Parlour. Can I rub you up the wrong way?" I made myself laugh with that one, anticipating Mother's indignant, (hurrah!) reply.

"You can do my shoulders if you like, they're killing me!" Louise laughed.

Oh my God! Now what will she think of me? I was convinced it would have been Mother.

"Any time you want! I thought that was my mother. I was trying to shock her."

"That's what they all say!" She replied. "I'll bet that's your new business venture!"

"OK! I'm busted. How are you?"

"I'm fine. Simon is picking me up at about 10-30, so I thought I would ring before he comes. We are supposed to be going down to the coast to have lunch somewhere."

"I bet Bognor Regis is a hive of activity in the middle of winter! I've always wanted to spend January watching huge waves crash against the coastline, while I stand freezing my essentials off!"

She began laughing. "Yes, he has some strange ideas at times!"

"Not the least of which is wanting you to move in with him!"

"Now, now! You're getting catty." She chided me.

"So, he is obviously back in your good books again. The other day, I thought you were about to leave him."

"I didn't say that. I know we discussed it and that was your advice, but I did say that I wanted to keep my job, didn't I? That doesn't mean my feelings about him have changed!"

Good!

"Yes you did, but you also agreed that it was prostituting yourself...."

Oh FUCK! Did I really say that out loud?

".... I didn't mean that the way it sounded. I didn't mean sexually... I mean... I believed you when you said you haven't slept with him... Oh...! My...! God...! When you get to the bottom of a big hole... stop digging!"

Fortunately, she was laughing her socks off!

"Oh Ben! You are so funny! I knew what you meant in the first place. You don't have to walk on eggshells with me, you know. I know that I'm compromising myself... note the change from prostituting to compromising?" She laughed again. "And I **am** compromising myself, because I really don't want to be with him. He is OK for company, most of the time, but I don't see myself married to him, or even sleeping with him. I just don't fancy him."

"Then you have a big problem. Staying with him is just giving him mixed signals. He thinks everything's OK and that his behaviour's acceptable to you, because you stay."

"So how do I get out of the relationship, without getting out of the job, clever clogs!"

"I never said I had the answer! My forte is pointing out the questions! Answers are a lot more difficult!" We laughed together.

"So if I want to know what is wrong in my life, I can always ask you? But God forbid I should ask you how to put it right?"

"That's about it in a nutshell. Glad I could be of assistance... oh, there goes my call waiting signal... can you wait a few moments?" I was hoping she could.

"It's OK, I have to go anyway. Speak to you in the week?"

"Yes. I'd like that. 'Bye for now."

The second call was from Mother, as if I didn't know.

"Hello, Ben. How are you?"

"On top of the world, Mother. How about you?"

"Note the time! Nearly nine o'clock!"

"Thank you, Mother. Very considerate of you."

"You were on the phone then, weren't you?"

"How do you know?"

"It rang more than four times without your answering thing coming on."

"Yes I was on the phone."

"So how come it is all right for other people to ring you early on Sunday, but not me?"

"It is not "all right" for anyone to ring me early on a Sunday! But when the phone rings, it rings. There is not much that I can do about it."

"Who was it, then?"

"That's a very personal question. What difference does it make?"

That's scared talk for mind your own business!

"None at all, but since you're cagey about discussing it, I would guess it was a girl!"

"It was not a "girl"! For God's sake, Mother, I am almost 35! I don't go out with girls, I go out with women."

"Aha! I thought so. Anyone we know?"

"Yes, as a matter of fact, it was. Louise. Remember? The one you tried so hard to frighten away?"

"I did not!" she said indignantly, (Hurrah! Used it twice! Ben 2: Word of the Day 0!). "I thought she was a lovely girl...er...woman! In fact, I have asked you since then, why you haven't got together with her."

"Exactly! She was so horrified by the mental state of my mother, that she did a runner and was never seen again."

"That is a blatant lie, if she has just rung you! So don't give me that rubbish... How is she?"

"She's fine. Well, actually, she is not."

I explained to Mother the situation that Louise finds herself in, and she was remarkably understanding and sympathetic. She advised me to play a waiting game and not jump in with both feet.

"If you do, you may be seen to be the home wrecker. It sounds as though this solicitor is doing his best to break them up, without your help. Just hang in there and be ready to pick up the pieces, when it happens.... As it almost certainly will."

Sometimes life throws up some surprises. I didn't expect Mother to be such a big help. I suppose she has had more experience of life than me.

So! I don't know everything, after all! Quelle surprise!

Things to be grateful for

1) Another phone call from Louise.
2) Unexpected sympathy and good advice from Mother.
3) Two days without work!
4) A night out with the lads in prospect!

Tuesday 30th January 2001

Word of the Day: Symbiotic... interaction between two organisms or parties, giving benefit to both.

Midnight   In bed

I have had an interesting couple of days. Last night, I decided to go to the Football Association referees training course. There will be a variety of instructors over the weeks, and the first of these were Paul Ainsworth and Martin White. I have to say that it did open my eyes. As Martin stated, in his introduction, the first few lessons are a bit boring, but necessary nonetheless. We learned about the field of play, (yawn!), and the ball and its relative dimensions and properties, (bigger yawn!). I really felt for Paul, with material like that to teach! It was very difficult to get a laugh out of it! However, we did have some discussion about football in general and refereeing, in particular. Martin promised that we would all learn something about the game that we didn't know and, as a starter, asked what the referee should do, in a game, if a player from one team shouted, "leave it" to a colleague, meaning his team-mate to leave the ball and let it run to himself. To a man, we all replied that he should be penalised, because you can't shout, "leave it," unless you shout the name of the colleague as well. He then pointed out that nowhere in the laws of the game, (and we must say laws, not rules, under pain of death!), does it outlaw calls of that nature, nor does it require a player to call the name of the team-mate. He said that any verbal call which puts an opponent off, will be penalised, while any call which does not put an opponent off, is allowable, provided it is not offensive or abusive. This was just one of the numerous players' and spectators' myths. He was right! We all learned something new, which we thought we already knew!

Today, Colonel Draper came out to speak to me. He asked if I would like to go back inside the base, if I was able to deal with Military Services directly. I said that I would like to discuss it, and he arranged for me to meet the contracts manager tomorrow. If all goes well, I could be back on base by Thursday, the first of the month. As they have no food on base at the moment, and I am not making enough money outside, it appears to be a symbiotic, (hurrah!), arrangement and, therefore, I trust that they will not ask for a large fee to be there.

Now there is a turn up for the books!

Sadly, I have not heard from Louise since the weekend and I am having a great deal of difficulty preventing myself ringing her. I want to follow Mother's advice, but it is not easy. I hope that she rings soon.

I did get another e-mail from Corinne, asking me if I would be free to meet next weekend. I have responded by e-mail, with a little white lie, that I have to attend a weekend event with the trailer. I must admit that I am reticent to meet someone to whom I have only spoken on the Internet, although she does seem like a nice person and very bright. The timing is not the best, either, with the possibility of Louise becoming available again. I really don't want to get involved with another woman, if Louise is about to do the sensible thing and dump Simple Simon!

Things to be grateful for

1) I enjoyed the first week of the referees' course.
2) If all goes well tomorrow, I will be back on base.
3) I was a good boy, and didn't ring Louise!

Wednesday 31ˢᵗ January 2001

Word of the Day: Circumspect... wary, guarded, cautious, judicious.

11-30 p.m. In flat

I met the Services contracts manager today, and Colonel Draper attended with me. They seem like a good bunch and, with the Colonel's help, we came to an agreement, which is far better than the deal I had previously. I will be required to pay a single fee, on a monthly basis, thereby removing the need for customers to sign for their food, or for my keeping a record of sales. Although they were not keen to rush things through, they did want things to run on a calendar monthly basis, so I will be back on base tomorrow!

Tonight, it was below freezing, and the paths were covered with frost. At one point, Brian Naylor, who is rapidly outgrowing his position as apprentice village idiot and staking a claim for the full title, made a slide on the asphalt in front of the hatch.

"Brian, if I fall over on that when I pack in, you are dead!"

"Yeah right! You'd have to catch me first!"

"And what makes you think I couldn't?"

"'Cos you're too old!"

The words were hardly out of his mouth, before I was through the rear door. In panic, he turned to run, slipped on the very product of his own misdeeds and came crashing down on the asphalt. I began to laugh, which elicited a predictable response.

"Fuck off, you bastard!" He picked himself up and limped off towards the shops.

I grabbed a handful of salt and sprinkled it onto the slippery surface that he had engineered, in an effort to make it safe for later customers, although the ice was thicker on the ground than customers this evening!

About an hour later, he returned. In an effort to show off, he ran from an area to the right of the hatch, intending to utilise the slippery area he had made earlier, to slide across my eye line and disappear to the left. Unfortunately, he was unaware that I had melted the ice with the salt, so he slid for about a yard, until his shoe made contact with the salted area. His soles gripped against the salt, causing his feet to stop dead, while his upper body continued its motion. He was launched forward and crashed in a heap, once again, on the pavement. I guess it just was not his night! When he returned, just as the pubs were turning out, he was a little more circumspect, (hurrah!).

Things to be grateful for

1) I have a new contract for the base.
2) I hope my finances are about to improve.
3) I enjoyed seeing Brian Naylor get his comeuppance!

<u>Sunday 4th February 2001</u>

Word of the Day: Inclement... severe, rough, detrimental, usually relating to weather

11-30 a.m. In flat

Mother managed to get me out of bed again, this morning, before eight. We chatted about the various comings and goings of her neighbours, whom I am supposed to remember and care about! As luck would have it, Dad is taking her to see an old friend of hers, who has recently been rediscovered and is living in Milton Keynes. Apparently, Mother hadn't seen her for over thirty years. She was walking around the Arndale Shopping Centre in Luton and Mother recognised her. It sounds as if this friend, Elsie, asked how I was.

"You remember Elsie, Ben. We were always together in those days."

"You said you haven't seen her for over thirty years, Mother. That means I would have been four, at best, maybe even younger. I don't even remember myself at that age, let alone Elsie!"

"Of course not! How silly I am!"

I wish I had been recording that call! She actually admitted that I had a point, for once!

"Anyway, I can't stand here gassing with you! We're going over to her place for Sunday Dinner. Her old man died about a year ago and left her well off, so she bought a bungalow in Milton Keynes."

Why would anyone do that?

"Is she into concrete cows or something?"

"There's more to Milton Keynes than concrete cows! There's a fantastic shopping centre for a start!"

And that is orgasm country for Mother, a shopping centre!

I left her to get on with preparations for her day out.

I am about to go for a lunchtime pint over the Red Lion and hope I might bump into Emily. That way I can find out how Louise is doing without ringing her.

11-15 p.m. Just back from Quiz night

Unfortunately, Emily was not at the pub this lunchtime, so I am still in the dark about the recent goings on at Chichester. The boys disagreed with my mother's advice very strongly and felt I should "go for it!"

"So what are you waiting for.... her to come running after you?" Brian asked pointedly.

"No, but I don't want to be pathetically chasing after her, while she is not ready to leave the guy she's with. You know she likes her job down there and, if she dumps him, he'll probably get her the sack."

"That's bollocks and you know it. If you want her, you've got to go for it."

"My mother agrees with me, that I should stay out of it until she's available. I don't want her to blame me, if it all goes pear-shaped."

"What are you, a mummy's boy?" Gordon piped up.

"No, I'm not. Far from it, but I know when she's right."

"Well, remember what I told you when you're out of the picture and regretting it!" Brian gave up on his line of persuasion.

"You should have come out with us last night." Jamie changed the subject. "We had a cracking time! Got pissed out of our heads in town."

"You know I had to work, you pillock! I can't afford to lose the turnover on a Saturday."

"He's right, though, we got completely rat-arsed!" Brian continued. "I was shitting myself about facing Maria when I got home!"

"Really?" I replied insincerely.

"Yeah! I got in at about two o'clock. Just after I got in, the cuckoo clock was striking two, so I made ten more cuckoo noises, so Maria would think it was twelve. I thought I'd got away with it too, but at breakfast she said, "What time did you get in last night?"

I said, "About twelve."

She said, "We need a new cuckoo clock."

When I asked her why, she said, "Well, last night it cuckooed twice, then said, "Oh shit!"; cuckooed 4 more times; cleared its throat; cuckooed another 3 times; giggled; cuckooed twice more; and then farted."

We all burst out laughing, and then Jamie said, "I bet she was well pissed off with you then? Anyway, I never noticed a cuckoo clock at your place."

"That is because it was a joke, you wassock!" I felt constrained to tell him. "Are you completely dim?"

"How the fuck am I supposed to know that, when he tells it like it really happened?" He whined.

"It's called using your intellect!" Gordon joined in again. "Oops, I'm sorry, I forgot. You haven't got one!"

"Where did you go?" I asked. "The gay bar again?" I chuckled to myself.

"Why don't you fuck off?" Gordon did not enjoy my joke.

"Methinks Mr Pinder doth protest too much!" I rejoined.

"Methinks Mr Arnold is a homophobic prat!" He replied.

"OK, you two. Now, now! Don't let's get our claws out." Brian was laughing at our exchange of abuse.

"I can't help it if he's gay, can I?" I couldn't resist one more jibe.

"I'll fucking hammer you in a minute!" Gordon was getting very hot under the collar.

"Hey, Gordon!" I said quietly. "It's only a joke, mate. Don't take it so seriously. You walked out with the hump last week. What's the matter? You know we mess about like that. You do it yourself, to the rest of us. Why take it so personally when you get some back?"

"No one's trying to say **you're** gay, are they?" He said more calmly.

"No one's saying you are, either. Not seriously. In any case, it wouldn't matter if you were. We're mates, it wouldn't make any difference to me if you were all gay."

"As long as you don't want to use my arse for a dart board!" Jamie tried to lighten the mood quite successfully.

My first two days back on base were hectic, just as I thought they would be. I have contacted Ashley and Stacey and, from Monday, they are back on the workforce. Thank God they are, because I can't cope with that much business on my own.

Luton haven't had a game for three weeks, because of the inclement, (hurrah!), weather. That must be the longest they have gone this season, without getting their arses kicked!

Things to be grateful for

1) A good start back on base
2) Stacey and Ashley are coming back.
3) Luton have gone three weeks without a defeat!

Tuesday 6th February 2001

Word of the Day: Can't think of one!

11-30 p.m. In flat

I went to the FA for the next instalment of the referees' course yesterday. It is getting a little more interesting now. I think I basically knew most of what we were taught tonight, though. Oh well, it will be another string to my bow if I qualify at the end of it.

There have been rumours flying about that Lil Fucillo is about to get the chop. How many different managers do Luton need in one season? If it turns out to be true, it must be a record. That will be four managers so far! The rumour is that Joe Kinnear is to take over. He would be great for the club, a very experienced manager.

Things to be grateful for

1) I'm enjoying the referees' course.
2) If Joe Kinnear comes to Luton Town FC, he would probably halt the slide towards relegation and keep us in division 2.

Wednesday 7th February 2001

Word of the Day: Guttural... raspy, throaty, deep

11-30 p.m. In flat

'Wayne and Waynetta' came to buy chips tonight. He was wearing a pair of khaki trousers, which had so many stains on them, they almost looked like camouflage pants. His hands were filthy, covered in engine oil and his face hadn't seen a razor for about a week.
I guess he has been working on his clapped-out Cortina, then!
His hair was matted and he and Waynetta made a matching pair. Between them, they could have kept a grease recycler in business for a fortnight. Their brood was with them, looking like an advert for refugees from a war-torn state. I also noticed that Waynetta is pregnant again.
Oh deep joy!
I really must stop calling them Wayne and Waynetta, before I do it to their face, by accident! Their real names are and Billy and Nina.
It is my theory, which is mine and belongs to me, that cackers are taking over the world! They are the most prolific of child producers and must surely bring the average IQ of the world down, with each generation. They always seem to find a mate of the same "species",

so I think that Darwin's theory of evolution is beginning to go into reverse!

"All right, Arnie?" Billy said, in that monotone, with which all cackers seem invariably to be endowed. "What's going on?"

"Not a lot," I replied. "I see you're having another baby?"

"Yeah! Didn't want it... Just happened."

"If you kept your cock in your pants, it wouldn't of!" Nina seized the moment.

"If you took your pills properly, it wouldn't of, neiver!" Billy shifted the blame back to her, exercising his wonderful command of the English language and its grammar.

"I'm not a fucking baby machine, you know..." She retorted.

I beg to differ!

"... I ain't 'avin' any more. You can do it yourself." She gesticulated with the universal signal for male masturbation. "You ain't coming near me again!"

"Don't be stupid!" He exerted the full measure of his intellect to the conversation.

"I mean it. I've done wiv sex. You can buy one of them dolls!"

Another customer had arrived and frowned towards me in disbelief at the discourse, which was taking place.

"Oi! 'Nita! I won't fuckin' tell you again!" Billy shouted at his daughter, who was rummaging through the Council rubbish bin.

Anita ill advisedly ran to him and received a cuff round her ear for her trouble. This caused her to start to scream, prompting another smack from her mother.

"Stop that noise or you'll get another one!" She bellowed. "Fuckin' kids... And you go and give me another one...? Bastard!"

Obviously, the way to stop a child from crying in pain is to inflict more pain. I hadn't realised!

I served his chips and asked, "Anything on them?"

"Tomatah sauce." He said gutturally, (hurrah!), with anticipation.

He drowned each portion with sauce and, as I wrapped them, picked up a number of chips in his filthy hands and proceeded to eat them. I struggled not to wince in distaste! He bolted the chips, and then let out a cry of pain.

"God! They're fuckin' 'ot!"

"Sorry, I didn't know you wanted cold ones. I needn't have cooked them, if I'd known!"

Nina laughed at my comment and could not resist a comment of her own.

"Course they're 'ot, you dick'ead! They've just come out of the chip fryer! Duh!"

Billy replied with a belch, and they left. The other customer screwed up his face.

"I suppose that would have been a compliment, if you were an Arab!" I laughed and continued to prepare his order.

I was disappointed to find, on my return home, that there is still no word from Louise. I may ring her, if I don't hear from her by the end of the week. However I saw, on Teletext, that Joe Kinnear has been appointed Director of Football at Luton.

What the hell does that mean? It is not the same as Manager. Is Lil for the chop or will they work together? No doubt we will learn soon!

Things to be grateful for

1) I'm not a cacker.
2) I will be dead before the cackers finally take over the world!
3) I think this Sarah woman has a point, in her book, about writing down what you are grateful for. It does make me feel better about myself.

Thursday 8th February 2001

11-30 p.m. In flat

Joe Kinnear today announced that he is in charge of all football matters, from Youth policy, to first team selection and purchase of players. When asked if that meant he was the new manager he said, "Yes you could say that. I am responsible for all football matters within the club."

I guess Lil's future is very much in doubt, then!

Sunday 11th February 2001

Word of the Day: Regale... entertain, divert vocally

7-45 a.m. Sleeping like a baby!

(telephone rings!)
Shall I answer it or not? I feel half dead and really don't want to move!
(Telephone switches to answering machine)
"Hello Ben!" Mother begins in a mischievous singsong tone. "I know you're there. Pick up the phone."
"Hello, Mother. How are things in your world?"
Cloud cuckoo land!
"Fine, thank you. How are you?"
"I'll tell you when I get some feeling back in my head."
"Why, are you drunk?"
"Of course I'm not drunk. It's 7 o'clock in the morning. I'm just still fuzzy from sleeping."
"Time you were up and about. It's a lovely day."
I felt a compelling desire to scream, tell her why I do not want to be awake at this time of day and strangle her, all at the same time, then, strangely, did none of the above!
"I'm sure it is, Mother. Now, to what do I owe this pleasure?"
"What about Luton yesterday? I bet you didn't expect that."

She was referring to the fact that, after a long arduous and multi-managered season to date, Luton managed an unforeseen 1-0 victory, away at Northampton.

"Yes it was brilliant, wasn't it?"

"But what about that other poor bloke. The Italian one."

"You mean Fuccillo? He's not Italian, he's English. I think his Grandfather was Italian or something."

Well? What's going to happen to him?"

"How should I know? I guess he'll either be offered a job or be kicked out. He's helping Joe Kinnear at the moment. No-one has been sacked yet, as far as I know."

She then deftly changed the subject to regale, (hurrah!), me with what she really rang to say.

"You should have seen that Elsie's place. It was fantastic."

"But it's in Milton Keynes. I'm surprised Dad found his way in and even more surprised he found his way out again."

"You wouldn't say that if you'd have seen it...." She then gave a fifteen-minute monologue, extolling the virtues of Milton Keynes, in general, and Elsie's place in particular. At one point, I was so close to falling back asleep, that she noticed my periodic grunts had stopped and she raised her voice.

"Ben? Are you still there?"

I regained immediate consciousness, but luckily, she did not question me on the information she had so unrelentingly dispensed, so I did not have to explain my lack of absorption!

I must ring Louise today. I am getting stressed not knowing what is happening down there.

Am I getting obsessed?

Things to be grateful for

1) Luton off to a winning start under Joe Kinnear.
2) Sunday off, and quiz night with the lads.

Monday 12th February 2001

Word of the Day: Pontificate... Hold forth, preach, sound off.

10-45 a.m. Bored! Have already been on the Internet again this morning!

I spent some time, yesterday, chatting on the Internet. Predictably, Corinne appeared and immediately began cajoling me, as I had not responded to her e-mails, nor been available for Internet chatting. It did not take long before she was also asking when we are to meet. Under such pressure, I reluctantly agreed to meet her next weekend, for a coffee at Tesco's coffee shop at Bar Hill. I am none too sure that this was altogether a good idea, but it is time to get it out of the way, as it were. She seems nice enough, but a bit pushy to say the least.

The lads were in good form last night, not so much in the quiz, but in the inanity of the conversation. We sat for an hour, after the quiz had ended, discussing the relative merits of the world, the universe and everything. They are a good bunch, and I like their company, but they have some strange opinions. The subject inevitably turned to matters sexual!

"So, how's your sex life, Ben?" Jamie enquired.

"Non-existent, thank you!" I replied truthfully. "Is that all you think about?"

"Just about! If God made anything more enjoyable than sex, he kept it for himself!"

"Fucking moron!" Gordon tendered his usual intellectual observation.

"Hah! You're not getting any either, then?" Jamie came back at him.

"It's not the be all and end all of life, you know! There are other things." Gordon continued.

"There speaks a man whose cock is all atrophied from disuse!" Brian joined in.

"And there speaks a man who has swallowed a dictionary, and who knows what it's like not to have sex, 'cause he is married!" Jamie redirected the ridicule to Brian.

"That'd be funny, if it wasn't true. The best way known to man to stop a woman having sex, is to marry her!" Brian said philosophically. "And mine is as frigid as a nun."

"Sam fucks like a rattlesnake!" Jamie boasted. "She's always ready for it!"

"So you keep telling us ad infinitum," I complained. "If she likes a lot of sex, I wonder who she's getting it from. It obviously isn't you... You're never there!"

"I keep her well supplied, don't you worry!" He replied defensively.

"But what about all these women you keep chasing after? She'll find out in the end, and you'll be dead meat, sunshine!"

"As long as she gets her share, she'll never know." Jamie said confidently. "Anyway, you know that Cindy from Low Fen? I gave her one last night. She practically raped me!"

"Some bloody conquest that was!" Gordon said cynically. "She's a raving bloody nympho! She's had most of the blokes in the village at one time or another!"

"Isn't that funny?" I pontificated, (hurrah!). "When a bird shags a lot of blokes, she's a nympho, but when a bloke shags a lot of birds, like Jamie does, he's just normal! A good bloke. Smacks of double standards to me!"

"Who do you think you are? Jerry Springer?" Gordon said, provoking my reply.

"At least I don't frequent gay bars!"

This drew laughter from all of us, including Jamie, until he realised that he was also in the gay bar, and the joke was on him too, whereupon he frowned and fidgeted in his chair.

"What are you saying?" Gordon asked aggressively.

"Calm down, it was only a joke. No one's calling your manhood into question." I tried to pacify him.

"I don't know!" Jamie intervened and laughed. "That Rhondda told me he couldn't get it up!"

"Fuck off!" Gordon came back. "I wasn't the one with the bloke!"

"Oooooooh!" We all made that high pitched, childish noise, which seems to be the traditional response, when someone "gets out of their pram.""

Gordon however, was not amused and left in yet another fit of pique.

"He is fine dishing it out, isn't he? He can't take it, though." Jamie began. "And it's true, anyway. Rhondda did say he couldn't do it."

"I wonder why that was?" Brian queried. "He doesn't go out with many women, does he? Perhaps he was just scared, or out of practice?"

"Probably. But we were a bit hard on him. No one likes their sexual prowess called into question." I observed.

"Oh, he's just too sensitive," Jamie had the last word on the subject.

I have just attempted to ring Louise and spoke to her mother. She is out with the moron! I told her mother to tell her I'd rung, but not when Simple Simon is around. She agreed that that was probably the best policy.

Things to be grateful for

I would have said a good night out, but it was spoiled for me when Gordon got upset and left. I might also have been grateful for speaking to Louise, but I can't because I didn't! (And she was out again with that Simon!)

Wednesday 14th February 2001

Word of the Day: counterpart... Corresponding person, opposite number

4-45 p.m. After another good day on base.

Things are looking very good on base. My two helpers are mucking in and proving very good value for money. The guys like them and they are very easy to work with, now that they have become used to my foibles! However, some of the conversation today did my head in! Four female Air Force members were conducting a discussion about their love lives and reporting what other people had said to them. The mind-numbing quality was due to their use of the words go and like to describe people talking.
"So he goes, *"How would you like to go to the movies?"* and I'm like, *"Movies? Are you kidding me?"* So he goes, *"What's wrong with the movies?"* and I'm like, *"If I gotta tell you then, like, forget it!""*
And I'm, like, Argghh!
All this modern, American jargon jars me! Mind you, it is no better when English people do it. If these women had have been their English counterparts, (hurrah!), then it would probably have been just as jarring!
"So he turned round and said, *"How would you like to go to the flicks?"* So I turned round and said...etc. You have a mental image of people pirouetting before they speak.
Luton won again last night, 3-1. I don't believe it, two wins out of two for Joe Kinnear, and both away from home. The team hasn't changed, so I don't know what it is he has been saying to them, but it obviously has worked. Probably "Get your arses into gear or you are out!"

Things to be grateful for

1) Excellent trade on base, even if I do have to put up with their Americanisms!
2) Luton win again!

Saturday 17th February 2001

Word of the Day: Litigious... given to going to law, possibly unreasonably.

5-00 p.m. Having watched the football unfolding on Sky TV!

I am ecstatic! Luton have won 5-3 against Swansea, who are in the relegation zone along with us, so, in effect, it was a six-pointer! Joe Kinnear is GOD! At this rate, we'll win the league, let alone survive relegation!

I had a lot of luck this morning. In the mail, I have been awarded, (I know not why!) a free weekend for two in a hotel of my choice, (provided my choice is one of those listed in their leaflet!), worth up to £80 per person. This sounds too good to be true, and it is. Since the £80 refers to the price per night for two people, bed and breakfast, the cost without breakfast is only £60. Since meals must be taken in the hotel and will be billed separately, including breakfast, you are not going to be saving much, unless you intended to eat at their incredibly overpriced restaurant anyway! Looking at their menu, if two people had the cheapest breakfast, and the cheapest item on the lunch/dinner menu, it would cost £80 for the meals, for two days. This means that the most you can save is £40, which is one third of the bed and breakfast price. You can walk into most hotels and get a discount at certain weekends in the year, often two nights for the price of one, and no fine print forcing you to spend more money! It is a moot point, anyway, when I have no one to take on a weekend away! However, more luck was to follow! Reader's Digest has written to me telling me I've won a prize, and a possible bonus, if I reply immediately, and a book worth £8-57. How lucky is that? And a scratch card came inside the newspaper, and when I scratched it, I have won a prize! All I have to do is ring up a premium rate number for about 5 minutes at £10-00 per minute, to find out what I have won! Probably all of a pound! And I got a letter from Which! Magazine with a free trial subscription, and a cheque for several thousand pounds with my name on it! Shame the small print says, 'if your number is drawn' on it! Come to think of it, it may have been Which! Magazine with the prize and bonus, and Reader's Digest with the cheque. One thing I do know is that it is a hell of a lot easier to subscribe to these magazines than it is to unsubscribe. If I accept the free book, no doubt I'll get another, every two weeks, for the rest of my life, unless I move house and don't leave a forwarding address! The whole junk mail thing turns my brain to jelly! Do they all think we are so dense that we cannot see what is happening? I guess enough people are, and do fall for it, to make it worthwhile or they wouldn't do it. I remember reading in the newspaper about several people in America, who received dummy prize cheques that were so realistic that they bought plane tickets, and flew halfway across America, expecting to pick up prizes that they hadn't actually won. I was only surprised the report didn't conclude, *"and murdered the customer services assistant, who explained that the draw had not yet taken place, and that the cheques were not real!"*

Talking of adverts, there are some really annoying, repetitive ones on at the moment. Every ad break seems to contain five ads which begin, *"Have you had an accident in the last three years that wasn't your fault?"* and, likely as not, three of them are for the same company! Am I alone in wishing that kid in the ad had been abducted by aliens? I'm fed up hearing his name and seeing the ad! Reports in the newspapers seem to suggest that these companies have a lot of dissatisfied customers, who get awarded large sums, and then find that they receive a fraction of it, after costs and commissions. Some even allege that they ended up owing more money in commissions and fees than they were actually awarded. I can't help smiling at the irony of that. Mind you, I wouldn't be surprised if a lot of those complaining had little cause to get compensation in the first place. These ads just fuel people's greed. We are turning into a litigious (hurrah!) something-for-nothing nation. I am glad I went directly to a solicitor over my claim, though!

Things to be grateful for

1) Being so lucky in all of these companies' draws! (NOT).
2) Deciding to go direct to a solicitor and not to a third party, over my ankle injury.
3) Luton 5, Swansea 3, 9 points in a week from 3 games.

Sunday 18th February 2001

Word of the Day: Eulogise... sing the praises of

10-00 a.m. Having breakfast

(Telephone rings!)
"Hello, Benjamin. It's me."
"I know. I recognised your voice, Mother!"
"Oh! You know people say things like that. It isn't meant to be taken literally!"
"I know that, too. I was being ironic."
"Yes... Well... Don't...! How about Luton, then? They won again!"
"I know, I can't believe it... any more than I can believe you waited until 10 o' clock to ring me!"
"You are so funny! Be careful you don't cut yourself on that tongue!"
"So? What's new with you, then?"
Oh! No! I did it again!
"Your dad took me to Milton Keynes again yesterday..."
"To see Elsie?"
"No to the shopping centre! It is fantastic there. You should go some time."

"Why on earth should I want to travel all that way, when there is a perfectly good shopping centre in Peterborough, ten miles away? Sometimes you amaze me with the things you come out with."

"But it has acres and acres of shops. Loads of them you don't see in Luton."

She went on in ecstatic tones eulogising (hurrah!) Milton Keynes, yet again, until I was bored rigid. I am ashamed to say that I told her that I was getting a call waiting signal and was expecting an important call and this might be it.

"Shall I call you back later?" I offered.

"No it's OK. We might be going out."

"OK then..." I began to do that strange manoeuvre, where you start distancing your ear from the phone, moving it towards its cradle, and laughed at myself as I did so.

4-30 p.m. Just back from Bar Hill Tesco!

I have just returned from meeting Corinne at Tesco in Bar Hill. She was nothing like I had pictured her. Then again, maybe I was nothing like she had pictured me. I got there at about 2 o'clock and wandered around outside the coffee shop, thinking I might get a quick glimpse of her before introducing myself, (or not, as the case may be!). However, she saw me before I saw her and attacked from the rear!

"Hello? Are you Ben?"

"Yes. You must be Corinne."

"All my life!" She said with a slightly nervous gesture.

"Would you like a coffee?"

She nodded in assent and went to take a seat, while I ordered the drinks. I made a few glances in her direction to form an opinion on her appearance, but each time I did, I caught her eye, as she was watching me constantly. We had a very basic chat, covering many of the staple enquiries about life history. I found her pleasant, if a little mundane and, while not in the supermodel bracket, quite attractive. I certainly wouldn't feel embarrassed to be seen out with her. We had a second coffee and talked some more until the Tannoy announcer declared that the store would close in 15 minutes. It was

3-45 p.m.

"Would you like to come back to my house for something to eat?" She asked tentatively.

"Umm..."

"Oh dear!" She seemed embarrassed. "Was that a bit too forward?"

"No, not at all! It's just that I have to work tonight and haven't really got the time." I lied.

"Oh. OK. Maybe another time?"

"Yes. That would be nice."

Nice? Oh my God! I am so bad at this!

I was not sure exactly what was being offered and, either way, I did not want to get tied up and miss meeting the lads for the quiz. However, I wouldn't mind seeing her again, for a proper date, but I don't intend to get into another situation, where I miss out on going out with Louise. I may have to keep Corinne at computer's length, for a little while, until I know what is happening down in Chichester.

Things to be Grateful for

1) Mother allowing me to get some sleep this morning.
2) A pleasant meeting for coffee with Corinne.
3) I got away in time to go to the Quiz tonight!

Things to be Ashamed About

1) I lied to Mother to get her off the phone.
2) I lied to Corinne about working to avoid going back to her place. I should have told her the truth, that I have a previous engagement. Why do I feel the need to do that?

Monday 19th February 2001

Word of the Day: Pariah... Outcast, exile, recluse

11-a.m. Still in shock!

Last night would have been very flat, as the quiz was boring, with only three teams in attendance, and only Gordon and myself from the Far Canal team. Flat, that is, if Gordon hadn't have dropped a nuclear bombshell after we left.

"Do you fancy coming round to my place for coffee, Ben?" He said.

"Well it's the best offer I've had all week!" I joked. "It's a bit unusual, though, isn't it? What's up?"

"Oh, I've had a traumatic week, and I just need to talk to someone. Brian and Jamie can't take anything seriously, and I need to be taken seriously at the moment. It's important."

We drove to his house, in our own cars, and he opened the front door into a welcoming hallway. He ushered me into a sitting room, and I sat in a very comfortable armchair. He left to make the coffee. For the abode of a single man, his house was very impressive. The decoration was immaculate and the furniture was expensive and very tasteful. He is obviously a very good housekeeper, or he employs one! He's also a bit of a dark horse, as I'm sure none of us would have expected him to be living in such palatial circumstances. He returned to the sitting room and presented the coffee, in a bone china coffee service. I had no idea that he was a man of such taste and refinement, certainly not from his demeanour when out with the lads. I was in mild shock already, but totally unprepared for the major shock which was to follow.

"Ben...?" He began, nervously.

"Yes...?" I said, equally warily.

"You know what we've been talking about lately?"

"Yes... All sorts of crap!"

"No! I mean, like last week."

I racked my brain, but didn't get his point.

"Remind me." I suggested. "My mind is a blank."

"About what happened in town. At the... Erm... gay club."

"Oh! You don't need to worry about all that banter. It's only done in fun."

"But I do... Have to worry about it, I mean."

"Why?"

"It wasn't the first time I'd been there."

"So what?"

"Can't you put two and two together? It is a gay pub; I've been there before; more than once; therefore it is a reasonable assumption...?"

"You mean...?"

"Yes, I do mean...! I am... gay."

He looked as shocked as I felt! I was dumbfounded for what seemed like ages.

"You're shocked." He broke the silence.

"I'll say I am! I had no idea."

"I had to tell someone. It's so difficult going out with you guys and keeping it a secret."

"Why the hell didn't you say?"

"Why the hell do you think? I thought you all hated gays. You're always poking fun at them."

"So are you! But that's all it is... Fun. It's just macho bullshit. No one hates gay people. I told you it wouldn't matter to me if they were all gay."

"Yes, I know. But it's easy to say that, when you thought I was straight. How do feel now that you know I'm not?"

"I really meant it. I don't care if you are gay or straight, you're one of my friends." I hesitated again as it sank in. "How did you keep it hidden for so long?"

"I've never told anyone. Not even my parents."

I suddenly realised the enormity of the situation.

"But... You told me?"

"Yes. I trust you. Please don't tell anyone else, though."

"But why can't you just be open about it...? God! Now I know why you've been running away when we were razzing you."

"Exactly. I just didn't know what to say."

"I don't know what to say either! Why have you decided to tell me now?"

"I met someone. Last week. In the same bar we were in before. We went out for a meal, and he wants to see me again. I don't know how to handle it."

"Same way you handle yours, I suppose!" Once again, I tried to cope with what I was hearing by using humour. He laughed, which was a relief.

"Seriously, though, do you think I should...? See him again, I mean?"

"You're free and single, why not, if you want to? Do you fancy him?" It suddenly flashed through my mind, that this was the first time I had ever spoken about gay issues directly with a gay person. Here I was, offering advice on a gay guy's love life! If you'd have told me that, 7 days ago, I'd have thought you were on tablets!

"Yes, actually I do. But, apart from one relationship I had when I was 20, I haven't actually been out with anyone, you know.... properly.... male or female. Not until the infamous Rhondda incident. Trust me to get the real woman, eh? How ironic is that? Mind you, I'm not particularly enamoured of blokes who dress as women, anyway."

"So when you were 20, was that a man or a woman?" I asked.

"It was a man. I had realised I was gay by the time I was 18. I just never fancied women at all. I was friendly with a guy I met at college, and we became really close. He told me, one day, that he was gay and that it gave him a problem, because he really liked me. He also said that he would have liked to go out with me, if I had been gay too. He asked if I was offended, when I was actually thrilled. I admitted to him that I had thought I was gay too, but was unsure how to broach the subject with him. You know, Ben, it is very difficult for someone who is gay, to form relationships, unless you go to a gay club. You could hardly walk up to someone in a pub, and say, "I fancy you." You would more than likely end up with your facial features rearranged!"

"I can see that!"

"Anyway, we were together for three years... Never lived together, but we were... A couple, you know? But unfortunately, he died."

"I'm really sorry." I felt quite emotional, having heard him pour out his heart to me.

"He drowned... In a boating accident...I was heartbroken. I was supposed to have been going with him, but I had a part-time job and had to work, so he went with a bunch from college. They'd been fucking around on the river, and he fell in, but nobody realised he couldn't swim. They'd all been drinking and everyone thought it was hilarious that he had fallen in, until they realised that he hadn't come up. They dived in after him, but they couldn't find him in the murky water. The police found his body downstream the next day."

"That's awful! What a horrible thing to happen... And you've never met anyone since?"

"I've met a few guys, yes, but I could never bring myself to go out with any of them. Not until I met Mark last week."

"Well, go for it, you silly sod. Why are you asking me?"

"If the others find out, they'll hate me, or make my life hell at the very least."

"I'm sure they wouldn't."

"Please, don't tell them!" He said, in a panic. "Ben! Please! Don't."

"OK. You tell them when you're ready. I won't say a word."

We went on to talk about Louise, and how I really want to go out with her, and about Jamie and Brian's attitudes to gay people, and how Gordon wanted to avoid being a social pariah, (hurrah!). Finally, I went home, still in shock, both that he is gay, and that he chose me to confide in. It puts his moodiness and his reactions to some of our discussions and banter into perspective, though. It also makes sense of a lot of things, which have happened in the short time I have known him.

Things to be grateful for

1) It is quite humbling that Gordon chose me to trust with his secret.

2) I am pleased for him that he appears to have found someone to go out with.

3) I'm also pleased for him, that he has had the courage to tell someone.

Wednesday 21st February 2001

Word of the Day: Protracted... prolonged, drawn-out

6 p.m. On the trailer.

The damned Land Rover would not start again this morning. It really does not like this cold weather. Even when I put the spare battery on, it was having none of it. I went to a Land Rover dealership, this afternoon, and looked at a Land Rover Discovery. It was priced at £6500, but I think it was a little over the odds, at that sort of money. I offered him £6000 and expected him to give me £1000 for my old heap. After some protracted (hurrah!) negotiation, he offered me £2000 for it, and £4000 to pay. Result! I signed the papers and he has sent them off. The Discovery is blue and has a diesel engine, but it is only a three-door version. If get rid of my old Renault 21, and the Land Rover, and replace them with the Discovery, which will do both jobs, I'll save on road tax and insurance by only running one vehicle, and on the constant spending to keep the Land Rover on the road. I'm going to pick it up on Monday.

Luton lost for the first time under Joe Kinnear on Tuesday. Oh, well, never mind. Walsall will probably win the division and get promoted, so it was no disgrace losing 3-1 to them.

Things to be grateful for

1) A new (to me anyway!) Land Rover Discovery.
2) A good deal, well struck! How clever am I?

Thursday 22nd February 2001

Word of the Day: Unscrupulous... unprincipled, immoral, devious

11 p.m. Just in.

Last Monday was the last session in the referees' course. It has been quite rigorous and opened my eyes to how little I knew about the laws of the game, considering I have been playing it for 25 years! Tonight was the written examination. They didn't tell us how we'd all done, but I am confident I did well enough. Stacey was kind enough to stand in, for an hour and a half, while I went to take the exam and, luckily, it was not too busy, so she coped very well. After my return, a customer, who was unknown to me, arrived and said, "I used to run one of these things!"

Now, I wish I had a pound for every customer who alleges that he used to have a trailer like mine, and who knows how I should run my business. However, this guy turned out to be my predecessor on the airbase, Patrick. He also had great problems dealing with the company on base and, like me, found them to be unscrupulous. (hurrah!) So much so that, when he received an offer for his business, from another operator on another airbase, he was glad to sell it and get out!

"Some days I know just how you must have felt!" I sympathised.

"I did pretty well out of it. I thought of a figure that I would like to get for the business, and then doubled it, and they went for it. I was quite shocked. You know how it is, when people start running off at the mouth, and you think to yourself, "Yeah, Yeah! Heard it all before!"? I was feeling pretty pissed off with life on base, and I didn't think the guy was serious when he said he would like to buy the business. So I thought I would give him a ridiculous figure to shut him up. If I had realised he was serious, I would probably have asked for far less. I had enough money to start an export business, and it is doing very well, at the moment. Do you go to any events? I used to, but they're a pain the arse."

"Not really! I do the Stilton Cheese Rolling every year, On May Day Bank Holiday, but that's about all. All the others want too much bloody money. You have to nearly double your regular prices to make it worthwhile, then all the punters think it's you that is ripping them off!"

He nodded in agreement.

"In millennium year," I continued, "I got a phone call from some moron who said he was organising a Millennium Ball. Down in Essex, I think it was. He reckoned there were over 30,000 going... I've heard that sort of bullshit before... And he wanted to know how much I would tender for a site. I mean... Millennium night! A once in a lifetime event. As if I wanted to work that night! I said, "5 grand." And he said, "Sounds about right, I'll send you a contract." I said, "As soon as your cheque clears, I'll sign the contract and send it back to you.""

Patrick was laughing.

"He was gobsmacked! "I'm sorry? My cheque?" He says. "I meant how much would you tender to pay us." I told him, "You're having a laugh! It will be millennium night. I'd want at least five grand in my hand to turn up, then if I made some money, while I was there, it would be a bonus. Do you know how much bar and restaurant staff are getting paid for that night? 40 to 50 quid an hour!" He admitted that I wasn't the first to ask for payment to turn up and said he would come back to me if he needed me! Needless to say he didn't, and I got completely rat-arsed at a big party in the village instead." I laughed.

"I don't blame you," Patrick responded. "I would have done at the same."

He seemed like a nice bloke, in fact, a lot of the guys on base, who were here when Patrick was here, have said that he was a good bloke to deal with.

Things to be grateful for

1) Stacy helped me out and did a great job.
2) The written referee exam is out of the way. I could be a qualified referee by this time next week!
3) I had an enjoyable conversation with Patrick. It is nice to discuss one's frustrations with someone who knows what it is like.

Friday 23rd February 2001

Word of the Day: Disastrous... ruinous, catastrophic

4 p.m. Sitting down with a nice cup of tea.

Mother kindly got me out of bed at 7-30 this morning.
"Have you heard about the foot and mouth epidemic?" She said excitedly.
"I haven't heard anything this morning, yet! This morning didn't even exist for me until the phone just rang!"
"Yes..." She continued, oblivious to my response. "They are worried to death over it. Several cases... All over the country. Apparently, some sick animals came in from abroad and went to a market. They were sold on to farmers all over the place. They might have to kill all the animals."
"I think you are overreacting. Surely it won't spread that quickly. One day - no cases, the next - so many they that they've got to slaughter the entire animal population of the UK? I don't think so! Anyway, not all animals are susceptible so it."
"What about your chicken? Won't it affect you?"
"I doubt it! Chickens don't get it. They get claw and beak!"
"Do they? Oh my God. Is it as bad as foot and mouth?"
"I think so. Their beaks drop off and they can't peck their corn!" I was struggling to stay deadpan.

"What will you do? Could you sell turkey meat instead?"

"No! They get it as well. Makes them walk with a limp!" I finally lost the battle and began to laugh.

"You cunning little sod!" It dawned on her that I was winding her up. "Why do I always fall for it? Seriously though, will it affect you?"

"I don't know. Until I hear it for myself, I don't know how serious it is. I suppose it might mean there's less beef about; so chicken prices might rise. We'll have to see. Wasn't there an outbreak once before?"

"Yes, but you were only a baby. They had disinfectant on the roads and everything. You weren't allowed near farms, and meat was in a very short supply."

"Oh! Great! If that happens, not only would chicken go up in price, but also there would be less of it about, if everyone were eating it instead of beef. I think sheep get it as well. I'm not sure. I don't know about pigs, either."

"See! Smart arse! It's not so funny now, is it?"

I had to concede that it wasn't.

Luton are away to Swindon tomorrow. They are in the relegation dogfight too, so they'll be fighting for their lives, just as we will. Should be a good game.

I have seen the news on TV. It appears that Mother was right. There is quite a panic about the foot and mouth cases. It could be disastrous (hurrah! For the word of the day but not for business!) for business!

Things to be grateful for

Not a lot by the sound of things!

Monday 26th February 2001

Word of the Day: Fluctuate... rise and fall, vary.

5 p.m. Stressed out!

Surprisingly, Mother did not ring yesterday. Maybe Dad took her on another Milton Keynes jaunt. She seems obsessed with the place at the moment.

The foot and mouth situation is escalating. Several cases were confirmed, over the weekend, and movement of animals is under curtailment. The price of chicken has already increased by 25% and is set to rise even further. The price of beef and lamb is soaring, even though the stock being sold currently was killed prior to the outbreak. Things in the catering industry are not good! I guess it is supply and demand. My main chicken supplier has agreed to hold my price, as it has been stable for a long while, and he doesn't usually raise or lower my price when wholesale prices fluctuate, (hurrah!), so that I can budget more easily. However, if prices rise too high and stay high, no doubt he will be forced to raise his prices.

I went to pick up my "new" Discovery this morning, as planned. I approached the dealer, who smiled nervously.

"Hi! I'm afraid I have some... erm... bad news."

"Oh, no! Problems with the finance company?"

"No. I haven't actually sent off the paperwork yet."

"What's the problem, then?"

"Erm... I've...er...sold it. The 3-door."

"What do you mean, you've sold it? How come? I thought we had a deal?"

"Yes, but someone rang out of the blue, over the weekend, and offered cash for it."

"So what?"

"Well, in this day and age, first money on the table gets the deal."

"So, what happened to the "gentleman's word is his bond"?"

"I'm sorry. What can I say? You could have changed your mind over the weekend, and I would've lost the sale. I've got another one coming in this afternoon. I think you'd like it better. You can have a look at it, as soon as it's off the trailer. It is coming in about four o'clock."

I was so angry with him that I could have cheerfully punched his lights out! I managed to keep my composure and walked out without speaking. I spent the day chuntering to myself, about what a two-faced, self-interested bastard he was, but at four o'clock, I went down and parked near enough to see what the new vehicle was like. When it arrived, despite my anger, I was hooked almost immediately. It was metallic maroon, in colour, and was a five-door version. It had a very high standard of trim, with bull bars on the front and running boards. It also had, I noticed, a private number plate, probably Irish. Against my better judgement, I went in to speak to him about it. He told me that it was in better condition than he had realised, and he wanted an extra £500 for it, compared to the other one. I pointed out to him that this one had a petrol engine, whereas the other one was diesel, so it would obviously not hold its price as well as a diesel, and so should be less expensive. He didn't appear to be shifting ground, so I said that I felt he owed me something, due to the underhanded way he sold the other one from under me, and turned to leave. He called me back and, eventually, he agreed to honour the price of the original deal. The paperwork was adjusted and sent off to the finance company, so I am hopeful of having a new vehicle tomorrow or Wednesday.

Yesterday's quiz night was a quiet affair. Gordon did not turn up, probably because of his revelations from last week. Ironically, not one word was spoken about homosexuality. In fact, Gordon was hardly mentioned either, other than to say that his absence was noticed and that they hoped he was not ill.

Things to be grateful for

1) My persevering personality in securing the original deal for the alternative vehicle.

2) A higher specification Discovery than I thought I would be getting.

3) The fact that Gordon did not turn up, so I did not have to deal with Brian and Jamie in Gordon's presence, knowing what I know!

<u>Wednesday 28th February 2001</u>

Word of the Day: Nominal... pertaining to names.

Approaching midnight.

I had a few laughs today with the Americans. One guy was doing his very poor impression of John Wayne, and that started a complete talent show among the group that was there at the time. It seems to me that your average American will open the fridge door and, as soon as the little light comes on, they will start performing. The conversation switched from film to music and on to TV. I paid compliment to the American sitcoms of today.

"Most of them are really funny. "Friends" is brilliant, but the old ones were dire. Totally unfunny! "The Lucy Show"? What was **THAT** all about? The American audience used to fall about laughing, but in truth, ...to English audiences at least...it was about as funny as fog on a motorway. I've seen trestle tables that were less wooden than that Desi Arnaz, or whatever his name was."

"Yes, well, the audience laughter was canned. No one in America thought it was funny either!"

"So why did it run for 150 years? Or did it just seem like it?"

"Because they owned the darned studio!"

"And another thing. You guys seem pretty intelligent to me, how come nearly all American detective programmes have to have a character read out the plot for you? Just to make sure you are up with the programme!"

"What the hell are you talking about, Ben?"

"You know, like Hawaii 5/0 or Columbo. About two-thirds of the way through, just as it gets interesting, some character will pop up and give a résumé and destroy the moment. *"You mean he thought that she was pregnant by Joe, when she was actually pregnant by Bill? But Bill never knew until it was too late, because she lost the kid, and Joe thought she had aborted **his** child, so he shot her dead?"* (I put on my best American accent, *and then changed to a southern drawl to reply.) "Yup! That's exactly what I mean!"* Oh that's OK then! I hadn't worked that out, all by myself, from watching all those events unfold! Duh!!!"

"Hey, Ben! What are you saying about Americans?"

"I'm saying that you probably don't need to be led by the hand by some producer, to understand a plot. Unless you do, in which case you're as thick as two short planks!"

They all laughed spontaneously.

"Hey, you guys! We should be honoured that we can come on base and have Ben go right ahead and abuse us. Some people have to travel miles to get that kind of service!"

"Only kidding guys!"

"Yeah, right! I'm not so sure about you, Ben! I think you enjoy putting us down!"

I laughed at the difference in meaning between our "putting down" to their "putting down!" The speaker thought I was laughing at his wit, so I let it pass.

I rang Louise from the trailer tonight, hoping against hope that she would not have **him** there with her. She was alone when I got through.

"Hi Ben!" She said breezily. "How are you?"

"I'm fine but more to the point, how are you?"

"I'm fine. The job is going well, except for the fact that the others in the office treat me with suspicion, because Simon makes it clear to all and sundry that I am **HIS** woman."

"Are you getting any more time alone, or is he still in your face every hour that God sends?"

"No! He's still round here every opportunity he gets. He still wants me to marry him."

"You can't marry him. You don't love him. It's getting worse. Before you know it, he'll be locking you in your room."

"Don't even joke about it. I will never marry him. He is just too possessive. He would smother me."

"So, at the risk of sounding like a broken CD player, why stay with him?"

"Don't, Ben! I know you are being logical, but it's not that easy."

"So you keep saying! You know I'd really love to take you out and have you as **my "woman"?**" I stressed the "my woman," as she had when referring to Simon's attitude.

"Really? You mean that?"

"Of course I mean it. The difference is that I would treat you with respect. I just wish you would come home! You have no idea how jealous I am of that guy.... Oh damn! I've got a customer. I'll ring you back in a few minutes."

"OK, 'bye!"

I promised myself I wouldn't say that, while she was still with him! Oh well. It's done now!

One customer became several and a few minutes became an hour, but finally, it went quiet and I rang again.

"Hello?" A cultured male voice answered.

Oh! Bollocks! I bet that is him!

"Hello, is Louise there?"

"Yes, who's calling?"

"It's Ben."

"Well, what do you want, **BEN?**" He placed an unnatural emphasis on my name.

"Considering I asked if Louise was there, I guess I want to speak to her! **SIMON!**" I returned the nominal, (hurrah! nice one!), emphasis.

"Oh! You know who I am, then? She **has** mentioned me?"

"Yes, in passing!" I taunted him.

"Why would she want to speak to **you?**"

"I don't know. Shall we ask her?" I was waiting for my flippant tone to provoke a reaction, but Louise was obviously there all the time, and took the 'phone from him, before he could respond.

"Hello, Ben." She said softly.

In the background I heard Simon say, in a less than cultured vocabulary, *"Tell him to fuck off, Louise!"*

Ha! Ha! 1-0!

"Stop it, both of you. You're doing my head in. Ben, I'll speak to you some other time, OK?"

"OK, Louise. I've got another customer anyway," I lied.

God! This lying business can get very easy! I must stop it before it becomes habitual!

I am not happy about this. She is obviously not happy about her situation and wants to be out of the relationship with him, but is still too scared to leave him. Oh well. I've said my piece for now. I'll back off again, even though it pains me to do so. I'm getting fed up with this whole mess.

Things to be Grateful for

1) A fun day at the base.
2) I managed a friendly chat with Louise earlier.
3) I managed to piss off Simon! Bonus!

Friday 2nd March 2001

4-00 p.m. Preparing for the Friday night rush.

I took the oral part of the referees' exam last night and passed with flying colours. I am now a qualified class 3 referee. Whether I've got the bottle actually to take charge of a game is another thing! Now that it is a step closer, the thought of it terrifies me.

I still haven't got the "new" Discovery. I asked the dealer to have it MOT'd, even though there was about a month to run on the old certificate, just to be sure that it was roadworthy. It was a good job that I did, because it failed the test. It needs new brake discs and pads and some work on the exhaust system. Unfortunately, no one seems to have a stock of the discs, and it won't be ready until Monday.

Sunday 4th March 2001

Word of the Day: Irritability... Tetchiness, bad temper

3-30 p.m. Just finished cleaning trailer.

I was up with the larks this morning. For some reason I woke up at about 7-30 a.m. I wonder if my internal alarm clock was expecting Mother to ring? If so, it was disappointed because, of all the days to ring later than usual, she chose the one when I was up and about at the crack of dawn. I was feeling rather moody earlier, which is not like me at all, when the call arrived at 9-30 a.m. We discussed, (or should I say "she orated while I listened"?), the developments in the foot and mouth outbreak. She did not bring anything that was new to me into the conversation, but I listened dutifully and ooh'd and aah'd at appropriate times. She revealed that I was correct in my assumption that she had gone shopping at Milton Keynes, last Sunday, and they had ordered a new three-piece suite, among other things, and the conversation eventually drew to a merciful conclusion, before my irritability, (hurrah!), began to show.

Luton got back to winning ways with a 3-1 victory at Swindon, in what was effectively a six pointer. I feel quietly confident now, that Joe Kinnear can save us from relegation, but he may need a few new faces, before transfer deadline day, in a couple of weeks time. The problem is, what decent players want to board a half-sunken ship?

Things to be grateful for

1) I got through this morning's conversation with Mother, while I was in a mood, without upsetting her.
2) Luton won again!
3) I need a pint and it's Sunday and quiz night!

Wednesday 7th March 2001

Word of the Day: Prophetic... predictive, visionary

11-50 p.m. Just finished for the night.

No one from the Far Canal quiz team turned up on Sunday. I hadn't a clue why that should be, but I joined in with the Norfolk Enchance team, whose name turned out to be prophetic! (Hurrah!). We did not win any of the rounds, but we had a few laughs.

I saw Gordon, in the shops, on Monday. He looked a little sheepish, which was unfortunate, as I don't want him to avoid me from embarrassment. I approached him and he seemed a little lost for words, so I invited him to the flat, and we had some coffee and a chat. It had the effect of breaking the ice between us, and I think he's more comfortable with having told me, now that we had chance to talk. He has promised to come to the quiz next Sunday.

I picked up my "new" Discovery on Monday, and I noticed it had an oil leak, so I took it back to him, and he gave me back my Land Rover, until he can fit a new seal.

I thought I would wait for the pub to turn out tonight, before leaving, as there was a function going on, and the pub was heaving with people. It was a good decision, as I had a very busy half hour or so when they came out.

Earlier in the evening Louise rang on my mobile.

"Hi Ben! It's Louise."

"Hi. How're you doing?"

"Not bad. Look, I rang to tell you that I have decided to tell Simon that I don't want to go out with him any more."

Result! At last!

"Thank God for that! I thought you'd never do it."

"I've got to. I can't stand it any more. I went to a colleague's house yesterday... A female colleague... And he went off his head at me. "Why didn't you tell me? I came round to your mum's and looked a complete fool not knowing what you were up to!'" She mimicked his whining protest. "I told him that it was none of his business because he didn't own me, and I thought he was going to hit me! I think he may have done, if we had not been at work."

"You've got to get rid of him, Louise. You know you must."

"I know. I've been sitting here winding myself up to do it. I thought that, now I have made my mind up, it would strengthen my resolve if I told you. You know? Make it difficult for me to back out?"

"Glad to be of help... And don't let him blackmail you over your job, either!"

"I've been thinking about that, too. The job's good, but it is not worth having to live in a prison, because that's what it's like. I'm going to tell him tomorrow, at work."

We said our goodbyes and I left her to pluck up courage to do the dirty deed.

Things to be grateful for

1) Good takings tonight.
2) Simon is history!
3) Simon is history!
4) Simon is fucking history!!

Thursday 8th March 2001

Word of the Day: Penetralia... innermost secrets, hidden recesses

3-00 p.m. Just finished for the night.

I could hardly wait to ring Louise, this morning, for confirmation that she had told Simple Simon to hit the road! I called, as soon as I had finished the rush on base, at about 1-45 p.m.

"Hi Louise, it's Ben. How'd it go?"

"I can't really talk right now."
"You could say if it was good, bad or indifferent!"
"Not the first, more the second!" She said cryptically.
"You mean it didn't go well!"
"Exactly."
"But you did tell him?"
"Oh yes, I certainly took care of that part, but thank you for calling, I'll speak to you soon. Goodbye."

Well, at least she told him! Fantastic news. I wonder if I should have the night off and drive down to see her? Probably a bit soon and a bit too keen! Oh well! I'll wait till tonight.

9-00 p.m. I Don't believe it!

I rang Louise about 10 minutes ago, as it has been quiet for about an hour.
"Hello?"
"Hi brave girl! Tell me all about it! You said it went badly. Did he get upset?"
"You could say that. Hang on a minute, I'll call you back." Her voice dropped to a whisper.

After a few moments she rang back.
"Hi, Ben! I'm in the bathroom, on my mobile. He's here. It didn't go according to plan. Look I'd better not be too long."
"What difference does it make, if you've dumped him? And why is he there?"
"It's a long story. I went in to work early, to tell him. When I told him, he went all teary-eyed and begged me to stay with him."
"So what?"
"He wanted to know why, so I told him I felt smothered, and he was too possessive. He begged me for another chance and said he promised he would be better. I was trapped."
"No you weren't. You had done the hard bit. You're going to stay with him, aren't you?"
"Well... I said I'd give him one chance to prove himself."

"He won't change you know? I give up! How many times are you going to...? Oh never mind!"

"I'd better go."

"See? You are still cowering away because you are scared of him. Nothing's changed and nothing will change!"

"Sorry...I know I've let you down."

"You've let yourself down. 'Bye."

"'Bye."

I am totally gobsmacked. I seem to be always fluctuating between ecstatic highs and plummeting depths of despair with Louise. I don't think I can take much more of this. I can't begin to understand what goes on in the penetralia, (hurrah! If I wasn't so pissed off by the subject matter I would be really pleased with myself for that word!), of her mind! I've had it! I'm not going to discuss this with her any more. She's made her bed this time! She'll just have to lie on it! I am not going to moon around, like a lovesick pony, waiting for Louise to get rid of that fucking little weasel. She has become an obsession, and it is stopping me getting on with my life. I am going to go online later and leave a message for Corinne and ask her if she fancies going out somewhere over the weekend.

Things to be grateful for

1) Having some sort of resolution over the Louise obsession.
2) My Discovery is ready for pick up tomorrow.

Sunday 11th March 2001

Word of the Day: Disingenuous... having secret motives

Midday. Devouring a large bacon and egg bap!

Mother was back to normal this morning and rang at 7-45 a.m.

"What about Luton eh? They're hopeless. Lost again! Millwall this time."

"Yes Mother, I am perfectly capable of reading football results from the television, all by myself, thank you. Shouldn't you be pulling the wings off flies or something, instead of torturing me?"

"That's a little unkind, isn't it?"

"Maybe it is, but you were winding me up."

Hang on a minute; she's done it again! She's teasing me and I end up feeling guilty!

"It **was** against Millwall, and they are top of the division."

"They are definitely heading for relegation this year! Luton I mean, not Millwall." She laughed at her own wit.

"Up until a week ago, I would have argued with you, but it seems a lost cause now, after all those home matches without a win. Can't we talk about something else?"

"OK. What have you been up to this week?"

"The usual. Work, eat, sleep. Oh yes, and Louise rang me to tell me she was dumping that solicitor bloke. Then when she's told him, he asks for another chance, and she gives it to him! What do you think of that?"

"Que sera. She sounds like another lost cause. You'd better say a prayer to Saint Jude."

"Why?"

"The patron saint of lost causes!"

"Are you sure?"

"I was, but now you've questioned it, I am not confident about it."

Ha! 1-1!

"Anyway, it's Catholics that pray to saints. We're not Catholics."

"You can be so frustrating some times. Why do you always take things literally when you shouldn't, and don't when you ought to?"

"Because I can!"

Ha! 2-1 to me!

I drew the conversation to a close, fairly quickly, while I was still ahead, and went for a shower to liven myself up.

My Discovery was further delayed by an absence of parts, or an absence of intelligence in the bloke who was supposed to order them! I picked it up, finally, yesterday morning. I have to say it is like a Rolls-Royce compared to the old Land Rover!

I emailed Corinne earlier in the week, offering to take her for a meal on Monday night. She wasn't keen on Monday, due to other commitments, and asked if we could make it over the weekend. It would be a damned expensive meal if I didn't work on Friday or on Saturday, so that only left Sunday. Maybe, I should have agreed to take her out tonight, but it is Sunday and the only chance I get to see the lads. I couldn't tell her the real reason, or she would probably have told me where to go! It had to be Monday, or a rain check. Unaware of the disingenuous, (hurrah!), nature of my request, she said she would try to rearrange her diary to be available tomorrow, but can't be positive until later.

Things to be Grateful for

1) I think I won the battle of wits with Mother this morning. It is quite eerie, though, how I'm never totally sure!
2) I have my new vehicle at last.
3) I have a date with Corinne on Monday, (probably!).
4) I remained free to meet the lads for the quiz tonight.

Monday 12th March 2001

Word of the Day: Succinctly... concisely, tersely, briefly.

11 a.m. Having a Bacon and egg roll for brunch.

I seem to be "into" bacon and eggs at the moment!

Last night was a bit on the difficult side for me, bearing the burden of knowledge of Gordon's homosexuality. It is certainly a two edged sword. On one hand, I feel quite humbled that he felt comfortable enough to confide in me, but on the other, uneasy with the knowledge.

The quiz went well, with the super team, the Far Canal, winning all three rounds and only just failing to win the money in the jackpot round. We only got one question wrong, "what is the play area called in fencing?" I had an inkling it was a piste, but was not sure enough to insist.

"Piste, my arse!" Said Gordon. "You're 'piste' if you ask me. That's what you ski on, you dumb arse!"

"Careful, Gordon, that is twice you've mentioned arses. Are you becoming arse fixated?" Brian taunted him.

I winced and Gordon raised his eyebrows at me, in an expression, which said, "see what I mean?"

"Why do you keep on about homosexuality, Brian? Are you homophobic or a closet homo yourself?" I asked him.

He laughed. "That's a good one. Maria would piss herself laughing if I told her that."

"At least she'd know why her knickers keep disappearing." Jamie added.

"Fuck off, Jamie, you nancy boy!" Brian resorted to his usual abuse, when reason fails him!

This banter continued for several minutes and Gordon remained noticeably quiet.

"What's up with you, tonight?" Jamie asked Gordon.

"Nothing," Gordon replied succinctly, (hurrah!).

"So, why so quiet then?"

"Because the conversation lacks a little intellectual quality."

"How do you mean?" Jamie asked innocently.

"Well, if brains were cotton wool, you two haven't got enough between you to make a Tampax for a canary!"

I was the only one laughing!

"You've been a right miserable bastard lately." Brian began. "I think you need a good shag to sort you out."

"Thanks for the offer, " Gordon replied. "But you're not my type."

By this time, I am nearly choking with laughter. I had never seen Gordon in such great form. I had to admire his sardonic wit, although, truth to tell, it was wasted on the other two, who resented my laughing and disliked being the butt of his sarcasm.

"What was it you said the other day, Brian?" I re-entered the arena. "It's OK dishing it out, but not so good when you get it back?"

Brian grunted, but had no clever riposte in his verbal armoury.

After the pub closed, and we had all finished talking, we made our ways to our cars. Gordon motioned for me to remain, with a flick of his head. I opened the door to my recently acquired Discovery, and Brian and Jamie drove off. I shut the door and returned to where Gordon was still standing.

"I know what you're going to say!" I jumped in before he had time to speak. "I told you so!"

"Well, I did!" He said. "I'm sure they have some idea, you know."

"I'm sure they haven't. In any case, so what if they did? I'm sure they wouldn't give a shit."

"I'm equally sure they would not want to know me, if they knew for sure."

"You know, you wouldn't worry what other people thought about you, if only you knew how seldom they did!" I repeated a quote that I had heard from that Dr Phil bloke on the Oprah show.

"Fucking hell! That's a bit profound for this time of night." He laughed. "But it's probably true."

I let him believe that particular pearl of wisdom was my own!

Things to be grateful for

1) An enjoyable night out.
2) Gordon managed to stay all evening without storming out!
3) Gordon managed to use his wit to silence the other two.

Wednesday 14th March 2001

Word of the Day: Imprudent... Irresponsible, unwise.

3 p.m. Sitting in reflection of the week's events

I still can't believe that Louise bottled it last week. I really thought she was going to do the right thing. Having finally plucked up the courage to tell him to bike it, she must realise how imprudent, (hurrah!), she has been, by succumbing to his pleadings. She has not rung since and, I imagine, that is because she feels stupid, having told me she was going to end it with him, then losing her resolve and caving in. I have come to a decision. I am not going to ring her again. Too often have I got my hopes up, not only that she is doing the right thing for herself, but that I might have a chance of getting together with her and seeing how well we get on in a relationship.

Corinne managed to free herself to come out with me for a meal on Monday. She is pleasant enough, but in the aftermath of my disappointment with Louise, it was probably not the best of ideas. It was a partial distraction from events, but I kept looking at her in comparison to Louise, and she just doesn't match up in my eyes. We had a steak, in Cambridge, and she invited me back to her place and, having 'rejected' her last time we met, I felt obliged to go. As I write this, I am aware that I was adopting a very chauvinistic attitude, and this was made worse by the fact that she was all over me when we got there. It was obvious that she wanted to go to bed, and I offered little resistance to the idea. In retrospect, it was probably an act of revenge on Louise, which shows a very immature attitude, and a disgraceful lack of respect for Corinne, and I feel terrible about it now. She was a very enthusiastic lover, though, and seemed to be oblivious to my mental confusion, so I sincerely hope she does not feel used.

It is bloody cold today, and I feel depressed and could care less if I worked tonight or not. I suppose I ought to, if only to avoid letting down my regulars.

Things to be Grateful for

Can't be bothered

Saturday 17ᵗʰ March 2001

Word of the Day: Vicissitudinous... pertaining to a change of circumstance, or accidental fortunate developments

11 a.m. Watching the snow falling outside.

I just saw, on teletext, that Luton's game today against Oxford has been postponed, due to the vicissitudinous, (hurrah!), nature of the weather. Luton's team would have been decimated by injuries, so it is for the best. Still no word from Louise, which is disappointing. I half hoped she would ring me and admit that she had made a terrible mistake and was running home to Marston Ferrars. Oh well, c'est la vie!

I have decided to get a doner machine on the trailer. I have had numerous requests from customers, both here and on the base, so I think it will improve turnover. I can just about run to a second hand one, and the company who supply the doner meat will install one free of charge and allow me to pay for it over three months. They are coming to see me on Monday morning.

Things to be Grateful for

1) Luton will not lose today!
2) It is cold and business is usually good when it is cold!

Monday 19ᵗʰ March 2001

Word of the Day: Pristine... immaculate, spotless, in brand new condition.

12 noon In possession of a doner machine in the garage!

The doner company rep has just been and was unable to fit the machine, as he is not qualified to work with LPG! I will have to get an authorised CORGI gas fitter to install it. I am less than amused. I told him I am not starting to pay for it, until it is in use and the company agreed.

Mother rang, yesterday, to invite me over for Easter, but I really didn't want to go. I persuaded her to come over here, with Dad, instead. It will be a bit cramped but I'll cope. We will finalise the arrangements next Sunday, when I travel over to visit, as it is Mothers' Day.

Last night at the quiz was abnormally normal. (Hurrah! I love paradox!). All was very quiet on the gay comment front. I think the ambiance of the previous week caused at least two of us to take a look at ourselves! I told them all how depressed I was, and they cheered me up in the usual manner, and I had to leave my Discovery in the car park and get a taxi home, as I was brain dead by closing time. Their advice was to give her the big heave ho and get on with my life. However...

As if by magic, just as I was steeling myself to take their advice, I arrived home to find the answering machine showing a message, which turned out to be from Louise!

"Hi, Ben! It's me. I'm at Emily's for a few days. I'll explain later. Any chance we could get together for a chat? See you!"

My heart began to beat faster, as my mind played with thoughts that my daydream at the weekend was coming true. In my semi-inebriated state, I forgot what time it was and rang Emily immediately.

"Hello? Emily? It's Ben. Is Louise there?"

"Yes, hang on... we're in bed."

"Oh shit, I'm sorry, I didn't realise."

"Hello?" Louise came on the line, sounding sexily husky, from being asleep.

"Hi, What's up? Is everything OK?"

"Of course it is. How are you?" She began to wake up a little.

"All the better for hearing your voice. What are you doing up here, then? Have you got your passport? You're a foreigner in these parts now, you know!" I was rambling!

"I don't feel like one. It feels like I've never been away...."

Good news!

"...I had a few days owing, so I thought I'd come up. You know, get away from things. Do you still have Mondays off?"

"Not usually, now I am back on base, but this is a four day weekend for the Americans, so I am not working tomorrow. Why?"

"How about we get together? I'd like to have a chat about things."

Not so good news! If she'd left him, she'd have said so by now!

"Of course. How about we go somewhere for a meal?"

"OK. I'd like that. Why don't you come round for lunch. Emily will be at work, so we can chat, then go for something to eat in the evening."

"That'd be fantastic. I'll look forward to it. Tell Emily I'm sorry if I woke her. Didn't think about what time it was!"

"OK. 'Bye."

I am about to make myself pristine, (hurrah!), for her, to keep that date.

Things to be Grateful for

1) The obvious! Having the afternoon and evening with Louise!
2) No work today! It is a down day on base.
3) I feel absolutely on top of the world!

Tuesday 20th March 2001

Word of the Day: Disparaging... unfavourable, critical, disapproving

10 a.m. Just got up!

I am not working at the base today, as I did not get to bed until almost 3 a.m., and I awoke this morning with the mother of all hangovers! I am pleased with the way the "date" went with Louise last night. I hope I made her feel like a woman should feel, when out with a man. I was also pleased with some of the news I received.

I went to Emily's at 12-30 p.m., for lunch, as agreed. Louise, who was wearing the most beautiful smile, greeted me. It lit up her entire face, made me feel really special and reminded me why I fancied her so much! It was so good just to see her again. We caught up on the local gossip and on what had been happening in her job, and I took the opportunity to try to clear the air over the Stella incident. Louise was very understanding about it, from my point of view, but had some very disparaging, (Hurrah), words to say about Stella's behaviour. She told me that Stella had been very aggressive and vulgar towards her and had behaved like a cat defending its territory, on that fateful day that Louise had arrived, unannounced, to visit me. Stella had told Louise, " He's my fucking boyfriend! What do you want him for? Why don't you just get the message and fuck off and find a man of your own, instead of hanging round mine, when he doesn't want you around? You had your fucking chance and blew it! Just fuck off!" Stella didn't wait for Louise to respond, but slammed the door in her face. I assured her that none of what Stella had said was true, but I admitted that I had been seeing her and that I had slept with her.

"I can understand that," Louise said. "I had left the area, and we didn't seem to be getting anywhere when I was here, so I am sure it was even more of a non-starter living in Chichester! But it is a bit "off" when you were calling me and saying that you wanted to see me. In fact, we had made arrangements to meet. Simon had been asking me out ever since I got down there, but I kept putting him off, because I felt I owed it to you not to see someone else, while you were trying to see me. I wanted us to get together and had come up, really, just to see you, to surprise you. It was me who got the surprise though, wasn't it? Seeing her in your flat, like the lady of the manor, was the last straw."

"I know. I'm really sorry. I have no excuses... I'm thoroughly ashamed of myself."

I gave her my most earnest winning smile and she laughed.

"Good! So you should be...! I've never slept with Simon, you know." She seemed to be claiming the moral high ground, and with some justification.

"You're joking?" I said incredulously.

"No. I'm not. You know I told you that I was not ready for anything sexual, when we went out that time. I wasn't lying."

"I guess not!" I said, and she began to cry, as the futility of her situation hit home. "Don't do that or you'll have me doing it!"

"You don't strike me as the weepy type." She laughed, as the tears welled in her eyes. "It's all such a mess!"

"I know. I can't believe you didn't get rid of him, while you had the chance." I scolded.

It was not the right thing to say, at that moment, and the tears overflowed and rolled down her cheeks.

"If you keep up that crying, I'll have to hug you!" I said only half jokingly. I wanted to hold her so badly.

"Someone needs to!" She sobbed.

Needing no second invitation, I took her in my arms and drew her close to me. She felt so right snuggled against my chest, and I kissed her tenderly on her forehead. She looked up into my eyes, then brushed her lips lightly against mine, then pulled away, as sanity took over.

"OK! Now, mister! Go home! I need a shower and several hours work, to make myself beautiful, if we are going out for dinner tonight!"

"You are already beautiful. You don't need to do a thing."

"Very gallant, sir! She said. "But full of you-know-what!"

Her tears had stopped and she had a smile back on her face, as I left and went back to the flat.

When I returned to pick her up, she looked a picture. Her make-up was not overdone, but just perfect, and her hair shone.

"You don't scrub up too badly, do you?" I teased her.

"You don't look too bad yourself!" She responded, looking me up and down, with a look of mock surprise.

We had decided to go to my favourite Indian restaurant, The Bombay Brasserie, in Peterborough. We enjoyed an excellent, leisurely meal and spent the time talking incessantly, on various topics that were totally unrelated to her situation with Simon, or to our attempts, in the past, to get together. I found her a very intelligent woman, which only served to elevate her, even further, in my esteem.

After the meal, I drove her back to Emily's flat, and I pulled up outside, at about
10-30 p.m.

"Would you like a coffee, Ben...? And I **mean** a coffee!" Her eyes sparkled as she spoke.

"Louise, I could think of nothing more desirable, than to partake of a coffee with you. Indeed 'twould be a fitting termination to a very agreeable excursion!" I said in my best aristocratic accent.

"Who the heck are you, posh bloke? And what have you done with Ben?" She laughed.

We went inside and Emily made coffee for us all, and we continued to talk for hours. It was just after 2 a.m. when Emily could stay up no longer, worrying that she would never get up for work in the morning, if she did not sleep immediately.

"Look, you two!" She said, as she left. "Why don't you both stop all this messing about, and get on with it! Anyone can see you are perfect for each other! You've been talking each other's ears off all night! Sort it out, for God's sake!"

"You've done your share of yapping too, since we got back!" I observed, but I had to agree with her. We really did hit it off. It is such a shame that circumstances have conspired to keep us apart for so long.

We took at least another half hour to say goodbye and, as I left, I had butterflies in my stomach. I wanted to kiss her so much, but was confused as to where I stood, in the overall scheme of things. Should I kiss her as a friend, or as a potential lover? Should I not kiss her at all? What if I tried to kiss her and she rejected me? That would be embarrassing! As these thoughts were surging through my mind, she solved the problem for me in a heartbeat, by hugging me and kissing me briefly on the lips.

"Thanks for a lovely evening," she said sincerely. "I can't remember when I enjoyed myself as much."

Things to be Grateful for

1) A fantastic evening out.

2) Getting to know Louise so much better in such a short space of time.

3) I think Simon's days are numbered. Move over, son, and let a man in!

4) She hasn't even slept with him!

<u>Saturday 24th March 2001</u>

Word of the Day: Stilted... artificial, overformal, stiff.

10 a.m. Just got up!

Louise is returning to Chichester today. I haven't seen much of her, since the night out, because she had to visit so many people while she was here. She has a lot of friends, in this area, and a few relatives too, but, in a way, it worked out OK, because I was working in the evenings. She came to the trailer and spent an hour chatting with me, between customers, on Wednesday, and came round to my flat for coffee, when I returned from base on Thursday.

We sat with our coffees for about twenty minutes, without saying very much. The atmosphere was a little stilted, (Hurrah!). I was loath to say anything, which might damage the bond we had built up on Monday. Eventually, we started to loosen up, and I gained enough confidence to ask the question, which had been burning in my head all week.

"How do you think it is going with Simon? I mean...his probation!"

"Probation?" She laughed. "You make him sound like a criminal."

"It **is** criminal, the way he treats you."

Nice one, Ben!

She laughed again. "You never miss an opportunity, do you?"

"I do try!" We both smiled at each other.

"I don't know, really. He has been quieter, almost reflective... and he didn't kick up a fuss when I told him I wanted to come up here, to Emily's, for a week. He has phoned me every night and seems very sweet and charming. I guess he's doing better than he was!"

Bollocks! That is not what I wanted to hear!

"So, how long are you giving it, before you make up your mind?"

"I don't know. I told him I'll give it a month, but my heart isn't really in it. I wanted to get away from him... and I think I still do."

Phew! That's more like it!

"So, why did you give into him and give him another chance, like that? Doesn't seem logical to me."

"Me neither, when you put it like that. Oh well, I promised to give him some time to change, so I suppose I'm stuck with it for now."

I decided not to badger her any more and let the matter drop. She is popping in to say "goodbye", before she leaves.

Things to be Grateful for

1) Louise sounds far from convinced about staying with Simon.
2) She has been very friendly while she has been up here.
3) She has gone out of her way to see me despite my working hours.

Sunday 25th March 2001

Word of the Day: Vacillation... indecisiveness, dithering, wavering.

6 p.m. Just back from Luton

Louise called in, as promised, yesterday lunchtime, before setting off for her current home. She bade me a disappointingly swift farewell, hugged me and said that she hoped to see me again soon. Then she was gone and I was left reflecting on the futility of persevering with my quest to go out with her. Once again, I decided, she would have to ring **me,** if she wanted to talk to me, as I am thoroughly disillusioned with her vacillation, (Hurrah!).

At 7-30 a.m., this morning, the telephone rang, startling me out of a deep slumber.

"Hello Mother."

"Hello, love!" She began brightly.

OK! What's she after? Something's up!

The shock of her 'niceness' induced immediate wakefulness! My mind focussed on what day it was, and I realised her motive! It was Mothers' Day. She was ringing to give me the opportunity to wish her a Happy Mothers' Day, at the earliest possible moment.

In her dreams! It is not going to happen!

"So, what's happening in downtown Luton, then?"

"The same as in every other town." She tried, cryptically, to jog my memory.

Ha! As if!

I pretended absolute ignorance of the fact, by sidestepping all of her hints and, after fifteen minutes of verbal fencing, the call was terminated with her final comment.

"Well if you haven't anything more to say, I'd better get on."

"OK, Mother, you do that, and I'll see you whenever. Love you! 'Bye!"

I got up and showered, but I felt as lethargic as a sloth. Suddenly, the realisation struck me that, last night, I had put the clocks forward for the beginning of British Summer Time and that I had lost an hour's sleep. When Mother had rung, it was still 6-30 a.m. according to my biological clock. No wonder I was tired! I began to get ready to travel to Luton to surprise her. I had ordered a large bouquet of flowers from a florist in Peterborough, which was due to be delivered to me, by 9 o'clock. It arrived almost on the dot, and I set off for Luton by 9-30 a.m.

A little after half past ten, I arrived, put the bouquet on the doorstep and pressed the doorbell. Then, I retired to a vantage point alongside the house. She picked up the bouquet and read the inscription.

'*To the best Mother in the world, with all my love from the best son in the world, Ben. Xxxxxx*'

As she took them in, I heard her say to my dad, "They're from Ben! Shame he didn't come over to..." Her voice faded as she shut the door. I rang the bell again and, this time, stood and waited until it opened. Dad answered it and, as he opened his mouth to speak, I hushed him, putting my extended forefinger over my mouth.

"Let me surprise her." I whispered.

I walked in ahead of Dad, and Mother was in the kitchen, attending the flowers.

"These are absolutely beautiful, George." She called across the kitchen.

I was standing in the doorway and replied, "I know he's my dad, but can't you tell us apart?"

She was quite stunned when she turned around, which was the plan, and she came over and hugged me, as if she hadn't seen me in years. She was near to tears and thanked me for the flowers, but said that seeing me was better than any amount of flowers. Dad rolled his eyes and shrugged his shoulders, in a gesture, which asked, "Will you ever understand women?" He followed it up by miming the act of poking his forefinger down his throat to induce vomiting, and I stifled a laugh.

"I saw that!" She barked, although I know she could not have, since she was facing the other way. Dad made a further face imitating a small boy caught in the act.

"Why didn't you say you were coming?" Mother regained her composure. "It serves you right! I've got nothing for dinner! I **suppose** I could stretch it to three, though."

"That would have made for a great surprise... telling you I was coming! And surely, if you've got nothing for dinner, it could stretch to a hundred and three. Everyone would still get nothing!"

"Good point!" Dad laughed.

"Don't encourage him, George!" She chided him. "He's bad enough on his own, without you helping him."

"Anyway, we're going out for dinner." I announced. "I've booked a table at "The Mill.""

"I'm not dressed for going out, look at me!" She protested.

"Mother, it is not eleven o'clock. I booked the table for one. Even **you** can get ready in two hours!"

"You cheeky little sod!" She said with a smile. "OK! George, make him some tea. I'm going for a bath."

Dad and I spent a quiet hour, drinking tea and discussing Luton's latest failure to win, drawing 1-1 at Peterborough on Saturday and remaining 22nd in the league table, out of 24. Mother returned looking very smart, if a little over-dressed, took one look at Dad and me and said, "Come on, you two, sort yourselves out. I'm not going out with you looking like that."

A mutual glance of resignation was exchanged between us, as we scuttled off to improve our appearance to Mother's satisfaction.

We had a very palatable Sunday roast dinner, and Mother was in her element, smiling broadly at the other diners. She was obviously pleased with her day, and Ben is in her good books for the time being!

I am about to get ready for the quiz, although my brain is still fuzzy from the lost hour's sleep this morning. I meant to give Mother some grief about ringing at such an early hour, but I clean forgot. Oh well, I imagine there will be other opportunities, if her track record is anything to go by! I'll let her off on Mothers' Day.

Things to be Grateful for

1) My clever ruse to surprise Mother worked a treat.
2) She was pleased with my efforts and had a lovely day.

3) I had the chance to speak with Dad for a good hour without interruptions!

4) I quite enjoyed the day myself, but I will never let on!

Monday 26th March 2001

Word of the Day: Popinjay... A fop, a conceited pretentious person

6 a.m. Up early and seething!

When I came home from the quiz, I had a message on my answering machine. It was Louise in serious distress and crying

"Ben, it's Louise. Oh God, I don't know what to do. I'm on my way home to Mum's. I daren't go home like this. Can you ring me? Please?"

I didn't know what to think, or what the hell had happened to her, but I rang her mobile immediately. It was switched off, so I rang her mother's house. Her mother answered.

"Hello, Mrs Burnham, is Louise there?"

"Yes. Of course she is. It's nearly midnight, I think she is in bed."

"She left me a message and asked me to ring her urgently. I'm sorry about the time."

"OK. I'll see if she is awake."

Louise came to the phone and, before she picked it up, I heard her mother say, "Don't be on the phone half the night. Do you know what time it is? I'm going back to bed."

"Hello? Ben?"

"Hello. What on earth's been going on? I was frantic, hearing you crying like that."

"Hang on a minute." She said quietly and I heard her shut a door, before returning to the phone. "It's Simon. He went berserk tonight!"

"Why? What's his problem?"

"He tried to rape me! That's what his problem is!"

"You're joking? I'll kill the bastard!" I felt the anger rising.

"I wish I was joking." I could hear the trembling in her voice. This was no joke.

"OK Louise. Calm down and take a deep breath, then tell me what happened."

"He was mad with me, because I didn't go to some posh dinner with him, on Saturday and, when I went round his place on Sunday, he gave me a right mouthful. He accused me of being up there just to sleep with you, and that I was just stringing him along. I told him I wasn't, and that nothing happened between you and me, but he didn't believe me. He said that if it was OK for you, it was OK for him, and he just pulled me to the floor."

"I'm going to punch his head in. The moron! Did he hurt you?"

"Yes he did! I was trying to fight him off, but he was too strong, and he ripped my clothes…" She began to cry.

"It's OK, sweetheart. Take your time, there's no rush." I tried to calm her down, but I was struggling to stay calm myself. "I know it's hard for you to talk about it. Are you saying he raped you?"

"No, but he was going to. I fought him and screamed at him, honestly I did."

"It's OK, sweetie, this isn't down to you. It's him. Don't blame yourself. You say he **tried** to rape you. What stopped him?"

"It's embarrassing."

"I know it is, take your time."

"He… I can't talk about it. I'm sorry."

"It must have been horrible."

"Yes, it was awful. He called me some disgusting names."

"Did you call the police?"

"No, I just wanted to be out of there."

"Don't worry, I'm coming down. Right now!"

"No! It's OK. I'll be all right. Get some sleep. We can talk tomorrow."

"OK. If you're sure? I'll be there, as soon as I can, in the morning. Don't you dare go to work tomorrow."

So, it looks like a little visit to Not-So-Simple-Simon is called for! The scheming bastard!

11p.m. Back home.

I drove like a maniac, this morning, to get to Louise. My mind was racing faster than the car. I could cheerfully strangle this toe rag of a lawyer. I got to Louise's parents' house at around ten and Louise was alone. As soon as I was through the door, I took her into my arms and hugged her tightly. She made no move to release herself for, what seemed like, minutes, and my heart was pounding. I'm not sure if it was from holding her or out of anger at the situation.

"Thanks for coming." She said. "I need someone to talk to, my parents would have gone mad!"

"I'm not surprised. I would hope they **would** get mad! You should have told them, I'm sure they would have been supportive."

"I couldn't, it's too embarrassing." She made coffee and we sat down in the living room. I asked her to begin at the beginning and tell me exactly what happened.

"I came home on Saturday, and he rang to ask me if I wanted to go to some dinner he was going to. It was a posh, black tie affair. I'm not keen on all that pretentious stuff, at the best of times, but I had been away all week and I just felt tired. I just wanted to stay in and relax. He wasn't very happy about it. He said, "You'd better be joking, or else..." and, "Who the hell do you think you are to embarrass me like this? It's a couple thing and I've told everyone you're coming, so you're coming!" He said he'd give me half an hour to get ready and he'd be round. I said, "At this short notice, I've got nothing to wear, and I'm not going to be bullied into it. You're always like this!" He said, "You haven't seen me for a week. I thought you'd be desperate to see me... and this dinner is £200 a double ticket. It was a surprise." I told him it was more like a shock, and I really was too tired for such a stressful night, and he should be more understanding, and he said, "Thanks a lot!" and hung up...

I held her hand reassuringly, kept quiet and continued to listen.

"...Then on Sunday morning he rang again, still in a bit of a strop. He said, "If I meant anything to you, you'd want to see me, when we've been apart for a whole week..."

Fair enough point. I'd feel the same! Especially if I'd just done in two hundred quid!

"...So I told him that I did want to see him, just that I would have been poor company at a 'do' like that, when I was so tired. He asked me to meet him for lunch, which I did, but he hardly spoke a word to me. I could tell he was still upset about it. Then, as we were leaving, he said that he had someone to see in the afternoon, but he would pick me up at seven, and we could go out somewhere. So all the 'wanting to see me' rhetoric was one-way traffic, wasn't it? He could have spent the afternoon with me, but went off to see someone, he didn't say who.

"And did he? Pick you up, afterwards?"

"Yes, but then he said that **he** was tired, so suddenly and inexplicably, the plans had changed, and he got a bottle of wine and drove us to his place, without a "by your leave!" He made a unilateral decision that we could have a quiet evening in. He had been drinking already; I could smell it on his breath. When we got there, he was behaving even more strangely. He poured us each a glass of wine and sat there staring at me, without speaking. I tried to start a conversation, but he just sat there... staring. I said, "You're scaring me. Stop it. Talk to me or I'm leaving." That's when it got really scary. He said, "You're going nowhere," and went out into the hallway and locked the front door, then came back in and began interrogating me. You'd have thought I was on the witness stand. He kept asking me questions about where I'd been all week, and who with, and what I'd done. Not like any normal person would ask you, you know? Like I'd committed a crime, and he was prosecuting me in court. I told him everything that happened, including 'going for an Indian' with you, and he got very upset when he heard that! He said, "I thought so! That's why you went up there in the first place, wasn't it?" Then he said, "OK, let's not beat about the bush! We've been pissing about long enough! Isn't it about time you came up with the goods? I think now is as good a time as any, don't you? Let's see what you've been hiding from me all these months." I said, "Not like this… please, you're frightening me." He said, "I bet your burger flipper friend didn't frighten you, did he?" I said, "No, we had a pleasant meal…and that **is** all we are…friends." He said, "Friends, my arse! You slept with him! Don't lie to me! Don't try to tell me you were with him all that time and didn't sleep with him. What's good for him is good for me! You've just been stringing me along. You get all the perks of my status, and I don't even get laid? He does nothing and gets to fuck you! Hardly fair, wouldn't you say?" I tried to protest my innocence, but he just shouted, "Shut up!" He was brushing my hair with the back of his fingers, and then, suddenly, he grabbed a handful of my hair and pulled it tight and said, " Well, **darling**! It's payback time!" I tried to leave but he wrestled me to the ground."

"But you said he didn't actually rape you?"

"No, but he ripped off my blouse and pulled up my skirt. Then he tried to get my panties off. His hands were all over me." She started weeping again. "It was horrible. He didn't wait to take his clothes off… just unzipped his trousers and tried to force himself between my legs. I kept struggling and kicking, but he forced me down and managed to get my legs apart…oh this is so embarrassing…"

"It's OK. You're doing brilliantly."

"… Just as I was resigned to it happening he… let out a gasp and shuddered violently and… and it… you know…. went all over my skirt…"

Although I was angry, and it was not a laughing matter, I don't know quite how I didn't laugh. I could not resist a wry smile to myself, though, partly out of relief that he didn't manage to penetrate her, but mainly at his shortcomings.

"…He called me some foul names, grabbed me by the arm and marched me out of the flat. I was still half dressed when he shut the door on me."

"It's OK. Everything is going to be all right. Are you sure you don't want to report this to the police? You really should, you know."

"He'd only say I consented to it."

"Has he marked you?"

She showed me the bruises on her arms and wrists.

"Where is his office?"

"Why, what do you want to know for?"

"I need to have a word with him."

"What are you going to do?"

"If I'd have been here last night, I would have gone and hammered him, but I had another thought, while I was mulling it over last night."

"You won't do anything stupid, will you?"

Moi? How rude!

I called at the office, gave my name and told the receptionist that I needed to speak to him. She spoke to him on an intercom and I heard him say, "Tell him to make an appointment." His voice was cool and controlled, very upmarket, even snobbish.

I told her to tell him that I was only in town for the day, and I may have to go for an interview with the police, later, and needed his advice before I did! He understood the implication of my words, and he said, "Ask him to wait. I'll see him at 1-30."

"I think that might be too late. I'd better go." I interjected. He heard my comment through the open intercom and said, "Sarah? Show him in now, please."

Sarah led me to an office, knocked lightly, then opened it, wide enough for me to get through, and shut it again without entering the room herself.

"Mr Arnold?" He said in a very superior manner.

He was taller than I had expected, lean, almost gaunt in appearance. He had angular facial features, small, piercing, blue eyes and an aquiline nose. His dark brown hair had a hint of grey, at the sides, but was somewhat overdone, in the styling department on top, and gelled backwards over the ears. It was a style in keeping with his arrogant demeanour. I had visualised him as a weasel, but as I looked at him now, he reminded me more of a reptile. There was a large antique oak desk and a number of highly polished wooden bookcases containing hundreds of legal tomes and sets of court proceedings.

"Simon isn't it? Is that Vaughan?" It occurred to me that I hadn't known his surname until Sarah had said, "Mr. Vaughan?"

"That's right." He held out his hand for a handshake and had a smug look of contempt on his face that told me just how superior to me that he felt.

How dare he offer me his hand after what he's done? He was lucky I didn't take it, twist it and break his arm!

I took him warmly by the throat, and a look of absolute terror came over him, and the colour drained from his face.

"I ought to punch your lights out. What the fuck did you think you were doing?" I let him go and he sat, defiantly, in his deep leather chair. I sat down next to him on a conference chair.

"I don't know what you're talking about."

"Of course you don't! That's why you saw me without an appointment and knew who I was!"

"She's nothing but a cock tease." He relented.

I guess that's posh bloke speak for a prick teaser!

"What makes you think that? How dare you disrespect her like that?"

"Disrespect her? Are you serious? We've been going out together for six months and she's never put out. She keeps dangling it like a carrot, and then when the heat is on, she comes over all virginal. She is nothing but a cock teasing little gold digger. A woman like that ought to be grateful that I am even bothering to trifle with her."

"Maybe she just doesn't fancy you!"

"So why is she still going out with me, then?"

"I think you'll find that she's not! Your little performance last night has put paid to any chance you ever had of getting into her knickers! She's not a prick teaser or a gold digger. She's got a problem, that's all. She has had some bad experiences with men…she's been traumatised by men trying to control her and abuse her. You trying to rape her won't have helped much in that department, will it?"

"It was hardly rape! I thought she wanted it."

"You just said she was a tease and was stringing you along. Make your mind up. Surely you can't have it both ways. In fact, you can't have it at all, if your rocket explodes before you get it docked…" I smiled a contemptuous smile.

"What has she been saying? I suppose she has spun you a right tale, the lying little cow."

"She told me **everything!** And I believe her. She even told me that you shot your load all over her, before you could carry it out. That is probably all that stood between you and a prison breakfast this morning, you stupid, arrogant bastard!"

"That's a lie!"

"That's what Clinton said, before he knew Monica Lewinsky hadn't been to the cleaners! I'm sure there will be some interesting evidence on Louise's skirt!"

His demeanour softened.

"You know how it is! I thought she wanted me to make a move. You know, you're a man of the world... sort of... take the decision out of her hands. Like she doesn't have to say "yes" or "no", you just, like, do it"

"That's bollocks and you know it! Did she say "yes"?

"Well, not in as many words!"

"So, which part of "no" were you having difficulty with?"

"OK, look...I know it could look a little bad to someone like you, but it wasn't like that. I just got a little bit carried away. Anyway, why does she play the virgin with me, when you're boning her? How do you think I feel... being played for a fool, while she's having a bit of rough with a glorified Ronald McDonald."

Someone like me? Ronald McDonald? Who the fuck does this pompous arsehole think he is?

"I'm not 'boning' her. In fact, I never have. I told you, she's got a problem. Didn't you ever discuss her past, or were you too busy talking about you and your "OK, Yah" brigade? Just because you have a bit of cash in the bank, doesn't make you better than anyone else and certainly doesn't give you the right to just take what you want."

"Oh, really..." He began in a patronising tone. "She knew what she was there for... I've only been keeping her on tap until I breeched her defences, old boy. Can't have a stuck up little social climber holding out on **me**. Anyway... it's hardly a hanging offence is it? She owed me..."

I could have punched those words straight back down his throat but resisted the temptation.

"... I have been splashing the cash for six months and....nothing. What does she expect? A man in my position has certain expectations of a woman. She is only a bit of sport, anyway. Thrill of the chase and all that. I just got fed up waiting. She's hardly what you would call marriage material, is she, old boy? I have plenty of other much more suitable female 'chums', who are desperate to please me, if you get my drift?"

"No. I think you know, as a lawyer, what this is. Indecent assault? Attempted rape? A court might even regard it as actual rape for all I know about the law. That will go down very well on your CV."

"OK Yah...!"

He actually said it!

"...I know it could look bad in a dim light and, if it ever got to court, it might prove a little sticky. But it is hardly likely to get that far, is it? It would only be my word against hers."

"Well, it's a good job I wasn't taping this conversation, then, isn't it?" I pulled the old 1980's vintage Dictaphone out of my pocket. "Oops! I was! Don't you just hate it when that happens?"

I was not sure whether it would work after all these years, but it certainly wiped the contemptuous smile off his face for a second!

"You'd never use it. That would be blackmail!"

I was so tempted to put on a James Cagney accent and use the cliché, 'Blackmail is an ugly word, see!', but I managed not to!

"No it isn't. You have committed a criminal offence."

"Arguably," the lawyer in him surfaced.

"Let's put it another way, then. I have evidence that makes a prosecution more likely than if it were just her word against yours?"

"Possibly, but then again, who would a court believe? The word of a woman like her, or a man of my standing? The litigation risk is quite considerable, old boy. The CPS would never run with it."

"I don't think it is appropriate that she works here any more, do you?"

"That is hardly your business, but I wouldn't allow her in the place, if she makes accusations like that."

I picked up the telephone.

"Do you think this is an emergency? Should I use 999 or the local number?"

"Don't be so fucking melodramatic," He replied. "What's your angle, anyway? What are you after, in all this? Money?"

"Of course not. That would be blackmail...and it would make me as bad as you. Louise has done nothing wrong here, has she? Why should her life be wrecked by someone like you?"

"She led me on."

"Did she?"

"In my opinion, but I suppose you would argue she did not."

"There is no suppose about it...and she can't afford to be out of work, can she?"

" What are you getting at? You don't think I'm going to let her work here after this?"

"Patience, Simon! Don't you think it would be nice, if you gave her...say, three months salary, in lieu of notice, to give her time to find another job...? Oh... and of course, the most glowing reference you have ever written?"

"You are living in a dream world, old boy!"

"Do me a favour, old boy! Don't keep calling me 'old boy'. It is a bit clichéd and pretentious for this day and age."

"Whatever you say, old boy. Oops, sorry, force of habit. No, it won't happen. That is blackmail. It is too much. The partners would never agree to it. They would want to know why I was deviating from company policy. I'll give her a month."

"Then perhaps we'd better tell them?"

"No! It is not in anyone's interest to do that. Anyway, they would simply close ranks and support me. How do I know that you won't go to the police anyway?"

"You don't. Ain't life a bitch?"

"I need guarantees."

"From where I'm standing, you don't appear to be in any position to demand anything. You have my word as a gentleman, and that's all you do get. Oh, and stay away from her. If I come back again, it won't be for negotiations!"

"You don't frighten me and you're no gentleman. You just want her for yourself."

"Well, you are not bothered about her. You haven't even asked if she is OK..." He opened his mouth to speak. "...Don't do it now, it's too late. As soon as your precious status is at stake, you'd sell your own granny! I despise people like you!"

"There's nothing to be gained from continuing this conversation, is there?"

"Probably not. So, do we have an agreement?"

"We'll see about that. I could argue that the tape incriminates you as much as it does me."

"But it is my evidence, and I can disclose as much, or as little, of this conversation as I wish. I'll watch developments with interest."

He opened his desk drawer and said, "How remarkable. I appear to have taped this conversation also. Maybe you are not as clever as you thought. Now get out!

I left, having had the smug feeling knocked out of me, although I didn't know what Louise was going to say. I hoped she wouldn't get annoyed that I had interfered.

I returned to see her and told her what had happened.

"What were you thinking of?" She asked. "You can never beat lawyers. How on earth did you even manage to get into his office?"

"The magic word seems to have been 'police'." I smiled at her.

"Well, I guess I'd better start looking for a new job." She smiled back and patted the back of my hand affectionately.

We went out for a drink at a local pub and talked about whether she would be staying with her parents, or coming back to Marston Ferrars, but she said that she did not want to make a decision at the moment, which was not what I was hoping to hear. After all my efforts, I thought she would have wanted to come with me and get away from the scene of her distress. I had to get back to prepare for work in the morning, but a thought came across my mind. I asked Louise to show me where Simon lives, and we drove to his apartment in a very flash neighbourhood. Louise stayed in the car, while I knocked the door, and he answered it, wearing a dressing gown. Upon seeing me, he tried to shut the door in my face, but I forced it open and went in. He was very jittery and was trying to hush me. A female voice called from another room.

"Your naughty little girl is sorry, now. Please forgive me. I'll do anything you want... to pay for my naughtiness."

The look on Simon's face was a picture. I opened what was a bedroom door. On the bed, was a virtually naked, young woman, tied by handcuffs to the bed head. She had a school tie around her neck and a gymslip up around her waist. In a bid to achieve some semblance of modesty, she drew her knees up and turned away, as best she could, but in doing so revealed a pair of bright red, recently beaten buttocks!

I turned to him and said, "You really are a disgusting pervert. I came here intending to beat some sense into you, but this is even better. I can see the court case now. Sadistic, premature ejaculating lawyer pervert in attempted rape." I turned to the young woman.

"I hope you didn't want a shag, darling. He'll come all over you before he gets it in!" I laughed and he lunged at me, striking me on the cheekbone. I touched it and saw that I was bleeding.

"Even better. Assault as well. I'll expect Louise to hear from you tomorrow, or **I** will go to the police."

The woman on the bed shouted at him, "Who the fuck is Louise?"

I looked him in the eye, winked at him and made a tutting sound. He swung at me again, but I just avoided the blow and sent out a straight right hand landing on the point of his chin. I know I shouldn't have done it, but it made me feel so much better...and it was self-defence!

Things to be Grateful for

1) Simon is off the case! Regardless of how it came about, it is ultimately for the best.
2) I am back in the frame.
3) I managed to get one over on a popinjay, (hurrah!), lawyer!

Tuesday 27<u>th</u> March 2001

Word of the Day: Disenchantment... Disillusionment, dissatisfaction, disappointment

6 p.m. getting ready for football

I am still angry, after meeting the haughty, self-worshipping Simon Vaughan. He really needed a good beating, and I had the opportunity and didn't take it. Mind you, it would have been stupid to do it in his office.

Louise decided to stay at her parents' house, for the time being, and that wasn't part of the plan, either. I thought she would have come back to the village, with me last night, and stayed with her sister, but it was her choice and she made it. I left quite abruptly, showing my obvious disenchantment, (hurrah!). The whole episode leaves me no nearer knowing where I stand with her now, than I did before.

Ashley is standing in for me tonight, while I go to watch Luton play at Peterborough. They will need to start stringing some decent results together, or we will be dumped into the depths of the basement division.

11 p.m. just back from football

Luton achieved a creditable 1-1 draw, but had opportunities to have won the match. There was an Ansafone message from Louise, when I returned.

"Hi, Ben. If you are there, will you please pick up the phone...? I guess either you are not there, or you aren't talking to me. I tried your mobile and it is switched off. Aren't you working tonight? You left in a bit of a mood with me, what's wrong? What have I done to upset you? Whatever it is, I'm sorry. I didn't intend to upset you. Is it because I'm staying here...?"

Very astute!

"...I just wanted to be with Mum and Dad for a while, just until I get my head together. I will probably come back to Marston Ferrers... Maybe soon. Please be patient with me..."

Patient? Are you having a laugh?

"... I really appreciated what you did. You made me feel really special, when I was feeling worthless. I can't thank you enough. Please ring me. Tomorrow? Please...? 'bye."

Her tone became pleading as she came to the end of her pretty little speech. I am still too pissed off to swallow it. I've heard enough rhetoric, in the last 24 hours, to last me a long time.

Things to be grateful for

1) At least she is out of Simon's clutches.
2) I didn't get myself put in jail.
3) Luton didn't lose tonight.
4) Ashley took a good sum on the trailer tonight.

Thursday 29th March 2001

Word of the Day: Turmoil...(again!) Mayhem, confusion.

6 p.m. getting ready for football

Paul came by today and we had a chat, as best we could, amidst the turmoil, (hurrah!), of a busy day on base. He was telling me how his Rover 600 project was nearly complete. He bought a flood damaged Rover from an auction, about six months ago. I saw it, when I was last at his house, completely stripped to the bare shell, with all the insides thoroughly dried out and stored at various parts of his house. He also drives an almost identical metallic gold Rover 600, which is in excellent condition. He has now finally rebuilt the interior of the flood damaged one, and it is ready for sale. However, he was driving his own Rover to work, during the recent floods, and tried to bypass a flood in the road, by driving along a sloping bank. Unfortunately, he became bogged down and slipped slowly down the bank into the floodwater on the road, thus creating a flood-damaged vehicle of his very own! He now has to drive the originally flood-damaged Rover, while he performs the same refurbishing operation on his own. Irony rules again!

I have not rung Louise and she has not rung me. I suppose I ought to, but I am nothing if not a stubborn bastard!

Things to be grateful for

I really can't think of anything today, or can't be bothered. I'm too depressed about my disastrous excuse for a love life. I even thought about hitting on Stacey today! In fact I'm still thinking about it!!

Sunday 1ˢᵗ April 2001

Word of the Day: Antagonise... Irritate, annoy, alienate.

10-00 a.m. At home in the flat

I woke up early, this morning, without Mother's assistance, and rang her.

"Hi Mother, how are you?"

"Fine thanks...but I'm worried now! Benjamin ringing his mother? Either something's wrong, or this is a real honour! I am speechless!"

"No you're not! That hasn't happened since you had laryngitis when I was a teenager, and even then you wore your arms out giving orders by sign language!"

She laughed.

"Even so, there has to be an ulterior motive. So, what is it?"

"Oh, ye of little faith!" I laughed. "Actually, I was writing in my electronic diary the other night, and the 'battery low' warning came on. I couldn't get batteries until the next day and, by then, some of the memory had crashed. I know I don't ring you very often, but I can't find your number."

"You are so stupid sometimes! We've had the same number for thirty years, except when they added an extra digit that time. Surely, you don't forget your own telephone number for all your childhood years?" She recited the number to me.

"April Fool!"

"What do you mean, April...? Oh, yes. I get it, it's April 1st. So you did know the number all the time! Very amusing, you callous little bugger!"

"Think about it, Mother! I just rang you on that number didn't I?"

"That's right! Take advantage of a poor old woman!"

"I'm sorry. I couldn't resist it. It's a dirty job, but someone has to do it. I get you every year, and every year, you say I won't catch you out again."

"Oh yes!" She seemed to suddenly remember something. "I was going to ring you this morning and tell you. We had a strange phone call for you, yesterday. A young lady."

"Really? What did she want?"

"She said that she's been trying to contact you for quite a while. Seemed very nice."

"Hang on a minute. Is this a wind-up? You're trying to get me back, aren't you? April Fool yourself, I didn't fall for it."

"Well, now you are an April Fool, because it's true! Hah!"

"As true as you're riding that camel!"

"OK! Ask your father... **George! Come and tell Ben about the phone call...!** He's coming."

No I couldn't do THAT joke with my mother!

"Hello? Ben? How are things?"

"Fine Dad, and you?"

"Oh...you know!"

"Ha! Ha! Is she keeping you on your toes?"

"Tell me about it!"

In the background, I heard Mother prompting him. "Go on, then! Tell him!"

"Yes it's true. A young woman called...oh, what was her name? Hang on, I wrote it down somewhere..." He left the phone to get the note and returned quickly. "...Here it is. Nicola Sherman."

"Never heard of her. So why was she ringing you instead of me?"

She said that she had been trying to contact you for some time, after she received something in a will. There's no need to worry, and she has some information that you might be pleased to receive."

"I haven't lived with you for over ten years! How come she was ringing you? Did she leave a number?"

"No, and I didn't give her yours either. Not without your say-so."

"Hmmm. I wonder if someone's left me some dosh?"

"It sounded like something along those lines. Good luck to you if it is."

"Is she ringing back?"

"I told her we would be speaking to you today, and she said she'd ring back in the week."

"OK. You'd better just give her my mobile, in case it's something dodgy. You never know, do you?"

"All right, son, nice to chat. See you soon." He handed the telephone back to Mother.

"So there you are, then. You believe your father, but not me, eh?"

"You have to admit that it does sound a bit fishy!"

I wonder what that was all about. Maybe an old relative has passed away and left me millions!

I told her about the visit to Louise's, and how I'd had a run in with Simon. She thought I was mad to get involved.

"One of these days, someone is going to knock you senseless, if you keep going into matters which don't concern you."

"But they do concern me. We're friends and I've wanted to go out with her for ages."

"You've been out with her. It didn't work, so move on with your life. She sounds like trouble to me."

"That's why they call a wife, "Trouble and Strife"."

"You are not thinking of marrying her, are you?" There was a hint of panic in her voice.

"Who knows, who can tell? What strange twists of fate are waiting for us around the corner?"

"You silly devil! You hardly know her."

"Exactly, so how can you say it didn't work out? It never had a chance to work out, or otherwise."

"Well, go your own way! You will anyway."

Too true, Mother! Too true!

After I had spoken to Mother, I rang Louise. She was upset that I hadn't rung her back earlier in the week. I lied to her that I wasn't upset with her and told her that I had tried to ring her a couple of times. (I admit that I felt guilty feeling like I did. It was only natural that she would cling to her mother after circumstances like that. I was being very selfish.) She told me that Simon had rung her and had apologised for his behaviour!

Alarm bells ringing in my head! The devious tosser!

"Don't tell me!" I ventured. "You've forgiven him, all's well and you are back together?"

"Don't be so stupid, of course I haven't forgiven him... And he didn't ask me to get back with him."

"What would you have said, if he had have asked you?"

"I'd have told him to take a running jump!"

"Good! I'm glad that's sorted out then!"

"He rang to arrange my termination pay. I've got to go into the office tomorrow to collect it."

More alarm bells! However, I am not going to voice my concerns, or I'll just make it worse.

"How much is he paying you?"

"Well, I've just had March's salary, and I haven't worked in April, so that worked out well. He's giving me two weeks pay, in lieu of the holiday I am owed, and one month's severance pay, in lieu of notice."

"I hope you told him to stick it somewhere very dark!"

"How could I? It's what I am entitled to. One month's notice. I left them, didn't I?"

"I think a court would rule rape by your boss, as constructive dismissal, don't you? I told him three months, or I was going to the police. This is entirely his fault, remember? Not yours. I'd take him for every penny I could. Better still, take the money he is offering and then go to the police. Then everyone has played it by the book."

"I can't do that, Ben. Look, I'm just happy to get out. The thought of him makes me feel sick."

So he gets away with it!

I decided, once more, not to antagonise, (Hurrah!), her any further and dropped the subject. We parted on friendly enough terms, but I did not ask her what her future plans were. She did say she would ring and let me know how she got on with Simon.

Luton lost a six pointer with Colchester and, now, start a run of four straight home games. They need to win them all, if they are to stay up. I am not hopeful!

Things to be Grateful for

1) I may be getting a legacy from someone.
2) Simon the snake makes Louise feel sick!
3) Tomorrow should see the last of Simon in her life! Yes!!!

Monday 2<u>nd</u> April 2001

Word of the Day: Naivety... Lack of sophistication, child-like innocence

Midday nursing a bruised ego!

The quiz was a waste of time last night. Only three teams were in evidence, so it was hardly any great shakes to have won all three rounds. The jackpot was ridiculously difficult, we only managed two right, out of six, so, it remains unclaimed yet again. Next week it is a maximum £60.

When I recounted the events of the visit to Louise, the lads were strangely supportive and unusually attentive. As I told them of the incident at Simon's flat, they became more animated.

"Yeeeeessss!" Jamie began the responses. "Good on you, Ben! The slimy shit bag deserved a good sorting. I'm surprised you didn't do him up big time!"

"Do him up?" I laughed. "What sort of talk is of that, for an educated man?"

"But did you give Louise one?" Brian returned to basics.

"Behave yourself!" Gordon shook his head in disbelief. "The poor girl's just been nearly raped. I should think that was the last thing she needed from Ben."

"A good seeing to would have done her the world of good." Jamie agreed with Brian.

"Well, I didn't." I disappointed the two of them. "Have you got no compassion, you pair of wankers?"

"I bet you've been the wanker this week, my son!" Jamie joked. "Had to resort to bashing the old bishop, did we?"

"We haven't all got bigger brains in our dicks than in our heads, Jamie!" I responded. "I'll taste the fruits of the delightful Louise, as and when the time is right. All in good time."

"I bet you a tenner you don't." He replied.

"That's a stupid fucking bet, you dickhead. It's one you can never win." Gordon interjected.

"What are you talking about?" Jamie was confused. (Not a difficult state to induce!)

"Think about it!" Gordon was annoyed with Jamie's naivety. (Hurrah!).

Jamie frowned, as he wrestled with the thought, but still couldn't work out why it was a silly bet.

"OK!" I said. "You're on! Ten quid says I do."

"Done!" Said Jamie and shook my hand to seal the bet.

"You have been!" I laughed.

"Why?" Jamie whined. "Will someone tell me what is so funny?"

We were all laughing.

"OK, genius!" Gordon decided to enlighten him. "So Ben shags the trouser stretching Louise, and you have to pay up, yes?"

"Yes!"

"If he doesn't, you collect, right?"

"Right!"

"Wrong!"

"I still don't get it!"

"How thick can you be? Next Sunday, we ask him if he's done the dirty deed, and he says "no, not yet." The week after: "no not yet," and so on. Next year, you're still asking him, and he is still saying, "no, not yet." How the hell are you ever going to collect? While they're both still alive, there's always a chance that he might shag her, and win the bet. You, on the other hand, can only win the bet, if Ben admits that he has failed, which he's hardly likely to do, or if Louise dies before Ben shags her. Moron!"

"Oh no! That's not fair. There has to be a time limit."

"But that wasn't the bet, was it?"

"You bastards. Why didn't you say something?"

"I did." Said Gordon. "But you've got a big mouth. Sometimes it is going to get into trouble, and this is one of those times. It's probably going to cost you a tenner to learn a lesson. I reckon that's cheap at the price."

Maria rang Brian, on his mobile, to tell him that one of the kids was ill, and so he left immediately. Jamie began to chat to a young woman, who had been drinking with a female friend all evening, but was now apparently on her own. He's got radar where unattached females are concerned. Gordon and I remained at our original table, and he began telling me about his new friend, Mark.

"We've been going out together for a couple of weeks now. It's getting quite serious. I really fancy him!"

"Have you... You know!" I was a little on foreign territory here!

"No!" He replied emphatically. "Not yet. But I am giving it serious consideration."

"Do you think he feels the same way?"

"He said he does. He wants to take it further."

"Well, if you both fancy it, go for it!"

"You don't feel strange, being mates with a poofter?" He looked scared at the prospect of rejection.

"I must admit, it's new ground for me, but no, of course not. You're still the same bloke, aren't you?"

"Of course I am!"

"Well, then."

He looked relieved, then added, "But you won't tell the others? You promised."

"You tell them yourself. When you are ready."

"I can't see that happening any time soon." He smiled.

Things to be grateful for

1) Gordon is the happiest I've ever seen him.
2) Louise should have her money by now and be free of Simon.

Tuesday 3rd April 2001

Word of the Day: Diatribe... verbal attack, tirade

4 p.m. After a very busy day on the base.

Louise rang last night and we had a heart to heart about her future plans. She went to collect her salary, as arranged, yesterday morning. Simon made her go into his office and, apparently, his behaviour was true to form. He asked her to reconsider dumping him and bad mouthed me at the same time.

"We have a good thing going. We don't need to break up over a misunderstanding. You can't blame me because you turn me on, now can you?" he said to her.

Louise told me that she just sat in disbelief, letting him drone on.

"You can't seriously tell me, that you prefer to be with that moronic burger man, rather than with me. I mean, for God's sake, what has he got to offer you? The man is virtually penniless! No social standing whatsoever."

She said that, at that point, she responded.

"He has a lot more to offer me than just material wealth. He is an honourable, caring person, unlike you. He never tried to force me to have sex with him, but he is more of a man than you'll ever be."

He threw the envelope, containing her severance statement, onto the desk in front of her in disgust and said, "This isn't over, you know."

He has overplayed his hand, because she has now decided to return to the village permanently, to get away from him.

Things to be grateful for

1) Simon has shot himself in the foot! (Although I'd like to shoot him in the bollocks!)
2) Louise is coming home.
3) She stood up for me, against his diatribe. (Hurrah!)

Thursday 5th April 2001

Word of the Day: Auspiciously... favourably, promisingly.

4 p.m. back at the flat

Tuesday was the start of Luton's long run of home games. It hardly started auspiciously (hurrah!) with a 1-1 draw against Reading. Things are looking very dodgy; they seem to have no confidence whatsoever. Foot and Mouth disease reached a thousand cases yesterday, and there is no sign of it easing up. On a purely selfish note, my supplier has maintained my chicken prices, so I can't complain. Jason has been moping about for a few days. If he's no better over the weekend I'll get him to the vet. It's not like him to miss his food.

Louise rang last night. She is definitely coming back to the village but is going down to Exeter for a while, to stay with her "other" sister. I didn't even know she had another sister. She is staying there for Easter, but she promised to ring me over the weekend.

Things to be grateful for

1) Louise is still coming home.
2) She is keeping in touch with me.

Sunday 8th April 2001

Word of the Day: Incoherent... confused, illogical

7-30 a.m. Why? Why? Why...?

Won't she let me sleep???

"Hello...?" I put on the best impression of being incoherent, (hurrah!), that I could muster. "....Who... who's.. er.. what's that?" I said with a husky, sleepy voice.

"It's me, Benjamin. Are you drunk?"

"Eh...? What...?"

"You are drunk! Still drunk on a Sunday morning? You must have knocked some back last night!"

"I am not drunk, Mother. I was working till 1 o'clock, and it was nearly three in the morning by the time I got to bed, so my body did not want to wake up."

"What were you doing till three in the morning...NO! Don't tell me, I don't want to know!"

"Trying to wind down, Mother. By the time I got back to the flat, it was nearly two, and by the time I'd had a coffee, and relaxed for half an hour, it was getting on for three."

"Well, no wonder you couldn't sleep. It's a bit stupid having coffee just before you want to go to sleep, isn't it? You drink coffee to stay awake!"

"You might, Mother. I just drink it because it tastes good and I am thirsty...! And it didn't keep me awake. I went straight to sleep once I hit the sack..."

The thing is... some old biddy rang me at 7-30 and woke me up, after only four and a half hours bloody sleep!

... But that is only four and a half hours ago."

"Yes, well, you should go to bed earlier and get up earlier."

That's easy for you to say when you've got bugger-all else to do!

"Yes, Mother, whatever you say."

"When you consider it appropriate, perhaps you would consider ringing me back. I have to get your dad's breakfast on now. I'll speak to you later. 'Bye!"

Why the fuck couldn't you have made him his poxy breakfast first, instead of ringing me? What are you? The alarm clock police?

I screamed the vitriolic remarks down the phone to her... after disconnecting, of course! I deliberately rang her back at twenty to two, because, I remember, all too well, from my childhood days that Sunday Lunch was always served at 2 p.m. precisely. Therefore at 1-40p.m. she would be running round the kitchen, like a headless chicken, draining spuds, making gravy and saving the Yorkshire puddings from scorching. Of course, my dad answered the phone!

"Hi, Dad. Is Mother there?"

"Of course she is… and you know exactly what she is doing at this precise moment, don't you?"

"Er…I would say… Straining the greens?"

"Spot on…!" He replied.

I heard Mother in the background shout, "Get off that phone, George, it'll be dished up in a minute. Who is it?"

"…It's Ben, he wants to talk to you…" He breathed a quiet snigger down the receiver.

"Not now, George. Tell him he'll have to ring back after we've eaten."

"She said…"

"I heard what she said. Half of Bedfordshire heard it. Tell her I want to speak to her right this minute, or else!"

"You tell her!" He laughed.

"Tell her what?" She eavesdropped from the kitchen.

"No. It's all right. I can't be bothered." I joked. He laughed again, just as quietly as before, and we conspirators against the female peril bade each other a fond goodbye. Eventually, she rang back and castigated me for not ringing her back after lunch, then found that she hadn't really much to say, for once, so I told her about Louise.

"Louise is coming home soon."

"Really?" She said, disinterestedly.

"Charming! You ask me what I'm doing and how I am, then when I tell you, you sound about as interested as I am in ironing!"

"Well! She's trouble, that one. You mark my words. I hope you're not thinking of marrying her! You'll soon get to know why they are called "trouble and strife" if you do."

"You already told me that, and I am not likely to be marrying her just yet, am I. Thanks to your wonderful performance, when we went out to lunch, she did a runner and hasn't been seen in Marston Ferrars since, so I hardly know her!"

(Poetic licence!)

"That wasn't my fault. I told you, I liked her. I thought you should have taken the chance while it was there, but I was wrong. She was on her best behaviour for me. She's too flighty. She's proved that now!"

Make a note: On Sunday the 8th April 2001, Mother admitted she was wrong!

"That's rubbish, Mother you don't know how rough it's been for her."

"Hmmm! We'll see."

There was little point in pursuing this conversation. She was in too odd a mood.

Luton contrived, yet again, to snatch death from the jaws of glory! Having led Stoke 1-0, they fell apart in the second half and lost 2-1. I concede defeat. We're definitely going down. Unless...

Things to be Grateful for

1) It is Sunday, a night out beckons.

2) Mother admitted she was wrong. Now there's fuel for a fire at some point in the future when I bring it to her attention!

Monday 9th April 2001

Word of the Day: Egocentricity... Self-interest, selfishness

10 a.m. just had breakfast

Louise rang yesterday evening, making me late for the quiz. She was at her sister's.

"Becky is the oldest. She has been married for fifteen years, but they've never had any kids. None of us has. I think Mum has just about given up on having any grandkids of her own!"

"So's mine, but you never know, do you? It could happen!"

"No, you don't. I always wanted to have kids, but I'm glad I haven't, with my track record!" She laughed, nervously. "Maybe one day, but I'm not getting any younger. I'm staying here with Becky and Matt, until Easter Sunday. I'll drive back to Mum and Dad's on the Sunday night, so I can spend the Bank Holiday Monday with them."

"I've got my parents up here for Easter, that should be a barrel of laughs!" I said. "When are you coming back here?"

"I'm not totally sure, but probably the week after. Emily says I can share with her, until I find another place, so I'm really looking forward to it."

"Do you think there might be the slightest chance that we might be able to see a little of each other, if you are moving back for good?"

"I very much hope so! It is one of the reasons I am coming back."

At last! A dim light at the end of the tunnel!

When I finally got to the quiz, there was a strange atmosphere, which I couldn't quite fathom. However, as the first fun round finished, Gordon moved to the bar to get a round in and Jamie motioned to me to follow him, as he went out towards the toilets. He didn't go into the toilets, but walked straight out into the car park and I followed him.

"Jesus! I had a shock last night!" He said.

"Why? What happened?"

"I was in town having a few jars with a mate from work, so, for a laugh, I took him to the gay bar we ended up at, when I went on the town with Gordon."

"And...?"

"Gordon was in there, as large as life, with a bloke!"

"So what? He was in there with you once!"

"Yes, but he wasn't holding my fucking hand, was he?"

"I don't know, I wasn't there!"

"Don't be funny! This is serious! I think he's gay!"

"I know, so what?"

"What do you mean, you fucking know?"

"I know he's gay. He told me."

"Well, why didn't you tell us?" He said, wide-eyed in disbelief.

"Why? What difference does it make?"

"Well, you know.... going to the toilets and that."

"You think he's getting his thrills watching you have a piss?"

"When you say it like that, it does sound a bit stupid, but it is a bit off-putting, isn't it?"

"Not at all. I was stunned when he first told me, but it doesn't mean I can't cope with it."

"Phew, it's a lot to take in, isn't it?"

"Yes, I suppose it is. Have you told Brian, yet?"

"Yes, I told him before Gordon got here."

"What did he say?"

"He doesn't believe it. He reckons I made it up."

"What did you do when you saw him in there?"

"What do you think? I legged it before he saw me. I didn't want him thinking that me and Parfitt were poofters, did I?"

The humour of his egocentricity, (hurrah!), hit me, and I laughed heartily. He wasn't worried about Gordon's feelings, finding out that he had been rumbled; more that Gordon might think that Jamie, himself, was there with a man, because he is bisexual!

Oh dear! That would never do, would it?

"Don't say anything yet." I suggested. "Let me have a word with Gordon first. Let him know he's been sprung! He wanted to keep it a secret, because he was afraid you'd do all that, "Backs to the wall, boys," stuff. Do you think you could try to show a bit of maturity, while he gets used to the idea that we all know?"

"I don't want to upset him, do I? He's a nice bloke. One of the lads, or should I say one of the girls?" He laughed a naughty schoolboy laugh, then said, "Sorry, couldn't resist it. Just the once!"

We returned to the quiz and had missed the first three questions of the drinks round.

"Are you two having an affair?" Gordon said, unaware of the irony of his comment.

I could sense the words, "That's rich, coming from you!" rising in Jamie's throat, but I caught his eye and he stifled his comment. After the drinks round finished, I said to Gordon, "Can I have a word? In private?"

We went out to almost the same spot in the car park that I had occupied when talking to Jamie, earlier.

"I've got good news and bad news." I said cryptically.

"OK..." He said apprehensively. "Give me the good news first!"

"You don't need to worry about telling the others you're ...gay." I said the word gay in a whisper.

"Why not?"

"That's the bad news! They already know!"

"How the hell did they find out? You didn't tell them? You promised..."

"No, I didn't tell them. Jamie was in town last night and so were you, apparently. With Mark, I presume?"

"Yes but we were in... Marinero's!"

"And so, very briefly, was Jamie and his mate. He saw you and Mark holding hands."

"Oh, shit. I'll have to go." He made a move towards his car, but I caught hold of him.

"Don't be silly. It's out now. YOU are out now. Just face it tonight and you are home free."

"I can't!"

"Of course you can." I started to lead him back into the pub, and he sat down silently, at the table. You could have cut the atmosphere with a knife, so I said, just loud enough for the three of them to hear, "It's OK. Gordon knows that we know, now let's get on with the quiz and discuss it later."

After we left the pub, we gathered near Jamie's car and chatted for about half an hour.

"Why didn't you tell us?" Jamie asked him. "You told Ben."

"I know. I had to tell someone, and Ben was the only one here that night. Besides, I would have chosen him to tell anyway, " he said, in a burst of honesty. "I was too afraid that you and Brian would take it badly."

"It was more of a shock seeing you in there holding hands with a geezer."

"By the way, Jamie, what were **you** doing in there, anyway?" Gordon enjoyed asking him.

"Don't start that old Malarkey! You know I'm not gay! I was telling Parfitt about that night, and we were right nearby, so I took him in to show him."

The conversation went very well and, as we all went our separate ways, it had become quite clear that the bond of friendship between the four of us was not going to be broken by this revelation. I think that even Brian and Jamie were surprised, themselves, at the matter-of-fact way they were able to deal with the news.

Things to be Grateful for.

1) Louise said her main reason for returning here was me!
2) I am freed of the burden of being the only one to know of Gordon's homosexuality.
3) Gordon is freed from the secrecy of it too.
4) Jamie and Brian took it extraordinarily well.

Tuesday 10th April 2001

Word of the Day: Diminutive... very small, minute, tiny

4 p.m. Just back from the vets.

My cat, Jason, was still off his food and kept pawing at his face, so I took him to the vet. She was a diminutive (hurrah!) woman, (well quite small!), in her forties, who found the problem instantly. He had a bone wedged in his upper palate. She cut the centre of the bone and one piece fell out while the other, which had broken the skin, needed gently coaxing with forceps. Jason spat and hissed, in a demonstration of how pleased he was not!

"OK! OK! It's all done! You're not that fierce, stop pretending!" She said to him, while stroking his head lovingly. Then she turned to me. "I hope you don't give him bones to eat!" She said, doing a reasonable impression of my mother. "Chicken bones like this one can be very dangerous. In some ways, it is a good job it stuck in his palate and he didn't swallow it. We could have had it stuck inside his stomach!"

I wanted to point out to her that I was not stupid and wouldn't have done such a dangerous thing, but I wasn't too sure whether she was joking or not.

"Of course not, he gets the best of everything."

"That'd be why he's overweight, then!"

"I can see you are not going to rest, until you can blame me for something!" I said, causing a wry smile to creep over her face. "It isn't my fault. I only put the food down; it's him that eats it! He should know better!"

"Well, there's an answer I haven't heard before! Seriously, though, he needs to lose weight. I'll give him some antibiotics, because that bone punctured his palate. He should be OK in a few days. It won't hurt him to be off his food for a bit. He could do with losing about a Kilo. I should think he's found a piece of chicken in a rubbish bag somewhere. It is not uncommon. If you get any more problems with him, give me a ring."

"Thanks."

"See the receptionist, she'll give you the bill."

"Give me the hump, more like." I replied with my tongue firmly in my cheek.

The receptionist printed a statement off the computer, and I reluctantly released two ten-pound notes and a fiver from my claw-like grip.

"God! I'm in the wrong business." I joked, not realising that the vet had followed me out into the waiting room. "No wonder she drives a Land Cruiser!"

"It isn't all profit, you know. I have to maintain the surgery and equipment..."

"Stop! I know! You're preaching to the converted. I have the same argument with my customers. I was only joking."

"Good job too. I thought I was going to have to sort you out!"

I had heard from some of my customers that the vet could be a bit direct and, having met her, I can see how they might have got that impression. She is a bit feisty. I like that in a woman! Her sense of humour is very dry and probably flies over some people's heads. However, she does not know Birmans, or more particularly Jason, because, as soon as I got him home, he wolfed an entire bowl of food in no time, as if he'd never been poorly. It is good to see him back to normal, even if the vet does think he's a fat git!

Louise rang last night. She asked me to get the local papers and have a look through, for her, to see if there were any jobs going in the legal field. She is getting very bored at her sister's, but feels she has got to sit it out, having said she would stay until Sunday. I wish I were spending Easter with her.

Luton are at home to Oxford tonight. Oxford are already definitely relegated, so they might be an easy touch for three points. One can only hope!

I got a letter this morning, stating that my Doctor is retiring and that I would be transferred to a new one. Dr. Gillian MacDonald. I wonder if that is Gillian as in Jill, female, or Gillian as in Gil, male? I've never had a female Doctor before. The letter asked for my medical card. I haven't a clue what that is. I'm sure I've never had one.

There is a message on the Ansafone, from Mother. She wants me to ring her. I'll do it tonight while I'm working. It'll give me an excuse to ring off if she goes on a bit!

Things to be Grateful for

1) Jason is OK
2) Louise is looking for work in the area so it looks as though she is definitely coming back.

Thursday 12th April 2001

Word of the Day: Divulge... give away, reveal, let slip

4 p.m. Back from the Base.

On base today, a customer was chatting about my business and how good it was to have some choice for lunch, after having to put up with the chow hall for so long. "How long you bin doin' this, Arnie?" He asked.

I am not explaining the name thing again!

"Getting on for five years, now."

"It sure is good to have somewhere decent to eat!"

"Thank you. It's always nice to be appreciated."

"So. Are you Turkish or Greek or something?"

"Something!" I suggested, but quite obviously to an unresponsive audience. "Just plain old English." I clarified the situation for him.

Why? Do I look like a Stavros Papoudopoulos or a Hassan al Hassan?

"No, I didn't mean... I mean... The kebabs thing. In the States, kebab guys are always Greek or Turkish."

"It's the same here, but no. I'm nothing as exotic as that, I'm afraid!"

He seemed embarrassed to have asked and was made more so, when another customer said, "Jeez buddy. They don't come anymore English than Arnie!"

Argghh!

Just after midnight.

Bob, the butcher, came by tonight. I haven't seen him in ages.

"Where have you been hiding, Bob?"

"I got a new job, in London. I don't get home till gone seven nowadays."

"What? In butchery?" I asked, innocently.

He laughed long and hard.

"I'm not a butcher! I work for an insurance company."

"Really? I'm sorry, I thought everyone called you, "Bob, the butcher.""

"They do. But it's not because I work with meat! It's because of my alleged lack of footballing ability!"

I must have had a look of confusion on my face, because he added, "I'm a defender who can't time a tackle. I get booked almost every game. The team I play for have all got stupid nicknames. "Fairy" Fox... he is scared to tackle; Chick McBride... short for "chicken", for the same reason; "Whiff"...that's Jimmy Smith, he always has a curry on a Saturday night then stinks the dressing-room out on Sunday morning; They call me Bob, "the butcher", because they reckon I cut people up when I tackle them."

I laughed at the silly names and changed the subject.

"Going anywhere for Easter?"

"Nah! Well, not for all of it. The missus wants to take the kids to that Viking place at York."

"The Jorvik Centre? That's a fantastic place. I went there a few months back with an American couple. York's a really interesting place, very pretty."

"Not on a fucking bank holiday, though! She wants to go on Monday, so I've got to get up at five in the morning to avoid the bank holiday traffic. I'm going to have the right hump! I've already decided!"

I laughed again.

"And then you've still got to come home, down the A1, with 100,000 other drivers, when you've finished!"

"Tell me about it!" He said, collecting his food into a carrier bag, before shrugging his shoulders in resignation.

"What're you going to do? You've got to keep them happy!"

Just as he left, Jamie turned up, out of the blue. I thought to myself, *"That's strange. He never comes here to buy food."*

I suddenly noticed he was ashen, and his eyes divulged, (hurrah!) that he had been crying.

"Whatever's up, Jamie?" I asked, with genuine concern.

"It's Sam. She's thrown me out."

"Had a lover's tiff?"

"No. It's worse than that. I left my mobile at home this morning and didn't realise until got to work. You know that bird, Sian, I've been seeing, over at Whittlesey...?"

I nodded as he spoke.

"... Well, she rang my mobile, at 8 o'clock this morning, just before Sam went to work. So Sam answers it, doesn't she? What are the chances of that happening? By all accounts, they had a lovely little chat."

"Oh, my God! Surely she could have said it was a wrong number, when she heard Sam's voice?"

"She didn't know I was living with someone."

"Oops! She does now!"

"Sam had a few words with her and found out that Sian didn't know I was engaged. When I got home she was really stoked up and ready to blow! She ranted on at me for half an hour... I couldn't get a word in edgeways... Then she told me to "Fuck off and don't come back!""

"What're you going to do...? She'll calm down." I tried to reassure him.

"I don't think she will. She has always said that she wouldn't stand for me doing anything like that. I don't know what to do. I'm devastated."

"Well, with all due respect, I imagine Sam is pretty devastated too!"

"Yeah, I know. It didn't mean anything. It was only a bit of fun. You know! Just a bit on the side. Sam's everything to me."

My conscience said, "you should have thought of that before you did it," but I managed to edit it, before opening my mouth.

"What were you thinking of? You must have known that she'd find out, sooner or later?"

"I know. It is obvious now. I am surprised she hasn't found out before.... But it was just sex." He added, as though that was justification for his behaviour.

"It may have been just sex to you, but women rarely see things like that! I'll bet Sian won't see it like that, either."

"I just rang Sam. She just hung up on me. I haven't even got anywhere to go!"

"You can doss down at my place, if you like, until you get it sorted."

"Thanks Ben, you're a mate! You couldn't have a word with her, could you? I think she'd listen to you!"

I couldn't imagine what I could possibly say, in mitigation of the ultimate sin in Sam's eyes, but I agreed to try. I gave him my key, and he went over to the flat.

After I closed, I rang Sam and spoke to her. She was in a very tearful state. Nothing I said, on the phone, seemed to help. Finally, I asked her, "Are you going to be OK?"

"Not really!" She sobbed. "How could he do this to me?"

"I know. It must hurt. I'm worried about you. Do you want me to come down?"

"I'm OK. I'll live."

"It might help if you talk it through with someone."

"I don't want to be any trouble."

"You are not any trouble. You and Jamie are friends. I hate seeing you both like this. I'll just put the trailer away, then I'll pop down."

"All right, thanks. I'll put the kettle on."

"It won't suit you, but go-ahead, if you think it will help!"

She managed a little laugh.

I arrived at the front door of the house, about ten minutes later. She opened the door and I could see that her eyes were red, from crying. We sat down in the living room.

"You know that he is in a state, too, don't you?"

"I find that hard to believe! He should be, though, the bastard. How could he...?"

She got up and went towards the kitchen.

"...Do you want tea or coffee?"

"Whatever you're having will do fine."

"I'll make coffee then."

I followed her into the kitchen.

"I think it was just one of those things, Sam. e really regrets it. It was just a silly mistake."

"Yes? And how many silly mistakes has he been making, exactly?"

Ouch!!

"None that I know of." I lied. I felt guilty about lying to her, but I just wanted to make everything all right between them. hey are a really nice couple. It is horrible seeing them like this.

"Men are all the same. Bastards!" She said, with a vengeance.

"Hey! Thanks a lot... don't forget, I'm a man too!"

She looked at me, softened and smiled, then said, "I wouldn't forget that. You're not so bad, I suppose!"

"Well! Thanks for the vote of confidence," I laughed. "I know Jamie sometimes seems like he's had a charisma bypass and is in need of serious wit therapy, but he's a good bloke, deep down."

"That's the problem. He's a good bloke. Good at doing what blokes do. He's got as much sensitivity as a smack in mouth."

"I think you're doing him an injustice, there."

"Do you? He goes off and fucks anything with a pulse, and I'm doing him an injustice? I don't think so!"

Got me there! Was she reading my mind? In all the time I've known her, I've never heard her swear. She must be really upset.

"What're you going to do? You've got a mortgage together and everything."

"Everything? We may have a mortgage together, but you see more of him than I do."

I have to admit that I don't know what they both get up to during the week. I see him mainly on Sundays.

She began to cry again, and, instinctively, I put my arms around her. After a few moments, she looked up and seemed to be moving towards kissing me. I was a little startled and moved away.

"What's wrong?" She said. "Are you scared of me? I always thought you fancied me."

"I do! That's the problem! I never, for a moment, thought that you fancied me, though! You are a beautiful woman and, in any other circumstances, I wouldn't hesitate; any man would be blind not to find you attractive. But not like this. I'd just feel as though I was taking advantage of you, while you were vulnerable."

Not to mention you might just be doing it to get back at Jamie, and that I cannot afford any more indiscretions in Louise's book!

She smiled and said, "You really are a sweet guy, Ben Arnold! Now, I think you'd better go, before I do something that we both might regret."

Whoa! I think she is right. I had better go before I let her!

I left to drive home, finding it hard to believe that I hadn't succumbed to the opportunity of sleeping with such a gorgeous woman. hen I got back, Jamie was asleep on the sofa, with Jason curled up, also asleep, on his chest. I didn't wake either of them. Jamie looked so innocent, lying there, like a little boy. Aren't looks deceptive?

There was a message on the answering machine, from Mother:

"Hello Benjamin, it's your mother. I could have sworn I left you a message, asking you to ring me. I realize you are a very busy man, and that your mother is way down in your list of priorities, but it would have been nice if you had replied. Then we might know what is happening tomorrow. What time should we arrive? Would it be too much to ask for you to give us a ring, when you get home tonight, and let us know?"

It was much too late to ring them now, but I need to ring them early in the morning. I can't really invite them over here, if Jamie is staying! Oh, what a mess!

Things to be grateful for

1) Jason is as good as new and back to his old self.

2) I did not disgrace myself with Samantha, (though I still can't believe it!).

Friday 13<u>th</u> April 2001- Good Friday

Word of the Day: Recalcitrant... rebellious, wayward, obstinate

11-30 p.m. in bed at Mum and Dad's house!

I rang Mother, early this morning, and explained the difficulty of Jamie staying at my place. I have to admit that I thoroughly enjoyed the exercise, because I got her out of bed.

One up to me, I think you'll find, Mother!

"What on Earth is wrong?" She said wearily, as she struggled to engage in semi-conscious thought."

"I don't know what you mean." I responded mischievously.

"What time is it?"

"6-15!" I replied brightly and enjoyed doing so! Time you were up and about! I've been up ages!"

"That doesn't mean we all have to be, does it?" She protested.

Don't you just love the irony?

"Pot to kettle, pot to kettle, anyone there?"

"What **are** you going on about?"

You do this to me every Sunday morning. I just got in first today!" I was feeling very superior! " I had to ring you early, because, when I got in last night, it was too late to ring you, then. I had to catch you before you set off."

I was going to cancel altogether, but she made me feel so guilty, that I ended up offering to go there, to them.

"That's what I suggested in the first place." She chastised me. "Now that I have got no food in the place, and I've packed our suitcase, you decide to alter the arrangements. You can be so inconsiderate at times!"

"What was I supposed to do Mother? Leave him on the streets?"

"That's where he deserves to be. Poor girl. Imagine being so callous to her!"

"Well, don't shoot the messenger! I didn't do it, I only told you about it."

"Hasn't he got a mother to go home to?"

"I don't know, I didn't ask him. I couldn't see him with no place to go, could I? I've got food in for us here. I'll just bring it with me. There's no need to have a cow!"

"It'll still have to be cooked, though, won't it? It means dinner is going to be very late."

"So what? We can have a snack for lunch, and then have dinner tonight. What's the big deal? Show some flexibility."

She humphed and grunted, but agreed, unwillingly.

Once I had rung Mother, I rang Samantha.

"Hi, Sam. How're you doing?"

"I'm OK." She replied.

"Have you calmed down any, yet?"

"Yes, but I'm still angry with him."

"That's not unreasonable, but what are you going to do?"

"Nothing! As far as I'm concerned, he can go jump off a bridge."

"You don't mean that!"

"Oh? Don't I?"

"Not really, do you? I think you two need to sit down and have a civilised discussion and sort this all out."

"The only discussion I want with him is about when he can pick up his things."

"He's here now. Wouldn't you like to talk to him?"

Argghh! – Stupid question or what?

She refused to speak to him, wished me a Happy Easter, and then hung up.

"Sorry mate! I did my best." I told him.

"Never mind. I know you did. Can I stay the weekend?"

"Of course you can. I'll be back Monday. Make yourself at home."

I don't remember having Good Friday on Friday 13th before! I guess it must have happened in my lifetime, but I can't recall it. I arrived in Luton at about 11 am, unloaded my Easter fare, including a ten-pound Turkey and some chestnut stuffing, and then delivered them to Mother's kitchen, along with my winning smile.

"Happy Easter, Mother!" I cried enthusiastically and pecked her on the cheek.

"What are you grinning at? You look like a Cheshire cat!" Mother greeted her recalcitrant, (hurrah!) son warmly, in her time honoured fashion!

Dad and I exchanged glances, raised our eyebrows and sat down without comment.

We sat around the television, with Dad and I trying to watch a film, but with Mother insisting on discussing various events and, of course, the state of my love life. The last time I tried to watch this film, I missed the ending because Mother phoned me. When I told her I intended to start seeing Louise, when she returns, she said that she was "keeping out of it!"

I'll believe that when I see it! And I still don't know how the bloody film ended!

Things to be grateful for

1) I got Mother out of bed this morning. Deep joy!
2) The chance to spend some quality time with my parents.

Monday 16<u>th</u> April 2001- Easter Monday

Word of the Day: Destine... to doom, seal the fate

Back home to sanity... NOT!

I went to watch Luton play, on Saturday. Dad came with me. It was his birthday and I hadn't a clue what to get him, but he came up with the idea that he would like to go to the match. It was the first time he had been to a Luton game for about twenty years. When we took our seats, he pointed out the changes in the stadium...

Stadium is a bit of an overstatement at Kenilworth Road!

... And how the main stand is just the same as it was all that time ago and, probably, for fifty years before that! It is now a fire hazard. The wooden framework was recycled from Noah's ark, if I remember correctly! Dad bombarded me with stories of "the good old days" when he was in his twenties.

"I remember 1959, cup final year!" His eyes lit up as he recounted the memories. "We beat Leicester 4-1 in a replay, here, in freezing weather. Allan Brown got a hat trick. He was Luton Manager a few years later, you know?"

I did know but I had to let him reminisce, uninterrupted. It was his birthday and being uninterrupted, while talking, was a new experience for him, having lived with Mother for 35 years!

"When we played up at Filbert Street, I caught the milk train up to Leicester, with my mates. We had a great day in town and, then, after we got a draw, we went on the booze until the early hours of the morning. Then we got the milk train back." He laughed as he recalled the memory. "I was still living with your nan and grandad. Boy, was I in deep trouble with your mother? I got in about 7 in the morning, still half-cut from the night before, and your nan was up and dressed, with a face like thunder. She told your mother next time she saw her, and she didn't speak to me for a week!"

Result, I would have thought!

"I bet you thought you'd gone deaf?"

He laughed. "Don't let her hear you say that. She still remembers it to this day. I'm sure she's convinced I was up to no good with a woman."

"And were you?"

"Of course I wasn't!"

"That's OK then. I didn't want to have to grass you up!" We both enjoyed the moment.

"I went to the semi finals as well. We were playing Norwich. They were a lot further down the leagues than us, third or fourth division, I think, but they were playing out of their skins that year. They held us to a draw down at Tottenham, you know! Then we beat them in the replay at Birmingham."

"Who was playing in those days? " I prompted him.

"Oh! Let me see. Ron Baynham, the England goalie, Allan Brown, Billy Bingham................"

He went on to name the entire Cup Final Team and described most of the play in the Final against Nottingham Forest.

"We never should have lost that game. It all turned for us when that Forest player broke his leg. There were no substitutes in those days, Ben. You could see that our boys looked sick when his leg snapped.

Dwight... Roy Dwight it was. He was the Uncle, or something, of Elton John! His real name is something Dwight."

"I wonder if he was an uphill gardener as well?" I let the words slip out.

"What was that?

"Nothing, just thinking aloud!"

"They were happy days," he said. "But within five or six years they'd gone from top division to bottom. When you were born they were in the third division I think. World cup year that was. We'd just got married and money was tight..." He stopped short.

He was suddenly interested in the match we were watching, and didn't speak for some time. I was ruminating on his last words. Then I had a rude awakening. I had never before given it any thought. If I was born in 1966 in May and they were married in 1965, in October, I must have been on the way, before they got married! Oh! My God! That is incredible. I know the sixties were supposed to be free love, and all that, but I just didn't see Mother as a sixties chick! I'll have to store that one up for future reference. (He said with a wicked grin!)

This game was about as exciting as watching paint dry, finished 0-0 and has probably destined (hurrah! I don't think!) Luton for relegation to the third division.

On Sunday, Mother spent just about the entire morning cooking the lunch, which I have to say was excellent! I played cards with Dad, interrupted at intervals by Mother, as she passed through the living room.

"Play the ace! Go on!" She told Dad,

"Thank you very much! I'll have to now that you've told him I've got it!"

Exit Mother, stage left, and tutting to herself. After an evening of Mother talking and us listening, while the TV spoke to itself, I finally got to bed at about 11 o' clock. I don't know if it's just me, but it seems that Mother always stops yapping when the ads come on and continues when the programmes start again.

I got up early this morning and headed back to sanity, or so I thought.

I got back to the flat at about ten and was dying for a cup of tea. I let myself in and headed for the kitchen. There was no sign of Jamie. I wasn't sure if he'd just gone out or had found somewhere else to stay. I opened the bedroom door, and there were clothes everywhere. I looked up and there, in the bed, was Jamie, fast asleep, alongside Cindy, the village bike, from Low Fen!

"What the fuck is going on?" I shouted angrily.

"Use your imagination!" Jamie replied, as he struggled to focus.

"OK, you Muppet! I'm going to get some milk from the shop, and I'll **imagine** you've both gone! When I get back, I'd better not **still** be imagining it! All right?" I stormed out. I haven't been so angry for ages!!

When I got back they had both left. The bedroom was still a tip, and I was still extremely annoyed that he had abused my hospitality. Wait till I see him on his own!

Things to be grateful for

1) I really enjoyed having my Dad all to myself for an afternoon. I think he enjoyed it too.

2) An excellent turkey dinner, cooked by my mother instead of me!

3) The rest from work has done me good.

Wednesday 18th April 2001

Word of the Day: Licentious... immoral, shameless, abandoned

9p.m. on trailer

Luton lost again at Wrexham on Monday. I'm losing interest. I really thought Joe Kinnear would save us from relegation. I guess it was just too big a job. I expect he'll be off in the close season, to some Premier division club.

I've just spoken to Louise on my mobile. She is still with her parents.

"I know I said I was coming back," she said defensively. "It's just telling my mum and dad. They have been really good to me, while I've been down here. They're going to be so disappointed."

"You mean you haven't even told them yet?"

My mouth is seconds ahead of my brain again, but in for a penny in for a pound.

"The longer you leave it, the harder it will be...and you haven't got a job at the moment. From my limited experience of speaking with your mother, she doesn't strike me as the type to let you languish at home, like a lady of leisure."

"No, she has mentioned it already...'don't you think you should be looking for something, dear?'"

"That's how to break it to her, then... tell her that you've found a job, but it's up here."

A customer came and interrupted the conversation, so I left Louise pondering my words.

The customer ordered his food, but was distracted by the personal CD player he had on. I could hear tinny sounds, like a miniature hi-hat cymbal being played, emanating from it.

"What're you listening to?" I asked politely.

"It's my CD player." He replied without the slightest hint of sarcasm.

Unkind thoughts, such as 'He would be out of his depth in a puddle', went through my mind, but he suddenly redeemed himself.

"Sorry, I was miles away. What a stupid thing to say. It's "The Corrs", he said.

"I like The Corrs, the lead singer has a very distinctive voice." I observed.

"Yes, I think they all do."

"When you're watching them, though, doesn't it make you think that somewhere in town, there's an Irish theme pub with no staff?" I gave him a lead by laughing myself, but a tumbleweed moment ensued. I hadn't realised that "The Corrs" were his entire raison d'etre!

He had just unredeemed himself, in my eyes, and reverted to nerd status, so I went back to unkind thoughts about his intelligence, and then served his food with a smile. As he left, the mobile began to ring.

"Hello, Arnold's Kebabs!" I said breezily.

"Hello," came the tentative response. "I'm looking for Ben Arnold."

"Why? What's he done?" I did not try to conceal my enjoyment of the 'lateral thinking' humorous remark.

"Sorry?" replied the caller.

"Nothing!"

The world is full of humourless people today. Or is it me?

"Ben Arnold?"

"I am he... it is me!" I replied in the same light-hearted manner.

"Oh!" She seemed taken aback. "Erm... it's Nicola Sherman here."

"Oh, yes. The solicitor who rang my parents?"

"Well, not exactly. I am not a solicitor, but I did ring your parents."

"I see. Dad said you have something for me, though? From a will?"

"Well, sort of. I'd prefer to tell you in person than on the phone. I would have written but your parents didn't want to give out your address..." She was becoming less defensive. "..... Why? Are you an axe murderer or something?"

Aha! She has got a sense of humour!

"Not recently. They never proved anything, but don't go digging under the patio." I joked again. "OK! When are you free?"

"Where are you situated?"

"Near Peterborough."

"Hang on, let me look at my diary... Ah! I have to go to Lincoln next Wednesday. I could drop by then. In the evening?"

"Well, I'm usually working in the evenings. Any chance of the afternoon?"

"I'll see if I can get my business in Lincoln done early. About 4 o'clock any good?" She asked.

"Spot on," I replied. "It's a date! I'll meet you in The Red Lion, in Marston Ferrars. You'll recognise me easily enough. Most of them are inbreeds with two heads. I'll be the good-looking one, without the webbed feet!"

"We'll see about that!" She said, almost assertively!

My mind began to wander, as I tried to picture her. She sounded very sexy and in charge of the situation, and I couldn't help seeing her, with enormous breasts encased in a basque, long legs in black fishnet stockings and high-heeled boots, and holding a riding crop!

Wow! Where did that image come from?

"Penny for them!"

My mind was dragged back from the abyss, in which it was wallowing, by the sound of the voice of one James Ryecroft.

"Oh! You decided to show your face, then?"

"I don't understand why you were so mad!" He continued.

"That's why you have an ex-fiancée, an outstanding mortgage on an ex-residence and an ex-sofa to doss on. You just have no concept of decency!"

Shit! That was a bit hard on him!

"That's a bit harsh, isn't it?" he whined.

"Harsh, but fair, I think you'll find, if you asked anyone with a modicum of morality."

"Oh, come on, mate. You'd have done the same. Sam wouldn't even talk to me. What was I supposed to do? Cindy was just a refuge."

"More like a fucking refugee, if you ask me."

I don't know what it is about Jamie. I think it is his naivety. He honestly doesn't mean any harm. He just doesn't think out the consequences of his actions, but just plods on, oblivious to the world around him. I tried, but I couldn't stay mad at him."

"Yes, she was a bit of a bowser, wasn't she? Mind you, she's up for a bit more than Sam was! If you know what I mean?"

"It was bad enough finding you in my bed, without the sordid details, thank you! Where are you staying now?"

"Ah, well. I'm at home with me mum at the moment. Hey? What about us sharing a place? You could get shot of the one bed hovel, and we could get a two-bed place. What do you say?"

If he had asked me that this time last year, I would probably have jumped at it. The way my love life was then, it needed all the help it could get, and Jamie certainly attracts women. I've moved on from there, though. I'm still hoping that Louise will come back, and we can get something going. I don't want to be sharing with a licentious, (hurrah!), predator, who would make her feel uncomfortable.

"It would never work!" I told him. "Louise would never go for it."

"Oh, so Louise makes all your decisions for you now, does she?"

"No, but neither do you. You can't even be trusted to make your own decisions!" I laughed at him.

However, it looks as though Samantha is sticking to her guns and not having him back. Fair play to her!

Things to be Grateful for

1) I managed to have a quick chat with Louise.
2) I am to meet the enigmatic Nicola Sherman next week. I may just have to give her one! (If Louise is not here by then.)
3) Against my better judgement, I've made it up with Jamie.

Sunday 22nd April 2001

Word of the Day: Exonerate... vindicate, absolve, free from blame

7-45 a.m. Sleeping like the proverbial log!

(telephone rings)

I fall out of bed trying to answer the phone, and I am not in the best of moods when I pick it up.

"Hello!" I barked.

"Goodness! Someone got out of bed on the wrong side this morning." Mother says in all seriousness!

"What do you mean, '**got** out of bed'? I was in it... fast asleep... and then **fell** out of it trying to get to the bloody phone!"

"All right, all right! There's no need for language!"

"How will we communicate, then? By smoke signals?" My mood softened a little, as I was amused by my own wit!

"Very clever, Ben.... I don't think! You know what I mean. I wouldn't have dared use language like that to **my** mother. She'd have slapped my face."

That is a spectacle I'd have paid money to see!

"Really? But then I don't suppose she ever rang you up in the middle of the night and made you fall out of bed trying to get to the phone!"

"She never had a phone."

"I rest my case!"

"What is the matter with you lately? You've been in a funny mood for weeks. You and your father were conspiring a bit too much, for my liking, when you were here for Easter, as well, come to think of it. You're like a pair of kids when you get together. God alone knows what you got up to at that football match. You're not safe to be let out on your own, either of you!"

If only you knew what I learned at that football match. You'd be horrified!

"Well, we weren't alone were we? We were with each other! Duh! So... To what do I owe this pleasure, Mother?"

"Do I need a reason to ring my only child...? And don't "duh!" me."

"On a Sunday morning at half past seven, yes you do!"

"Don't exaggerate, it's nearly eight o'clock."

"It is now, yes! But it wasn't when you... Oh why do I bother?"

"Have you heard any more from that Louise?"

"That Louise? Mother, that is a bit disrespectful. Especially as you have met her. She's a very nice woman."

"I've told you. She's too flighty for my liking."

"Well, you are going to have to get used to her. She's coming home to the village, and I'm going to go out with her."

"Marry that one and you'll soon rue the day! You know what they say? Marry in haste, repent at leisure!"

"Have you swallowed a copy of the Oxford Book of Naff Sayings? They also say "There's many a mickle maks a muckle!" and I don't know what that means either! Anyway, who says I'm going to marry her?"

" I can read you like a book, Benjamin Arnold! You'd marry her, just to spite me!"

"My word, we **are** paranoid this morning, aren't we? I can assure you, that I would not tie myself up in marriage to anyone, just to score points against a third party. Not even if the third party was you, Mother!"

"You mark my words is all I'm saying!"

"Promise?"

"What?"

"Promise that it's all you're saying?"

"I can't stay arguing with you all morning, I've got to get breakfast"

"Fine, Mother. I'll speak to you later, then. 'Bye"

Luton managed to lose, yet again, 2-1 at home to Bury. If they lose again, on Tuesday, at home to Rotherham, they are mathematically certain of relegation.

12 noon in the Red Lion

I thought there might be a few people in for Sunday Lunch, but I am sitting here, making notes, like Billy No-mates! I just rang Louise. Her mother seemed less than pleased to hear my dulcet tones!

"Hello?"

"Hello."

"Oh Hi, Mrs Burnham. Is Louise there?"

"Yes she is. I suppose we've got you to thank for this?"

"For what?"

"Louise going away again."

"Well, all children fly the nest sooner or later, don't they? She **is** over thirty! Why? Is that a problem?"

"She was happy down here, in that job. Why couldn't you leave well enough alone? I know you had a go at that nice solicitor she was going out with. Simon. They were very happy together. He could have given her a good life. Why did you have to come and spoil it?"

He could have given her a good hiding!

"I think he spoiled it himself, Mrs Burnham. Anyway, I don't want to fall out with you. Can I speak to her please?"

"She's here..."

"Hello? Ben?"

"Hiya!"

"What've you been saying to mum? She's gone off crying."

"It was her. She told me off for spoiling it for you and Simon the Snake!"

"Oh, I see... I haven't actually told them the full story... sorry."

"So, I've got to be the bad guy, for ever, in their eyes? That'll make for a good start to the relationship!"

"Oh! Are we going to have a relationship, then?"

"Are you saying that you don't want one?"

"I'm not saying anything. I was just checking!" She laughed at her wind-up.

"We could have one if we lived a bit closer!" I said tentatively, awaiting her disclosure of the news that her mother had inadvertently leaked.

"Well...we might be a bit closer from next weekend. I am moving in with Emily. So how would that assist a relationship?" She said excitedly.

"Well it can't do any harm!" I teased her. "I'll have a think about it and let you know when you get here!"

"Ooh! You cheeky devil!"

The teasing remarks continued for a few more minutes, then I asked her if she was going to tell her parents the truth about what happened with Simon.

"I will…at some point. I promise."

I accepted the promise that one day may exonerate, (hurrah!), me in her family's eyes and we arranged to meet next Saturday, for a drink at lunchtime. I have decided that I will not work on Saturday. This is too important to mess up yet again!

Things to be Grateful for

1) Louise is coming home!
2) Louise is coming home!
3) Louise is coming home!!!

Monday 23rd April 2001

Word of the Day: Entreat… plead, implore, beg

10-00 a.m. Head pounding but half way through a sausage sandwich!

The atmosphere at last night's quiz was very peculiar. It didn't last long, because a mass walk out occurred, before the quiz even began. Everyone was still coming to terms with the fact that Gordon is gay, and Jamie was trying to pretend that he doesn't care about his self inflicted split with Samantha. Then Brian, who ought to have known better, began dishing out abuse to anyone, with whom he came into contact.

"You plank!" Said Brian to Jamie. "You're always saying that Samantha is right where you want her. Keep her well supplied with sex and she's happy. Well you certainly got that wrong, didn't you? I wonder who's keeping her supplied now."

"Leave it, Brian. He doesn't need you to tell him he's stuffed up!" Gordon defended Jamie.

"OK gay boy, keep your panties on!" Brian replied.

"Come on, Brian. What's wrong with you tonight? A bit of fun is OK, but show a little sensitivity." I entreated, (hurrah! Good one!).

"You're just as bad, burger man. Your tart teaching you to get in touch with your feminine side, is she? You'd better move in with our Gordon, here. You could exchange recipes!" He laughed loudly, but was the only one finding his aggressive mood funny.

"I don't know what the world is coming to," Brian continued. " One minute we have a really good little group going. The next thing you know, one of them has decided to go trouser diving; another's so depressed he makes everyone else feel suicidal... and he's only got himself to blame for the shit he's in; and the other's lost all sense of humour and he's behaving like a bloody agony aunt. I reckon I'm the only one who's still sane, here! The fucking lunatics have taken over the asylum!"

"If you feel like that about it, why don't you fuck off, then?" Gordon said with a raised voice.

"No! Bollocks! If you don't like the truth, then you lot fuck off!" Brian was adamant.

"People who live in glass houses shouldn't throw stones!" I ventured.

Oh, God. I am turning into my mother!

"What **are** you talking about?" Brian was having none of it.

"You want to look at your own life, before you start criticising other people. That's all." I continued.

"What do you mean by that?" He wanted to know. "What do you know about my life? I'm the only normal one here. I'm married with two kids! You can't keep a bird for five minutes. He's as bent as a nine bob note, and he's so insecure he has to shag anything warm, with a pulse!" he pointed to each one of us in turn.

I wanted to put him in his place, and I had the ammunition to do it, too, after my little heart to heart with Maria, but I realised that I was getting in too deep and did not wish to break her confidence. I decided that I was not enjoying the atmosphere that Brian had generated, and there was little sign of his tirade abating, so I stood up.

"Look, Brian, I don't want to get into all this. I think you must have some problem of your own to be so fucking disagreeable tonight. I suggest you address it, instead of taking it out on your mates! I, for one, don't need it. I'll see you when you feel like being a bit more sociable." I moved towards the door.

"Well done, Brian," Gordon said, clapping his hands in mock applause.

"Oh, why don't you all piss off, if you feel like that about it!" Brian said with finality.

The other two followed me out. I noticed that Jamie had said nothing in his own, or anyone else's defence. This was singularly abnormal.

"What's up, Jamie? You're very quiet." I began." This break up has had a bigger effect on you than you're letting on, hasn't it?"

"Yeah. I don't know what to do with myself. I've had a different bird every night this week, and all I can think of is Sam."

"Is there nothing you can do?" Gordon asked.

"No. She won't even talk to me. I rang her yesterday and she just said that she wanted me to collect my stuff and put the house on the market."

"Fucking hell!" Gordon seemed shocked. "That sounds a bit terminal!"

"It's worse than that!" Jamie went on. "I went round this morning to get a few things. Everything I own was in suitcases at the door, and there was a for sale board outside the house."

"I'm sorry, Jamie." I tried to console him, but he was extremely morose. "It looks like you're going have to accept the situation and move on, mate."

"I guess so," He said quietly, then in a sudden burst of energy and enthusiasm shouted, "Bollocks to everybody! Let's go down The Lion and get totally rat arsed!"

We did not need a second invitation and drank more than we should have. This is why my head feels like my brain has been wrung out, my throat is sore from the unusual way my stomach chose to divest itself of its contents in the night, and I am finding it hard to focus my eyes this morning.

Things to be grateful for

1) Soluble Paracetamol.
2) I don't have to work today.

Wednesday 25th April 2001

Word of the Day: Haughtily... proudly, arrogantly, self-importantly

6-00 p.m. Mind in a whirl and totally bewildered!

Luton lost 1-0 at home to Rotherham last night. Rotherham are almost certainly going to be promoted, while Luton are now definitely relegated. It is hard to accept that, having been in the top division and winning the Littlewoods Cup only twelve years ago, we have come to this. It is so depressing!

I have just returned from the Red Lion, and I am in total shock at the news I received. I went across at about a quarter to four to meet the mysterious Ms Sherman at four, as agreed. The pub was very quiet. Although it is open all day now, there are never many people in between about three and six o'clock. Three locals were sitting at the bar, and there were a few in the pool room. The barflies nodded as I ordered my beer. I took my half of Tetley's Smooth and sat in the corner to read the newspaper, while I waited for her.

At four, on the dot, a young woman walked in alone. It had to be her. The three at the bar had been engrossed in deep conversation, but stopped talking when she entered. She scanned the room and caught my eye. I smiled and she immediately realised that I must be the one for whom she was looking. She was much younger than I had expected, tall and slim, with natural-looking, long, blonde hair, which swayed as she approached, its tips reaching down to her waist. I noticed that she did not possess the voluptuous breasts that I had previously fantasised over, but she was **adequately** endowed in that department. Fortunately, neither was she wearing the basque, nor carrying the whip!! Instead, she looked quite businesslike, in a white blouse and a navy blue suit, the skirt of which hung modestly, at about knee length. I would have placed her in her early twenties; too young to be a fully-fledged solicitor, I would have thought. The three locals at the bar turned to follow her with their eyes, as she walked over to me. One puffed out his cheeks and blew out his breath, indicating how attractive he thought she was, although she did not see him do this, as her back was to him. He was not wrong, though; she was quite stunning.

She held out a trembling hand for a handshake. I took it in mine and shook it warmly.

"Hello," she began; her voice had a slight quiver as she spoke. She cleared her throat. "Mr Arnold?"

"Ben," I replied. "Ms Sherman?"

"Call me Nicola...well Nicki. Not many people call me Nicola apart from my mum..." She stopped in mid flow.

"Are you OK?" I asked. She was looking a little distressed.

"Yes, I'll be fine, thanks."

"Anyway, I'm sorry. How rude of me? Let me get you a drink."

"Thanks...JD and Coke please."

I bought her drink and brought the Jack Daniels to her with a can of Coca Cola, so that she could add the quantity that she preferred.

"OK, then!" I said directly, as I felt the adrenaline rush that my anticipation had caused. "Perhaps you'd like to tell me what all this is about."

"All right. Do you remember a young woman by the name of Carole Sherman?"

"Er...no. I don't think so...Why? Is she suing me or has she left me something in her will?" I said jokingly."

"In a way," she smiled. "She has left you something. It depends if you like what I'm going to tell you about her!"

"Carole Sherman? You're a Sherman. Would this be a relative of yours?"

"Yes she is...was ... my mother."

"Was? I take it she is the one who passed away?" I said softly.

She nodded.

"I'm sorry to hear that." I condoled with her. "But how do I come into the equation? Is she a relative of mine?" I was confused. Someone I don't remember leaving me a bequest in her will?

"Not exactly…Look there is no easy way to say this…" She seemed to take a deep breath searching for courage, "…I am your daughter… at least, I think I am."

There was a deafening silence born of total astonishment. I am sure that, tomorrow, my chest will bear a bruise as a result of my chin hitting it, with some force, as my mouth opened in amazement. I could not find any words to reply. Each time I tried to say something, the words scrambled in my head, and my mouth rejected them as inadequate.

"I'm sorry…" She broke the silence. "I can see you're shocked."

"No, no. It is not your fault. It **is** one heck of a shock though, you're right!" I regained the use of my mouth. "Wow! My mind is spinning. I don't want to offend you, really I don't, but… what makes you think that I am your father?" Then as the myriad questions came thick and fast into my head, I asked, "If it is not a rude question, may I ask how old you are?"

Of course it's a rude bloody question!

"Nineteen." She replied.

Inappropriately, my thoughts wandered to Jenni, who had also been nineteen, and the realisation that I had slept with a woman young enough to be my daughter. Then I voiced the logic, which had led to the question, having mentally calculated my age at her conception.

"Are you sure…? I don't mean are you sure you're nineteen, of course you are…I mean are you sure it's me you are looking for? I would only have been about sixteen…no, probably fifteen."

"Yes, I am sure. Mum told me that you were only fifteen…she was nineteen."

Argghh! There's that number again. Nineteen!

"Oh my God!" My memory processed the information and located the relevant period in my life. "Carole! I do remember a Carole. She used to live in Crawley Road."

"That's her." She was looking misty-eyed, as though she was fighting back the tears. "I'm sorry, it's a bit emotional for me. I've wondered about my father all my life, and it's just overwhelming to think that I'm actually meeting him after all these years."

"I smiled at the use of the term "all these years" from one so young. I placed my arm around her shoulder and pulled her head on to my shoulder and squeezed her supportively. I looked over her shoulder and saw the men at the bar watching us. I could see what was going through their minds.

"It's not beyond the realms of possibility that I **could** be your father, Nicki, but it seems unlikely. We only ...er...were only..."together"... once, if you know what I mean."

She smiled at my obvious embarrassment in discussing such personal matters with someone, who, after all, was a total stranger.

"When I went to see her the following week," I continued, "she told me that she was seeing someone else and that I'd been a mistake. She said she needed time to think things through and that she would ring me the next week, but she never did. I was quite heartbroken, I remember. She was my first...you know... my first time and all that! I was quite besotted with her. After a while, I went to her house to see what was happening, and her mum said she had gone away. To Lancashire or somewhere."

"It all fits in with what she told me. As I grew up, with no father... she never married you know... and I became more and more inquisitive, she gradually built up the picture, until she had told me almost everything. She told me she met you at a party and liked you a lot, right away. She hadn't got a boyfriend... that was a lie to let you down gently."

"Why? Why lie? I don't understand."

"I'm coming to that. She was young and naive. Things were different in those days..."

"Steady! I'm not that old!" I protested.

She smiled. "I know, but people are so much more... what's the word I'm looking for...? Worldly?... at nineteen nowadays."

"You think so? You should see some of my customers when the pub turns out on a Friday night!"

We both laughed. She had a very gentle demeanour, which was very likeable.

"Well, she was nineteen and living at home with her parents and she hated it. My grandad was a real tyrant, apparently, but it's hard to see it in him now. I can wrap him around my little finger."

I didn't doubt it for a minute!

She went on. "She wanted to leave home, but he wouldn't let her. Can you imagine that today? It would never happen. Anyway, she couldn't see any way out of it. Her prison, she called it. She dreamed up a scheme to escape. She thought that if she were pregnant, grandad would throw her out, and she would be free. *"He would never have suffered the stigma of a child of his having a baby out of wedlock!"* she told me, *"Imagine what the neighbours would think."* She had always wanted to have a child of her own, and so she decided to do it. She said that as soon as she met you, she knew that you were the one she wanted to be my father. She called you her "pretty boy". I remember her telling me that you were very pretty for a man, and you were not at all macho and aggressive."

"I don't know if I should be flattered or insulted!" I laughed.

"I think you should be flattered. She said that she wanted her child to be good-looking and gentle."

"I think she succeeded!"

"Thank you. You are most kind, sir." She said with an air of affectation.

"But, as I said, we only slept together once. If she wanted me to be the father of her child, you'd have thought she would have done it a few times at least, just to be sure. How can you be sure that I am your father, from just the one... erm.... time?"

"You were the only one she slept with. She said that after the party, you went out together a few times, to the cinema and for a drink, and then you slept together. You didn't tell her your age, until after you had been to bed with her, did you? She was horrified. She thought you looked much older, and you had taken her into pubs for a drink, so she assumed you must be at least eighteen."

"Yes, well, I was over six foot by the time I was fourteen, so I must have been 6'2" by then."

"When she found out your age, she lost her nerve. She thought you were too young for her and also realised that having a baby was probably not a good idea, when she thought it through. But it was too late to change her mind. A few weeks later, she found out she was already pregnant. She told me that you were the only person she slept with until after I was born, so you are the only possible father."

"But why didn't she tell me?"

"She never intended to tell you to begin with. It was her decision and she wasn't about to ask you if you minded! So she certainly wasn't going to tell you, once she found out you were only fifteen. She said it wouldn't have been fair to you. Anyway, she got her wish. As soon as he found out, Grandad packed her off to his mum's in Preston. She told me all about you and that your name was Ben, but she said she couldn't remember your surname and that she'd never known where you lived. I just accepted it. When she knew she was dying, she wrote me a letter to be read when she was gone. She left it with the solicitor who was holding her will."

"When did she pass away?"

"Last year, August 28th. Nan and Grandad were devastated. They still haven't got over it. They still cry when we talk about her. I'm living with them now. I'm not home much; I'm a flight attendant. I work out of Luton Airport a lot, so it's quite convenient."

"How did your mum...er... die?"

"She had cancer. It was in her ovaries. There was nothing they could do for her by the time they found out. She was scared of doctors and hospitals. She didn't go when she knew something was wrong, and when she did it was too late. She passed away quite quickly after she was diagnosed. That was what was so shocking for us all. It was all over so quickly. We didn't have a clue she was seriously ill. She just kept saying she was tired."

"I'm sorry." I didn't know what else to say. I changed the subject. "What were you doing in Lincoln then?"

"I had to drive a colleague home from the airport. She was on leave and was going back to her parents for a week, but she hasn't got a car at the moment."

"Two birds with one stone, then?"

"Yes, it was quite handy."

"So, it has taken you, what... eight months to find me?"

"Not exactly. I didn't act on the information until after Christmas. Then I found your house in Luton straight away. It wasn't exactly difficult, your family still live in the same house!"

"Oh, yes. So they do!" I said ironically and we both smiled.

"It took a while for me to pluck up the courage to ring the house, and even more to ring you. I've been shaking all week since we organised this meeting.""I'm not that fearsome!"

"No. I can see that now! I'm just glad to have found you."

"Oh my God! This is so scary. I can hardly believe it. I've never had any kids."

"Yes you have," She smiled. "You just didn't know it."

"Would you like to see Mum's letter?" She asked.

I felt strange about reading someone's personal dying words to someone else, but I have to admit to having been curious.

"I would love to... if you don't mind. It seems a bit voyeuristic though, somehow."

She handed me the letter.

"I'd really like you to read it," She said sincerely.

I opened the envelope and removed the carefully hand written letter. As I read, I realised it had been a mistake. It was full of personal stuff, which really made me feel intrusive. It ended with Carole's confession that she had lied to Nicola about not remembering my surname, and explained her reasons for keeping it secret. It certainly all fits. I could well be this girl's father. Seriously, though, I have to say that there was a lump in my throat, as I read her words. I found it hard to conceive that someone would be so desperate as to do such a thing.

My stomach churned as the excitement and shock of the news sank in, even as the darker side of my brain doubted that it was true.

"Wow!" I said to her. "That is quite something. I have always wanted a child of my own, but somehow I envisaged one about this size!" I indicated the size of a babe-in-arms.

We continued to discuss her mother's life and how she had been brought up. The time flew by. At half past five, she said that she had to leave, as she was due at the airport at ten, and she had to go home first to prepare.

"Do your grandparents know you are here?"

Oh my God, I never thought. Mum and Dad are also her grandparents!

"No! I didn't want to upset them. I thought I'd find you and see what the reaction was before telling them."

"You are a naughty girl!" I came over unexpectedly fatherly. "Meeting a strange man on your own could have been dangerous... and you didn't even tell anyone where you were going. Don't you ever do that again!"

"I'm not likely to go searching for my father again, am I?" She laughed. "But thanks, it is nice to know you care!"

"And you have two more grandparents now!"

How the hell do I break this to THEM?

"Of course. But one step at a time. What should I call you? Ben? Dad?"

"I don't mind. Whatever you are comfortable with. But for God's sake don't call me Arnie!"

"I'm sorry?"

"Long story! I'll tell you another time." I smiled.

"OK. Well, look. I'd better go."

We stood up and I hugged her and kissed her cheek. She kissed mine in return. It was one of the most wonderful moments of my life. I really feel like her father, although it also seems weird. But how the hell **do** I tell Mother?

Not at all until I'm sure in my own mind! That is for sure!

She left and I sat down again feeling deflated by the anticlimax of her departure.

Barfly one said, "Hey, Ben! You dirty old bugger! She's a bit young for you isn't she?"

"No! He likes them, young, don't you, Benny boy!" said number two.

"Don't be so disgusting!" I said indignantly. "She is my daughter!" I continued full of pride. I puffed out my chest, held my head high and walked out haughtily. (Hurrah!).

Things to be Grateful for

1) I have a daughter!
2) She is beautiful, articulate and seems to be a very gentle person.
3) Mother has a grandchild.
4) This news is going to strike her speechless.
5) How potent am I? Scored a bull's-eye first time!

Thursday 26th April 2001

Word of the Day: Politic... diplomatic, prudent, wise

11-00 p.m. In flat

Trading on base was extremely brisk today. Stacey certainly earned her money! I was so tired when I got home that I fell asleep for an hour and a half.

This evening was steady and there were plenty of hiatuses to recuperate from the busier moments. At about eight o' clock, Louise rang my mobile, to tell me that she is coming home, on Saturday, and hopes to arrive around midday. We arranged to meet at the pub for lunch. I decided it would be more politic, (hurrah!), to delay mentioning Nicola, for the time being. I think it is more tactful to discuss something as monumental as this in person. The same must also apply to telling Mum and Dad.

At around 9-30, Nicola called. She had just returned from a round trip to Spain and, now, has two full days off, which she is anticipating with delight. She asked how I was feeling about the situation, having had some time to digest the information. She seemed genuinely concerned for my feelings. I told her I was thrilled at the prospect of having a daughter. I did **not** tell her that I spent most of Wednesday night wrestling with all the understandable doubts and misgivings about the news; in fact, a downright suspicion of her mother's motives, before coming to the conclusion that Carole had nothing apparent to gain by lying. After all, she revealed her secret in a letter, to be read after she had died. I could not see how Nicola had anything to gain either, unless she was going to try to hit me for a big loan or something, but since she is grown up and self-sufficient, I can't imagine that is her aim. It is not as though I am being chased for child support! She seems such a level headed and personable young lady, and I felt guilty at doubting her, especially as I could see her resemblance to me. So, I accept, wholeheartedly, that she is indeed my daughter, and all that remains now is to reveal the fact to Mother…And of course Dad and Louise!

Nicola said that she was going to sit her grandparents down tomorrow and tell them her "fantastic news". I divulged the imminence of my 35th birthday, next week, and she asked if she could come over to help me celebrate it. I was very excited at the thought of seeing her again. A customer arrived, inconveniently, causing me to terminate the call.

As I did so, she said, "OK! I'll look forward to seeing you next week. 'Bye, Dad." I almost wept with emotion, when I heard those words for the first time in my life.

I said "Almost!"

I felt my eyes filling up and took some kitchen roll and wiped them, before the customer noticed. Arnold boys don't cry, do they? I must go to Luton, on Sunday, and break the news to Mum and Dad; it is only fair to them.

Things to be Grateful for

1) Louise is finally coming back.
2) The first thing she wants to do is see me.
3) Nicola wants to visit on my birthday.
4) She called me Dad!

Things to be scared about!

1) Telling Louise.
2) Telling Mother!

Sunday 29th April 2001

Word of the Day: Inconsequential... trivial, insignificant

11-00 a.m. About to leave for Luton

I met Louise for lunch at the Red Lion yesterday. She looked a picture, much less troubled than when I saw her last. She was very pleased to see me, too, and was in a very touchy-feely mood! It was as if every time she made a comment, she rested her hand on mine and then patted it gently, as she sat back after speaking. I found it strangely endearing. After we had eaten, I asked her what her plans were for the day, and she admitted that she had none, other than unpacking her belongings into her sister's spare room. I decided that the sooner she learned about my recently acquired offspring, the better, but lost my bottle and left it to be done in private, rather than here in the pub.

"Why don't we do something tonight?" I suggested.

"Don't you have to work?" She replied with an accusing smile.

"I can live with not working on your first day back." I successfully smiled my winning smile.

"You know best." She smiled back. "What did you have in mind?"

"Nothing specific. Whatever you want. The world's your lobster!" I winked at her.

She laughed generously at my deliberate malapropism.

"How about we get a take-away and a bottle of wine and just relax a bit? I could do with unwinding. I don't much fancy getting dressed up to go out tonight, after all the stress of leaving Mum and Dad."

"Suits me!" I agreed, intentionally ignoring the parental minefield reference.

We went our separate ways, and I headed for the sanctuary of the flat. I realised, as soon as I had walked in, that we had omitted to discuss the venue for our evening's revelries, so I rang her.

"Hi, Emily, is Louise there?"

"I thought she was with you...wait on, she's just arrived..." I heard Louise call "Hello," in the background. "... Can't you bear to be parted from her for five minutes?" She teased.

"I need to check something with her, that's all!" I said.

She laughed at my defensiveness. "It's OK she's here. 'Bye for now."

"Hi, Ben. What's the problem?" She trilled airily.

"Hiya! No problem. It's just that we didn't decide where we were eating tonight."

"Oh! Right! Listen, I know it's a bit cheeky..." She began in a whisper."...But is it OK if I ask Emily if she wants to eat with us? It's a bit awkward being my first night with her."

"Of course I don't mind," I tried to hide my disappointment. "Go ahead!"

"Emm!" She nearly deafened me, shouting through to another room. *"We're having Chinese tonight! Do you want some?"*

"No! You're all right!" I heard Emily shout back. *"I'm going clubbing with some mates from work. We're eating in town first!"*

"She's going out..." She said to me returning to normal volume. "... So, your place or mine, big boy?" Her Mae West impression was less than convincing, but the sentiment hit the mark.

"It's up to you."

"OK!" She had made up her mind. "Here, then... Then I won't have to walk home when I'm tired!"

After a supreme effort to make myself look passably attractive, I rang her again, at about six, to ask what she would like to eat. I took a note of her choice and ordered it, by telephone, to be picked up at 7-30 p.m. I bought a bottle of Australian Cabernet Shiraz, at the Off Licence, picked up the food and arrived just after 7-30. Emily was wearing a very short skirt and a skimpy low-cut top and was just putting on a jacket ready to leave, apparently on a manhunt!

"Don't do anything I wouldn't do, you two!!" She joked, as she passed me in the hallway.

As the witty retort, "Is there anything you wouldn't do, dressed like that?" sprang into my mind, I realised, just in time, that I didn't really know her well enough, yet, to make a joke like that without the risk of offending her, so I refrained from voicing it.

Louise and I spent the evening feeling very comfortable in each other's company, eating our meal and demolishing the entire bottle of red; although I was constantly in trepidation of what her reaction would be, if I ever plucked up the courage to tell her about Nicola. We talked and talked mainly about inconsequential, (hurrah!), matters, just relaxing and laughing. I told her about Jamie's saga and that one of the seemingly most macho of the bunch has turned out to be gay, but she confessed that she really didn't know them that well. Finally, I summoned the nerve to divulge the secret to end all secrets, my previously unknown daughter. Unfortunately, the right words would not come into my head, and I lost the momentum. She began to speak and the moment was lost.

Oh well! I'll leave it till later!

As it got later, the conversation began to dry up a little, and I thought about telling her then, but again I bottled it! Instead, I told her I was going to see Mum and Dad, in the morning, and said that I ought to get some sleep. She walked me to the door, holding my hand as we went. I turned to kiss her goodbye. I was expecting a rather quick kiss but it was a long, lingering, loving kiss, which quickly aroused us both.

In fact, I could have hung my coat on the front of my trousers!

As we broke for air, we kissed again, in a similar passionate embrace, holding each other tightly as we did so. This time, when our lips parted, we simultaneously sighed in surprise at the intensity of it, and I said, almost involuntarily, "Wow!"

"Wow, indeed!" She agreed.

"I'd better go," I said reluctantly. "Shall I ring you tomorrow?"

"You'd better!" She warned, laughing as she spoke.

I kissed her forehead and she stepped on tiptoes to kiss my cheek, then I left.

I returned home on cloud nine and spent much of the night thinking about her, how beautiful she is and the passion of the kiss goodnight. I wondered what might have happened if we had been a little more adventurous, earlier in the evening, but, in a way, I was glad we didn't push things along too quickly. I remembered the last time we became excessively amorous, and it had been too much for her. I don't want to create a problem. As much as I want to make love to her, I think I'll wait until she shows me that she is ready. I don't want to lose her now!

I was up at 6 a.m., being unable to sleep, after the lustful thoughts of Louise gave way to more apprehension over telling Mother about Nicola. I wished I had gained some practice by telling Louise. As I contemplated telling Mother, it felt as though a thousand butterflies were having a fly-past in my stomach. I tried to convince myself that she would be overjoyed at being a grandma, but I wasn't succeeding! What if the shock gave her apoplexy? Dad will take it in his stride, I think. In fact, when he digests the details, he'll probably be pleased that the next generation is already in place! As the clock took, what seemed like, three hours to tick round from 6-30 to 7-15, I made some tea and toast and then picked up the telephone.

"Hi, Mother! How's tricks?"

"Excuse me? Do I know you?"

"Very funny. I could always ring off and wait for you to ring me back. Then you could pay for the call."

"And how, exactly, would that differ from the norm?" She replied sarcastically.

"Who the Hell is Norm?" I countered.

"OK! Truce!" She was laughing.

"Truce!" I concurred with her. "Anyway, listen! I have good news!"

"Really? And what's the bad news?"

"Who said anything about bad news?"

"Whenever you say that you have good news, there is always bad news as well!"

"Oh, ye of little faith," I said laughing. "No! There is no bad news, just good!" I continued with all the enthusiasm I could muster. "I'm coming over later."

" I thought there was no bad news...! Ha! Ha! One to Mother!" She joked. "Hmm! You're coming over, eh? She mused suspiciously. "I wonder what for?"

Her sarcasm baffled me.

"To have dinner with my parents?" I said quizzically.

"I see. So it's nothing to do with the fact that a certain person is having a certain event later this week?"

"OK! I give up! You have totally lost me. Have you been messing around with Ouija boards again?"

"So you are not coming over to collect your birthday present, then?" She finally disclosed where her mind had been foraging.

"Oh! I get you! No… It's nothing like that. I had forgotten it was my birthday. I just wanted to see you... but if you would rather I..."

"No, no!" She interrupted... ***1-0 to me I think! Ha!***

"...If you say so, who am I to disbelieve you?" Her tone was that "knowing" tone, when someone thinks they know something, but probably doesn't, as in this case!

This especially applies to Mother, who has a black belt in jumping to conclusions! In fact, it is probably the only exercise she gets!

"Well, you believe what you want, Mother. I won't bother, then. I'll leave it until you are in a more sociable frame of mind!"

"Don't be so stupid!" She came back at me in a panicky tone.

2-0! I'm getting good at this game. Mind you, I had the best teacher in the world! It must be painful when your student takes over as the master!

"We'd be pleased to see you. You know that."

"Then don't try to make me out to be some devious schemer."

"I was only teasing you. Where's your sense of humour today? Hasn't it woken up yet? Mind you it is a bit early!" She enjoyed her little joke!

"I still have it," I replied. "It's just that I've had a lot on my plate recently. I'll tell you later."

I told her I'd be there at about 1-30 p.m. and she said that she could easily stretch their Sunday roast to three people.

Thirty-three, if I'm any judge!

Oh well! Here goes nothing!

Things to be Grateful for

1) Soon the secret will be out, for good or for bad!
2) Ha! Ha! I will get my birthday present.
3) It's Sunday and quiz night. I can't wait to hear the latest goings on in the complicated lives of my teammates!

Monday 30th April 2001

Word of the Day: Placating... pacifying, soothing, calming,

11-00 a.m. Trying to make the flat look a little less like a bomb-site!

Louise is coming round for lunch today. I've planned nothing else for the day, so I hope we can spend a long afternoon together and, who knows, maybe the evening too. I wish I'd told her about Nicola, last night. She will wonder why I didn't.

I arrived at Mum and Dad's, at around one o'clock yesterday and, as usual, Mother was making a drama out of cooking the Sunday lunch. Dad got me a can of beer, and we passed the time of day with the usual, "how have you been doing?" conversation. Mother, not to be left out, made sporadic interruptions. We answered her, when appropriate, and then resumed our own conversation. Lunch was a quiet affair. I was contemplating the best way to break the news. Should it be gently, or straight from the hip? In the end, it was over the head with a shovel!

"Mother...! Dad...! You know you have always wanted grandchildren? Well, you've got one!" I blurted it out with no-frills.

"Don't be silly!" Mother responded. "How can we have **got** one? You mean you've got someone pregnant? Is it that Louise girl?"

Dad remained silent. He looked like a stunned mullet.

"No. I haven't got anyone pregnant, least of all Louise. At least not recently."

"What **is** he going on about?" She said to Dad, referring to me in the third person as though I were invisible.

"I'm going on about your granddaughter."

"Ah? So it's a girl?" Mother smiled, I wasn't sure why!

"OK! Now listen. It is a very odd story..."

Mother opened her mouth to speak, and I held up my hand to stop her, and then continued.

"... Someone I went out with, a long time ago, had my baby, but didn't tell me. We split up and that was that. I didn't know anything about it, until the other day. The young lady, Nicola, who rang you asking for my number, was my daughter."

I paused to let Mother speak, but she was speechless.

There's a first time for everything!

"How long ago?" Dad asked. "How old is she?"

"19," I replied. "I can't even have been 16!"

Dad smiled an inscrutable smile.

"Wow!" He said. "We've got a 19 year-old granddaughter?"

He was genuinely excited, probably, as I predicted, at the fact that the new generation of Arnolds is already in place!

"Are you sure it's yours?" Mother found her voice.

"What do you mean 'it'? She's 19, she's hardly an 'it'. And, of course I'm sure! I wouldn't be telling you otherwise, would I?"

The shock of the news gradually subsided, and Mother warmed to the idea. I told them all the circumstances surrounding the conception, and Mother had real compassion for Nicola.

"Poor child!" She said. "How could anyone bring a child into the world in those circumstances? It's just plain selfish!"

"I'm sure she felt she had no choice, Mother." I tried to defend Carole.

"She sounds like a trollop to me! How old was she?" She said angrily.

I laughed at the archaic language. I haven't heard that word since my gran died!

"She was only 19."

"It's no laughing matter!" She continued. "Only 19? Rape. That's what it was, if you were only 15. What was a 19 year old woman doing seducing a 15 year old child?"

"It was hardly that, Mother, and I did volunteer!"

Dad suppressed a giggle.

"You were still only 15. That's too young, by law, to give consent. If you were a girl of 15, they'd have put a 19 year-old boy in prison for doing that."

"But I'm not... And the poor woman is dead, so it's a moot point anyway. She didn't know I was 15. That's why she dumped me when she found out."

There was no placating, (hurrah!), her on the matter, so I ceased resistance, in the time honoured Arnold manner, and merely shook my head in frustration. Dad realised I had done so and nodded his approval of a good decision. Deep down, they are both quite quietly pleased that they have a grandchild and have expressed a desire to meet her.

I should hope so too!

Just as I was about to leave, Mother gave me a small, gift wrapped box and a birthday card, with the instructions not to open them until my birthday.

I went to the quiz with anticipation last night. I wanted to know what was happening in the lives of Jamie, Brian and Gordon and couldn't wait to impart my news. I arrived, later than usual, just as the quiz commenced. Brian was not there. I guessed that he was too embarrassed, by his disgraceful behaviour, last week, to show his face. There was no time for small talk, as we set about answering the questions to the best of our ability. As the first fun round ended and the question master was swapping around the answer papers for marking, Brian walked in, as though nothing had happened. We fared very well in the quiz, as usual, finishing second in the first fun round. We won the drinks round and the second fun round but, once again, failed to scoop the jackpot. Once the quiz was finished, Jamie confronted Brian.

"What was all that crap about, last week?"

"Yeah! I know. I'm sorry. I had a bad week." Brian was much more subdued than he had been last week.

"I should think so, too!" Gordon joined in. "You were like a bear with a sore head."

"Maria asked me for a divorce. He said sombrely.

"Really?" I said. I could barely believe it.

"Yep! That's what she said. Totally out of the blue."

"So, are you getting divorced or not?" Jamie was predictably direct, showing his customary lack of compassion.

"I don't know. We've talked more this week than in the previous five years! She's just about tolerating me now! I'm on probation!"

"Probation, my arse!" Jamie rejoined. "She needs putting in her place. You want to put your foot down, mate!"

"You're well qualified to give advice." Gordon cut in, sarcastically. "I suppose you put your foot down and put Sam in her place? That's why you're living with your mum!"

"Bollocks!" Jamie resorted to his habitual response when he's been an arse, and has had it pointed out to him.

"You remind me of a joke, Jamie." I began. *"A petite woman married a bloke just like you. On their honeymoon, the bloke gives her his trousers and says, "Put those on." She says, "Why?" He says,*

"*Just do it!*" *So she puts them on. He says, "That's the first and last time you ever wear the trousers in this marriage!" So she hands him a tiny pair of her knickers and says, "OK! Now you put these on!" He says, "Are you kidding? I'll never get into those." And she says, "And while you've got that attitude, you never will!"* We all laughed except Jamie.

"Yeah! Very funny, burger man! We've all heard it before." Jamie was less than impressed, then turned to Brian with some more useless advice.

"You'd be better off giving her the sack, anyway. Look at me since I got rid of Sam. I've shagged about a dozen different birds in a couple of weeks. Give 'em the four 'F's! Find 'em, feel 'em up, fuck 'em and forget 'em! That's my motto, now."

"That's brilliant! You really haven't got anything to recommend you as a human being, have you, Jamie?" Gordon observed.

"Tosser!" Jamie replied, exerting the full force of his wit.

"Well, if you want to stay with her, Brian, you'll have to make some changes in your life. She's obviously not happy about something." I counselled.

"Yes, I know. We've just been existing... we hardly talk to each other lately." He admitted. "I think we will be OK, though. I'll make sure we are."

"Good on you, Brian!" I supported his resolve. "What about you, Gordon?"

"What about me?" He replied.

"How's your life?"

"I'll tell you later," he said. "If you're interested. I don't want to broadcast it."

"Well, thanks a lot!" Jamie was offended that Gordon didn't show trust in the whole group. I decided to defuse the tension with my own news.

"Well, lads, you are looking at a fully fledged father!" I announced.

"You what?" Jamie came back at me. "How do you work **that** out?"

"Duh! It's not difficult! You know...? You have a shag; the woman gets pregnant; nine months later she has a baby. Bingo, you're a dad!"

"When did all this happen?" Brian asked. "You never told us!"

"Twenty years ago! She's 19. Turned up out of the blue last week."

"You're having a laugh!" Jamie said, disbelievingly.

"No, it's true. Her mother died last year and only told her who I was in a letter she left with her solicitor. My daughter only got the letter after her mother died.

"My daughter! Listen to him! He's giving it large already! I bet she must be a right bowser, though!" Jamie joked.

"Do you want a smack in the mouth?" I was surprised by my immediate anger. "You Muppet!"

"Don't get out of your pram, burger man. I was only joking. I mean... look how ugly her old man is!"

Rather than effect upon him the violence he deserved, and probably get myself barred from the pub, I ignored him. In fact, I don't think I spoke to him again, for the half hour or so that remained, before we all left. Gordon stood alongside me at the bar, as we placed our last orders, and said in a whisper, "Mark and I are thinking of moving in together."

"Isn't that a bit quick? Are you sure it's what you want?" I replied, equally quietly.

"Oh! It's not definite. We're just considering it as a possibility."

"Oh, right." I did not pursue it. It is his business and I'm no expert on gay affairs. Mind you neither is Gordon!

Things to be grateful for

1) Mum and Dad took the news better than I had dared hope!
2) The reason for Brian's strange behaviour came out tonight and it looks like he and Maria are reconciling their differences. I hope so.
3) The lads now know about Nicola.

Things to be wary about

1) Louise is still blissfully ignorant of my fatherhood!

2) Jamie has turned into a bitter and twisted excuse for a human being. I really don't like him very much of the moment.

Tuesday 1st May 2001

Word of the Day: Disparity... inequality, inconsistency

4-00 p.m. Back from the base.

Louise came for lunch yesterday. We had a real heart-to-heart! She told me some more recollections of the story of the incident with Simon. It obviously re-opened the wounds, not only of that episode, but also of others in her life. She told me that, being the middle child of three daughters, she always felt unloved and unwanted, particularly by her father. Apparently, Rebecca, the eldest could do no wrong, and Louise would always be blamed for any differences between her and her older sister. Her dad always took sides, but never with Louise. She always felt the odd one out. Emily, being the baby, could get away with anything, and again, if there were any argument between Louise and Emily, Louise would be punished and told that she should know better, being older than Emily. She said, "It's funny that that argument didn't apply where Rebecca was concerned." She is obviously still bitter about it and has been psychologically scarred for life. Her main childhood recollections centre on her father smacking her for things she hadn't done and constantly bellowing at her. She could recall no loving attention from him at all. I'm no psychologist, but I think in cases like that, the child either goes wild, because any attention is better than no attention, or they end up with low self-esteem. Obviously, as far as Louise is concerned, she ended up the latter. It is not difficult to see why she keeps getting involved with controlling bullies. Her father provided the role model for her future men friends by the disparity, (hurrah!), he showed in his affection for his children.

I hope that, now she is with me, she can learn to realise that we are not all bullies and woman beaters!

I had hoped that we could spend the whole day together, but she got a telephone call on Tuesday morning, asking her to go for an interview at a firm of solicitors in Peterborough, at 3 pm, so she had to leave, at two, to get ready. I thought she might come back here afterwards, but she had planned to go out with Emily. She is coming here on my birthday, though, so I must tell her about Nicola soon.

Things to be grateful for

1) Louise let me get quite close to her innermost emotions today. It showed a lot of trust and affection.

2) She got an interview so she is definitely looking to stay in this area.

3) She is coming to visit on my birthday.

Wednesday 2<u>nd</u> May 2001

Word of the Day: Adulation... admiration, respect, worship.

4-00 p.m. Back from the base.

We took a lot of money on base today. It more than made up for lost trade on Saturday, caused by my absenteeism, to enjoy an evening with Louise. An air force guy, who said he had been worshipping her from afar, ever since she had been working for me, propositioned Ashley. She seemed a little embarrassed by his adulation, (hurrah!), so I stepped in with a humorous comeback.

"That's it!" I teased him. "How rude are you? You come here, trying to steal my bird?"

"Oh! Sorry, Arnie. I didn't mean to... Hey! You're pulling my chain!" He suddenly noticed the wry smile on my face.

"Yeah! It's part of my job description. You guys are just so easy to wind up!"

Ashley was quite gentle in explaining to him that she was in a relationship. She was quite sweet really.

The United Nations arrived to order, a little later on, at least the Italian and Spanish contingent. I was telling them my old stock story about English people shouting at foreigners, if they don't understand English very well, because they think it helps them understand the message if it is louder. Jose Miguel said that Americans are actually funnier then the English. Apparently, according to him, they not only shout, but also add an 'o' on the end of various English words and seem to believe that it miraculously turns the English into Spanish or Italian.

"Excuso. Which wayo to the bathroomo?" He mimicked the American practice.

The spectacle of the Spaniard imitating pigeon Spanish, in a Spanish accent, was so absolutely surreal that it had Ashley and me in stitches!

Things to be grateful for

1) Plenty of business on base today.
2) A good laugh with United Nations crew.
3) Tomorrow is my birthday. I am looking forward to this one much more than I did the last few!

Thursday 3rd May 2001

Word of the Day: Hedonistic... self-indulgent, self-gratifying, pleasure seeking.

10 am looking forward to a lazy day off

The telephone rang at an ungodly hour this morning! It was 5-05 a.m.! There was only one possible reason for it... I picked it up...

"Hello, Mother."

"Ha! Ha! How did you know it was me?" She said brightly.

"Who else would ring in the middle of the night and pretend it was normal behaviour!"

"At exactly this time... thirty-five years to the day... I was lying in a hospital bed, feeling as though a steam roller had just run over me." She said dramatically.

"Thank you for sharing that, Mother. Is that why you ring me, every week, at the same time? To get your own back? Must I pay for the rest of my life for the results of your sexual misdemeanours?"

"Don't be like that, and don't be so vulgar! I wanted to say "Happy Birthday" right on the exact time of your birth. I though you'd be pleased... and I don't ring at this time every week, don't exaggerate!"

"OK maybe you don't. Perhaps it just seems like it! Thank you for your felicitations, Mother. Can I go back to sleep now?"

"You don't want to do that! Get yourself up and about and enjoy the day!"

"When it **is** day, I will, OK?" I softened the remark with a little laugh.

"OK! I'll talk to you later. Have a good birthday."

"I'm sure I shall."

So! Today is my birthday! Happy birthday to me, again! Well, when I woke up this morning (for the second time!) I was not dead...

Although, for a minute or two, I was not too sure!

...So I must be 35 years old! Looking back, it has been quite an eventful year. Things have changed quite dramatically for me and generally for the better, I think. Firstly, I will not be spending the evening of **this** birthday with nothing better to do than sit in an aluminium box, looking out onto some bushes, waiting for customers to grace me with their presence, as I did last year! I **now** have a woman in my life and a 19 year-old daughter. With any luck, both aforementioned beauties are coming today to help me celebrate my 35th birthday in style!

Provided I can pluck up courage to tell Louise, before they meet each other!

In the mail, this week, I received no fewer than 14 birthday cards, which I have displayed on the bookcase, along with the one from Mum and Dad. I have opened my present from my parents, which turned out to be a very expensive looking gold signet ring with my initials, BA, on it. Now, either they have spent a lot of money on a beautiful present, or they picked it up as a free gift from British Airways!

Does my wit know no bounds? Well! The thought made me chuckle, anyway!

I began my day by treating myself to a cholesterol bombshell for breakfast: Three rashers of bacon; two fat succulent pork sausages; two fried eggs; mushrooms and tomatoes; all garnished with the greasiest fried bread I could muster. I'm feeling very hedonistic, (Hurrah!), and somewhat slothful and why not? I am now lying decadently, on my sofa, with a full stomach, awaiting the arrival of my daughter to continue the pampering forthwith! I can feel my arteries hardening; maybe Louise can arrange a similar fate, later, for another part of my anatomy.

But not in front of Nicola!

10-30 am Just noticed the 'message received' light blinking.

The first part of that scenario is not going to materialise, because I just listened to an Ansafone message from Nicola. It was left overnight. She is on a long haul flight from the US, and it is delayed, so she doesn't think she'll be back in time to see me on my birthday. She said she would probably call over at the weekend, so I don't need to compromise a nice birthday afternoon with Louise, by rushing into telling her I have a daughter.

Result! Oh! The intrigue of it all! I wish it were all sorted out!

6-30 pm WORKING ON TRAILER!

I give up, submit and surrender! The whole day has gone completely pear-shaped, and the devil has, most certainly, farted in my face, yet again! What a complete nause-up this has been for a birthday.

Firstly, Nicola isn't coming, but that, at least, would have taken away the pressure of divulging the dreaded secret to Louise. Then, at two o'clock, Nicola duly showed up, without warning, having got back sooner than she thought! That was a nice enough surprise, in itself, but it did nothing for the health of my heart, as it seemed that they were destined to meet, without Louise having prior knowledge of Nicola's existence. Well, maybe it was fated to happen like that. Not my fault!

Nicola is a very thoughtful girl. She had seen my Greenbay Packers hat, when she was last here, asked me about it, and I had related the story of Craig's generosity. As a birthday surprise, while in the USA, she bought me a Packers football shirt! I was gobsmacked.

"Where did you get this? It's a great present!" I said sincerely.

"I was in Chicago and I saw it at O'Hare airport. It is the right team, isn't it?"

"Certainly is!" I said, kissing her cheek.

In her rush to get here, she had driven straight from the airport and arrived, still wearing her uniform and carrying her flight bag. I have to say, she looked a picture, very smart and attractive.

A real chip off the old block!

I made her a coffee, and we chatted about her latest journeys. I suggested a bottle of wine to celebrate my birthday and, as I was about to nip to the off-licence, she asked if she could freshen up and get out of her uniform. I got out my best towels, (both of them!), for her, and went out in search of the fruit of the grape. While I was out, I filled up with petrol, ready for the morning, and returned full of the joys of life.

Nicola, wrapped in my fluffy bath towel, but with an ashen face, greeted me. She told me that a woman had knocked on the door, who had seemed startled when Nicola answered it. It didn't require Einstein to deduce who it might have been.

"Oh my God, was it Louise?" I asked, shaking my head in the hope that that might somehow elicit the opposite answer to the one I was expecting.

"That's what she said."

"Damn! Were you dressed like that?" I winced at the thought of Louise's reaction.

"Er...yes. I'm sorry." Nicola said sheepishly.

"It's OK, it's not your fault. But you can imagine what she was thinking! What did she actually say?"

"She said something like, *'Oh, no, not again! Tell Ben, Louise called.'* She handed me a carrier bag with some food in it, and said, *'You'd better have this. I hope you're a good cook! It looks like he's having a happy enough birthday without me intruding.'*

"I said, *'it isn't what you think...'* but she just walked away, before I could say anything else. I couldn't chase after her, only wearing a towel."

"Don't worry. I'd better ring and explain."

I rang Emily's house and someone picked up the phone.

"Hello? Louise...?" (Click). The phone was slammed down.

"Look. Will you excuse me a minute?" I said to Nicola. "I'll only be a minute. I'll just drive round and see her. I need to get this sorted out."

I drove to Emily's, but there was no answer when I knocked.

What is it with me? I manage to get into trouble even when I've done nothing wrong!

I returned to the flat. Nicola greeted me with two messages.

"The phone rang twice while you were gone," she smiled, as she poured us some wine.

"Firstly, can you ring your mum, and then someone called... Stella?"

"Oh, God. No! I can't cope! Has some perverse god of ridicule got me down for a target, today?"

"What did Louise say?" She asked.

"Nothing. She wasn't there. What did Mother want?"

"To wish you a happy birthday?" She said with a soft sarcastic smile. " I'm guessing?"

The phone rang again.

"Hello, Mother!"

"Mother? That's nice!" Said a voice with a vaguely familiar American accent. "It's Jenni! Happy birthday!"

Whoa! That was a shocker!

"Oh. Right! I had forgotten it was my birthday for a minute. How are you?" I instantly felt guilty that I haven't e-mailed her since the Louise thing was back on again.

"I'm fine. I've got some great news. I have to come back to the UK on TDY in a coupla months. Maybe we can get together?"

Oh shit! What do I say now?

"Yeah, that'd be great."

Fantastic! And what if everything is 'all systems go' with Louise?

"I'll look forward to it!" She replied. "Anyhoo! Just rang to say 'happy birthday', gotta fly, work to do, and this must be costing a fortune! Don't get too drunk!"

That might be the answer. Get totally pissed and block all this out!

Not wishing to have my mother on my back...

How much room can there be back there? It's getting bloody crowded!

...I rang her.

"Hi Mother, you raaang?" I mimicked the voice of Lurch, from 'The Addams Family', much to the amusement of the intrigued Nicola.

"Yes, I did. Where were you? How embarrassing to have a strange woman answering your phone."

"That was no strange woman! That was your granddaughter!"

"Oh! I wish I'd have known. I could have chatted to her until you got back."

Oh dear, how sad, never mind!

"Yes, that would have been nice!" I lied.

"Anyway, I have a surprise for you." She said with an ominous air.

How much do I not like the sound of that?

"Really?"

"Yes, really. You remember Mr & Mrs Cope?"

"No!"

"Yes you do. He was a special constable...used to play cricket at Wardown Park."

"I still wouldn't know him, if he wore stockings and suspenders and painted his face blue, every third Wednesday, Mother." Nicola was giggling and I made a silent conspiratorial gesture to her to 'Shush.'

"You can be so perverse at times, Benjamin. His name was...."

"Cope!" I butted in, before she could finish.

"Yes, very smart!" She admonished. "He was called David... he's dead now, anyway. It was a lovely funeral, though. I think it was done by the Co-op. Lovely flowers, I remember."

"Happy birthday, Ben! I've got a surprise for you. It's a story about a dead bloke you've never heard of, and what a good job the Co-op did of planting him!"

Nicola was beside herself laughing at my sarcastic riposte.

"Don't be so sacrilegious! That's a terrible thing to say about the dead." Mother was horrified.

"It's OK, Mother. It was just a joke. I'm sure he's past caring now, whoever he was."

"Don't start that again. You **do** know them. Anyway, listen. They had a daughter called Debbie, who you were at school with... and she...."

"I was not at school with any Debbie Cope, Mother."

"Yes you were, it was the junior school. She'd be about.... 37."

"Well, she would have been in the bloody fourth year when I was in the first. How the Hell would I have known her?"

"There's no need for swearing, Benjamin. **She** knows **you**!" She was not to be dissuaded from this story.

"OK, Mother. You win. What about her?"

"She's been divorced for three years and hasn't been out with a man since."

"And your point is...?"

"I've invited her for tea on Sunday, so you can meet her!" She said with an excited satisfaction in her voice.

Beam me up Scotty! Someone get me out of this! Warp Speed!

"Hang on, I'll have to hang up. There's someone at the door." I lied. "Speak to you later, Mother!"

I put the phone down and let out a huge sigh, through puffed cheeks.

I told Nicola the gist of the conversation and how Mother persists in doing things like this. She laughed and laughed.

"I can't wait to meet her." She said, apparently sincerely! "She sounds a hoot!"

"Ah! But you wait till she finds out **you're** single," I warned her." She'll be trying to fix **you** up next. See if you think it's as funny then!" We both collapsed in laughter.

Ten minutes later, the phone rang again.

"That'll be Mother again!" I forecast.

"Hello?"

"Hello, Ben. Still up to your old tricks I see?" Stella's gentle Norfolk accent began.

"What do you mean by that?" I replied indignantly.

"I rang earlier? Who's the lucky lady?"

"It's a long story! I haven't got time to tell you right now!" I tried to deflect the inquisition!

"Oops...sorry! Am I cramping your style?"

"Not exactly, but it's complicated."

"I'll bet it is! So, how's my birthday stud, then? Sounds like you are having a good day!"

"You don't know the half of it," I said. "Anyway, how are you doing? Are you married, yet?" I replied, cautiously diverting the subject to her.

"No! I'm not marrying that idiot. I can't believe how stupid I was to get back with him. He didn't take long to remind me of why I went to the Lake District to get away from him!"

"... And now you are having his baby! That's not the best way to get him out of your life, now is it? How's the pregnancy going? You must be getting quite big, by now?" I winced as I said it.

"I'm nearly seven months. It's getting a bit uncomfortable...." She seemed to be looking for sympathy.

You're looking in the wrong place, sweetheart!
".... And my breasts are enormous! You'd love 'em like this!"
If I could reach them!
There was a (pregnant?) pause. When her comment did not elicit a response, she continued.

"You know, it really could be yours. In fact, I'm convinced it is. I just can't be 100% sure." She said in a whining tone.

"You're joking! I thought we went through all that ages ago." I snapped incredulously.

"Can't we get together and discuss it?" She persisted.

Is my picture hanging on a poster, somewhere, in an ad for a Home for Unmarried Mothers?

Having a baby? Don't know who the father is? Ring Ben Arnold! He came down in the last shower!

"Oh Yes! Louise would love that, wouldn't she?"

"So, you're still with that scheming little cow?" She said, unaware of how irony rears its head in unlikely places! "How would she feel about the little playmate you've got in there now?"

"That's not very kind, is it? She hasn't done anything wrong here, and neither have I, for that matter." I defended Louise and myself.

"I don't care about her. I care about me and this baby... and you." She added me as an afterthought. " I've stopped working now, so I could come down and visit... or you could come here. That would be easier for me, with this lump to carry about. Then we could discuss things."

"I don't think so, do you?" I was having trouble believing this conversation. "There isn't really very much to discuss, is there?"

I said I would ring her when I had more time, just to get her off the phone and extricate myself from the situation. While I was on the phone to Stella, Nicola had dressed and returned to the sofa, as I finished the call. I gave her a look of confused resignation to the disaster that was my birthday. We had another glass of wine, and she suggested that she ought to go and let me sort out this confusion. I protested and asked her to stay longer. She appeared pleased that I wanted her to stay and seemed to settle back into the sofa. There was a soft tapping on the door.

"I'll answer it this time!" I said, laughing, and went to the door. Standing there, greeting me with a smile and handing me a card, was Samantha.

"Happy Birthday, Ben." she began. "How old are you? 55?" She laughed impishly.

"No, but it bloody feels like it! What a day I've had."

"Me too, want to talk about it?" She offered.

I didn't know how I would explain who Nicola was, so I kept Sam on the doorstep.

"Another time, maybe?"

The words were no sooner out of my mouth than Nicola appeared at the door and said, "I really ought to be going." She was carrying her uniform on a hanger and her flight bag was over her shoulder.

When she saw that there was a different woman at the door, Nicola gave me a knowing look, then smiled. It was, however, nothing to the knowing look Sam gave me, upon seeing Nicola! Nicola kissed me on the cheek and said that she would ring me very soon, and then left. I ushered Sam in and shut the door.

"I hope I wasn't interrupting anything!" Sam said mischievously.

"You know you weren't!" I said, pretending to be offended. "She's a relative."

"Oh, right. So... is there anyone special to spend your birthday evening with?" She queried.

"There was supposed to be, then the wheels fell off!" I began to outline the sorry tale of the day's developments. Sam had also had a bad day. Jamie has been harassing her with phone calls and, it seems, she can't get him to accept that they are finished. Their house sale has fallen through, too, just before contracts were due to be signed.

"We are real mates in adversity, aren't we? She said. She leaned back and rested her head on my shoulder, then kissed me, gently, on my lips.

Holy shit! What was that all about?

"Would you like a glass of wine?" I mumbled nervously.

"Mmm! Please... You remember you once said... that you had always fancied me?" She said with a serious note.

"Er.... yes..." I replied with trepidation. I could feel my heart thumping in my chest.

Where is this leading?

"Well, **I'm** free and single." She cuddled up to me. "What is happening between you and Louise? Is it on or off?"

Yet again, I am torn between immediate gratification and doing the right thing! I am sorely tempted to give in to it! She is gorgeous!

If I were to give in, I would lose all chance of making things right with Louise, and it would be the end of my friendship with Jamie. I couldn't do it.

"It's very much on." I lied. "She's going to laugh her socks off, when she realises that it was a relative she was jealous about. Anyway, as much as I'd love to go out with you, we are in that "off limits" category, aren't we? Can you imagine what it would do to Jamie?"

"Bugger Jamie! He's history. You know what he did to me. Are you so naive as to think he would even hesitate, if the situation were reversed? He wouldn't give your feelings a second thought!"

"Yes, but he's still my mate, and he still loves you. I reckon you still love him as well. Imagine how complicated it would get, if we slept together, and then you and Jamie got back together. It would be too weird."

"I guess." She said resignedly. "But I won't ask you again!"

"I'm going to hate myself when you're gone." I said truthfully.

She got up and left. I was unsure whether she was miffed with me, or not, but the door shut behind her with a bang. Another problem I could do without!

After she had gone, I tried again, unsuccessfully, to ring Louise who, quite obviously, was not in any mood to talk to me. It was her loss! I was annoyed enough to write her off for the day. Gordon rang to wish me a happy birthday and asked me if I would like to join him and Mark for dinner. In my present state, I am not ready for **that** giant step, so I said, "I'm a bit busy at the moment. Another time, maybe?" I rang the other two lads in turn, to see if they fancied a birthday night out. Brian daren't come out, as he is currently trying to dissuade his wife from divorcing him, and Jamie is going out, shagging anything female that stays still long enough for him to mount; that's if he can stop stalking Sam! In a fit of pique, I decided that I was not going to spend my 35th birthday sitting, drinking alone in my flat, and that I might as well site up the trailer and work. At least I'll get some money in.

So! I am now 35 years old...

Bigger Gulp!

... **STILL** living and working in, what has again become, a shag-free zone in rural Cambridgeshire. (Despite supreme efforts to rectify this situation and offers from inappropriate partners!) And I am, once again, stuck here sitting in an aluminium box, 12' x 7'6", staring out into the twilight at a hedgerow through a hole in the side.

OH DEEP JOY! *I really feel like running away from the whole bloody lot! There's only so much a mere mortal can deal with at one time. Gordon's life seems uncomplicated compared to mine. Perhaps I should become a... No...! perhaps not! I doubt gay relationships are any less complicated than straight ones!*

Whilst ruminating upon the disastrous chain of events, which had killed off my birthday as a celebration, I noticed an advertisement, on the village notice board, for a week's trip to France. I could do with a break and considered going. But, then again, I can't really afford it, and France would be a whole lot nicer, if it wasn't full to the gunnels with the French!

11-30 pm back at the flat

I tried to ring Louise, about half a dozen times, while I was on the trailer. She hung up on me the first time, and then refused to pick up the phone, until just before closing time. Finally she answered it.

"Hello, Louise, don't hang up, I can explai....." CLICK!

I'm beginning to lose patience with her! There's only so much a bloke can take. It's quite ironic how she finds it so easy to be assertive with me, when all the other men she has ever known seem to walk all over her unhindered!

I feel like the whole world is closing in on me. Unfortunately, my usual place of refuge, the gents, is totally inadequate for my current set of circumstances!

Things to be grateful for

You must be joking!

Saturday 5th May 2001

8-30 am somewhere several thousand feet over France

Despite my promising myself that I wouldn't do it, I tried again, yesterday, to contact Louise. She wasn't answering and, even if she had, I would probably have merely succeeded in making myself look more stupid and desperate than I already did. I finally succumbed to the urge to flee! I persuaded Mrs. Roberts, next door, to feed Jason for me and, despite the lack of funds, took up a very good offer on the Internet, to spend 7 days in the Costa del Sol. It was cheap enough, but I haven't got too much spare money to spend. I hope my "flexible friend" doesn't snap under the pressure!

Gordon drove me to the airport, and I am looking forward to a week of total escapism and complete anonymity. A place, (unlike "Cheers"), where everybody **doesn't** know my name! I know that my problems won't disappear while I'm gone, and I'll have to face my dragons...

All of them!

... sooner or later, but I'll cross all those bridges when I come to them. If Louise won't talk to me, there is not much I can do about it. I tried! Maybe a week of cooling her heels will do her good! When I get back, she'll either talk to me, or she won't.

Reclining, with my back rest down, sipping some Southern Comfort over ice...

Who the hell put ice in it? The only thing you EVER put in a Southern Comfort is another Southern Comfort!

… And, with the hum of the jet engines in the background, I still feel aggrieved that Louise would not even listen to my explanation, but to be honest, right now, I haven't got the energy. She's no Scarlett o'Hara and I'm certainly no Rhett Butler, but the way I feel right now…."Frankly, my dear, I don't give a damn!"

Printed in Great Britain
by Amazon